asner

BACHELOR'S PUZZLE

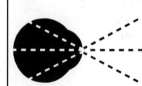

This Large Print Book carries the
Seal of Approval of N.A.V.H.

Bachelor's Puzzle

Judith Pella

THORNDIKE PRESS
A part of Gale, Cengage Learning

Detroit • New York • San Francisco • New Haven, Conn • Waterville, Maine • London

GALE
CENGAGE Learning™

LIBRARY OF CONGRESS CATALOGING-IN-PUBLICATION DATA

Pella, Judith.
    Bachelor's puzzle / by Judith Pella.
      p. cm. — (Thorndike Press large print christian fiction)
(Patchwork circle ; bk. 1)
    ISBN-13: 978-1-4104-0587-6 (lg. print : alk. paper)
    ISBN-10: 1-4104-0587-7 (lg. print : alk. paper)
    1. Women — Fiction. 2. Swindlers and swindling — Fiction.
3. Quilting — Fiction. 4. Oregon — Fiction. 5. Large type
books. I. Title.
PS3566.E415B33 2008
813'.54—dc22
                                               2007049483

Published in 2008 by arrangement with Bethany House Publishers.

To the Columbia County Piecemakers Quilt Guild who I would like to think are the descendants of quilters like those in the Maintown Sewing Circle. Thank you for the inspiration of your enthusiasm in the craft of quilting, but most especially thank you for your friendship.

AUTHOR'S NOTE

The setting of this story is Columbia County, Oregon, which is an actual place. I debated about using a real place because it is easier and often safer to create one's own setting. But I chose the real county for a couple of reasons. First, I've always been told to "write what you know," a rule I often break, but this time I went with it. I have lived in Columbia County for several years and know parts of it well. But mostly I chose it because it is a lovely place — in a rustic, somewhat threadbare sort of way. It is past its heyday, but that is what gives it its particular charm. It is very pretty country here with the Columbia River on its north-western border and forests and farmlands dotting the rest of the county. It is still quite rural despite its proximity to Portland — the county seat is only forty-five minutes away from the city. I thought it would be fun to pay tribute to my home in this way.

That said, I must go on to emphasize that except for some place names, ambiance, and general historical facts, I have fictionalized a great deal of what you see in these pages. People and incidents are spawned entirely from my own imagination. Maintown, its residents, and events are especially my own creations. Nevertheless, when you have so many characters in a story, it is difficult not to accidentally appear to hit upon a real person. But believe me, if you see someone familiar in this story, it is truly just that — an accident. As always, however, I have tried to stay true to the life and times of the people and places.

ONE

Columbia County, Oregon
April 1882

Ada Newcomb drove the buckboard this morning so she could be sure to arrive early at the schoolhouse. It was a bit hard to handle for her petite frame, but she had too many things to carry to ride a saddle horse. How she wished they had a better family wagon, perhaps a nice little Rockaway carriage like the Parkers drove. But Calvin had been forced to sell the more comfortable, though older Barouche last year because fickle weather had played havoc with the crops, making harvest thin and pennies tight. The buckboard was fine, and there was more room in it for the whole family.

After unhitching the horses and taking them to the adjacent stable, Ada pushed open the schoolhouse door, gratified to see that she was indeed the first to arrive. She set to work immediately putting things in order. Friday after school Miss Stowe, the teacher, knowing the Sewing Circle would meet on Sunday, had instructed some of the older boys to push aside the desks and move the quilt frame into the open area. Now Ada saw to it that enough chairs were set about the frame. Only six sewers could fit comfortably, and since there were nine women in the group if everyone showed up, three would sit out and do handwork, then "spell" the others every so often. She hoped all would be present today, for not only was it her quilt to be quilted, but she had important news. Smiling, she glanced toward her sewing basket sitting on a chair. Peeking out from among the scraps of fabric and spools of thread was the corner of an envelope.

It wasn't often such momentous tidings came to their town, so she was pleased as punch that she could be the bearer. Emma Jean Stoddard would be livid that the news hadn't fallen into her hands first, for she was the chairwoman of the Maintown Brethren of Christ Ladies' Aid Society and most looked to her as the leader of the Sewing Circle, as well. But when her husband, Albert, had resigned as head of the board of deacons due to failing health, Emma Jean had lost some of her, albeit tacit, power.

Ada's Calvin was now chairman of the deacons and was also on the county board representing the four Brethren of Christ churches in the area. Thus the letter from denomination headquarters back East had come to him. It informed the church that a new circuit preacher had been appointed and would arrive within two months. The beauty of it was that the quilters were meeting before the deacons, so the duty of revealing the contents of the letter naturally fell to Ada. Calvin had tried to make Ada keep a lid on the news, arguing that the church leaders — meaning the men — should hear it first. But Calvin had given up after only one try because, after twenty-two years of marriage, he knew he could not make his wife do anything she was not quite willing to do in the first place.

Well, it was only right that the women were the first to know, for were they not the backbone of the church? Half the women had to practically threaten their menfolk to get them to attend church, while the other half had to at least nudge theirs.

The schoolhouse door opened, bringing in Jane Donnelly with a gust of wind. She shut the door quickly behind her. It was the month of April in Columbia County, Oregon, where spring in the northwestern part of the state could be as fickle as a young man's fancy.

"Is it raining?" Ada asked. Rain would certainly deter some of the women from attending.

"No, and I don't think it will until tonight," Jane said, straightening her bonnet. Though a bit on the plump side, she was still quite pretty for a forty-year-old matron. "At least that's what Tom says. He says he will probably have to delay planting until next week."

"Oh, well, of course," Ada said as noncommittally as she could. Everyone knew Tom Donnelly would use any excuse possible in order to put off work. But Jane, bless her, always tried to give the man the benefit of the doubt.

Jane set down her basket, untied her cloak, and hung it on a wall hook. Ada had stoked the fire in the stove, warming the large room a bit. They were fortunate to have use of the schoolhouse when it wasn't needed for the children. There was plenty of room here to set up the quilt frame. Ada fondly recalled when she was a girl in Maine and the ladies went from house to house for their quilting. She thought it was so much cozier in a home and was usually a far more festive occasion. The hostess would prepare special

12

food, and later, when the menfolk came home, there would often be a huge supper and dancing. Now the ladies just brought their own lunch in a pail like the children did for school because there were no cooking facilities in the schoolhouse. Ada also brought her apple spice cake to share.

It had been Florence Parker's idea to keep the best frame at the schoolhouse and meet there on Sundays when there was no church, which also met there once a month when the circuit pastor came. The reason was clear to Ada. Though Florence had one of the nicest houses in town, it was never what you'd call tidy. What a waste such a house was on someone like Florence.

"Shall we start to load the quilt onto the frame?" Jane asked.

"Yes, let's do so."

As Ada fetched her thread and pincushion from her basket, she asked, "How come you're here already, Jane? I am the hostess today, so I had to come early."

"Tom was going to St. Helens, and that was my only transportation. I'll have to leave when he comes back through."

Though St. Helens was only about seven miles from Maintown, where Ada and the other women lived, the trip took a few hours because the roads were so bad. In any case,

Ada didn't expect Tom to return before the quilters finished. The man was known to take his own good time about things and to frequent St. Helens's taverns.

"I can give you a ride home if we're not finished. I have to go right by your place anyway."

"That's kind of you, Ada. But . . . well, I've already made arrangements with Tom, and if he has to stop for nothing, he won't be much pleased. Thank you, though."

Ada had already marked the quilt top with a design, a task usually done beforehand; then she and her daughters had basted the layers together — the top, cotton wadding in the middle, and backing fabric of inexpensive wash goods. She'd been working on the quilt all winter and was quite proud of it. She couldn't help waiting expectantly for Jane's praise as she opened it and spread it out on the frame.

"Oh, Ada! This is simply lovely. It's fine enough for a special bed or even a dowry chest."

"It's far too plain for that," Ada said modestly. "I just did it to keep my hands busy. It's not even laid-on work. But I did save scraps for years to get enough indigos and pinks." The pattern was a rendition of Delectable Mountains, a blend of pinwheels and feathered stars. Dark blue and pink made the triangle shapes, with muslin for the sashing. Indeed, she did intend it to be an everyday quilt, though her elder daughter, Ellie, had admired it and said she'd be proud to have it in her hope chest. Both of Ada's daughters already had their wedding quilts, and they were each spectacular enough to take your breath away. Ada had been working on those quilts for years and had been pleased when she finished her younger daughter's, Maggie's, six months ago. Both girls were of marrying age, but there really had been no hurry to finish Maggie's because she had more interest in climbing trees than in finding a beau. Ellie, on the other hand, would surely be needing hers soon, since nearly every boy in the county had an eye for the nineteen-year-old girl.

"What will you do with it, then?" Jane asked.

"Calvin and I can use a new cover for our bed. The old one is so worn."

"I can help you take apart the old quilt so you can reuse the wadding," Jane offered.

"Yes, I should do that. Why be wasteful?" Ada felt a little sorry for Jane, whose ne'er-do-well husband forced her to be so frugal.

While they talked, they laid the bottom of

the quilt over one of the frame poles and began sewing it to the ticking. They were rolling that edge onto the pole when the door opened again and Emma Jean Stoddard strode in. Petite and compact in size, she was tiny in every way except the force of her character, and her presence seemed to fill the large room. Ada noted a momentary frown on the woman's face; perhaps she was disgruntled that she hadn't been first to arrive. But that was immediately replaced by a smile, not exactly false but too well-practiced to be entirely genuine. Emma Jean took seriously her place as leader of the Brethren of Christ Ladies' Aid Society. She believed it was her duty to be kind, considerate, and in general a glowing example of godliness to all the women.

"I'm so sorry I'm late," Emma Jean said, but there was little apology in her tone.

"We're just early," Ada said. "I wanted to make sure the quilt was here in time."

"Oh, well —"

Before she had a chance to finish her remark, the door opened again and three more ladies breezed in: Mary Renolds, whose white head towered over all those present; Louise Arlington, the youngest of the group; and Nessa Wallard, the largest member, in girth anyway, of the Maintown

16

Sewing Circle, though somehow her retiring personality often made her seem invisible.

Chatter now filled the schoolhouse. Everyone busied themselves in finishing the loading of the quilt onto the frame. Polly Briggs and Hilda Fergus scurried in, bringing with them the first drops of rain. Last to arrive, after the quilt was loaded and the women had settled into their places around it, was Florence Parker. She was always late and always had one exciting excuse or another for her tardiness, all usually justifiable, but Ada wondered how so many mishaps could befall a single person. Secretly she thought Florence just relished making a grand entrance.

"Oh, my goodness!" Florence exclaimed, slipping off her cloak and giving it a shake. "You won't believe what just happened. The wind spooked one of my horses, and my buggy went into a ditch. If Able Jenkins hadn't been riding by just then, I might never have gotten here. Thank goodness, the buggy is undamaged. It's practically new, you know."

"Here's a seat for you," Emma Jean said with a long-suffering gesture of her hand toward an empty chair adjacent to the frame. The last to arrive were always the first to sit out.

Florence slipped into the chair, looking over the quilt as she did so. "Fine work, Ada," she said.

Perhaps only Ada noted the disingenuous sound of her praise. Florence held such a high opinion of her own work she'd never admit that Ada was an equally skilled quilter, if not superior. Nevertheless, Ada basked in the compliments her quilt received.

"So, Ada," Emma Jean said, "how shall we quilt it?"

"Nothing fancy," Ada replied modestly. "It's just for everyday —" A chorus of protests interrupted her, which she allowed to continue for a few moments — to be polite, of course — before she added, "Really, if we keep it simple, we can finish it today and move on to Polly's wedding quilt for her daughter."

"But I'm not finished with it yet," Polly said.

"Still, I think we only need to outline the small triangles," Ada responded, "with concentric lines, maybe a half inch apart on the large triangles. And as you see, I've marked a simple rope design in the sashing."

"I just love this quilt block," Hilda said.

"The name is from *Pilgrim's Progress*" came the small voice of Nessa Wallard. She seemed to wilt when all eyes turned to her.

"I didn't know that," Hilda said.

"Well . . . a line in the book goes something like, 'They went till they came to the Delectable Mountain. . . .' " Nessa's cheeks tinged pink as she spoke.

"My mama made a quilt with this design when she came over the Oregon Trail in 1840, more than forty years ago," put in Mary Renolds. "Then, of course, they thought California and Oregon were the Delectable Mountains."

The conversation continued as the women took their spools of heavy cotton thread from their baskets, popped thimbles onto their fingers, and threaded their needles. Since the design was simple Ada said they could just "eyeball" the outline stitches and the other lines.

Fingers flew nimbly across the quilt while the ladies chatted about things of interest — cooking, gardening, and their families. Ada decided it was time to make her announcement but waited as Polly recounted how her son-in-law-to-be, son of a prominent Portland banker, had invited the whole family to their palatial home in the city. Ada didn't want to be rude and break in, even though the story dragged on and on. Finally she decided Polly had monopolized the group long enough. She took a breath.

Just then Florence Parker spoke. "Everyone, I just can't wait a moment longer. Polly, I'm sorry, but I'm about to burst."

"Florence, I have some important news, too," Ada cut in boldly.

"Not as important as mine," Florence said. "Really, let me finish. You'll see."

Ada bit her tongue and braced herself for one of Florence's stories of some wild escapade. That woman did think her dirty laundry was cleaner than anyone else's.

"Nathan was in St. Helens yesterday," Florence continued rather breathlessly, her eyes flickering every now and then in Ada's direction, probably to make sure she didn't interrupt. "He ran into Bob Fulton, the chairman of the Columbia City deacon board, who told him we were finally getting a new circuit preacher!"

Ada nearly bit her tongue as she restrained a gasp of shock and dismay. She refused to show anyone that Florence had upstaged her, yet she was almost certain Florence sent a very brief triumphal glance in her direction.

All the ladies responded to the most welcome news with excited chatter.

"What do you know about him?"

"When will he get here?"

"Where will he live?"

Florence responded to these questions with a blank stare. Ada gathered back her aplomb and just couldn't help feeling smug. She knew the answers to most of the questions, but she thought she'd make Florence squirm a little. Anyway, revealing her knowledge would only reveal how Florence had usurped her.

At last she let her voice cut through the chatter like a knife through cake. "He should be here in two months, maybe sooner."

"What? You knew?" Emma Jean asked, as though realizing just how much she had fallen from the inner circle of things.

"Of course, Emma Jean. Calvin is the chairman of the board of deacons. The letter from the denomination came two days ago."

"What else do you know about him, Ada?" Jane asked.

"Yes, tell us everything," Polly said.

Ada refrained from looking at Florence but knew the woman was staring, slack-jawed. Nevertheless, Ada didn't want to be the sort of person to feel triumph at another's fall. "Well, his name is Reverend William Locklin, and he's from Oak Hollow, Maine."

"Why, that's not a hundred miles from my hometown!" Mary exclaimed.

Many of the settlers of Maintown were from Maine, thus the name of the little settlement, though the post office had erred and dropped the *e* when giving the official name. Still, Ada had never heard of the town in Maine, but Mary was not from the same region of the state that many of the local settlers had come from.

"Does he have a family?" Emma Jean asked.

"No, he's a single man," Ada replied. "Fresh out of seminary to boot." She paused to let this best bit of information sink in. She could almost see a light go on in the eyes of the ladies with marriageable daughters. Who wouldn't want a minister for a son-in-law?

"I suppose he will be living near one of the other churches?" Hilda asked. She had a twenty-two-year-old daughter who was getting uncomfortably close to becoming an old maid.

"As a matter of fact," Ada replied, "Calvin has gone over to the Copelands' to inquire if the pastor can board there." Everyone knew that the Copelands, the oldest and one of the most affluent families in the settlement, had the largest house in Maintown. And since their children had all grown and moved on, their house was often used as a boardinghouse.

"He will live in our community, then," said Hilda.

The honor of this wasn't lost on them because the last two circuit riders had settled closer to the other churches. There were only four churches in the circuit — at Deer Island and Columbia City, which were close together, and at Maintown and Bachelor Flat, neighboring hamlets a two-day ride from the other two. But since Deer Island and Columbia City were closer to the larger town of St. Helens, the ministers always preferred to live in that area. It also meant that those two churches got an extra Sunday service. This time Calvin had lobbied for Maintown and won.

The women discussed what it would mean having the pastor boarding in their town, and several suggestions were made of ways to make the man feel at home. They would all, of course, open their homes to him for meals. He might tire of Ursula Copeland's cooking, and besides, the woman was getting up in years and refused to take in help, so no doubt she would welcome the break.

"I have a wonderful idea," said Florence, speaking for the first time since she had lost control over events. "Let's make him a welcome quilt!"

"That's an excellent idea!"

"But do we have time?"

"What pattern shall we use?"

Now Florence seemed to have all the answers. She must have been thinking of this all along, though she made it sound as if the idea had just struck her. "It should be a sampler. Each family should make a block, perhaps something to capture that particular family's identity."

"We'll have to involve other quilters on the circuit to get enough blocks," Louise said.

"That would make it too complicated and take too long," Florence replied. "Each of our families can make two blocks. That should be enough."

"That's all right for you, Florence. You have a daughter to help and a sewing machine," Louise said. "My children are little and can't help. I don't think I'd have time to make two blocks."

Ada thought she'd have time if she did something simple, but of course she'd want to do something special. "I've got two daughters who are excellent quilters." Ada knew that was stretching the truth a bit because Maggie hardly knew one end of a needle from the other, but she could sew a fairly straight seam. "We can do three blocks."

"This reminds me of something that happened in my hometown when I was a girl," Emma Jean said. "We got a new, unmarried pastor, and all the young women decided to make him a quilt with the intent — don't you know? — of impressing him with their handiwork so that one might win his heart."

"Did you win his heart, Emma Jean?" asked Jane.

"Well, I'm not married to a minister, am I?" she replied testily. "Back then I was not nearly the accomplished quilter that I have become."

It seemed as if all the ladies in the group with young marriageable daughters concentrated especially hard on their fingers, which were still busy with the quilting, refusing to catch anyone's eyes. Ada wondered why they just couldn't be honest about it. There were at least two men to one female in the county, especially if you counted the men who came seasonally to the lumber camps. No girl, not even Hilda's homely daughter, should have too much trouble finding a man. But what Christian girl doesn't dream

25

of becoming a pastor's wife? Ada knew she'd be pleased right down to her toes if Ellie won the heart of the new reverend.

Two

Portland, Oregon

Zack Hartley was not a man to reflect often on the state of his life, and as a fist slammed into his ribs, he sure wasn't about to start now. But he did have to wonder how his sorry self could get into so many messy scrapes.

Slam! A fist made contact with his person again.

He struggled hard against the second man who held him.

"No one welshes on a loan from me, Hartley," said yet a third man in the dark alley down by Portland's waterfront.

"I . . . tell . . . you . . . it ain't my fault!" Zack grunted, though he knew the words were lame and Beau Cutter, boss of one of the town's crime rings, wasn't really listening. Zack was going to die in this alley, or at least get a few bones broken, and all because of a woman.

27

"Ain't he cute?" Cutter sneered.

"Let's finish him off, boss, and get outta here before —" Ron Sinclair, Cutter's right-hand man was suddenly cut off as a shout came from the end of the alley.

"Hey! What's going on down there?" someone yelled.

"Mind your business," Sinclair shouted back.

"This is my alley, so it is my business, and I'm sick of you hoodlums causing trouble."

Zack thought the fool was coming into the alley.

Crack! A gunshot burst through the night air. The shot nearly parted Zack's hair, though he thought it had been fired into the air, not specifically at him.

Sinclair and Cutter hit the cobbles of the alley. The fellow holding Zack did not let go of his captive but swung him around as a shield. Zack could vaguely see Cutter and Sinclair scramble on hands and knees toward the passerby.

Everything started happening fast. Zack struggled against his captor. The other two hoodlums were tussling with the fool pass-erby. Zack heard a clank of metal — the gun falling from the stranger's hand onto the cobbled alley. Zack saw a flash of metal. Maybe he could get to it if he could break

28

away. But his arms were held fast. Only one part of his body was free, and since he was a man who had lived by his wits all his life, though some argued he had but few, he knew what he had to do.

With all his might he slammed the back of his head into his captor's nose. He heard a crack and hoped he had broken the cretin's nose, but at least he caused enough pain for the man to loosen his grip so that Zack was able to break free. Jerking quickly to his right and in the same motion dropping to the ground, his hand made contact with the gun.

Maybe his luck was finally changing.

He heard a few grunts from the other struggle. Then there was a hard thud, and the sounds of struggle suddenly faded.

Before anyone had a chance to regroup, Zack fired a shot into the air to get their attention, then leveled his aim at Cutter. "Okay, Cutter," he warned. "The next shot is for you. Call your boys to heel."

"You heard him, boys," Cutter said.

Sinclair moved cautiously to where his boss was now standing. The man who had held Zack also struggled to his feet and hobbled in that direction. In the moonlit alley Zack could see blood dripping down from the nose of his captor.

"Throw down your weapons," Zack said. Vaguely he thought about the passerby, but since he'd heard no more from that one, he thought the fellow was unconscious from the scuffle.

When he heard the sound of a couple guns and knives hitting the cobbles, he added, "Look, Cutter, I'm going to get you your money back, but you know as well as I that I can't do it if I'm dead. I need two days. I ain't no welsher."

"What can I say? You're holding the gun."

Zack wanted a more formal agreement. He didn't want this scoundrel hunting him down again when maybe no one would be around to save him.

"Just say you'll agree to give me time." Even holding a gun aimed at the man's head, Zack didn't feel much in control. He began backing up to get closer to the alley entrance in case these blackguards realized he wasn't as tough as he was trying to sound.

"I thought some harpy cleaned you out," Cutter said, "so how you ever gonna produce that kind of dough again? That's one hundred dollars. I bet you never seen that kind of money before."

"I'll get it. Don't worry." Zack took another step back.

"Two days, Hartley, then you're gonna pay, one way or another."

Zack felt his boot brush something, and before he realized what it was, he stumbled over the obstacle — the body of the fallen passerby! He wobbled like one of those spinning tops he'd played with as a kid. He swung his arms to control himself, and forgetting about the gun in his right hand, his fingers twitched, and the weapon fired.

He heard a yell. He'd hit someone!

"Ronny! Ronny!" Cutter's voice.

Oh, man! He'd shot Cutter's second-in-command!

Somehow Zack regained his balance, managed to clear the body, and was racing toward the alley entrance when he heard Cutter shout again, "You're a dead man, Hartley! After him!"

Late at night the waterfront district wasn't exactly teeming with people, but a running man was still apt to draw attention — even more, a man running and waving a pistol. Zack wanted to throw the thing away but knew he had to hang on to it so long as Cutter and his boys were after him. He'd never much liked guns and seldom used them. He'd never shot a man before. Had he really killed Sinclair? The idea sickened him, despite the fact that the man was a

31

dirty lowlife. But he couldn't think about that now, not when he could hear pursuit loudly behind him.

He turned a corner, hoping to lose them, but could still hear the pounding of boots on the street. What would he do if the police turned up now? Maybe they'd let him go in the interest of getting a bigger fish like Cutter. Maybe the cops would pinch all of them and throw them all in the calaboose. Cutter would get off because he could afford a lawyer, while Zack would rot.

Zack ran down so many streets that he soon became confused, but when he paused a moment for breath, he could no longer hear the sound of pursuing feet. Had they given up? More likely they were so sure they'd find him that they didn't have to chase him. They knew he had no place to hide. He knew few people in this town and fewer still who would lift a finger to help him. He'd met Darla at the Three Aces Saloon on Front Street just after arriving by stage from Seattle a couple of weeks ago. He was a drifter, and as he had in Seattle, he stayed in a place only until he became bored or got into trouble, which was usually long before it ever became like home. He'd known no real home since he ran away from his ma's place in Kansas when he was twelve years old. His mother, a widow, had remarried a fellow who brought three of his children — spoiled brats, the lot of them! — into the house. Zack's new stepfather thought Zack's only use was to wait on the other kids hand and foot. Ma didn't stand up to the man because she needed to be taken care of, even if it meant sacrificing her son. At first Zack was too young to do anything about it, but by age twelve he'd taken all he could, so he lit out on his own.

One thing and another brought him west. He'd been up and down the Pacific Coast from Ensenada, Mexico, to Alaska, chasing one get-rich scheme or another or just wandering. He had acquired a pair of very itchy feet.

What was he going to do now? He sure as shootin' didn't have any money, maybe two bits at the most. Back at his room in the cheap hotel where he was staying he had a couple bucks, but Cutter knew the place, so he couldn't go back there.

He sure couldn't expect any help from Darla now that she had found someone else. How could he have been fool enough to trust her? He wasn't a greenhorn kid anymore. He'd been around. He was twenty-four, not twelve. But all she'd had to do was blink those pretty blue eyes of hers, toss those silky brown locks, and shimmy in that fancy silk dress, and he was lost. He should have known better than to get involved with a saloon girl.

When he had arrived in Portland, he'd had some money from working for a Seattle boss named Duncan Falk, who was mostly a hoodlum. But the man also had several lucrative legitimate enterprises, and Zack collected "protection" money from local businesses, making a healthy percentage in return. It was one of the best-paying jobs he'd ever had. Then one of the businessmen failed to make his payments a couple of times and Falk ordered Zack to "teach the man a lesson," not unlike the lesson Cutter had just tried to teach Zack in the alley. Zack had no stomach for breaking a fellow's legs, so he hightailed it out of town. You didn't just quit working for men like Falk; you either disappeared or you ended up dead. But he'd been able to leave Seattle with his belongings and several hundred dollars in his pocket.

He got as far as Portland, met Darla, and decided to stick around awhile. But Darla had expensive tastes. It wasn't long before Zack had spent most of his cash on her. That's when he decided to try his hand at poker in order to beef up his stash. And that's what forced him to borrow the money from Cutter. The irony was that the minute he started losing at poker, Darla promptly found another fellow.

Cutter had given Zack five days to pay back the money. Zack used his last few dollars trying to win back the money at the card table. He was close after three days but lost big on the fourth. Maybe he would have made better use of that last day by hoofing it out of town, but he was beginning to grow weary of all the running. He thought if he could pay back Cutter, he might be able to stick around Portland for a while, maybe make some real friends, maybe meet a decent woman. The words *settle down* still made him a little weak in the knees, but not nearly as bad as they once had.

Now he regretted that decision. He just couldn't get a good hand dealt to him. And before he knew it, Cutter was hauling him into that dark alley on the waterfront in order to get his money — out of Zack's hide if nowhere else.

And now, here he was, running for his life. He might have been able to finagle two extra days out of Cutter and maybe figure some way around the debt. But Cutter would never let him off now, not after having shot his second-in-command, probably his best friend.

His only choice now was to get out of town. The big question was how! He had no money, and even if he did, he knew Cutter would be watching the train and stage depot. If he could steal a horse — he'd also lost his horse in the poker game — he might be able to slip away, find back roads, and head to some remote place where he could lie low for a while, maybe find a job so he could get some money. He sure couldn't get far on two bits. As soon as he had a little bankroll and his trail had grown cold and Cutter had forgotten about him, then he could head to some big city like San Francisco and really lose himself.

THREE

Maintown, Oregon

Maggie Newcomb eyed the pile of hay. From her vantage in the barn loft, it looked pretty far below, but oh, so tempting. She tried to reason that she was nearly eighteen, far too old to be leaping into hay mounds. Yet that very thought propelled her forward. She ducked her head out the loft window opening. There was no one around. Dad and Boyd were planting potatoes. Georgie, of course, was in school. Mama and Ellie were at the back of the house hoeing the garden. Maggie should be helping them and, in fact, had been sent to the barn to fetch the bag of seed corn. She'd noted the prime mound of hay on her way and had climbed into the loft just to see what it looked like from up high.

It looked perfect.

Years ago Ellie would have been right beside her. Now, at the ripe age of nineteen,

Maggie's older sister had gone all feminine and too girly for such boisterous fun. If Georgie were here, he'd do it with her. No one would yell at him for it, either, though he was fourteen. But Mama would surely light into Maggie for jumping. She was trying mightily to turn Maggie into a lady like Ellie.

Trying and failing.

Maggie stepped to the edge and launched herself out, hurtling straight into the middle of the sweet-smelling hay!

"Oowee!" she cried as she landed with a scratchy swoosh, sinking deeply into the great yellow mass.

"Margaret Edith Newcomb!" It was Mama's voice, though muffled by the hay wall surrounding Maggie.

For a fleeting moment Maggie considered staying put — the hay was so much more welcoming than her mother's commanding voice. But the moment passed quickly, and she knew she could not hide from Mama, so with flailing arms she propelled herself out of the nice hiding place.

"Uh . . . hi, Mama." Maggie sputtered the words through a mouthful of hay.

"Look at you!" Ada Newcomb all but wrung her hands. "I sent you a good while ago to fetch the corn. What is the matter with you, girl? We have work to do. I want that corn in before it rains." Reaching up, Ada plucked a few bits of straw from her daughter's honey brown curls. "Your braids have come loose, and your hair is all a tangle. You better watch out, Maggie! I'm going to send you to Mrs. Dubois' Finishing School yet."

Ever since Maggie finished high school last summer, that was her mother's constant threat. Maggie had managed to wheedle out of it thus far, mostly because Dad was on her side. Not that he usually got his way around Mama, but for some reason he'd been able to stanch the flood of Mama's threats.

"Mama, no! Please!" Maggie tried to sound convincingly abashed. No sense revealing that she knew what an empty threat it was.

"The school did good by Ellie. Why, she has blossomed into a fine young lady!"

"Well, you know Dubois ain't even the principal's real name."

"*Isn't.* And I don't care what her name is. She does an admirable job with —" Ada stopped abruptly. "Oh no, you don't! You're not going to make me forget why I've come looking for you. We have work to do. Come with me and let's get that corn."

Maggie followed her mother back into the barn, a grin plastered across her face that her mother couldn't see — Mama didn't have eyes in the back of her head, no matter how much it might appear differently. She'd managed nicely to deflect her mother's wrath.

Maggie got the bag of corn, and together they returned to the garden patch. Ellie was hoeing rows at the back of the garden for the corn seeds. Even in her work clothes — a faded blue calico skirt, dirty at the hem where it brushed the ground, and an old blouse — with her yellow hair neatly tied back in a braid, she looked like the beauty she was, her movements always graceful. But Maggie didn't think it was all Mrs. Dubois' work. It just came naturally to Ellie.

Maggie self-consciously brushed more straw from her overalls — no dress for her unless she absolutely had to wear one!

"Aren't you a sight!" Ellie said, pausing a moment in her work to take in her hay-covered sister. "What'd you do? Fall into Dad's hay mound?"

"She didn't *fall*," grated Mama.

Ellie laughed. "Couldn't resist temptation, could you?"

"Aw, shut up," Maggie said.

"Margaret Edith!" screeched Mama. "Don't you speak that way!"

"Is that a drop of rain I feel?" Maggie asked, wiping a hand across her nose.

"Oh, come on. Let's hurry!" Mama now urged, once again deflected from her rebuking.

When Maggie drew close to her sister, Ellie said under her breath, "There's no rain, Mags."

Maggie smiled covertly and Ellie giggled. Maggie could not be mad at her sister for long. Yes, it irritated her to no end that Ellie was so perfect, but it wasn't really her sister's fault, and most of the time she didn't even seem to realize her inborn perfection. Maggie and Ellie were such good friends they just couldn't stay angry at each other.

They managed to plant all six rows of corn before the rain began, but by the time they'd put away all their tools in the barn, they had to run to the house to keep from getting soaked. After they cleaned up, it was time to get supper. The rain would force the men in from the potato fields early, too, but they would have chores in the barn to keep them busy awhile. Mama seemed to have something on her mind and looked relieved when she saw Dad and Boyd head to the barn.

She gave Maggie potatoes to peel and Ellie some carrots and turnips to peel and cut
up while she punched down the bread
dough and laid it on the board for a final
knead. When all hands were busy — hands
always had to be busy for Mama's satisfaction — she seemed ready to discuss what
had been bothering her. Maggie feared she
might be getting more serious about that
finishing school and braced herself.

"Girls, I had a rather interesting quilting
bee yesterday," Mama began. "I wanted to
tell you about it sooner, but with one thing
and another, the time just slipped away."

"Mama," Ellie said, "now that I am home
from school, maybe I could come to the
Sewing Circle meetings."

"Oh, you wouldn't like it, dear. We're all
old ladies, you know."

"Louise Arlington is only five or six years
older than me."

"Still, you'd be bored, I'm sure."

"I could learn so much from you ladies."

"Ellie," put in Maggie, "you can't really
want to sit around with the biddies — now,
Mama, don't get ruffled! You said yourself
that you're all old ladies."

"Well," huffed Mama, "by comparison to
Ellie is all I meant. I'll talk it over with the

other ladies."

This last statement seemed reluctant. Surely Ellie, who was so smart and wise, must know Mama wanted this time for herself. Maybe Ellie realized it, after all, because she let it go at that.

"Anyway," Mama went on, "we are going to be getting a new pastor, and the Sewing Circle thought it would be a nice gesture if we made him a welcome quilt."

"That's a nice idea," Ellie said. "At least his wife will appreciate it."

"The thing is, he is a single man, a young man, if I take the information about him correctly." Mama gave Ellie a funny look and then added for emphasis, "A young, unmarried minister."

"Oh, Mama!" Ellie's cheeks turned pink.

"What — ?" Maggie began, then stopped as understanding dawned. She burst out laughing. "Mama's gonna play cupid. Ellie and the preacher, sittin' in a tree —"

"Enough, Maggie!" Mama broke in.

"I don't even know the man," Maggie went on, unable, as always, to resist the urge to push just as far as she could, "but I already feel sorry for him. I bet every biddy in Maintown, probably the whole county, is gonna put their daughters on display —"

"That will be quite enough, Margaret

43

Edith!" Mama demanded.

Ellie said, "You make light, Mags, but . . . well . . . young, unmarried ministers don't come along every day."

"I thought you fancied Colby Stoddard, or was it Elisha Cook, or Kurt Lambert? Or do you just want all the bachelors in the county?"

"I'll leave Colby for you, sis." Ellie grinned.

"Me? Don't do me any favors. Anyway, Colby is so sweet on you he doesn't even know I exist, not that I'd care if he did."

"You both should be getting more serious in your search for a husband. You don't want to end up like Hilda's poor daughter, Iris," Mama said.

"End up?" groaned Maggie. "She's only twenty-two. I want to wait at least that long till I even think of marriage."

"Don't be silly, child." Mama gave a slap to the lump of dough before dividing it into two chunks. "Iris is so homely, it's no wonder the men don't give her a second look. But you two — yes, *both* of you!" — she added this last with a pointed look at Maggie — "are such pretty girls, you'll have no trouble finding nice husbands. Ellie might be married already if we hadn't sent her to Mrs. Dubois, but I believe that was for the best, because there is now no reason why you shouldn't aspire to the cream of the crop."

"Like the minister," Maggie said.

"I've always thought it would be wonderful to be a minister's wife. What a wonderful way to serve God!"

Ellie's gaze grew dreamy. No doubt she was imagining herself leading the choir, playing the piano, and being loved by all her husband's congregation.

In truth, Maggie could imagine it of her sister. Ellie would be a perfect minister's wife. And if it left Colby Stoddard free — well, it didn't matter. Maggie had no interest in Colby anyway.

"So," Mama said, as if a profound decision had been made, "back to that quilt. Each family in our church will make one or two blocks as time permits. I volunteered to do three, since Louise won't have time for but one. We decided that it will be a sampler and the blocks will be the quilter's choice. Each should be twelve inches and blue the main color. Blue because it is for a man."

"Any blue, Mama?" Ellie asked. "I mean, there are so many different shades."

"We thought a variety of shades would be fine. We'd use a navy, we thought, for the sashing. We are hoping to have the blocks finished in three weeks."

"Three weeks? That's not much time."

"He's coming in less than two months, probably sooner. We need time to put the blocks together and quilt it. And it might be a nice touch to do some kind of appliquéd border."

"Oh, Mama, I saw the most wonderful quilt border in *Godey's* this month."

"I saw one, too. I'll bet it's the same one. That could work very nicely. If we all work together, and I'm sure some of the other ladies would help, we might have time —"

"Mama," Maggie edged in, "what is all this 'we' talk?" She eyed her mother warily.

"Well, of course, we will each make a block," Mama said.

"I don't want to snag the minister," Maggie protested. "Besides, you know I'm a terrible stitcher."

"The purpose of this quilt is not to snag the minister," Mama said with as much conviction as she could muster, though they all knew otherwise. "It is to welcome him."

"Uh-huh," grunted Maggie.

"Well, we are all going to make a block. You can do something simple for yours."

"Why do I always have to do what I hate to do?" Maggie lamented.

"Because," Mama replied, "you were born

a girl, and that is your lot in life."

After dinner Ellie and Mama went off to look at patterns. Maggie helped Georgie with his arithmetic. She liked schoolwork far better than stitching! And she far more enjoyed listening to Dad and Boyd talk about the gearing up of the lumber camp after winter than hearing her mother and Ellie prattle about patterns and the new fashions in *Godey's*. But when she and Ellie went up to their room to get ready for bed, she couldn't help feeling out of sorts. She didn't really fit in with Dad. He, and especially Boyd, would laugh if she tried to offer her opinion about lumber and such. Nor did she fit in with Mama and Ellie. Part of her really wanted to, but another part balked because she didn't have the talent or innate interest they had in household matters. Though she could cook if she had to, she didn't enjoy it, and her fingers were clumsy with a needle and thread, not to mention that she grew bored easily.

"Ellie, would you make my block?" Maggie ventured as they slipped beneath the covers of their four-poster.

"Mags, you've got to make a block. It wouldn't look right if you didn't, especially if I made two."

"You don't believe that hogwash about

making the quilt to impress the pastor, do you?"

Ellie wiggled under the covers to find a comfortable spot. "No, not really . . . but — I don't know, it could happen that way. He could see the fine work and how lovingly it was done and maybe want to get to know that particular girl better."

"And, my dear sister, what if our young, unmarried minister is fat as a hog and has crossed eyes and warts?"

Giving that new idea some thought, Ellie shuddered, then said, "How good a quilter is Iris Fergus?"

They both burst out laughing.

Dad called from across the hall, "Girls, keep it down. It's late."

More quietly, Ellie said, "But he could be handsome. Anyway, looks aren't everything."

"So you'd marry a wart-faced hog if he was nice?"

"Well, I'd have to draw the line at the warts."

The girls laughed again but more quietly.

Maggie said, "You could have Colby with just a wink of the eye."

"He's nice and good-looking. But . . . Mags, it is really important to me to marry a man with a strong faith in God. I can imagine us reading the Bible together and then having long discussions about what we read. He would ask me to offer opinions of his sermons. We would pray together. It's the kind of life that would be perfect."

"Then you better catch the minister because I doubt any of the other fellows around here would give you that."

Ellie gave a very solemn nod.

Maggie added, "I'll make the block if you think it would matter. At least anything I stitch will never win him over."

"Oh, you're not so bad. We'll find you a good block. Something special but not too hard . . ." Ellie pursed her lips in thought, but even she was hard pressed to think of something that could fit the bill.

"Wouldn't it be just my luck if he went for the non-domestic type?" Maggie said drolly.

"You could do worse."

"The only good thing about that would be the look of shock on the biddies' faces. I'd make a spider web block if it wasn't so hard. But maybe I should anyway, since the quilt is just a big man trap."

"It's a welcome quilt."

"And believe me, Mabel Parker, Sarah Stoddard, and even Iris Fergus will be just as intent as you in *welcoming* the new pastor."

"Mabel and Sarah are the best young quilters in the church," Ellie said with some trepidation.

"Not better than you. You're almost as good as Mama, and she's the best quilter in the church."

"Not if you ask Florence Parker."

"What is it between Mama and Florence? You'd think they were dogs after the same bone."

"All I know is that something happened when they were girls on the wagon train from Maine to here."

"Probably a fight over a man."

"Do you think — ?"

"Girls!" came Mama's voice. "Put out your lamp. It's time for bed."

The sisters looked at each other and shook their heads. Their mother couldn't have heard. Maggie blew out the lamp and snuggled down under the covers. She had a feeling she was going to need all her rest just for the stitching alone, not to mention for what promised to be an interesting next few weeks.

FOUR

The house was quiet with everyone gone. Dad had decided to try to get to St. Helens before the next storm. He needed a harness repaired before he could finish the planting. Mama needed groceries, and Maggie decided to go with them. Boyd was over at the Wallards' paying court to Nessa's youngest daughter, Kendra. Georgie was again at school and not happy that the whole family would be off having fun while he was "imprisoned" all day. Ellie tried to comfort him with the fact that she was going to stay home, but he countered, rightly enough, that she had a choice.

She didn't know why she had chosen not to join the others. St. Helens was a good seven miles away, so trips there were not frequent, since it took several hours to drive there and back in the wagon. But she wanted some time without distractions to get started on her block for the welcome

51

quilt. After she finished her chores — mixing the bread dough and setting it near the stove to rise, sweeping, and mending — she got down Mama's box of patterns. She loved this box, and Mama had promised her that one day it would be hers. Maggie had no interest in it, but Ellie loved not only the patterns themselves but also the rich history most of them represented. There were some patterns cut from magazines, some yellowed and quite old; one had a date of 1842 — it was forty years old! Older than Mama. There were several blocks made of cloth that Mama or one of her forebears had pieced together in order to remember a certain pattern.

Many of the patterns had been passed down through Mama's family. Grandma Spooner, Mama's mother, was the best quilter and stitcher ever. How Ellie loved to visit her in Deer Island and look at her quilts and learn from her! But that was even farther away than St. Helens, so they didn't get there more than once every few months. Now that Grandpa Spooner had passed on, there was talk of having Grandma move in with them, but Grandma wouldn't hear of it. She liked keeping her own house. Mama didn't push the idea, because every time the subject was raised, Dad would mention that his parents were getting up in years, as well, and though Scappoose, where they lived, wasn't quite as far as Deer Island, it was still hard to visit them and care for them properly. Mama would sooner burn down her house than have Mother Newcomb, as she called her, and not in a fond way, live with her. Grandma Newcomb could be difficult. For one thing, she was a good quilter, too, but there was not a single pattern in Mama's box from her, and there wouldn't be as long as the woman lived. According to Mama, Grandma Newcomb was jealous that Mama was a better quilter than she was. Moreover, she had never thought Mama a suitable match for her son.

Ellie often wondered what a future mother-in-law might think of *her.* She sometimes imagined how the mothers of the young men she was interested in would accept her. Colby Stoddard's mother, Emma Jean, scared her most. That woman ran her home like a military camp, with herself as the general. Her husband was only a colonel, if that. No wonder her daughter Sarah was so shy. Colby was a rebel except he was always polite and respectful in his mother's presence. Away from her, he was a wild one. That's probably why Maggie, much as she refused to admit it, was sweet on him. And why most of the girls, including Ellie, were to some degree taken with him. He wasn't a truly bad sort, just fun-loving, and Ellie did like that about him but not enough to risk having Emma Jean for a mother-in-law. Maybe if she really loved Colby, it wouldn't matter who his mother was.

The new pastor's family most likely would be far away in Maine. It might be she'd never meet them unless they had the means to take the train west sometime. She wondered again what he was like. She made a picture in her mind of a tall, handsome man about twenty-five years old, with dark hair and deep-set dark eyes intense with both humor and wisdom. Oh, how those eyes would gaze upon her with love! She would work at his side. She had always wanted to start a Sunday school in their church. Oh yes, she could see it now. She would lead the little children, and he would lead the adults. And together they would serve God, building a wonderful church and congregation that would become known throughout the county for its faith and good works.

Stop it this minute, Ellie Newcomb! How you spin silly daydreams.

More than anything else, she wanted her own home and family. Looking around at her parents' home, she imagined having one like it. She loved the simple frame house with its whitewashed siding and covered front porch. Dad had built the house himself, with the help of neighbors, of course. It was two stories, the bottom floor one huge area for the kitchen, dining, and living areas, though at Mama's insistence there was a small separate room for a formal parlor. Upstairs were the four bedrooms. There was no indoor plumbing except in the kitchen, the one thing Ellie would change in her own home. She'd have an indoor bathroom with a big bathtub, maybe even with hot and cold running water.

Not on a pastor's salary, you won't! she told herself in an attempt to bring her fancies down to earth.

She concentrated once again on the patterns in Mama's box. The pattern showing was a LeMoyne Star, or as her mama called it, Lemon Star. Maybe she should do something simple like that. She really should refuse to get caught up in a competition that was not only unseemly but could become downright unsavory if it went too far. But she had always been taught to do her very best, and she could do far better than the Lemon Star.

Thumbing through a few more patterns,

she paused at one called Tree of Life. This was also pieced but more difficult by far. And there was a lovely spiritual meaning to it. It consisted of a tree trunk with nearly fifty tiny triangles for leaves. But since she especially enjoyed laid-on work, maybe she could make a more representational tree with a gnarled old trunk like the willow in their yard. Could she work that in blue? Oh, of course. She'd make a sky and perhaps an entire scene of the house, the willow, a couple of birds.

Jumping to her feet she went to Dad's writing desk, found some paper, and sketched out her idea. Then she began to wonder if Mama had a scrap of blue that would work for the sky. She went to the scrap box and was digging through that when she heard the wagon rattle into the yard.

Within a few moments, the house seemed to burst into life.

"Looks like you've been hard at it, Ellie," Mama said as she strode into the house with an armful of packages and took note of the scattered patterns and scraps of fabric.

Ellie hurried over to help. "Just looking through your patterns."

"Find anything?"

"I've got some ideas."

"Ooh!" Maggie exclaimed, holding up Ellie's sketch. "Looks like you're Leonardo da Vinci creating a masterpiece."

"Put that down. You'll mess it up!" Ellie demanded, feeling a little embarrassed. Down deep she knew she had gone too far with the drawing.

Mama ambled over. "That's really nice. I know I've got some brown for the tree."

"What's all this?" Dad asked, coming in just then.

"It's for the biddies' man-trap quilt," Maggie said before Ellie could respond.

"What?" Dad truly had no idea what she was talking about.

Quickly Ellie said, "Oh, it's nothing, Dad. Just a welcome quilt the Sewing Circle wants to make for the new pastor."

Dad looked at Mama.

Mama said, "Maggie, would you put down Ellie's work and finish bringing in the groceries?" It wasn't really a request, but Maggie was obviously reluctant to obey just as things might be getting interesting.

"What are you ladies up to?" Dad asked Mama.

"We are just making a welcome quilt."

"What has Maggie gotten into her head — ?"

"Maggie, scoot!" snapped Mama, and this

time Maggie leaped toward the door.

"Stay put, Maggie," Dad said quite firmly. Everyone held their breath, for it wasn't every day he so openly disputed Mama.

"Calvin, now, don't get your dander up," Mama said with a laugh. "Goodness, you know what a kidder Maggie is."

Maggie, who had stopped short at the door, made a protesting sound, but before she could say anything, Dad spoke. "I was afraid of something like this. I knew there was gonna be trouble when I showed you that letter and your eyes lit up like the Columbia steamer at night."

"Whatever do you mean, Calvin?" Mama said with another laugh.

Ellie defined it as a nervous laugh.

"We've got a bachelor minister coming to the county," Dad said. "That's like luring a poor fly into a web."

"Oh, Calvin, really!"

"Ada, I am the chairman of the board of deacons, and I must set an example for the church. I insist that this family behave in a seemly fashion with the new pastor. You will not parade our daughters about like tavern hussies!"

Dad never used words like *insist* and *will not* around Mama, not to mention a word like *hussies.* This was serious.

"We are only making a quilt, dear," Mama said in a rare contrite tone.

"I'm going to tend the animals," Dad said, then strode past Maggie and out the door.

Maggie started to follow him.

"Don't take another step, Margaret Edith!" Mama hissed.

Again Maggie stopped short.

"Put the new sack of flour in the bin," ordered Mama. "Then it is time to get supper."

"But Dad will need help."

Maggie never did know what was good for her.

"Georgie will be home soon," Mama said tightly in a tone that broached no argument.

Reluctantly, like a convict marching to the gallows, Maggie picked up the sack of flour Dad had brought in and carried it to the bin in the sideboard.

Ellie closed up the pattern box, straightened up the scrap box, and put everything away. Then she went to the kitchen to help with supper.

"Mama, is Dad right?" she asked. "Is it so terrible to want to impress the new pastor?"

"Your father is just being a man, which simply means he doesn't understand how things are, especially in the area of love and marriage. But what he truly doesn't understand is that we are only making a welcome quilt. No man ever married a girl because of a quilt."

That didn't take into consideration the unspoken implication of the quilt, but logic did tell Ellie that her mother was right. A quilt would never affect a man's heart. Still, she felt bad, not because of the quilt but because she knew her father was upset, perhaps even upset and disappointed with *her.* What he thought about her meant too much to her to feel comfortable with that.

"Mama, do you mind if I go out and . . . help Dad?" she asked.

"Well, just until Georgie gets home —"

"That's not fair!" protested Maggie. "You told me I couldn't go out —"

"Ellie did her chores today while you went to town and played. And it was you who put your father into a sour mood in the first place."

"What happened?" Ellie asked.

"Nothing. Go on and help your father," Mama said.

Mama's tight lips and the flash in Maggie's eyes gave Ellie the feeling she really didn't want to know, so she grabbed a coat from the hooks by the door and went out.

Dad had brought the horses into the barn and was forking hay into their stalls.

"Can I help, Dad?"

"Why, you haven't worked in the barn since you came back from that fancy finishing school your mother sent you to." He seemed to place special emphasis on those last few words. The school had been Mama's idea, though Ellie had wanted to go.

Ellie rubbed Jock's white face. He and Samo were their wagon team. "I can rub the horses down for you."

"Georgie will do that, honey. Why don't you just get on with why you came out here?" He smiled and didn't seem mad at all.

"You're not mad anymore?"

He shrugged. "Not much."

"I don't want you to think ill of me, Daddy."

"I would never, Ellie. You are the finest daughter a man could ask for. You have always made me proud."

"Well, this thing with the quilt —"

"I know your ma put you up to it."

It would have been easy to let it go at that, but Ellie knew it would neither be fair nor honest. "Daddy, the quilt was Mama's idea, or at least the Sewing Circle's, but . . . well . . . I have to admit it kind of has an appeal. That is . . ." Pausing, she turned so she could look her father in the eye. "I

wouldn't be opposed to marrying a minister
—"

"Ellie, not you —"

"He's going to marry someone, Dad. Why not me?"

Instead of answering right away, Dad paused in his work and gazed at his daughter. There was sadness in that look but maybe some understanding, too. He reached up and touched a lock of her hair hanging loosely around her shoulders.

Finally, he spoke. "I reckon I don't really mind the ladies making a quilt. Maybe I don't even mind them trying to snag the pastor, though I feel mighty sorry for the lad. No, that's not what perturbs me. I guess I'm just realizing my little girls are growing up — well, truth be told, they are grown-up. After what happened in town today and now this silliness with the quilt, I know it won't be long till I'm gonna have to hand you over to another." He stopped, his lips trembling a little.

"Much as I have always wanted my own home and family," Ellie said, "that's the part that troubles me, too. Leaving you and Mama isn't going to be easy. I love our family and our home. But we'll always be near each other. I'll make sure of that."

"Just as long as you marry someone

worthy of you. A good man, a Christian man who treats you right." He bit his lip. "I don't worry so much about you, Ellie. But that Maggie. If she takes up with that no-account —" He stopped, lifted the hayfork, and impaled another load of hay for the horses. "Maybe Maggie ought to marry the minister. That'd settle her down some. But she's so young. . . ." He seemed to be talking more to himself than to her.

Ellie wanted to remind him that Maggie was only a little more than a year younger than she was. She wondered what in the world had happened in St. Helens that had him so riled but thought better of bringing any of that up now.

"Dad, I know God will lead me to the perfect husband," she said instead. "And I won't marry anyone you don't approve of."

"Then let's just leave it in God's hands."

It wasn't until that night after they had crawled into bed that Ellie could ask her sister about the trip to St. Helens. She put out the lamp and spoke in whispers because she was sure this wasn't going to be a discussion they wanted Dad to overhear.

"So, Mags, tell me what happened in town," Ellie said.

The moonlight coming in through the window revealed Maggie rolling her eyes.

"Dad went off like a lit fuse just because I was talking with Tommy Donnelly. He actually said he didn't want me 'keeping company' with Tommy. Can you believe it?"

"He said 'keeping company'? Those words?"

"Tommy is just a friend."

"You're probably his only friend. He never had any friends in school."

"I tried to tell that to Dad, that he himself always taught me to be nice to the less fortunate. Well, all he said to that was 'Less fortunate *girls.*' "

"Well, I can see Dad's concern," Ellie said. "Tommy always was . . . an odd sort. Kind of sullen and . . . I don't know. I can't put my finger on what makes him odd, but I'm not the only one who thinks so."

"He is odd, and I can't help feeling sorry for him. But to 'keep company' with him? Really!"

"You can't be too careful now that you're getting older."

"Another reason I hate getting older." Maggie squirmed under the covers. "And you know what's worse? Mama agreed with Dad."

"Agreed?"

"Jane Donnelly is Mama's best friend,"

Maggie went on, "so it seems kind of disloyal. She said Tommy takes too much after his father."

"Mr. Donnelly is almost always drunk and scowling like he's got a real mean streak. And he never comes to church. I've heard rumors that young Tommy drinks spirits with his father."

"Tommy hates his father," Maggie said. "The man beats him and makes him work like a slave when he, that is, big Tom, don't hardly lift a finger. Dad called big Tom shiftless, and I believe it. But Tommy is different. He doesn't want to be like his father, he truly doesn't."

"Sometimes a boy can't help turning out like the only example he sees." Ellie felt some fear rising up in her. "Mags, you're not sweet on him, are you?"

"Goodness, no! I feel sorry for him is all. You may not think looks are important in a husband, but I do, and Tommy, bless his heart, is as homely as they come. A bit slow-witted, too."

"Be careful around him, then."

Maggie gave a quiet chuckle. "You sound worse than Dad. Even Mama said it'd be okay to invite him to church."

"Won't be the first time we've tried."

"He could change."

"Maybe Georgie or Boyd could invite him."

Maggie gave a testy sigh. "He'd just consider them two-faced, and he'd be right. They have never been nice to him before."

Ellie thought it was time to change the subject. "Dad was all sad because he realizes we are growing up and will be married soon."

"He don't have to worry about me! I'm years away from that."

"Still, it's sweet, isn't it? And you know what else? He said he feels sorry for the new pastor with all the girls going after him."

"Yes. There's a man who is doomed even before he sets a foot on the powder keg."

FIVE

Dad announced that on Sunday, two weeks after Mama's Sewing Circle had decided to make the welcome quilt, the family would go to Scappoose and attend Grandma and Grandpa Newcomb's church. This was the last weekend in April. The family usually visited their grandparents on the third weekend of the month.

"One good thing to come of having no pastor of our own," Dad said, "is that we get to spend an extra Sunday in the month with Grandma and Grandpa."

Ellie was sure she saw a twinkle in his eye as he said this with a pointed look toward Mama.

Mama said nothing. She could hardly protest going to church, could she? But no doubt she was perturbed that Dad had to make such an embellished point of the matter, since they had been following this routine since they had lost their pastor.

Eight months ago, Pastor McFarland, their former minister, had suffered a stroke while riding the circuit. He fell off his horse and broke his leg and died a week later from the trauma. He was seventy years old and probably should have given up the circuit long ago. Most likely he had hung on because, as they soon learned, ministers were not exactly falling off trees in the Brethren of Christ Church. In those intervening months it had been quite a hardship on the church members in the county. Many letters had been sent to headquarters back east, but word always came back that there just were not enough available ministers.

Most of the church members in Columbia County visited other denominations when they could, but distances were so far it was usually quite an ordeal to get to another church. Nevertheless, the Newcombs now went to Scappoose two Sundays in a row.

The church was another bone of contention between Mama and Grandma Newcomb. Dad had been raised Methodist and Mama was Brethren of Christ. When they married and moved to Maintown, there was already a Brethren of Christ Church there, so that's where they became members. Grandma once said right out that she thought that's why Mama had pushed for the move to Maintown. Ellie did not know if that was so. She herself could see little difference between the two churches; in fact, she thought the Brethren were an offshoot of the larger denomination.

Saturday morning the family boarded the wagon. Dad had put up the frame and canvas cover because it looked like it might rain on the way. He and Boyd rode up front, and the rest of the family rode in back under the canvas. Dad had spread a layer of hay on the floor, and Mama had laid a couple of quilts over that so the ride would be a little more comfortable. Ellie tried to sew, but the bouncing of the wagon prevented her from doing the fine appliqué work she needed to do on her block for the welcome quilt. Maggie had a book to read, but after a while she had to put it down because the jostling was making her sick. She still hadn't chosen her block, and Ellie knew she would put it off until the last minute.

Georgie was restless and kept trying to say a tongue twister he'd just learned. "Theophilus Thistledown, the successful thistle sifter, in sifting a sieve full of unsifted thistles, thrust three thousand thistles through the thick of his thumb."

He drove them crazy with it until Maggie

tried to stuff a handful of hay into his mouth. Mama, who had amazingly dozed off, woke to the yells and scuffles and made the two sit as far apart as one could get in a small wagon.

About the time it began to rain, Georgie started with riddles. "Two brothers we are, great burdens we bear, by which we are bitterly pressed. In truth we may say we are full all day but empty when we go to rest."

"Shoes," said Maggie, barely giving him a chance to finish. Her tone was smug.

He tried another and another, and she quickly guessed them all, taking the fun out of it for him, and he finally fell silent. It wasn't long afterward that they pulled into Grandma and Grandpa's place.

They lived out of town a couple of miles on Cater Road. Grandpa had been a logger, only farming enough to feed his family, unlike Dad, who farmed a sizable potato crop for income and also had started working part-time at the sawmill last year when the crops were bad. Hearing the wagon rattle over the driveway of their house that was nestled in a nice grove of fir and cedars, Grandma and Grandpa came out on the porch and waved.

As the family bounded out of the wagon, the chatter began.

"Thought you might be coming today," Grandpa said. He was in his seventies, an older version of Dad. His hair was thin and white, whereas Dad's was still brown and thinning only in a few places. They were the same size, or would have been if Grandpa didn't have a stoop in his back that caused his head to jut forward, making him a few inches shorter than Dad. But their eyes were the same, as was the timbre of their voices. They had the same quiet, easygoing personalities and the same smile. It was very easy to love Grandpa.

Then there was Grandma Newcomb. In a way she was a lot like Mama, though Ellie knew Mama would never believe that. Perhaps Mama more resembled Grandma's shadow, a softer, gentler version of the older lady. Both women spoke their minds and appeared to wield the power in the family, but Grandma's words seemed much sharper than Mama's. It was like the saying about a person's bark being worse than their bite. That was often true in Mama's case, but Ellie knew from experience that it was not so for Grandma. No one, not even Maggie, could manipulate Grandma. Her bark had bite, and one better not forget that.

Grandma and Mama didn't look at all alike, either. Mama was shorter than Ellie but a bit on the plump side. "You try having four babies and still keep your girlish figure!" she'd say if anyone even hinted that she should drop a few pounds. Her hair was brown and her eyes green like Maggie's. She was pretty even for a thirty-nine-year-old matron.

Grandma Newcomb was tall, at least as tall as Dad, and what Ellie would call big-boned, though not fat. Her hair and eyes were gray, iron gray. She always wore her hair in a chignon, not the fashionable kind that Ellie liked to wear sometimes in the middle of her head. Grandma's was low on her neck and looked as though she was wearing a big spoon. Her everyday dresses matched exactly except in color. One was dark brown, one dark blue, and one dark gray. When she wore the gray one, she looked a little like one of the bullets in Dad's carbine. All her dresses had shirtwaists and long sleeves, with the only adornment being an ecru lace collar at the high neck. For special occasions she had another dress that was dark green. Now, as she waved from the porch, she was wearing the brown dress.

"Girls, let's get these quilts and bring them in so they can dry," Mama said.

"Oh, those old things," Grandma said as

the first quilt was pulled from the wagon bed. "Do they have to come into the house?"

The quilts were by no means Mama's best, but Grandma made it sound as if they'd been used in the barn for birthing a calf.

"I'll lay 'em out in the barn," Dad said in a conciliatory tone.

Amazingly, Mama didn't argue.

"I'll take care of them," offered Boyd, a little too eagerly, Ellie thought. He hopped up into the wagon and grabbed the reins.

"You hang them over a clean post," Mama instructed through gritted teeth. "Carefully."

"I'll help!" Georgie said, spinning around toward the barn.

Mama laid a hand on his shoulder. "No, you won't." Poor Mama had the look of a sea captain on a sinking ship that everyone was quickly abandoning.

One thing good that could be said about Grandma was that she was an excellent cook. Even Mama had to admit that. And since they had been making a habit lately of coming on the last two weekends of the month, she surely had been expecting them. The meal she spread out before them that evening was fit for Christmas. Roast venison, potatoes, and her canned green beans, which she had a way of seasoning so that even Georgie ate them. She brought out her pickled beets and Ellie's favorite, pickled carrots. For dessert she served apple and currant pie.

Too bad the conversation at the table wasn't as nice as the meal. Mama was quiet, but not quiet in a polite, demure way. It was more like if she said one word, she'd erupt like Mount St. Helens — which was across the river in Washington State — had done twenty-five years ago. Grandma went on about how appalling it was that the Brethren of Christ had left them high and dry without a minister for so long.

"The Methodists would never have left us without a pastor for eight months," she said. In fact, her church had it pretty good, because their pastor managed to have a service in Scappoose twice a month.

"It's a small denomination, Ma," Dad said.

"You should join our church," Grandma insisted. "You attend here once a month anyways, and now twice. I see no reason why you couldn't drive down here every weekend and spend it with us. We see so little of you."

Ellie heard a sound from Mama's end of the table, more a grunt than words.

74

The women all helped clean up after dinner, receiving constant instructions from Grandma. "No, don't put it there. Over here, Margaret. Ada, this pot isn't quite clean. Give it another scrub. Give the cloth a good shake outside, Eleanor."

It wasn't as if they hadn't been helping in her kitchen for years, but somehow they never seemed to get it right enough to please Grandma. Ellie had the feeling that she, Maggie, *and* Mama were all children being scolded. Mama was tight-lipped through it all. Ellie could remember a time when Mama would talk back to Grandma, but that had always brought so much contention that in the last couple of years Mama seemed bent on following the path of silence when humanly possible.

The men were sitting by the hearth talking about lumber, the crops, the weather. The women, after the dishes had been done, sat around the table. Ellie and Mama took out their sewing. Maggie glanced longingly at the men, and for once even Ellie wished she could talk lumber with them. Grandma was doing her mending.

"What's that you're working on, Eleanor?" Grandma asked. She always used their formal names.

"We're making a welcome quilt for our

new pastor." Ellie held up her block, on which she was just finishing the house. She still had the birds and tree to do.

"That is quite fancy, dear. The man's wife will be thrilled to receive it."

"He's not married," Ellie said, groaning inwardly as she felt the heat of pink rise in her cheeks. She prayed Maggie did not pipe up with her take on the matter.

Luckily, Grandma could not see Ellie's face in the poorly lit room. "An unmarried minister! I suppose you could not expect more from the Brethren of Christ."

"I think we are fortunate to get a man who will be able to start new here and make this truly his home," Mama said.

"All the young girls in the county will try to set their hooks into him," Grandma said. "It could become quite scandalous."

Maggie giggled.

"Goodness!" Grandma exclaimed. "Don't tell me you girls are already setting your sights on him! You mustn't behave shamelessly." She looked at Mama. "Ada, I hope you take a firm hand with these girls in this matter."

"Really, Mother Newcomb, I would never dream of encouraging such behavior in my daughters," Mama said, then snapped her mouth shut as if fearing to say more.

Sunday morning dawned with the first real promise of spring in weeks. It wasn't raining, and there were patches of blue amongst the gray clouds. Mama said it would rain later, so they shouldn't linger after church but head right home. Grandma insisted they stay long enough for a midday meal. Dad said they'd probably have time to eat. As always, he walked the precarious line between trying to please both of the most demanding women in his life.

The Methodists of Scappoose also met in their schoolhouse. The nearest actual church was in St. Helens. Built in 1853 on a bluff overlooking the river, it had been the third church structure built in Oregon Territory. Today, the rest of Columbia County still lagged in this regard. Maybe under Maintown's new pastor they would build their own church and no longer have to share with the school.

Ellie couldn't see how Grandma Newcomb could be so puffed up about her church. Mama wasn't the only one who said the folks of Scappoose preferred to work or frequent its saloon rather than support its church. Why, last summer the tent meeting held in Dutch Canyon just outside of town had been very poorly attended.

As Ellie took a seat on one of the benches,

she saw that the Stoddards had also chosen this Sunday to visit the Scappoose Methodist Church. After the service while the congregation stood about in the school yard visiting, Ellie sought out Sarah Stoddard. She noted that Sarah's brother, Colby, was visiting with a group of men. He winked at her as she passed, and she tried to ignore him.

Sarah was standing by herself looking around as if she didn't know where to go. She was so shy that she had trouble, even at the Maintown church among friends, going up to people and visiting. Ellie had no such problem.

"Hi, Sarah," she said. "It's nice to see a familiar face."

"But you come here all the time, don't you?"

"Yes, but it never feels like home."

"Mother's sister lives here and attends this church," Sarah said, "but we don't visit her much."

"What did you think of the service?"

"They don't sing as many hymns as we do. That's my favorite part."

Ellie knew that Sarah was quite an accomplished pianist. Ellie had taken some piano lessons at Mrs. Dubois' school but hadn't progressed very far. She realized that was a drawback for her because pastors' wives often assisted their husbands by leading the music in the church. However, there was no piano in the Maintown church, so that wouldn't be a problem.

"I agree," Ellie replied.

Silence followed. Sarah seldom initiated conversation, so the responsibility was left to the other person, and Ellie found it wearisome, much as she liked Sarah and wanted to be her friend.

There was one subject Ellie wanted to raise, but she didn't want to appear anxious or make it seem overly important. Nevertheless, she was dying to know what pattern Sarah was doing for the welcome quilt. Along with her many other accomplishments, Sarah was an excellent stitcher and probably one of the three best of the young girls in the community, Ellie and Mabel Parker being the other two.

Finally Ellie said as casually as she could, "So, Sarah, are you making a block for that welcome quilt? The one for the new pastor?"

"Mother didn't give me a choice." Sarah's voice held a distinct edge.

Had she actually tried to object, to stand up to her formidable mother? Ellie couldn't imagine such a thing. "You didn't want to make one?"

"Well, I . . ." She looked down at her clasped hands, her fingers twisting. "Of course, I welcome the new minister. I just . . . well . . . I hope that our mothers don't . . . you know . . . become pushy."

"I know what everyone's saying," Ellie said, "that we're trying to snare the minister."

"Aren't we? That is, they, the Sewing Circle?"

"Maybe he'll be looking for a wife." Ellie remembered what Grandma Newcomb had said. "Most ministers are married, and it probably is the best situation for a church."

Sarah had a bit of a desperate look on her face. She was a pretty girl with dark brown hair that fell in perfect waves to the middle of her back. She had large brown eyes and creamy skin without a single freckle, a fact much envied by Maggie who, especially in summer, was plagued by more than her share. But Sarah was Ellie's age and, as far as Ellie knew, had never had a beau, nor did the local boys go after her. It seemed they didn't even know she existed, and she did nothing to change that. She was probably the only true shrinking violet that Ellie knew of except maybe for Nessa Wallard. If life were perfect, Mrs. Wallard would have been Sarah's mother, for she'd have been able to understand a shy daughter. Instead, Sarah's mother was the bossiest lady in town, always pushing poor Sarah, not subtly either, but it was so obvious to all. Mrs. Stoddard pushed and Sarah usually responded by becoming even more shy.

"Mother wants me to do a Rose of Sharon design because of the spiritual meaning," Sarah said, no doubt initiating conversation just because of the sudden awkwardness.

"You haven't started your block yet?"

"Well, I started one like Mother wanted . . . but, maybe I won't use something so showy. I'm also working on a Sawtooth Star. I'll decide later." They both knew who would make the final decision.

Ellie was almost embarrassed to tell Sarah her design. "I'm doing a scene of our house and front yard."

"I bet it's beautiful."

"Maybe too showy, though."

"Oh, Ellie, I didn't mean . . . that is, you shouldn't . . ." She fumbled around a moment, then finished as if she were making a huge confession. "I don't want to win the pastor!"

"It's not as if our blocks will win him, Sarah." But Ellie was no more convinced than Sarah, else she wouldn't have decided to make the intricate scene.

"It's not our blocks. It's our mothers."

"Your mother can't make you marry someone you don't want to marry."

Sarah just replied with a look that said, "You do know Emma Jean Stoddard, don't you?"

Before Ellie could say more, a male voice interrupted. "Well, if it isn't the prettiest girl in the county!"

Ellie responded coyly, "Why, Sarah, doesn't your brother think highly of you?"

"I'm not talking about my ugly sister, Ellie, and you know it," Colby said.

"You take that back about your sister, or I won't speak to you at all," Ellie retorted.

"Oh, beautiful sister," Colby intoned with little sincerity, "why don't you take your beautiful and lovely self thither so I can be alone with this second most beautiful girl in the county?"

Sarah rolled her eyes at her brother but dutifully scooted away. Ellie noted she just went to another corner of the school yard to again stand alone.

Colby continued, "Ellie, I'm feeling kind of hurt. You've been ignoring me since my last proposal of marriage."

Ellie gasped and quickly looked around. She had told no one, not even Maggie, about the fact that Colby had proposed to her twice since her return from Portland.

Assured no one was near enough to over-hear, she said, "Colby, it wouldn't be proper for me to keep encouraging you, now, would it?"

"But to cut me off completely?"

"There are plenty of other girls around for you to pay attention to."

"I have eyes only for you." Pausing, he focused such an adoring gaze at her that she tingled in spite of herself. Then he went on, "Why would you reject the most hand-some, lovable, kindest, most perfect man in the county, maybe in the whole state?"

"I'm looking for a *modest* man," she deadpanned, then giggled.

Why, indeed, was she rejecting him? Tall, dark-haired, features chiseled like a Grecian statue, he very well might have been the most handsome man in the state. And though his words were rather immodest, she knew he was just joking — well, mostly. He was always making fun and kidding around. He made her laugh, but he made her tingle, too. Was that love? She just didn't know. What else could she be looking for?

As if he could read her mind, he said, "Don't tell me you are holding out for that new minister like all the other girls?"

"Oh, Colby, how could you say such a

thing?" She felt her cheeks flush.

"I fear my greatest rival is coming to town, and I can't do a thing about it. I'll wager that even if he's as ugly as a horned toad, the girls will flock to him. But, Ellie, I thought you were deeper than that."

"Well, I . . . I . . ."

Just then Maggie walked by. Ellie grasped her arm and reeled her in like a fish on a hook.

"Maggie, is Mama anxious to leave?" Ellie asked.

Ignoring the question, or perhaps she just didn't hear, suddenly caught as she was in Colby's brilliant orbit, Maggie said, "Hi, Colby." Her tone was meek, even shy.

"Hi ya, Mags. What you been up to?"

"Oh . . . uh . . . nothing much," stammered Maggie. Then she seemed to pull herself together and added with a little more aplomb, "Been busy working on the new pastor's welcome quilt."

"Not you, too, Mags!" Colby exclaimed with mock dismay. "I thought you, at least, would have the sense God gave you."

"We all want to welcome him," she answered innocently.

"I hate the fellow even before I've met him."

"Colby! You shouldn't speak so about a

man of God," Ellie said, truly appalled.

Recovering from her brief bout of shyness, Maggie jabbed, "Ellie doesn't want anyone insulting her future husband."

"Maggie!" Ellie squealed.

Colby frowned a little.

Maybe he saw beneath the jibes and jokes and realized it might be more serious than he thought.

"But have no fear," Maggie added glibly, "I have no interest at all in the minister."

Furious, Ellie began, "No, she's only interested in —"

"There's Mama waving," Maggie quickly cut in.

Ellie could have pressed on with her own tease, but didn't. She thought it would truly mortify Maggie if anyone even hinted at her interest in Colby, especially since he was so oblivious of it.

Though Mama hadn't really been waving, both sisters bid Colby adieu and hurried off to where their parents were saying their own good-byes and preparing to leave.

"How could you?" Maggie hissed under her breath.

"You're surprised after what you said about me?" countered Ellie.

"Well, I was just joking."

"And I wouldn't have been?" Ellie arched

a brow. Why couldn't Maggie be mature enough to admit to her feelings for Colby?

"You would have embarrassed Colby," Maggie said instead.

"But not you?"

"Oh, shut up!" With that Maggie hurried ahead and spoke barely another word to her sister until long after they got back home from Scappoose.

Six

The Maintown Sewing Circle always met on the second Sunday of the month, a day that was quickly approaching. Maggie had to find a block pattern and get it done.

Two days before the meeting she lugged out Mama's pattern box and began riffling through it haphazardly until Mama scolded her to take care with the precious patterns.

Defiantly, as if she were actually threatening her mother, Maggie said, "I'll do a nine-patch."

"You most certainly will not!" Mama said unequivocally. "You can do better than that, and you will."

"She could have done better if she hadn't put it off," Ellie said.

Maggie picked up the pincushion to throw at her sister's smug face.

"Don't you dare!" warned Mama, who seemed never to miss anything.

Reluctantly Maggie put down the pincushion, and her goal became to choose something that looked spectacular but was incredibly easy to make — if such a pattern existed. She also wanted to make sure that whatever she chose already had templates made. She'd never get it done if she had to make those, as well. She looked for nearly an hour — what with several distractions pulling her away. Eventually she narrowed it down to two: a Grape Basket pattern that was pieced with all triangles, which were irksome to make but within her ability to do so, and a Grandmother's Fan pattern. Setting the curved fan into the background piece would be tricky, but she thought she could manage it. She'd always liked the various basket blocks best, so the decision was hard to make.

When Mama came to the kitchen table where Maggie was sitting with a dozen patterns spread out in front of her, she pointed at the fan. "I think you should do that. I heard both Louise and Polly are making baskets."

So, with Mama having made the decision for her, Maggie went to the scrap box. And there she still was a couple of hours later, surrounded by piles of scraps, not that she had spent the whole time looking for fabric. She'd been distracted by the seed catalog, had raided the cookie jar, then spent some time searching for a hair ribbon she remembered she'd lost. Another time she jumped up thinking she heard a bird hit a window. She went outside to see if the poor animal was in the dirt, which it wasn't, but their dog Gypsy came up with a stick, wanting to play. Maggie tossed the stick a few times until Gypsy lost interest. Maggie hurried back into the house when she thought she heard Mama coming. It turned out to be just her imagination.

Mama and Ellie had gone to the garden to work. Mama was giving Maggie incredible leeway in her chores, a fact that drew more than one dirty look from Ellie. After all, Ellie had made a beautiful block and finished it in plenty of time while not missing any of her chores.

"Oh, Maggie! What a mess!" groaned Mama when she finally did come in to punch down the bread dough.

"I can't find enough blues," Maggie complained. She was going to use a muslin background but wanted to make each fan blade a different blue. She needed seven, but just when she thought she'd found the right scrap, it was too small. Mama's scraps were just that — leftovers from other quilt projects or salvageable pieces from old clothes and such. Any larger lengths of fabric, a few store-bought goods or some of the finer bits from old clothes, were put on a separate shelf and touched only at one's peril.

Mama washed the garden dirt from her hands and then went to where Maggie was sitting cross-legged on the floor. Mama knelt down beside her. "Here's an idea," she said. "Do the third blade in from each side in a dark navy and you won't need so many different blues. I'll give you a bit from the material we bought at the dry goods store for the sashing. Then it will tie the block to the sashing. Doing that, you'll only need five blues."

Maggie had the five blues. "That would work." It amazed her how in five minutes her mother could solve a problem that had stymied Maggie for hours.

"Could I have a little more of the navy for the fan base?" she asked.

"Then it would be lost in the sashing. Why not make the fan float on the background?"

When it came to quilting, Mama could be ever so resourceful and creative.

"I'll cut what you need off the sashing material. Luckily I have it here, since I bought it."

"You bought new material?" This was a

rare occurrence for Mama, as well as for the other ladies, and Maggie was again impressed as to how special the Circle considered the quilt.

"Everyone will reimburse me. It won't even put a dent in our egg money," Mama said, taking a length of dark blue material from a shelf in the cupboard where her sewing things were stored. She cut from this a thin strip that would be exactly enough for the two blades. "Now, take care with this, Maggie. It's all I can spare."

Maggie had never used new fabric in a quilt, so it was with great reverence that she took possession of the small bit of material.

"Before you get started on that, we need your help in the garden," Mama said. "Clean up the rest of the scraps. Put the pieces you're going to use in my sewing basket, then come outside."

For once, to show her appreciation of her mother's patience, she did as she was told. But spending the rest of the afternoon in the garden put her seriously behind in her work on the block. She didn't get back to it until after supper. When the table was cleared, she laid out her scraps of material and the templates, got a pencil from Dad's writing desk, and began the task of tracing the templates onto the material. She tried to be so careful in her work that the concentration began to give her a headache, made worse when remembering she had only tomorrow to stitch the thing. Her eyes were getting sore and blurry from the dim light of the kerosene lamp. She glanced toward her sister, who was stitching another quilt top she'd put aside when they started the welcome quilt. Ellie was pointedly ignoring her.

Maggie was near to tears by the time she finished cutting out her pieces. "Mama," she whined, "I'll never finish this tomorrow!"

"Ellie and I will do your chores for you —"

"Mama!" Ellie protested. "That's not fair!"

"Your sister is doing her best."

"She wouldn't be in this pickle if she hadn't put it off to the last minute. She'll never learn her lesson," Ellie argued in a most high-and-mighty tone.

"I don't need anyone's help!" snapped Maggie. "I'll get the block done and do my chores, as well. So there!"

Dad, who was sitting by the hearth sharpening his belt knife, grunted. Mama shot him a meaningful glance, though Maggie wasn't sure what it meant until Dad quietly said, "I told you this quilt was going to cause trouble."

"It is not the quilt," Mama countered. "It is these two girls who have forgotten their Christian values. 'Do unto others as you would have them do unto you!' " She swung her gaze toward Ellie.

Ellie never liked to be reminded that she was less than the most perfect Christian around. She seemed to shrink visibly. "I guess I can do a few extra chores," she mumbled.

"That's better," Mama said.

Maggie wanted to insist that she could do it all but knew better than anyone just what hogwash that was.

The next day, after pricking her finger a hundred times and ripping out stitches more often than she felt necessary because Mama kept saying she could do better, she finished the block. She decided she was going to rename it The Stupid Fan. Mama turned the block over and examined the back with a critical eye. When she pronounced it acceptable, Maggie knew she'd meant "acceptable for Maggie." The stitches were not of a uniform size, and in a couple of places she'd veered off her guideline, causing a bit of a pucker. With great magnanimity Mama said of those less-than-perfect places, "They'll quilt out."

Maggie breathed a sigh of relief that she was not going to have to rip out any more stitches.

Ellie complimented the block, too, and sounded sincere. She was not really a vindictive girl. Maggie said she would do extra chores to make up for the last two days.

Mama laid the three blocks out on the table. She had done the Bowtie pattern, since the quilt was for a man. It had a very simple look, but Maggie knew its set-in seams could be difficult, though not for Mama, of course. It was obvious she had purposely chosen a plain block so that Ellie's would shine all that much more. Which it did. The house really looked like the Newcomb house, with whitewashed sides and everything. The sky was blue, and there were two birds done in a darker blue. The willow tree was breathtaking. She'd done the trunk in several different shades of brown, so it had depth and looked real. Ellie had appliquéd green leaves on the tree, at least a dozen of the tiny things. Had Maggie done the scene, she would have made it in winter in order to eliminate the extra work of the leaves. Ellie had even put in the swing that hung from one of the stout branches. The final touch was a tiny version of their dog, Gypsy, prancing across the green grass. If this were a contest, Maggie thought Ellie would win hands down.

Ellie seemed to sense what her sister was thinking. "Mama, it's too much, isn't it? I went too far. I didn't think I was so vainglorious. I shouldn't have used green. That makes it stand out all the more."

"Don't you worry, Ellie," Mama cooed. "We never said only blue was to be used. Just that it had to be the predominant color. And your sky is definitely the main color. I happen to know Mary Renolds is making a brown and green Tree of Life against a blue background. Now, don't worry so."

The next day the three Newcomb women took the wagon into Maintown, only a mile away, to the schoolhouse. Today, the Sewing Circle was welcoming all female church members who had wanted to participate in making the quilt. There were a couple of women who were not stitchers but had been invited to make blocks with the help of the Sewing Circle. That brought the grand total of blocks to twenty, which would make a very ample-sized bed quilt.

When the Newcombs arrived, the place was already a buzz of activity, but no one had revealed their blocks yet because Mrs.

Stoddard wanted to wait until everyone had come. As usual, the last to get there were Florence Parker and her daughter, Mabel.

"I'm sorry I'm late," Mrs. Parker said breathlessly. "My new sewing machine was delivered yesterday, and I thought I would just fiddle with it a little this morning. Before I knew it, Mabel was telling me it was time to go!"

Maggie's gaze shot to her mother. Mama had been talking with Mrs. Donnelly, and suddenly her face froze. Maggie knew her mother had been saving extra egg money for a year in order to buy a sewing machine. It just didn't seem right that Mrs. Parker should get a new machine when she had a perfectly good one already. Mrs. Parker and Mrs. Renolds were the only ladies in the Circle with machines.

Maggie immediately wondered what Mrs. Parker would do with her old machine. Maybe Mama could buy that one?

All the ladies were asking Mrs. Parker about her machine. She invited them to visit anytime to try it out. Maggie didn't think she was too awfully boastful until Mama asked what she would do with the old machine. Mama's voice sounded funny as she asked, kind of strained and forced.

"Mabel has her eye on it," Mrs. Parker

said. "But — oh, Ada, I forgot. You've been saving your egg money ever so long to buy a machine, haven't you? Maybe you could afford one now if you bought an old machine like mine."

"I'm not interested in your old machine," Mama said, her voice as frosty as her expression. She looked as if she was about to say more when Mrs. Donnelly broke in.

"Oh, Ada, can you help me a minute with this . . . uh . . . with my block? One of the seams is puckered." Mrs. Donnelly nudged Mama over to a table where her sewing basket sat.

There was a little more conversation about the machine, but Mama added no more. She and Mrs. Donnelly looked absorbed in fixing Mrs. Donnelly's block, but they were also whispering to each other. Maggie had the feeling Mrs. Donnelly was soothing Mama. Maggie remembered that when Mrs. Renolds got her machine, Mama was as happy for her as she would have been for herself. Mama couldn't be jealous, then. It must just be that old rivalry between her and Mrs. Parker.

For once Maggie was glad when Mrs. Stoddard took charge and steered the meeting to its purpose.

"Now for the moment we have all been

waiting for!" she announced. "Let's reveal our blocks."

She had pushed aside all the desks and placed a large old quilt, made of a faded blue cotton, on the floor. In an orderly fashion the women filed up and laid their blocks in rows on the quilt. Maggie was surprised at how beautiful the whole was and how uniform. No one block, not even Ellie's, stuck out like a sore thumb.

After giving all the blocks a quick scan, Maggie began concentrating on the blocks made by her friends. Sarah's was a Rose of Sharon, a pattern of laid-on work with four long stems and four shorter stems radiating out from a center flower shape, each stem also having a flower at the end. Her stems and leaves were green, the flowers in different shades of blue. The work was unquestionably fine, but Maggie had seen this pattern done before to better effect using red for the flowers. However, Maggie well knew she was not one to be critical.

Kendra Wallard, Nessa's daughter, who was between Ellie and Maggie in age, had also done a block, but since Boyd was seriously courting her, she wasn't interested in snagging the minister. She had made a LeMoyne Star, with each of the points alternating dark and light blue. Iris Fergus made a Bear's Paw or, using the Quaker name, the Hand of Friendship. Finally, there was Mabel's block. Surprisingly, she had not done laid-on work, which was probably the best way to set a block apart and emphasize a quilter's skill. Her pattern, Sunburst, was probably the most difficult one of all, for it was a small sunburst inside a larger one, and each sunburst had two layers of points radiating from the center circle. There had to be thirty points in the smaller one alone!

Well, no question. Mabel won the prize and probably the minister, as well. Everyone else realized this, too, and were congratulating her. Maggie told herself that quilts don't win husbands. But Mabel had more than fine stitching in her favor. Though not exactly beautiful, she had a way about her that made you forget her large nose and somewhat crooked teeth. She had beautiful auburn hair that was always fixed stylishly. And she never wore anything that wasn't store bought. Which made it even more of an irony that Mrs. Parker had the best sewing machine around — she never sewed clothing. The Parkers were half owners of the sawmill, so they had money. Still, Florence Parker always looked frumpy and threadbare and their house was unkempt.

All the family's riches must have gone directly to Mabel's closet. Not to mention that she had a brother in a fancy Eastern college.

On top of that, Mabel was naturally graceful like Ellie. She always knew the right thing to say. Her responses now to the ladies' praise was perfectly balanced, not too embarrassed, not too prideful. She was the exact opposite of her artless mother. And she was Ellie's stiffest competition in the "battle" for the minister. Maggie thought it was funny that it should come to that, since their mothers had always been such rivals. No one knew why, and maybe the two women had even forgotten over the years the dispute that had pitted them against each other. But it wasn't going to help matters for their daughters to now become rivals. Though in truth, Mabel and Ellie had always been nipping at each other's heels to be best in school, in play, and of course in stitching. This didn't mean they weren't friendly, if not best friends. It just meant one or the other was always first.

Maggie was glad she wasn't going to be involved in this newest competition. She could just sit back and enjoy watching the fur fly.

The ladies spent some time moving the blocks around to find the most pleasing arrangement. This bored Maggie to no end because she thought it had been fine in the first place. Since this was a task only for the Sewing Circle, the younger women watched and chatted together, some quietly voicing their ideas but none brave enough to interfere with the ladies.

"Which is your block?" Mabel asked Maggie.

Maggie thought she probably knew but was fishing for a chance to make some condescending remark. Maggie vaguely pointed toward her block. "That one."

"You did a nice job," Mabel said, not waiting for more specific directions. "Your stitching is coming right along."

Only Mabel could make an insult sound like a compliment. Maggie wanted to say that she wasn't desperate enough to make the best block in the quilt, but even she couldn't bring herself to be that catty. Besides, Mabel always treated her like a child and would probably think such words a childish outburst rather than an insult.

"We've all outdone ourselves," Sarah Stoddard said.

"It's going to be a beautiful quilt," Ellie added.

"That preacher better appreciate it," Iris said.

Maggie thought it was probably because of such comments that Iris wasn't married yet.

Once the women agreed on the final arrangement, the blocks were numbered by pinning a scrap of paper to them. Then everyone took up the blocks and began sewing on the sashing, a dark blue calico, which Mama and Jane had cut out earlier into one-and-a-half-inch strips, since the sashing was going to be one inch wide. This same fabric would also be used in the border. This was all handwork, but Mrs. Parker made a point of saying that if her machines — she seemed to emphasize the plural just a bit — weren't so heavy, she would have brought them.

One of the ladies had brought an iron, which she heated on the school stove, and carefully pressed the sashed blocks as they were finished.

The final rows were being sewed together when the door opened and Dad came in.

"Knew I'd find everyone here," he said awkwardly. He would never have ventured in among the "hens," as he called them, unless it was important.

"Is something wrong, Calvin?" Mama

asked, concern in her voice.

"No. I just came from the post office, and there was a letter from denominational headquarters."

Maggie could almost hear all the ladies suck in air and collectively hold their breaths.

"He's not coming," a small voice ventured. Mrs. Stoddard would be the only one to not hold her breath.

"No, no!" Dad chuckled.

It appeared to Maggie that he had enjoyed their initial dismay and had waited just a tad longer than necessary to reassure them.

"It's good news. Reverend Locklin has departed his home in Maine and should arrive here by the end of the month."

There was a general gasp and then the ladies burst into chatter.

Mrs. Stoddard said, "We'll never get this quilted in time."

That pretty much summed up everyone's concern. The Sewing Circle didn't meet again until the second Sunday in June, and the minister would surely be here by then. They could just give it to him later when they finished. Someone even suggested that. But Maggie imagined that Mama and some of the other ladies had visions of fixing up the reverend's room at the boardinghouse with all the finery they had assembled together, along with a couple plates of cookies and the *pièce de résistance* spread out upon the bed. The quilt just had to be there to greet him, to *welcome* him, as it was meant to do, upon his arrival.

"I have an idea," Mama said. "Let's meet at my house this Wednesday for a quilting. I've got a decent frame. If the weather is nice, I'll set it up outside. If not, I can clear room for it in my parlor." Mama loved for people to know she had a special parlor, though it was seldom used even for company.

A few of the women had prior commitments that day, but enough of the others could come, so the date was set.

Maggie sidled up to her sister. "What do you think of all this?" she asked quietly.

"What do you mean?"

"It is suddenly happening very fast. In six months someone could be married to that minister. It could be you, sis."

Rather than turn pink as Maggie thought she would, Ellie turned white.

"S-six months!" She shook her head. "He's a minister, Mags. He wouldn't move that fast?"

But that final sentence was a question, a rather desperate question at that.

SEVEN

The old nag was lame, limping along as if she was going to collapse at any moment. Zack was tempted to get off and walk the pitiful beast. He was far enough out of town so that he could be fairly certain Cutter hadn't discovered his tracks — not yet, at least.

But it was still hard not to feel the press of urgency upon him. For the last several days he'd been trapped like a rat in Portland, unable to leave because he had no money, no transportation, and because it seemed Beau Cutter was always just one step behind him. He'd been running and looking over his shoulder for days, and that feeling was hard to shake.

Zack didn't have a lot of qualms about stealing. It wouldn't be the first time, though he'd done so mostly for survival when he was younger. He didn't want the law after him, as well as Beau, so he'd held off stealing a horse. Some still thought horse thieves ought to be hanged.

At least he didn't have to worry about the law where the shooting of Ron Sinclair was concerned. Cutter would have had too much explaining to do if he'd reported the shooting. Zack had learned two things about that melee in the alley. First, the passerby had been killed in the tussle, neck broken or something. Second, Sinclair was dead, too. The two bodies had been left in the alley, and the police drew the conclusion that the two had killed each other. There were many holes in that conclusion, such as the missing gun, but none seemed to implicate Zack. So the police were probably off his back. But Beau Cutter wasn't going to rest until his friend's killer was found.

Zack finally got a break when he slipped into a livery stable to spend the night — that's how he'd been existing the last few days, hiding in one hole or another. Anyway, in the back of the stable was the broken-down old nag, a sway-backed mare, long in the tooth and probably half blind. No one was going to miss her. They would probably raise more of a ruckus over the missing saddle, but Zack made sure he took the oldest one he could find.

Zack was now ten miles northwest of Portland, traveling along back roads. The town of St. Helens was about twenty miles ahead. Maybe he could find a way to earn some traveling money there. The town was right on the Columbia River, and he hoped he could earn enough for passage on one of the boats heading to the coastal town of Astoria. That plan had risks, though, because Cutter worked the river trade and might have sent word ahead to have the port watched.

Zack still thought his best bet was to eventually head south to San Francisco. He'd lived there longer than any place and had some connections there. The only reason he hadn't headed in that direction in the first place was that he'd once mentioned to Cutter that he knew people there, so when he'd tried to take that road in one escape attempt, he had run into some of Cutter's boys and had barely escaped with his life. Cutter would expect him to go to Frisco; therefore he had to do the unexpected. Once he had some cash, he could keep heading west from St. Helens to Astoria and then follow the coast down to California.

He was mulling over all these possibilities when he spotted the riderless horse. A nice chestnut mare with a good saddle. He hobbled closer on his own nag, but the chestnut was skittish and backed off. Zack dismounted, tied his reins to a tree branch, then tried to approach the chestnut on foot.

"Come on, girl," he said soothingly. "I won't hurt you." He reached out a hand as if he held a nice lump of sugar.

Hearing groans, he glanced back at his nag, thinking the animal had finally keeled over, but she was just standing placidly chewing grass. The sound came again, rising just above the sound of the wind.

"H-e-l-p!" The word was distinct.

Zack searched through the thick growth of brush, heading toward the direction of the sounds. He nearly tripped over the prostrate form. The man groaned in pain.

"I'm sorry, fella," Zack said. "I didn't see you."

"I'm hurt bad," the man said.

Zack pushed back some of the brush, revealing a man only a couple years older than himself. His hair was reddish blond, his skin sunburnt and freckled. His face was clean-shaven — baby-faced was how Zack would describe him. He was wearing wire-rimmed spectacles that were knocked askew on his nose. His clothing was Western attire, and except for some travel wear, looked to be almost new. It also looked like the kind of clothing bought in a dry goods store by someone in the East who wanted to dress like a cowboy.

"Where you hurt?" Zack knelt down by the man.

"I can't move my legs. I . . . I think my back is broke." The man's voice shook over the words, and rightly so, because if they proved to be true, they were probably a pronouncement of death.

"Nah," Zack said, as if he knew anything, "probably you're just numb from the fall. How long ago?"

"About an hour. I heard something crack as I fell."

Zack said nothing, realizing the man's words might be true after all. He jumped up, went to his nag, got his water canteen, and returned. "Here, you probably need a drink."

The man indeed was very thirsty and drank greedily, but immediately after doing so, he vomited, nearly choking in the process. More unsettling to Zack than the choking was the bright red vomit. Had to be blood. The man was horrified and sputtered on about how embarrassed he was. Zack tried to soothe him. He didn't know what else to do. The crack the fellow had heard might have been a rib breaking and puncturing some vital organ. Either way, the man probably didn't have long.

"How'd you fall?" Zack asked in an attempt to distract the man from his plight.

"A snake spooked my horse. I'm not much of a rider. I just wanted to see some of the countryside before I settled into my job. I'll have to be on a horse a lot, and I thought I should get all the practice I could."

"What job is that?"

"A circuit-rider minister . . . up in Columbia County."

"You're a preacher?" Zack didn't know why that surprised him. Truth was, the man looked like a preacher, at least far more so than a cowboy.

The man nodded, but another spasm of pain prevented him from speaking.

"I wish I had some whiskey to give you," Zack said.

"I don't touch strong spirits. But . . . but . . . thanks anyway."

"Portland's probably ten miles back, and the next closest town's a good twenty miles away," Zack said helplessly.

"I know." The man lifted his hand and laid it weakly on Zack's arm. "I know I'm going to die. I am ready to meet my Lord." He licked his lips.

He was obviously thirsty but refused another drink from the canteen, no doubt fearing a repeat of before.

"I don't have any right asking this of you. . . . Do you think you could stay with me? I don't fear death, but I don't want to be alone."

Zack had been wondering what he should do. He was not coldhearted enough to just leave the man to die, though there didn't appear to be much else to do. He supposed it wouldn't hurt to sit with him until he passed. Maybe doing a good deed for a preacher would get him into heaven, though going to heaven had never been of primary concern to him. Still, it couldn't do any harm to increase his chances. His ma had been a religious sort and had brought him up properly. She'd made him attend church every Sunday, and he'd been taught to fear burning in hell above all else, though in his adult life he'd balked at such foolery.

"Sure," Zack answered. He wouldn't be delayed long.

"Thank you. What's your name?"

"Zack."

"I'm William Locklin. Where you from?"

Zack was always careful about giving out personal information, but he figured anything he said now would die with Locklin.

Also, he couldn't lie to a man of God.

"I'm from Liberal, Kansas, originally," Zack said. "But I been out west for nearly twelve years — Mexico, California, Oregon, Washington, even Alaska."

"I always wanted to come west," William said. "When I was young I dreamed of being a cowboy. Who would have thought being a minister would finally get me here? Who would have thought I'd die just a week off the train."

"You should have taken the packet from Portland to St. Helens," Zack said. "The river is the best way to travel around here."

"Like I said, I wanted to see the country and get more accustomed to riding." Pausing, William started coughing. Blood flecked his lips. When he settled, he added, "Yes, I should have taken the boat. The river would have been pretty."

"Hey, I been thinking," Zack said. "Maybe I could rig up a litter and pull you behind a horse. We could get to St. Helens in a couple of days —"

"I'll die if you move me."

Zack wanted to argue that he was going to die anyway, but a man had a right to choose his way if he had that chance. If it were Zack, he'd take any chance he could if it promised even another minute of life.

Maybe that was the difference between being ready to die, as William claimed to be, and being a sinful reprobate like Zack.

They kept talking until the sun began to set and then Zack built a fire. It was a chilly spring night, but at least it wasn't raining. In these parts spring was as unpredictable as a young mule — sun and rain constantly exchanging places, though rain usually won out. But he liked this region well enough. The rain made it unbelievably green. Summers were warm and winters cold with some snow, but nothing like he remembered from his childhood in Kansas. Yes, it was nice country here. He wouldn't mind staying awhile, but, of course, that was impossible now.

Zack ate a little food he had in his saddlebag and offered some to William. The man didn't want any. Instead, he told Zack he could have what was in his saddlebags, too.

Later, Zack finally was able to get hold of the chestnut's reins and brought both horses closer to the camp. Then William said he'd had a carpetbag on the back of his saddle that had fallen off during the spill. Zack searched the area before it got too dark, finally found it, and brought it back.

"My Bible is in there," William said. "C-could you read to me from it? Maybe . . .

the Twenty-third Psalm." It was becoming more difficult for the man to talk.

Zack fished the black leather-bound book from the carpetbag and, with the minister's help, found the passage and began to read by the light of the fire. He read one psalm after another for about an hour until his voice got raw. As he read, his thoughts focused not on the words coming from his mouth but rather on what he would do next. He thought about money-making schemes, about San Francisco, even about Darla and finding her again and how he'd get back at her.

After he quit reading, a deep silence descended upon the men. Zack never much liked silence, and he was tired of his thoughts. For a while he busied himself with making Locklin comfortable. He got William's bedroll and laid it over him when he began to shiver, and when that wasn't enough, he spread his own over William, as well.

"I'm so cold," William murmured.

Zack was cold, too, but said nothing and tossed another branch on the fire. To get his mind off his morose thoughts, off the cold seeping into his bones, and off the nearby chill of death, he started talking.

"You been a minister long?" he asked.

"You don't look old enough."

"Just out of the seminary. Worked as an assistant pastor in Boston for a while. What do you do, Zack?"

"I drift. Find whatever work interests me. I've done it all. Cowhand, bartender, seaman, stevedore, hotel clerk — I'll be honest with you, William, some of the stuff I've done ain't always been legal." He didn't know why he added that, but there was a certain temptation to be totally honest with a person you knew you would never see again, at least not in this life.

"I guess you've had a hard life," William said.

"Is that an excuse to break the law?"

"No, of course not. Do you regret the things you've done?"

"Not everything. Maybe some. I don't think I'm a bad person."

"I don't think you are, either. You didn't have to stay here with me."

"If our places were changed, and I was lying there like you . . . well, I'd be mighty afraid to die."

William smiled. "I was afraid when I first fell, before you came along. I didn't want to die just as I was starting a new life, but now I see it is God's will. Maybe it is easier to accept . . . not that I have much of a choice in the matter." William tried to chuckle at his jest, but it came out as an unsettling gurgling sound.

"Doesn't it make you mad?" Zack asked.

"God has used me as He would, and now He is ready to take me home. I don't know why, but I know He must have a good reason for it, a righteous purpose." William's voice trailed away. There was another long span of silence.

Zack lay back on the hard ground and started to nod off. Then he heard his name.

"Zack! Zack!"

At first he thought it was his dreams. His ma was calling him; Darla was calling him, begging his forgiveness; Beau Cutter was calling and pointing a gun at him. Finally, there was something like a burning bush emitting his name in heavenly tones. That's what finally pulled him from sleep. It scared him awake!

It was Locklin calling him. Zack went to the prostrate form. The man was trembling uncontrollably. Zack noted that the fire was down to embers. He realized he'd done more than nod off. He must have slept for a few hours. The sky was already lightening in the east. He tossed another branch onto the fire and then turned back to his patient.

"That'll help," he said as the fire shot up

a nice flame.

"Zack, I'm afraid!" Locklin said.

"I'm here with you," Zack replied, though he didn't think that would be much comfort. It was all he had to offer.

"You've done so much for me. I hate to ask something else."

"What do you want, William?"

"C-could you t-tell them what happened to me? They'll wonder. . . ."

"Who's that? Your folks?"

"It's only my father left and a brother, but I'm not close to them. It was my mother's death last year that freed me to come west. . . ." He paused to catch his breath, coming in fits and starts now. "Someone should notify them. Also, the folks at my new church. It isn't far, and you are heading in that direction."

"Sure, I can do that." Zack thought he could just write a letter, but he wasn't about to disappoint a dying man.

"Maintown is where I was to stay . . . arrangements made. Calvin Newcomb would know."

"Where's Maintown? Never heard of it."

"Not . . . surprised. Backwater town . . . all the hamlets around there are, except for St. Helens."

"I'll find it."

"Thank you. God will bless you for this . . . I know."

Locklin was quiet for a while except for the rattle of his breathing. Zack could not help thinking a backwater town was just what he was looking for. The only problem was that a stranger would stand out in a small village. That's why he'd been heading for the larger town of St. Helens, though it was more likely Cutter might eventually look for him there, or word of his presence there might somehow get back to Cutter.

Suddenly he realized he no longer heard Locklin's rattled breathing. He leaned close and could feel no puffs of air from the man's nose, nor was his chest rising and falling. He pressed his ear against Locklin's chest and could not hear a heartbeat.

So it was over for the minister. Poor unlucky sot. To die so young just as he was starting a new life, and for no good reason. Just because he'd bought a skittish horse. To die alone with no friends around — that was the worst. Probably how I'll die, Zack thought bitterly.

But he was not a man to entertain bitterness and melancholy for long. He jumped up and began gathering more wood for the fire. Last night he'd found some coffee and a pot in Locklin's saddlebag. He could use a nice strong cup of the brew right now. While he was fixing it, he began to wonder what he should do next.

The idea came to him as naturally as breathing. Thinking up schemes was what he did best. He would not stick out as a stranger in a small village if he came with a purpose — if, for instance, he was the new circuit rider.

"You're crazy, Zacchaeus Hartley!" he said aloud, as if hoping the sound would punch some sense into him.

Yet he grew certain it was a perfect ruse. Locklin had mentioned that the people on his circuit were all strangers and knew nothing about the minister except that he was young and green. It would excuse any of Zack's failings as a minister. Zack had been to church often enough as a kid to draw upon that knowledge to get him by. He could do it, for a couple of months at least, until his trail had grown cold. It wouldn't earn him much money, but that wasn't as important right now as getting Cutter off his back.

He turned to the minister's body. Now that the sun was up, he saw that death had indeed taken the man. His face was pale almost to the point of grayness.

"Listen here, Locklin," Zack said to the

body, "I don't mean you no disrespect, okay? I'm desperate, and I don't see where this'll hurt anyone. I promise in a couple of months I'll write your father a letter, and I'll let the people on your circuit know, too, about what happened to you. I'm just going to borrow your identity for a while, not steal it."

Feeling like the worst criminal but not deterred, he searched through the man's pockets. He found a wallet with a few dollars in it. He told himself that if he used the money, he would replace it all when he could and send it to Locklin's father. He also took Locklin's boots because his own were old and beat up and he figured a minister would have newer ones like Locklin was wearing.

His next task was to bury the man, for he couldn't ride into town with a body. That would raise too many questions. He found a place secluded among some brush and loosened the soil with his knife. Luckily, it hadn't rained in the last couple of days, so it wasn't too muddy. Then he cut a stout branch, sharpened the end with his knife, and used it to finish the hole. He made it deep enough so that no animals would disturb William Locklin's eternal rest.

When he finished the grave, tossing the

last bit of earth over it, he fashioned a marker from branches. He put no name on it, of course, but he would draw a detailed map of the grave's location so it could be found again later if anyone wanted to pay their respects.

He was about to turn away but knew the least he must do for this man was to say some "words" over his grave. He searched his mind for things he'd heard in the past.

"Dust to dust, ashes to ashes . . ." He shook his head. That didn't sound right, nor was it very comforting. Finally, a bit lamely, he said, "God is love."

"You better get used to the lingo," he told himself, "if you are determined to go through with this fool thing."

He made himself look through Locklin's carpetbag. It didn't feel right, but he decided he should dress more like Locklin. His own clothing was too worn and "lived in." He found Locklin had two extra suits of clothing. One was a black broadcloth Sunday suit. The other was an outfit similar to the one Locklin had been wearing. Zack stripped down to his union suit and then slipped on Locklin's "cowboy" outfit. The shirt and pants were a bit tight. Locklin had been more slightly built, but luckily Zack had lost a few pounds since he'd been on the run from Cutter. Next he found shaving gear in the carpetbag and put it to use shaving off his mustache. He'd been wearing it for several years because he thought it made him look older and kind of mysterious, but it was best to alter his appearance in case Cutter had circulated a description of him. Besides, a minister shouldn't look mysterious. He also took the razor to his hair, cropping it up to the nape of his neck and then shaping the sideburns, as well. He'd gotten pretty deft with a razor — he'd rarely been able to afford a barber.

He stood back from the tiny mirror to get the full effect of his new look. He thought he could pass very well as a minister. His brown hair and eyes and tanned skin were a far cry from Locklin's pale hair and face, but that shouldn't matter to a bunch of strangers.

Zack rolled up his own clothes with his boots and stuffed them into the carpetbag. When he finished with this scheme, he would walk away in his own clothes. He could not even begin to imagine just how naive that notion was.

EIGHT

Ellie enjoyed gardening almost as much as stitching. Though normally she didn't like getting dirty, there was something quite satisfying about digging in the rich soil, planting seeds, anticipating the harvest of fruits and vegetables and flowers.

Today she was working alone. Mama had Maggie in the house doing the spring cleaning — hauling out rugs and ticking and beating them, scrubbing floors, cleaning out cupboards. However, it was just about time for lunch, so they might be preparing that now. Dad had come in from the field a few minutes ago. Ellie had a few more weeds to pull and then she would take a break also.

It was the end of May, and the rain had finally let up. The sun was showing its face more frequently, doing the newly planted garden great good. Shoots of carrots and radishes were already sprouting. When Ellie had plucked the last weed, she took the pile to a wheelbarrow and dumped it in with the rest, then brushing the dirt from her hands, she headed in.

As she turned the corner of the front yard she saw a rider approach. She could tell instantly he was a stranger, and suddenly she was more self-conscious of her old dirt-stained dress than she would have had the rider been a well-known neighbor. She brushed at the blue checkered gingham to loosen some of the caked garden earth.

"Hello, miss," the rider said.

"Hello," Ellie replied.

"This here the Newcomb place?"

"Yes, it is."

"Calvin Newcomb?"

"That's my father."

"I was told to ask for him." The rider dismounted his chestnut mare. "Is he home?"

"I'll go get him."

"Thank you very kindly."

Ellie was too polite to succumb to her curiosity and question the man. If it had been Maggie, she would have found out everything: Who are you? What do you want with my dad? What's your name? They didn't often get strangers up this way. Maintown was off the beaten track from anywhere. But it was possible the fellow had come to work in the sawmill or the lumber camp, which had recently started up again after its winter lull. He looked the type — young and strong. But he was dressed too nicely. Most of the lumbermen were rowdy types, and Dad was adamant that his daughters stay far away from the mill. And they never went to the camps. If the mill workers were as handsome as this stranger —

"Miss?" the man said. "Something wrong?"

Pink infused Ellie's cheeks as she realized she'd lingered a bit too long in her musings. "Oh no. I'm sorry. We don't get a lot of strangers up here. I'll be right back."

"I think your pa will be expecting me," the man said. "Tell him it's the new minister."

"The minister? Oh . . . my . . ." She felt the pink deepen and burn. She groaned inwardly. He was going to think her a complete dolt. "Please come with me," she said, trying to salvage what poise she had left.

Dismounting, he tied his horse to a post and followed her.

Zack knew a minister shouldn't be so intently studying the lithe figure that walked slightly ahead of him. But he couldn't help it. He was certain he had landed on his feet with this scheme. She was mighty pretty, with cornflower blue eyes, hair like bits of sunshine. Oh, was he partial to yellow-haired beauties!

And the way she blushed when she'd looked him over made him feel sure she had a favorable opinion of him, as well. Yes, this whole minister thing might not be so bad after all.

Whoa, boy! What are you thinking?

He reminded himself of what had happened the last time he had been dazzled by a woman. That was less than a month ago. How could he forget? Women, even a girl-woman like this one, were trouble. He'd be ten kinds of a fool to let himself be distracted. He was going to have enough problems convincing these people he was a man of God.

No women! he told himself firmly. Especially no farm girls whose daddies owned shotguns and would as likely shoot a preacher as he would a drifter for dallying with his daughter.

As they walked up to the house, the girl called, "Mama! Dad! We have a visitor!"

That brought the folks out to the porch. The father was a slightly built man, four or five inches shorter than Zack, though with a bit of a paunch in front. He looked to be in his forties, with thinning light hair, a pleasant enough face with a pale mustache that drooped over his mouth. The woman that came up behind him was shorter by far and a little on the plump side. She had brown hair, braided and coiled at the back of her head. She looked about forty and pretty in a matronly sort of way. They were dressed simply, like the farm folk they were.

"Dad, Mama, this is Reverend Locklin," the daughter said.

Calvin Newcomb grinned. His wife smiled.

"You're finally here," Newcomb said. "This is a grand day. Come on in."

Just then another young woman appeared in the doorway. "What's going on out here? Lunch is getting cold," she said in a somewhat impudent tone.

She was another pretty thing. Curly brown hair, green eyes. He could tell by the flash of those eyes and the tone of her voice that she was probably a spunky one. Zack peered over her shoulder into the house. How many more daughters did Calvin Newcomb have hiding in there?

"Maggie," Mrs. Newcomb said, "mind your manners. This is the new minister."

The girl named Maggie looked him over a

sight more frankly than the other daughter had.

"Well, I'll be!" she muttered.

Zack had no idea what she meant by that.

"And I best mind my manners, too," Mr. Newcomb said. "I'm Calvin Newcomb, and this is my wife, Ada. And these are my daughters, Maggie" — he nodded toward the one in the doorway — "and Ellie."

"I'm very happy to meet you all," Zack said with formal politeness, just as he figured an Eastern-bred minister would talk.

"We also have two boys," Mrs. Newcomb added. "Our Boyd is a few years younger than yourself, but he is out working at the lumber camp. During the season he is usually home only on weekends. Our youngest is Georgie, that is, George, who is fourteen, and he's at school."

"I'll look forward to meeting them," Zack said as they filed into the house.

He was greeted by a cozy home, simple but not poor. The Newcombs were obviously not wealthy, but they were comfortable. What he noticed most were the fragrant smells of fresh-baked bread and stew, or something tangy and meaty. He realized he was starved for decent food, and it had been a very long time since he'd had any home-cooked food. Luck was surely with him to have arrived in time for lunch — well, maybe more than luck, since he'd hurried along the last part of his journey in hopes of such good fortune.

Out of the corner of his eye he noted Mrs. Newcomb take Maggie aside and whisper something to her. Maggie seemed to balk at first; then with reluctance she turned and left the house.

"Maggie had an errand to run," explained Mrs. Newcomb somewhat sheepishly.

Mr. Newcomb laughed. "I'll wager you've sent her like our own Paul Revere to raise the hens into action."

"Oh, Calvin, really! What will our guest think?" She pulled out a chair at the table. "Please have a seat, Reverend. And I hope you don't mind, but I know the other church members will want to meet you. Just a few folks, nothing formal."

"But Reverend Locklin has no doubt been riding all morning," Mr. Newcomb said, "and is tired."

"I am anxious to meet everyone, as well," Zack said.

"I've suggested they stop by the boarding-house after lunch to meet you. Just for a few minutes. I know you need your rest."

Zack laughed good-naturedly. "What else would I do for the rest of the afternoon? I certainly have no need of a nap."

After lunch Mr. Newcomb hitched up the wagon and he, his wife, and daughter boarded. Zack followed on his horse. While the men had been outside preparing the transportation, the women had apparently taken a few moments to clean up. They were wearing different dresses, not Sunday best, but not work frocks, either. Down the road a short distance a woman stood on the side of the road waving. Newcomb stopped.

"Can I ride with you?" the new woman asked. She was about the same age as Mrs. Newcomb, a bit taller with a pleasant face and also obviously a farm wife.

Everyone scooted over on the wagon seat to make room.

Ada Newcomb said, "Reverend, this is Jane Donnelly, one of your congregation."

"I am so pleased to meet you, Reverend!" the woman said with quiet sincerity.

"As am I, Mrs. Donnelly," Zack replied.

He was warming easily to his role. He put on his best manners and speech, maybe not exactly Eastern quality, as no doubt the real Locklin would have had, but he figured it was close enough for these farm folks. He'd learned fancy manners when he and a friend from England had once tried to pass themselves off as English nobility so they could live off of a rich San Francisco socialite for a couple of months.

He and the Newcombs proceeded a mile or so down the road until they came to what was obviously the center of Maintown, which consisted of a schoolhouse — where about twenty children were playing in the yard — a post office that also had a small store inside, and a few frame houses. Zack had ridden through this area earlier on his way to the Newcombs' and had stopped at the post office to ask directions. Mr. Newcomb mentioned that the church met in the schoolhouse.

Mrs. Newcomb added, "We've been trying to raise money to build a separate church building but haven't near enough yet. Our old minister, dear Pastor McFarland, was too aged to lend much energy to the project."

Zack read in that oblique statement that a young, strapping fellow like himself ought to perform miracles in that project. Zack did not respond, merely appearing as if it had gone over his head. He'd be long gone before any building could be raised.

They stopped in front of one of the larger houses on the edge of the town center. There were three wagons parked there and two horses tied to a post. The welcoming committee, he supposed.

Maggie Newcomb was sitting on the front step but jumped up when they arrived. As they walked toward the house she spoke quietly to her mother but loud enough for Zack to hear. "This is the best I could do in the time you gave me." Her tone was defensive. "Most of the men were gone, but this is for the women anyway."

Ada Newcomb quickly shushed her daughter, noting that Zack could hear. Maggie shrugged. She didn't seem much cowed by her mother's scolding.

"The Copelands, who live here," Mr. Newcomb was saying, "had to go out of town for a few days, but knowing you might arrive at any time, they said you should make yourself at home. The church ladies have fixed up your room."

There were about a half dozen people in the entryway to greet them; only one was male. Introductions were made, but Zack hoped they didn't expect him to get the names straight. The only one that stuck was the other man, Albert Stoddard, an older fellow in his fifties, probably one of the church elders. Then they led Zack upstairs. The women were chattering with excitement. One of them, who was a tiny thing, shorter than Mrs. Newcomb, swung open the door to one of several rooms that lined the hall. The sudden burst of light into the darker hallway indicated the room had a western exposure, for the sun was moving toward its descent.

He was greeted with a cozy room, not overly small. It had a nice upholstered chair and footstool, a dresser and a washstand, a desk and a chair, and a huge four-poster bed. Zack had carried up his carpetbag, which he now tossed upon the bed.

This action was met with a chorus of gasps from the women.

Brow knit with confusion, he asked, "Is something wrong?"

"Oh . . . well . . . uh . . ." began the petite woman, who seemed, despite her diminutive stature, to be the leader of the group. "I'm sorry. We don't mean to be rude, Reverend." She gathered back her command of the situation as she spoke, and Zack had the feeling he was being scolded. "But we ladies wanted to make a special presentation to you."

"I'm very touched," he said, still confused.

He noted that Maggie had opened her mouth to speak, but her sister jabbed her in the ribs with an elbow, and the girl clamped her mouth shut.

"The ladies of the church," said the

woman — Zack still could not remember her name, but he was sure once he found out he would never forget again — "wanted to welcome you in a special way, so we all joined together to make you this quilt." She motioned with a sweep of her tiny arm toward the bed.

Suddenly Zack realized his error and quickly snatched up the carpetbag. "How thoughtless of me!" he exclaimed, then perused the bedcover. "You made this . . . for me?" He shook his head with awe. "It is stunning! And, you may not believe this, but you should because I am the minister and I don't lie, but blue is my favorite color."

The women all fairly preened with his words. Feeling he was on a roll he went on, gushing so effusively even he began to wonder about his sincerity. "I have never seen such fine work. My mama used to make blankets like this, but never this fine. You must tell me which of you did what part. And please tell me your names again so I can truly remember."

"This one is mine," said the petite woman as she pointed to a design that had squares in the center and petal-like things in each corner. "I am Emma Jean Stoddard. That block," she added, pointing to another, "was made by my daughter Sarah, who . . . well, couldn't join us today."

Zack was no expert, but he could tell the daughter's block was one of the most intricate in the quilt.

The other ladies then pointed out theirs: Ada Newcomb, Jane Donnelly, Nessa Wallard, Florence Parker, and the only other young person in the group besides the Newcomb girls, Mabel Parker. Zack was rather surprised to note that the most intricate blocks were made by three of the daughters, not the older and presumably more experienced women. He also noted that one of the females had remained silent.

"Maggie, you didn't show me yours," Zack said.

"Oh, it's nothing to speak of." She waved vaguely toward the quilt. "That one."

He wasn't sure exactly which she had indicated, but he said, "It's beautiful."

"Well, it's nice of you to say anyway."

Zack gazed once more upon the quilt, and he was truly awed and touched. These people had certainly gone the extra mile to welcome him.

With real emotion that surprised even him, he said, "I am truly overwhelmed. I have been here only a few hours, and you have already made it feel like home to me. I thank you all very much!"

Before the group departed he was offered a dinner invitation from each family for the evenings during which the Copelands were out of town. He was also shown around Mrs. Copeland's kitchen so that he could make himself at home in the morning. When his hostess returned she would prepare his meals. In the meantime, she had left several loaves of bread, eggs in the cooler, and a canister full of coffee beans.

After everyone departed, he went back upstairs to his room. This was better than any hotel he'd stayed in and even better than the rich estate in San Francisco he'd lived in while posing as an English lord. This was better because of its homey feel. He had never really felt comfortable in the mansion. He didn't realize until he sank down into the upholstered chair that it had been far too many years since he'd known anything like a real home, like his mother's house. He could enjoy this for a few months. But no more than that, he told himself, for it might start to make him feel too caged in.

He looked around and noted all the little touches the ladies had done for him. The porcelain wash pitcher and basin were almost new. The dresser scarves were quite fancy. There were even a few books on the shelf by the desk. Never had anyone been so thoughtful toward him. It gave him a peculiar feeling he couldn't quite describe.

And later that night after taking dinner with the Stoddard family, when he slipped beneath the bedcovers, under that fine quilt, the feeling returned. There was something about being warmed by a cover stitched with loving hands.

He was indeed a fortunate man.

But the contented sigh that rose to his lips was suddenly wiped away like a harsh wind yanking a tree up by its roots. The good feeling inside him became like a ball of lead as he remembered that the quilt had not been made for him at all but for a man who lay in an unmarked grave.

NINE

"I don't see why I had to come!" Maggie said as she trooped up the walkway to the Copeland house.

"I'd feel brazen coming by myself," Ellie replied.

"But Mama made the cookies and told you to come," argued Maggie. "She said she'd heard Mabel was going and maybe some of the other girls."

"For once don't argue, Mags."

"Personally, I think it is shocking for all the girls to come to a single man's home unchaperoned!" Maggie did her best Grandma Newcomb impression.

Ellie rolled her eyes but said no more because they were at the door. She raised her hand to knock. In a moment the door was opened by Reverend Locklin himself.

"More visitors!" he exclaimed. "How pleasant. Come on in, please."

The Copeland house was unlike the Newcomb home in that the front door opened into a foyer off of which was not one but two parlors. Reverend Locklin led them to one of these. Maggie saw they had been preceded by Mabel and Iris. Greetings were exchanged and the reverend bid them to have a seat. The Copelands also had very nice furnishings — chintz-covered chairs, a velvet divan, and intricately carved tables and such that could have fit into a palace.

"My, oh my!" Reverend Locklin said as Ellie handed him the cookies. "More goodies. You ladies are going to have me bursting out of my duds."

"Looks like you're already doing that," Maggie said.

"Maggie!" scolded Ellie.

"She's right," chuckled the minister. "I bought these things right out of seminary when times were lean, and so was I!"

"Surely your carpetbag is not all your baggage. You'll have more clothing when your trunk arrives," Mabel offered.

Naturally Mabel couldn't imagine traveling anywhere without at least one trunk.

"My trunk . . ."

For a moment it looked as if the reverend was hearing an entirely different language.

"You never know about shipping these days," he added with a nervous chuckle.

Maggie couldn't think why he'd be nervous. Perhaps he was ashamed of his impoverishment. She frowned a bit, and at just that moment Reverend Locklin's eyes met hers but quickly skittered away. She hoped he didn't take her frown wrong. Yet it would only make matters worse to mention it.

"The next time someone goes to St. Helens, they will inquire at the freight office," Ellie said.

"You know, Reverend Locklin," Mabel said, "my mother is an excellent seamstress. Perhaps she can alter your things for you."

"If she's so good, Mabel," queried Maggie, "why don't she sew any of your clothes? My mother, on the other hand, sews and alters our things all the time. She'd be happy to help out."

"Well," Mabel replied, "my mother would if she *had* to."

"Well, then," Reverend Locklin said diplomatically, "I shall speak to both of them. If my . . . ah . . . trunk does arrive, it will contain plenty of work for both of them."

As the reverend placed the dish of cookies on a table, Maggie also noted a two-layered chocolate cake and two loaves of bread. The other ladies had had the same idea as their mother: a way to a man's heart is through his stomach.

"I was just about to get tea," Reverend Locklin said. "If you'll excuse me, I'll be right back."

"Let me help you, Reverend," offered Mabel.

"Thank you, but I can manage. You ladies relax. You are my guests." He then left.

Maggie had the feeling he was trying to escape, and no wonder, the poor fellow being attacked only a day after his arrival!

When they were alone, Mabel said rather sheepishly, "I suppose we all had the same idea."

At least she didn't try to hide behind lame excuses. It was best to be open about their intentions, though it could be disastrous if the reverend knew.

"It is our place to be sociable," Iris said.

"Yes," added Ellie, "to make the pastor feel welcome."

"Come on, girls!" Maggie said with disgust. "At least Mabel is honest about it. The fly is being drawn into the web."

Mabel smiled at the jest. She was always so confident and self-possessed. "It doesn't make sense to pretend otherwise. But, Maggie, I am surprised you are here. Aren't you far too young for the man? And in any case, I thought you were more interested in fishing and tagging after that awful Tommy

Donnelly."

Maggie felt as if she had been slapped, and after she had tried to compliment Mabel! She was furious on so many levels. She hated it when the older girls treated her like a child, especially when she was smarter and probably more mature than any of them. She also rankled at the insult of her friend Tommy. But mostly she was mad because Mabel was right about her disinterest and she indeed hated being here. However, for her sister's sake, she could say nothing.

"Yes," put in Iris, "leave the minister to real women."

"As if he'd be interested in girls as desperate as the bunch of you!" Maggie retorted.

"He definitely won't be interested in a child," Mabel said.

Maggie glanced at her sister, thinking some defense might be forthcoming from her, but Ellie was quietly looking down at her hands. She had made Maggie come, even made her put on a dress, and now she had nothing to say! Maggie decided then and there that she would show all of them. She would go after the minister. She would catch him even if she didn't want him. Then she'd free him to go to one of them as second choice.

Finally Ellie spoke, "Everyone, please, let's

not get so disagreeable about this. Maggie isn't interested —"

Just then Reverend Locklin returned carrying a heavy-laden tray, which he set on the table in front of the divan. He reached for the teapot.

Maggie fairly jumped forward. "Let me do that, Reverend. It is woman's work, you know," she said in her sweetest tone. These girls had no idea just what she could do if she put her mind to it. And as for Ellie, if she had been intending to finally support Maggie, the effort was paltry and too late.

"I must say," Reverend Locklin said, "I have never been made to feel so welcome in any of the parishes I've served in."

"I thought we were your first parish," Maggie said.

"Oh, well . . . yes, my first *regular* parish is what I meant," he said. "Of course, in my . . . uh . . . training I served as an assistant in several churches."

"Most of us knew that," Mabel said, "but you see, Maggie is too young to understand the workings of the church. My mother says you served in Boston."

"Yes, a wonderful church."

"Pastor Markus was a friend of my grandfather," Mabel said. "Though my branch of the family comes from Maine, my grandparents were originally from Boston. I have an aunt there with whom my brother is staying. My brother, Reverend, is attending Harvard."

The Parkers always managed to find a way to slip that bit of bragging into every conversation. Evan Parker had been away for three years attending law school, and before that he'd gone to a private preparatory school in Portland, thus, if Maggie didn't know better, she would almost think he was an imaginary family member they conjured up just to brag about.

"Anyway," Mabel continued, "Grandfather went to school with Pastor Markus."

"And what a dear old gentleman he is. I learned so much from him," Reverend Locklin said.

"You knew him then, before he passed?"

"For a short time, but he made a great impression." The reverend reached for the dish of cookies. "Please, help me eat these." He passed the plate around.

Maggie took a cookie and nibbled on it thoughtfully. Reverend Locklin did not look at all comfortable. Maybe his stint with the old minister hadn't been as pleasant as he let on. Maybe he simply felt as if he was being badgered with questions. Mabel could be overbearing. Maggie decided she could do herself great good by rescuing the man.

"Reverend Locklin, will you be able to find your way around the circuit?" she asked. "It's a bit far-flung. It is a good fifteen miles from here to the farthest point in Deer Island."

"I do have a map."

"I know the countryside fairly well. I could guide you if you like."

"Thank you so much for the offer," he said. "I'll speak to your father. He probably has made some arrangement along this line."

He seemed to emphasize "your father," and Maggie realized she had gone too far. Of course an honorable man, much less a minister, wouldn't agree to ride over the country with a girl unchaperoned.

"You'll find your first church easily enough," Iris said, "since it is right here in Maintown."

"That is right," Reverend Locklin said, "you are the first Sunday of the month. And the fourth, I understand from what Mr. Newcomb told me."

"Yes," Mabel said. "Since you live here, that's how it works out. If you lived in one of the other towns, they would get two Sundays. So, you see, we are very fortunate." Mabel flashed a most beguiling smile.

"Bachelor Flat is the second Sunday," Maggie put in, mostly to distract the reverend from the glow of that smile, "but it's not far. You could ride there and back in a couple of hours. Deer Island and Columbia City are a good distance away, though near each other and so share the third Sunday, one in the morning and one in the afternoon."

"We are so looking forward to the service," Mabel said. "Many of us — those who wanted some churching in the interim since Pastor McFarland's death — have had to attend other denominations. We will be happy to hear preaching from our own for a change."

"Have you a topic for your sermon?" Iris asked.

"A topic?" Reverend Locklin's voice rose slightly on the word *topic*. He cleared his throat. "I'm working on it."

"Only two days away! We are so excited," Mabel said.

"Two days . . ." he said.

Maggie thought she detected a sudden pallor in the man's expression. Of course he'd be nervous about speaking before a new congregation.

They chatted for a while longer, though after the mention of the sermon, the reverend seemed a little detached and distracted. Maggie wondered if he was like her and had put off an unwelcome task until the last minute. She would think giving a sermon would be a minister's favorite thing to do.

Finally Ellie rose and said they had taken too much of the reverend's time. She thanked him for the tea. Maggie realized then it was the first time Ellie had spoken since the tea had been served. That was odd. Ellie wasn't exactly an excessively talkative sort, but neither was she shy.

In any case, when Ellie took her leave, the others were all but forced to do so, as well. They had been there longer, and it would seem as if they had taken even more of the minister's precious time. He tried to hide it, but he seemed relieved when he walked the group to the door. Iris reminded him that he was to have dinner at their house that evening.

It was a long walk home, but fortunately Mabel and Iris had ridden horses, so Maggie didn't have to put up with their company. She and Ellie had been forced to make the mile trek on foot because Dad couldn't spare any horses. Maggie tried to talk to Ellie as they walked, but her sister was still very quiet. It was almost as if she was mad about something, yet it was only Maggie who had a right to be mad.

"You didn't hardly say a thing today," Maggie said. Even if Ellie didn't have a right, Maggie did not like her sister to be mad at her.

Ellie shrugged.

"Reverend Locklin is going to think you don't like him."

"It doesn't matter," Ellie finally mumbled.

"What do you mean?"

"I never felt more foolish and more ashamed — at myself for being there and at the way the rest of you threw yourselves at him. Even you, Maggie!"

"I made a block for the quilt. I guess I have a right to go after the minister."

"What changed you?"

"It doesn't matter!" Maggie tried to mimic Ellie's earlier words.

"You are right. It doesn't matter."

"What happened to you, Ellie? You said someone has to marry the minister, so it may as well be you. You've dreamed of being a minister's wife. Don't you care any longer?"

"I won't compete with my friends, especially with my sister. That's all."

Suddenly ashamed of her earlier anger, Maggie confessed, "I was just mad at Mabel and Iris for saying I was too young."

"You've said yourself you are too young. You are only seventeen."

"Mama was married at seventeen and expecting her first child."

"What do you want, Maggie? Are you interested or not?"

"Well, I'm sure not gonna let the likes of Mabel and Iris get him."

Thoughtfully, Ellie said, "Once you said you felt sorry for the minister before you even met him. Well, now *I* feel sorry for him. It's not right what we are doing."

"It would have been better if he'd been short, fat, and ugly," Maggie said, trying to lighten the mood.

"He's none of those things, that's for sure." There was a dreaminess in Ellie's tone. "But I no longer want to be part of the frenzy."

"You'd be the best one for the job, Ellie. You'd make the best minister's wife."

"But now I see he's a real person, not just a title and an image. I realize I want a husband to love, not just one to give me status. It wouldn't be fair to him. He must also want a wife who will love him for who he is and not for the position he can offer."

"But such a handsome real person!"

"I know you are not that shallow, Mags."

"And I know you would never snag a man

just for what he can offer you." More reasonably Maggie added, "But you will never know if there is more to it than that if you don't get acquainted with him first, just like we know a quilt isn't going to win him. Ellie, you need to do that much."

"I'm not going to buzz around him like a bee at a honeycomb."

"Of course not. It isn't your way."

They continued walking in silence. Maggie realized her angry resolve before was just bombast. She'd do much better to keep encouraging her sister. Either way, she was going to make certain it was a Newcomb who walked down the aisle with the minister.

Zack barely closed the door behind his female guests when panic seized him.

A sermon!

It hit him like a pickax between the eyes. In two days he was going to have to lead a church service and deliver a sermon. This shouldn't be a surprise to him. He'd known on some level that such things would be expected of him if he pursued this crazy scheme, but he had chosen to minimize those thoughts.

Now questions bombarded his mind. What goes on in church, or specifically, this church? How do you lead whatever goes on? What would he be expected to say? Would they want him to pray? Would people come forward like in a tent meeting he had attended once with his mother?

What had he gotten himself into?

Frantically he paced around the Copeland parlor until he noticed the tea things and grabbed them up in a futile attempt to distract his thoughts. But they would not stop. In two days everyone would realize he was a complete charlatan. They'd ride him out of town on a rail, maybe get him arrested. Was it against the law to impersonate a minister?

Dumping the tea dishes in the kitchen sink, he raced from that room to the foyer and sped up the steps two at a time. It wasn't too late to flee.

He threw open the door to his room. He could pack and be long gone before dark. But the first thing his gaze lit upon was that quilt on his bed. These people had gone to a lot of trouble to welcome him — well, to welcome Locklin. Still, they wanted a minister. They wanted him to be the minister. And the first precept in any confidence scheme was to make your mark *want* what you had to offer. He had these people where he needed them.

His worst mistake now would be to panic. He could do this.

He sucked in a deep breath and made his mind calm down and think logically. He was a good salesman. The only good thing his stepfather had ever had to say about him was that he could sell shoes to a legless man. Once he had sold snake oil and done pretty well at it until the law ran him out of town.

Religion was just fancified snake oil. And wasn't a sermon just a sales pitch?

Still, to sell something you had to know your product, and it would be nice if he didn't have to study theology for the next two days to come up with something. Then he remembered there had been some books in Locklin's carpetbag. He grabbed the bag, but before he tossed it on the bed, he carefully folded back the quilt. The ladies were going to want this back in acceptable condition when he left town.

Inside the bag he found the books, four of them in addition to Locklin's Bible. There was a two-volume set called *Exhaustive Exposition of the Old and New Testaments.* They were hefty, and Zack hoped he didn't have to read them. The third book, not much smaller than one of the huge "Exposition" volumes, piqued his interest: *The Sermons and Essays of Robert E. Markus.*

The fourth was a small book titled *Brethren of Christ Manual for Ministers.* This he ignored for the time being but thought it would be useful. For now he focused his attention on the book of sermons.

Zack smiled, noting the author was Markus, Locklin's apparent mentor. And it also appeared as if that scallywag Locklin might have had the same idea that now occurred to Zack. All he had to do was memorize these sermons. There were enough to keep him going for months, even years. The book was broken down into themes such as salvation, giving, forgiveness. Then there were sections for various holidays like Easter and Christmas. There was one whole section devoted to the Sermon on the Mount. Zack wondered if that was for outdoor meetings or something. Curious, he opened the book to that chapter and found it was broken down into several sermons, each with a Scripture heading.

The first: "Lay not up for yourselves treasures upon earth . . . but lay up for yourselves treasures in heaven. . . ."

Zack quickly moved on from that one because he wasn't sure he could preach that with a straight face.

Next: "Blessed are the meek, for they shall inherit the earth."

He'd heard that saying before but never knew it had come from the Bible. He passed that one because he didn't want to risk offending any in the audience who didn't happen to be meek.

"Ye are the light of the world. A city that is set on a hill cannot be hid."

He glanced at the sermon that went with this, and it was mostly telling the listeners to be better Christians. Maybe he could do that. Everyone wanted to be better. But should he be telling them to be better when he didn't even know them?

Fanning the pages his eye lit upon the words, "Consider the lilies . . ." Intrigued, he read more, "they toil not, neither do they spin."

The sermon basically said not to worry, to trust God. He liked that. It had a positive ring to it. Sitting at the desk, he read it through and decided to use it. Then he set about to memorize it. This was another of his assets. He could quickly commit anything to memory. His mother had often told him he was too smart to be a farmer.

But was he smart enough to pull off being a minister? He, and everyone else, would know on Sunday.

TEN

The first Sunday in June was sunny and warm. In the best of circumstances this would bring out large numbers to the Maintown church service. The fact that this was the new minister's maiden service meant that every living creature in the area would attend if humanly possible. Some even came from the Bachelor Flat church because they didn't want to wait till their service the following Sunday to meet the minister.

There were about fifty people seated on the benches that had replaced the desks in the schoolhouse. Calvin Newcomb had said there were normally twenty or thirty who regularly came to the church service. Nerves like Zack had never known before attacked him. He was certain all the words he had spent the last two days memorizing were no longer in his head.

He walked up to the pulpit. Mr. Newcomb had told him that Clyde Lambert, known throughout the county as a fine wood-worker, had built the elaborately carved pulpit in hopes of one day having a proper church building to put it in. Zack gripped its oaken sides so as not to reveal how much his hands were trembling.

"Good morning, ladies and gents . . . ah, gentlemen . . . that is, brothers and sisters . . ." He groaned inwardly. Right from the get-go it was a disaster. But he plowed ahead. "My sermon today is taken from the book of Matthew, chapter six, verse twenty-eight." He'd been trying not to make eye contact with the people, looking over their heads instead, but he couldn't help noticing some movement from the Newcomb bench. His gaze flickered in that direction. Mr. Newcomb had an odd look on his face.

Then something in Zack's brain seemed to lumber into place. You don't start the service off with the sermon! Mr. Newcomb had come by on Saturday and spoken with him about the order of service, but Zack had been so worried about forgetting the words to the sermon that he'd forgotten all else. Well, now was the time to play his "greenhorn" card.

He uttered his most disarming chuckle. "So sorry, my friends. I am simply too anxious to regale you with my silver tongue!" He chuckled again, and to his relief a responding chuckle rippled through the audience. "First, however, Mrs. Renolds will lead us in a hymn." He nodded toward a white-haired woman in the front row, and she rose and walked to the front.

"Thank you, pastor," she said. She opened the book in her hands. "Let us sing 'Come, Thou Fount of Every Blessing.'" She blew into her key finder and then began to sing. She was the only one with a hymnal, but she had chosen a song that everyone knew well. Despite all her attempts, the tune was sung off-key. Unfortunately, the church lacked a piano or an organ.

Zack mouthed the words of the song as best he could. He had not had a chance to memorize any hymns. After the song, he welcomed Mr. Newcomb, as chairman of the deacons, to offer an opening prayer. Zack found the paper on which he'd written the order of the service, and things fell into place after that. He was glad the offering plate was passed before the sermon, for as the time for that performance drew near his nerves returned.

Reminding himself of snake oil, he took to the pulpit. He had written out the sermon so that it would appear as if it was his own work, but he never referred to the pages in front of him. He spouted Robert E. Markus's words flawlessly, and as he did so, he scanned the audience to make eye contact with various individuals in the congregation. He remembered this was an important sales tool.

The service closed with another hymn and then a short song called the "Doxology." Zack knew enough to walk down the aisle at the end of the song and stand at the door to receive his congregants as they filed out. He beamed at every spoken compliment.

"Fine service, Reverend."

"Wonderful sermon."

"Your words spoke to me!"

He put his memory to work once again as he asked each person their name. He even learned the names of the children. Next time when he saw them, he'd impress them by calling them by name. Yes, this was going to work out fine!

Just then a fellow came up and shook his hand.

"Mornin', Pastor. I'm Stan Wallard and this is my wife Nessa." He was a husky, ruddy fellow, his Sunday duds taut around his girth. His wife, whom Zack recalled from the welcoming committee the other day, was rather rotund herself, but Zack barely noticed her as she stood behind her husband.

"Good morning, Mr. Wallard. Pleased you could come," Zack replied, returning a firm handshake.

"I got a question for you."

"Feel free," Zack said broadly, then remembered who he was and how dangerous questions could be. But he couldn't refuse in any case.

"Well, a fellow down at the mill where I work — he's a heathen, if you ask me. Anyway, something about Solomon came up, and since you mentioned him in your sermon, I figured you'd know about it. I was telling him about how two women claimed the same baby and that Solomon decided who the real mother was by saying he'd cut the child in half and give half to each woman. He figured out who the real mother was when she said to spare the baby and give it to the other woman. This man said I was making up the story, or at least that it was never in the Bible. He bet me a whole dollar I was wrong. I could swear it was true, but me and the missus tried to find it and had no luck. Is it from the Bible, Pastor? And if it is, can you tell me where so I can show him?"

At first, the only response Zack could muster was a blank stare. Then his mind started working. He'd heard a similar story but hadn't really known it was from the Bible. He did recall mentioning Solomon in his sermon but couldn't recall the reference. His memory was good for rote memory but not for interpreting what was memorized. He certainly hadn't been paying much attention to what he was actually saying.

Solomon . . . Solomon . . . ?

"Pastor?"

Zack had to speak or give up now and run for it. He had to take a stab. So what if he was wrong. Ministers didn't have to know everything. But the story did sound like something biblical.

"Of course it is from the Bible, Mr. Wallard. You tell your friend." He waited for protest from the others still waiting to greet him. Surely Mr. Newcomb, who was next in line, was knowledgeable of such matters. But the man made no comment, and Zack began to relax.

"He'll need more than that. What book and such?" Wallard asked.

Zack groaned inwardly. He was good at thinking on his feet, but this was more like a test in school.

It was Mrs. Newcomb who came to his rescue. "Why, Stan Wallard, you can't be expecting the pastor to use the Bible to settle a bet, now, can you?" She scolded as she would her own child.

"A dollar ain't nothing to sneeze at," Wallard said defensively.

Now Zack had the means to escape his predicament. "Yes, I simply cannot approve gambling in any form, and especially when it tries to use God's Word as a parlor game."

"I'm sorry, Reverend," said a sincerely repentant Wallard. "Didn't think of it like that."

"I'm sure you didn't. It was an honest mistake." Zack smiled to show the man he didn't think less of him for it. Zack had known a minister once who would spit hellfire at anyone for the least error, but even as a fake minister, he didn't want to be that way.

When the Newcomb family filed by, Zack greeted them heartily. He already knew these were among a handful of families that formed the backbone of the church.

Mrs. Newcomb smiled warmly. "It was a lovely sermon, Pastor!" she said pointedly, her eye skittering briefly toward the Wallards. "I was especially moved by your story about your dog, Bones. I had a dog just like him when I was a little girl. How trusting our pets are indeed! How sad that yours ran away."

"Maybe someday I'll be in a position to have another dog," Zack replied. He himself had never had a pet, especially one so trusting and faithful as Markus's little beast.

"When you settle into your own home," the woman said with a smile that definitely held a deeper meaning. Mrs. Newcomb may have believed she was being coy, but from the first moment he had met her, he had not missed her all too obvious references to his singleness. Logic told him that a young single man could fall prey to the designs of the young women in the community, but he was determined to fend them off for a couple of months. Yet what about their mothers? If Mrs. Newcomb had her way, he'd be married in two weeks, much less two months!

The two younger men in the family followed their mother. Boyd Newcomb was personable enough, as was the youngest, Georgie.

"Reverend," Georgie said, "if you like to fish, I can show you all the best fishing holes in the county."

"I am very fond of fishing. I shall call upon your expertise as soon as I am settled."

Maggie Newcomb shouldered her way forward next. "I taught him everything he knows," she said. "And I know a few places he doesn't."

"Well, very good, then." He didn't know how else to respond to that.

"And it was a very good sermon. Great, really!" She smiled.

Zack read the good-natured mockery in her tone. He wished they could go off together and have a good laugh about the fiasco. He figured he could easily enjoy Maggie's company.

Ellie Newcomb was more reserved, almost detached. While all the other girls practically threw themselves at him, she was aloof. And it bothered him. In fact, he was far less surprised by the other girls' aggressiveness. He'd always had a way with women and believed there was not a one he could not beguile. Yet here was a pretty girl who showed no interest in him at all. He hoped he hadn't in some way offended her, because she would hold some sway with her important family.

She offered only a brief greeting and then moved on. While Zack pondered this, Mr. Newcomb came, the last to leave the church. He'd had to collect the offering money from the plates.

"I'm sorry it didn't go as smoothly as I had hoped," Zack said. He sensed this man would be more impressed by humility than false bravado.

"It was a fine service, Reverend."

"Thank you for saying so."

After Newcomb went off to greet another parishioner, Zack had a few moments alone while the people lingered in the school yard and greeted friends. He studied the group and knew these were good people. They were for the most part simple farm folk. Even the more affluent families, like the Copelands and the Parkers, were warm and friendly. He didn't much enjoy hoodwinking them.

His gaze lit upon Maggie, who was talking to a young man about her own age, a homely, freckled fellow with brown hair that had several cowlicks. Pretty Maggie could do much better. Not far from her he observed her sister, Ellie, talking to a young man and a young woman whom he had met, Colby and Sarah Stoddard. Their mother was the pushy, domineering woman he was already coming to know well.

Zack was a sharp observer, if nothing else, and he did not miss the besotted manner in which Colby Stoddard looked upon Ellie. Ellie seemed quite comfortable with him, laughing and talking easily. They had probably grown up together. Zack found himself looking upon this Colby fellow as a competitor.

Whoa, boy! he told himself, none of that kind of thinking. But he knew he was the kind of man who relished a challenge, which was probably why he was going to stick it out here and tackle this performance as minister with all he had. He also knew that if he had a hundred women bowing down before him, he was going to go after the one who wasn't. But he couldn't go after anyone, he reminded himself once again.

"Hey, Maggie."

"Hi, Tommy! It's good to see you in church," Maggie said, mostly because she knew as a Christian she should encourage someone like Tommy, who was probably a backslider. She was never comfortable with "witnessing" or, as her mother called it, "sharing her faith." She felt it was hard enough for her to keep herself on the "straight and narrow," much less badger others about it.

"My ma said I had to come and see the new minister. I told her that if my pa didn't have to come, I shouldn't have to either. When she said, 'Pretty please,' I figured I ought to have a look-see."

Tommy Donnelly was a funny-looking kid, Maggie decided, now that she really studied him. Freckled face, slightly bucked teeth, hair that stuck out all over his head, and a kind of slow way of talking that made you wonder if he was ever going to get all the words out. It made her mad that people made fun of him and shunned him, but — she hated to admit this — it made her just as mad that people would think she'd be sweet on him. How could she be friendly to him without people getting the wrong idea?

"So what did you think of the minister?" she asked.

"Don't know him but for the words he spoke. He'll do, lessen he tries to browbeat me into comin' to church."

"But that's his job, Tommy. Anyway, what do you have against church?"

"People are all phony. Look at 'em. Not a one but you is come up to say 'hey' to me."

"Don't I count? I'm a Christian, you know."

"You're different."

"I heard the reverend greet you. He called you by name."

"Like you said, that's his job."

Just then some laughter rose briefly above the din of voices. Maggie glanced around and saw it had come from Colby. He was talking to Ellie and seemed to be enjoying himself. Now that Ellie was no longer interested in the minister, did that mean she was going back to Colby? All the more reason for me to get the minister, Maggie thought bitterly.

"Now, there's the worst of the lot," Tommy said.

"Huh?" Maggie had all but forgotten his presence, blinded as she had been by Colby's light.

"That Colby Stoddard. You know, I seen him the other day in town, and I said, 'Hey, Colby,' and he walked right past me as if I wasn't even there. You better tell your sister that just because he's a pretty boy don't mean he's worth spit."

Maybe some of what Tommy said was true, but she still believed there was more to Colby than met the eye. She would have liked a chance to find out for sure.

Ellie smiled at Colby's raucous laughter, though inwardly she thought he seemed to be trying too hard to appear casual and careless. He didn't have to try to be those things, for she'd always thought them his nature. He must be feeling insecure about something. Was it because he'd had his first look at the new minister?

Ellie had to admit Reverend Locklin was

every bit as handsome as Colby. She glanced toward the schoolhouse door. The reverend was standing alone quietly observing the visiting people. He turned his head slightly, and she quickly jerked her gaze away. She felt she had been doing that all day, trying to steal covert looks at the minister. She didn't know why she kept wanting to look at him. Or why she had in the last three days constantly caught herself thinking about him.

He was good-looking and quite person-able, but she wasn't certain about his talent as a minister. He had not handled the service very smoothly. His sermon had been good enough, though he had obviously memorized it and repeated it by rote. She had sensed no real passion in his words, almost as if they weren't his words at all. Of course she reminded herself that he had no doubt been very nervous. He would need time to warm up to the task. Perhaps he would appreciate some constructive criti-cism. All he had heard after the service was how wonderful it was. No one would risk offending him with the truth, yet how else would he ever learn?

Maybe she should speak to her father about it. He would know the best way to handle the matter, and perhaps he might even wish to venture forth with some honest words of evaluation for him. More than likely Reverend Locklin would appreciate some criticism because surely he would wish to improve. Perhaps she could work it into another conversation she wanted to have with the minister. Since her return from finishing school she had been thinking of starting a Sunday school for the children but had never had a chance to speak with Pastor McFarland about it. Now would be the perfect time to introduce her idea.

Just then Mabel Parker sallied up to the minister. Ellie found her teeth gritting suddenly, so she swung her attention back to Colby where it belonged. It was terrible to have all this flirtatiousness present on Sunday. That was no doubt why Grandma Newcomb thought it was unseemly for a church to have an unmarried minister. Ellie decided this wasn't the right time to speak with the pastor — everyone would think that she, too, was just flirting.

Ellie's mother also probably had the right idea about getting the man married off as soon as possible. Then everyone could concentrate on their Christian faith. Perhaps Ellie ought to help promote Mabel's cause. Then she thought about Maggie and how she was suddenly determined to catch the minister. Ellie didn't have a good feeling about that. Maggie was too young and of the wrong temperament to be a pastor's wife. That was why Ellie couldn't support her sister. It had nothing to do with jealousy.

ELEVEN

On Tuesday William Locklin's trunk arrived at the Maintown post office. Zack borrowed the Copelands' buckboard to pick it up. He was in the post office, which adjoined the little store, when he noticed a head of brown curly hair bobbing above a shelf of cookery. Finishing his arrangements with the agent, Zack headed into the store.

"I thought that was you," he said to the owner of the curly brown hair.

Maggie Newcomb smiled. "Hi, Reverend. I got to get my mama some thread. This store doesn't carry much in general, but with all the stitchers around here, they do keep plenty of thread."

"I've come to pick up my trunk," Zack said.

"So it arrived after all?"

"I guess I worried for nothing."

Mrs. Brown, the postmaster's wife who kept the store, turned back to the counter with a handful of spools. "What color did your mother want, Maggie?"

"Something dark is all she said."

Maggie didn't appear pleased that she would have to choose between several dark threads.

With a shrug, she pointed to the one in the middle. "That'll do."

"Last time you bought your mother thread she had to come back to return it." There was a slightly censorious quality to the woman's tone.

"Then you'd think she'd learn her lesson sending me," Maggie countered as she plopped her nickel on the counter and plucked the spool from Mrs. Brown's hand.

The woman mumbled something about respect as she dropped the money into a cash box and gave Maggie her change.

With a roll of her pretty green eyes, Maggie gave another shrug. Together, she and Zack exited the store.

"Say, Reverend, now that you have all your things, maybe you'd be able to spare something for my mother to alter. I know she'd be happy to do it."

Zack hesitated because once Locklin's things were altered, they would become more and more Zack's. But with all the good food he'd been fed these last few days, the need was becoming rather urgent, and he certainly could not afford to buy anything new.

"Yes, I'll get some things ready," he said.

"Well, aren't you leaving in a couple of days for your circuit? If you give me something now, it could be ready by the time you get back."

"Well . . ."

"Your trunk's right here. No time like the present."

Indeed, Zack noted that the agent had carried the trunk out to the wagon. Still, he hesitated. He was reluctant to get his first look at Locklin's belongings in front of anyone. Who knew what was in that trunk? Yet logic told him Locklin couldn't have anything too awfully suspicious.

He strode to the trunk perched in the back of the wagon, but as he reached for the fasteners, he suddenly realized it could be locked. How could he explain not having a key? Unfortunately, his hands moved faster than his mind, and he gripped the clasp and gave it a tug before he could stop himself. Much to his surprise, it flew open. The trusting minister had seen no need to lock the thing. Right on the top was a black broadcloth suit identical to the one in the carpetbag. He pulled it out and quickly shut the lid.

"Let's start with this," he said, thrusting the suit toward Maggie.

"My mother is going to need you as well as the suit — you know, for measurements," Maggie said.

"That's right."

"Do you have time now?"

"I suppose I do." Zack saw no use in fighting the situation any further. "I'll follow you in the buckboard."

"I walked."

"Then climb aboard, and I'll give you a ride."

Reaching the Newcomb house, Zack left the wagon in the yard with the horses still hitched. He figured the measuring shouldn't take too long. Maggie led the way into the house. Mrs. Newcomb was in the kitchen peeling potatoes. She greeted him cheerfully as she put down her work, dried her hands on her apron, and shook his hand. Ellie was sitting by the hearth stitching. She also greeted Zack pleasantly but with a detached air about her.

"I'd be happy to do your alterations," Mrs. Newcomb said after Maggie explained the reason for the impromptu visit.

While Maggie sat at the kitchen table observing, Mrs. Newcomb gathered various supplies, then took the suit and examined it.

"This shouldn't be too difficult," she said. "Of course, it's harder to let out than take in. But there is a generous seam allowance, and elsewhere putting in a gusset or two should do the trick. But whatever prompted you to purchase suits that are easily a size too small for you?"

Zack decided the earlier explanation he'd given the girls about being thinner when he got them wasn't going to be enough for Mrs. Newcomb. "Well, Mrs. Newcomb, I am embarrassed to admit my impoverished background."

"Pride goes before a fall, Pastor," Mrs. Newcomb said. "You should know that."

"It has always been a thorn in my flesh. I am working on it, however." He offered a smile begging for her sufferance. "When I was in seminary I had a classmate who was better heeled than I but perhaps not as determined in the profession of the ministry. He finally decided to drop out, but not before he'd already invested in two somber suits more . . . ah . . . suited to the calling of Christ than to the life he wished to embark upon. I was in need of proper suits but without the means to buy new. He offered me an excellent price, which I could not refuse, though even then they were a bit snug."

"What about your other clothes, Reverend?" Maggie asked.

Zack groaned silently. That girl was sharp. He was going to have to keep an eye on her.

"Again, I could never afford clothing tailored specifically for me. I took castoffs from friends and bought secondhand clothing to meet my needs." He didn't want to appear too quick with ready answers, so he shrugged. "I suppose I have never cared overly much about my appearance." To Mrs. Newcomb he said, "I am happy they are salvageable."

"I'll have to take measurements," she said.

"Of course."

She hesitated a moment, then awkwardly asked, "Could you remove your jacket?"

He did so. The jacket was his own, and it fit decently, but its removal revealed that the blue cotton shirt under it was so tight, the buttons were nearly popping off.

"Please hold out your arms?" Mrs. Newcomb asked.

She picked up her tape measure and held it along the length of one of his arms, careful to keep it about two inches away from touching him. Throughout the process she was very careful not to touch him, and once when she did accidentally bump him, she apologized profusely. When it came time to measure for the fit of the trousers, she became extremely flustered. Zack had the feeling she was not a woman to flinch easily, and he felt sorry for her.

Finally she said to her daughters, "Maggie, Ellie, don't you have chores to do outside?" Maggie started to protest, but Mrs. Newcomb said firmly, "Maggie, you have weeding to do in the garden. And Ellie, take your stitching outside and take advantage of the better light. Now, scoot!"

With a little grumbling on Maggie's part, the girls obeyed. Obviously, Mrs. Newcomb didn't want an audience for the task ahead, much less her impressionable daughters.

She finished the job as quickly as possible, carefully writing down her measurements on a scrap of paper so she would not have to take them again. Zack was both amused and sympathetic. Maybe it would have been better for her if she had known he was not a "holy man" but just some coarse drifter. He was as relieved as she was when the thing was done.

"I'll have these ready for you when you get back from your circuit," she said. "And if you have anything else, feel free to send it over."

"Thank you. Perhaps I can leave some shirts and trousers with Mrs. Copeland for one of your children to pick up next time they are in town?"

"That is an excellent idea. I know you must have much to do before leaving. Calvin has been busy preparing, as well."

"I am thankful you can spare your husband for a few days to help me find my way and introduce me around."

"Well, the crops are in, and he can afford to miss a few days at the sawmill, thanks to God's blessings. I know he's looking forward to the trip. He has a brother in Columbia City we don't often see."

Zack bid Mrs. Newcomb good afternoon and stepped out onto the porch. He first noted that Maggie was nowhere to be seen. He enjoyed her company and wouldn't have minded spending a little more time with her. He turned and saw Ellie seated on a rocker at the end of the porch. He had turned quickly enough to catch her gazing at him. Her cheeks grew pink.

"Reverend Locklin," she said, acknowledging him, poised despite her discomfiture.

"Hello, Ellie."

She smiled a greeting and then looked back at her sewing in a way that seemed almost dismissive. But Zack wasn't one to be easily dismissed. He walked closer to her and leaned against the porch rail in a comfortable manner that indicated he wasn't going to be leaving anytime soon.

"Looks like you are enjoying yourself," he said with a nod toward the sewing.

"Yes, I am."

"You do very good work," he said, not letting himself get frustrated with having the entire responsibility for the conversation. "The piece you made for my quilt is truly marvelous."

Her eyes jerked up. "You remember which one I made?"

He liked that his comment had taken her by surprise. "The one with the house and tree. In fact, now that I think about it, I believe you made the actual front of your house and that tree yonder. It's just like it. Except the dog isn't in the yard today."

"Gypsy is off with Dad."

"You are very talented," Zack said. "I've seen pictures of famous artwork, you know, by people like Michelangelo, Rembrandt, and such. What you do with cloth is art like that."

"That's a bit much, Reverend!" Her cheeks turned even more pink.

"I don't suppose I could get you to call me William?"

"That would not be proper," she said shortly.

"It's funny that it is all right for me to call you Ellie, but because I'm the minister, you can't use my given name. That's a rule I don't like much."

"I don't know what to say, Reverend Locklin." She put special emphasis on his title and surname as she spoke them. He thought that if he weren't Locklin, if he were just himself, she'd have no problem calling him Zack. But then he had that niggling sense there was more to it than propriety.

"Do you dislike me, Ellie?" he asked suddenly.

"No, of course not! What would give you that idea?"

"Everyone but you seems to go out of their way to be friendly to me."

"Does everyone *have* to like you?"

"Ah, ha! So you don't like me?"

"That's not what I said. I just . . . it's just that . . . you are . . . I mean —" She broke off, looking more flustered than her mother had when she'd had to slip that tape measure around his waist.

He realized he was enjoying the moment, especially because she was a lot prettier when some of the frost had melted away from her.

"You know, Ellie," he said with just the right touch of sincerity, "I don't need everyone to like me, only those who are of admirable quality. I think you are the kind of person whose esteem I would greatly regard."

"Thank you, Reverend."

When she said no more, he found he had to initiate conversation once again. "Tell me about what you are making."

"Oh, it's nothing special. I don't even think it has a real name. It's just a diamond mosaic. I've been working on it for years whenever I have a free moment."

She turned her work so he could see better. It was a series of hexagon shapes sewed together so that it did take on the shape of a diamond. There was a darker hexagon in the center surrounded by a number of light-colored hexagons, each one made out of a different print. This was then surrounded by a number of darker hexagons.

"It really does look like a diamond. Did you make up the design yourself?"

"No, it's an old pattern. It goes by other names, such as mosaic and honeycomb. My grandma in Deer Island has a similar quilt that I am copying, except for the colors. Hers is really beautiful, in dark and light blues." She became surprisingly animated as she talked about her work. "I couldn't get enough to do just one color, so I have many colors. I trade scraps with other ladies to get a variety and my grandmother lets me raid her scrap box when I visit. I've got fifty diamonds done."

"And they will all be connected together eventually to make a blanket?"

"I'll connect them with more hexagons, maybe green, but I'm not sure yet."

"How will you know when to stop?"

She laughed. "Last time Mama looked she thought I had plenty. But then I find another scrap I think would be pretty and decide to make just one more. It started out as a doll quilt when I was nine. Soon it will generously cover a four-poster."

"And you never get bored doing it?" This truly amazed Zack. He was never one to stick long with anything, preferring always to move on to something new.

"Well, I have finished other quilts in that time. I've got eleven quilts in my hope chest."

"Eleven quilts? That seems like a lot."

"They're not all quilted yet."

"What are you going to do with so many?"

"Quilts are always needed," she replied. "Eleven does seem like a lot, but I have one more to go until . . ." She paused, her cheeks pinking once again. "Well, Mama suggested I make twelve. It was a tradition when she was young for a girl to make twelve quilts for her wedding." She seemed to get hold of herself and continued. "Anyway, I always seem to return to my hexagons. I don't know, maybe I'll never finish because I so enjoy making them."

"It seems to indicate an admirable quality in you, like faithfulness or loyalty," he said.

They were quiet for a few moments. Ellie appeared uncomfortable receiving compliments. Then she went on, "Reverend, I'm glad we've had this chance to talk."

"Then you no longer dislike me?"

"I didn't dislike you in the first place." Pausing, she seemed hesitant to continue. She looked at the work in her lap and then finally back up at him. "I have a confession to make."

"Now, Ellie, you know we're not papists, and I do not require confession from you," he responded lightly.

"It's not that kind of confession . . . not really. But the more I see you and get to know you, the more I feel it is wrong to deceive you."

Zack squirmed uncomfortably on the rail. This genteel, innocent young woman could hardly have a deceptive bone in her lovely body. He almost wished she did and that she was trying to dupe him in some way. Then he'd feel less guilty about his own dishonesty.

"I can't imagine you deceiving anyone, Ellie," he said.

"It isn't just me, it's — I'll make myself very unpopular around here for telling you, but I should tell you, shouldn't I? Even if others would be upset."

"You must follow your conscience."

"I think it's the right thing to do." She let go of her work and clasped her hands together. She still seemed hesitant as she went on. "When we learned we were getting an unmarried minister, well, many of the ladies hoped that he . . . that is, you . . . might look upon one of the unmarried young women in our community in a particularly . . . well, favorable way."

He tried to look appropriately shocked. "You mean they hoped to win my affections?"

"Yes, with a mind, of course, toward . . ." She sucked in a breath before saying the final word, ". . . matrimony!"

"They hoped I would choose one of the local women for my wife?"

"Yes, Reverend!" Her pretty features

contorted with anguish. "I hope you can forgive them. I believe their hearts were pure in this. Most felt you would eventually marry someone, so why not one of them?"

"Which ladies, might I ask?"

"Well . . ."

"Every unmarried lady in Maintown?"

"Probably in the entire county!"

"Except for you?"

"I . . . well . . ." She wrung her hands and shifted in her chair, rocking faster and faster as she did so. "Perhaps even I for a time."

"So all you dear Christian women were scheming and plotting after me?"

"Oh, you must think us horrible and evil!"

Crossing his arms over his chest, he stared down at her sternly for a moment, just long enough to get the most out of her discomfiture. She probably didn't deserve him toying with her so, but he sensed she was a bit full of herself and might just need to be cut down a notch or two. Perhaps it was a little payback to all women for those, most recently Darla, who had hurt him.

Finally he laughed, not cruelly but as good-naturedly as he could.

"You are not angry?" she asked.

"Nor am I completely without a clue. We even had a class in seminary about husband-hunting parishioners."

"A class?" Suddenly she knew he was teasing. "You did not! But I deserve your taunts for having any part in this at all."

"Maybe you do a little. But at least you eschewed the hunt. Probably because you decided you didn't like me —"

"I do not dislike you!" she exclaimed.

"You're sure?" He mocked her, but gently.

"If you keep teasing me, I may change my mind." She smiled smugly.

He chuckled. "Well said!"

"But, Reverend," she said, becoming serious again, "what will you do about this situation?"

"I suppose . . . I'll let God's will be done!" Slowly he was learning this religious business. He was pleased with his answer.

"Yes, of course."

"I've enjoyed our conversation, Ellie," he said. "Now I best take my leave so I can prepare for my journey. First, I should like to bid your sister good day, as well."

"She is in the garden. Go that way to the back of the house." She lifted a hand to point the way.

Ellie watched the minister walk away. She could not help wondering if there was a connection between his declaration of doing God's will and then immediately seeking out Maggie. Could he be sweet on her?

Why not? She was pretty and fun loving. Mama always said that once the boys realized Maggie was a girl, that is, once she let them realize it, they would be after her in droves.

But Reverend Locklin?

Ellie felt a pang in her stomach. Maybe it was jealousy. But it was her own fault. She had given up the . . . what was it? Competition? Anyway, she had backed off by her own will.

Did she now regret it?

Reverend Locklin was unlike any minister she had ever known. Granted, the ones she had known had all been older family men. Reverend Locklin — William — was only a few years older than she. He teased her and jested with her. It was almost as if he was flirting. Oh, surely not! Even young ministers did not flirt! But more unsettling than that — she had enjoyed it. She liked his easy laughter and the glint in his eyes when he made fun of her.

Her stomach had been in terrible flutters throughout their entire conversation.

She was glad he was taking off on his circuit soon, for if not, she'd be tempted to find some excuse to go see him. To present him with another dish of cookies, perhaps, or to loan him a book she enjoyed, or to get more of his clothing for alterations. She would be as shameless as Mabel and Iris and even Maggie.

She considered the minister's words: "Let God's will be done." That's what she wanted to do more than anything. But did it mean to hide in a corner and do nothing? That was a question she'd normally ask her pastor, if he hadn't been the one to prompt it in the first place.

TWELVE

The next Sunday the Sewing Circle met at the schoolhouse. This time Polly Briggs's quilt was spread out on the frame. She had finally finished her daughter's wedding quilt.

"I suppose the arrival of the new pastor spurred me on," she said.

"So when is the big day?" Mary Renolds asked.

"Claudia has her heart set on the first Sunday in July."

"That's just three weeks away."

"Have you spoken to Reverend Locklin yet?" asked Emma Jean Stoddard. "He hasn't mentioned anything about it."

"I wasn't sure if I would get everything done in time," Polly said. "I just finished the quilt, but that wasn't as important as Claudia's dress, which she simply couldn't decide on. We went to St. Helens last week, and she finally chose a pattern and material, but by then the reverend had already departed on his circuit. But I can see no problem. He'll be here on that Sunday."

"What's the dress like, Polly?" Ada asked.

"It is a pattern similar to a gown we saw in *Godey's.* It has a fitted bodice that goes a few inches below the waist with twenty crochet-covered buttons down the front. The overskirt drapes across the front, and the underskirt is flounced and shirred —"

"Yes, I believe I saw it, as well, in the magazine," Mary said. "Very elegant."

"What material will you use?" Florence Parker asked.

"There wasn't time to order anything from Portland," Polly said regretfully, "but the St. Helens mercantile had some lovely lawn. Lace and ribbon will dress it up."

"I have already purchased several lengths of silk for my daughter's wedding," Emma Jean said. "I don't want to be caught unprepared."

A few brows arched at this. Most believed Sarah Stoddard would never marry. And the comment didn't make poor Polly feel any better, either, since her daughter had been engaged six months ago and there should have been plenty of time to order something else. Nevertheless, Ada did not want to mention that she also had stored away enough silk to make a wedding gown for one of her daughters, the first to marry. It might just bring up the situation with the minister, and Ada didn't wish to dwell upon it. Ada was disappointed that Ellie seemed to have no interest in the minister. She had done everything she could and certainly couldn't force Ellie to woo the reverend. But Ada didn't see why her daughter felt as she did.

Jane Donnelly, in her usually kind way, offered to Polly, "I'm sure the trims will add an elegant touch." She was always diplomatic.

Ada had noticed that Jane had been especially quiet today. Once or twice when she first arrived, it had almost seemed as if she was on the verge of tears. Ada had wanted to ask her what was wrong but had curbed her curiosity. She knew Jane would have been mortified if she had broken down in public, even among her closest friends.

"Your fingers are going to be raw before the month is out," Ada said to Polly. "But your quilt is wonderful. It is one of the nicest basket quilts I have seen."

The basket blocks were set on point, alternating with plain white squares, while the basket itself was made of several small triangles with a curved handle. Each was of a different fabric with a white as the background.

"Claudia requested baskets," Polly said.

Polly had already marked the plain white squares with a feathered wreath pattern. She said the baskets could be outline stitched. Everyone found their places around the frame. The ladies worked together like a well-oiled machine. Stitches were small and uniform; even Mary's were nice despite her failing vision and arthritic fingers.

When the part showing on the frame was finished, Emma Jean said, "Shall we roll?" and a new section of quilt was rolled into view. The nine expert quilters would finish the quilt that day. Their work was not slowed or compromised by their steady stream of conversation.

They talked about their children and grandchildren, for those fortunate enough to have them. They shared recipe ideas or cleaning hints. They talked about mutual friends and relatives who were not in the Circle, and they steadfastly refused to call this "gossip." But by far the main topic of conversation this meeting was the new minister. They all had mostly good to say, although there was some criticism about his inexperience.

The subject of the minister prompted Ada

to mention a somewhat related topic, though she was careful not to make it appear related.

"I've been wondering about something," Ada began casually. "Ellie has shown an interest in joining the Sewing Circle. I know we've talked before regarding our daughters, and there never was a consensus. But several of the girls are older now. . . ." She let her words trail away, encouraging comments from the others.

"I still worry that the quality of our work will suffer if we invite the inexperienced," said Florence. "Not all the girls are as proficient as your Ellie or my Mabel."

Ada tried not to wince at the implication, but she knew Florence was referring to Maggie. Instead she decided, for Ellie's sake, to meet the problem head-on. "I can assure everyone that Maggie has absolutely no interest in joining this group."

Chuckles rippled around the frame, and there could be no doubt they had all been thinking of the problem of Maggie.

"That is not the only problem with the suggestion," Emma Jean said. "We determined from the beginning that the group would be open only to married women."

"This Circle could be a wonderful opportunity for the young unmarried women to learn from us," Jane said. "Not only quilting but about being good wives and mothers."

"Would you want someone to be learning on your quilt?" Florence asked. "Do you want a quilt full of toenail catchers?"

If it had been anyone else protesting, Ada might have just laughed it off. She knew better than any that Maggie's quilt stitches were indeed big enough to catch a toenail. But it rankled that the protest came from Florence. She was certain her words were pointed against Ada and her daughters.

Just to be ornery, Ada said, "So it would be fine if an inexperienced *married* woman wanted to join?"

"It seems to me it should be," Jane said, loyal friend that she was.

"There should be some way to assure quality," Florence insisted.

"Maybe we should test everyone with an interest to join," suggested Polly quite seriously.

"I know I would have failed such a test when I joined you two years ago," Louise said.

"And look at your work now!" said Jane triumphantly.

Indeed, Louise, at only twenty-five, had done rather rough work at first, but even in the beginning it had been far better than Maggie's.

"Girls should be learning to quilt at home, not here," Polly said.

Hilda agreed. Ada saw the group splitting on the issue: Florence, Polly, and Hilda against opening up to younger members; Ada, Jane, and Louise clearly on the other side. But Ada had seen old Mary Renolds nodding in response to comments made by Ada's side.

"That is a very good point, Polly," Emma Jean said, taking her stand with Florence and the others. "Also, we don't have enough space around the frame as it is."

"No one seems to mind taking turns," Ada responded.

Nessa had not weighed in with any definite opinion. Ada hated to put shy Nessa on the spot, but she happened to know that her daughter Kendra, who was all but engaged to Boyd, also had an interest in joining the Circle. No doubt Nessa had remained silent not only because of her shyness but because Florence was a good friend of hers.

"Nessa, what do you think?" Ada asked.

Nessa's cheeks pinked as all eyes swung toward her, but she didn't shrink away. "Well, none of us is getting any younger, you know. . . ." Her eyes flickered toward

Florence before she continued in an apologetic tone, "Well, we're not! New blood couldn't hurt."

"We could be selective," Louise said. "By invitation only."

"And deal with the hurt feelings of those who feel left out?" Florence asked.

"I didn't think of that." Louise backed down.

"Ladies," said Emma Jean, "if I remember right, this is where this same discussion left off two years ago. We all came together quite naturally because of our mutual love of stitching. That was a good ten years ago, wasn't it? There were ten of us then, but Betsy and Margaret passed on, and that's when Louise filled one of the empty places. Nine has been a good number."

"So someone has to die before someone new can join?" snapped Ada.

"I'll accommodate you soon enough," Mary said with a chuckle.

"You have taught me so much, Mary," Ada said. "I wish my daughter could learn from you, as well. Isn't one of the purposes of a group such as ours to spread our passion for stitching to others? We have done just that, with several young women now showing the same passion. Yet they are closed from joining us." Ada couldn't help if her voice trembled a little as she spoke, for even as the words came she realized how much this truly meant to her. At one time she thought the Sewing Circle was her little escape from home, a time for herself. But now she realized what a joy it would be to have her daughters involved.

"There is no need to get emotional," Emma Jean said.

"I'm sorry," Ada replied, not meaning it but trying to make peace.

"I suggest that we table this issue for a bit," Emma Jean went on, sounding very presidential. "Let's take a few weeks to think about it, and we can discuss it later."

Much later, Ada thought sourly, probably never. Florence would see to that, especially since Mabel, as good a stitcher as she was, had no interest in the Circle. She was far too sophisticated for a simple country quilting bee.

Ada was quiet the rest of the afternoon. She ate little of the midday meal she had brought in Maggie's old lunch pail. She was even silent about another topic of business she had wanted to mention. The quilting bee at her home to finish the pastor's quilt had been so successful that many of the women had talked about making that a regular feature of the Circle, that is, to have two meetings a month, one on the second Sunday at the schoolhouse as always, and another at a home on a weekday. It would be a way Ellie could attend when it was at their house simply because she was home. But Ada was afraid if she brought that up now, it would be put down by Florence and her cronies just for general purposes. She decided to wait to mention it until it had a better chance of succeeding.

When it was time to leave, Ada saw that Jane's husband had not arrived to pick her up.

"Where's Tom?" she asked.

"Oh, I walked today," Jane said a little hesitantly, as if she didn't want to admit it.

"Well, then, ride with me. We haven't had a chance to visit for a long time."

Jane climbed up next to Ada in the wagon seat, and they started up the road. It was as fine a spring day as one could hope for in these parts. Blue sky, warm sun upon the skin, gentle breeze, sweet fragrances of new growth in the air.

"I'm still fuming over that Florence Parker!" Jane said. "Sometimes I think she takes the opposite side of you just to be contrary."

"That's not the only reason," Ada said.

"I know you two have a past, but that was

years ago when you were girls."

No one knew the whole story behind Ada and Florence's rivalry. Jane knew a lot but not all, and Ada wanted to keep it that way. It would do no one any good to dredge up the past. Ada had prayed about it and tried to find peace about it, at least with God, but she doubted there would ever be peace between her and Florence. Once she had tried to confront Florence, but she had refused to talk about it, practically denying there was anything wrong in the first place. Ignoring it was probably for the best.

"For a while during the discussion today," Ada said, "I toyed with the idea of starting another sewing circle. But I just can't do that. We have our differences, but there is still a deep bond of friendship between us all. And such a split might even cause a split in the church. That would be disastrous."

"Maybe the young girls should start their own group."

"I fear that would be just as divisive."

"At least you don't need the group to share your love of stitching with your daughters," offered Jane. "How I wish I'd had a daughter —" Her voice broke off suddenly. Ada glanced over at her friend and saw her dash a hand against the corner of her eye.

"What is it, Jane? Something has been troubling you all day."

Jane sniffed. "I didn't know it was still so close to the surface. It is hard to have only one child and then to feel him slipping away."

"Sons do grow apart from their families."

"It is more than that, Ada. Before I left for the Circle this morning, Tom and Tommy had a huge fight. Tom is so hard on the boy, and the beatings don't help. He is going to push Tommy away. It used to be when Tommy was little that he'd run to me after his father . . . ah . . . disciplined him. Now, he goes off by himself. I . . . I think he blames me as much as his father."

"That can't be." Ada glanced once more at her friend; then fearing to be distracted from the road, she reined in the horses and eased the wagon over to the side and stopped so they could talk more easily. "He probably just feels he is too old to run to his mother. You know how boys are."

"Maybe."

"I'm sure that's it. I feel the same from Georgie, and he is younger than Tommy."

"Ada, I'm afraid Tommy will run away!" Jane ended in a barely restrained sob.

Ada reached over and laid a comforting hand on Jane's shoulder. She didn't know what to say. Yes, she had felt a small gulf form between herself and her boys as they grew older, but never had she believed they would leave home prematurely. Once Boyd had indeed run away. He had been ten and mad when his father wouldn't let him drive the wagon on an icy morning. He had been gone only a couple of hours, returning in time for lunch. Ada knew it was much different for young Tommy, who was treated so harshly by his father. Her heart went out to Jane.

"Has he said anything serious about running away?"

"No, but he goes off by himself more and more. I just know one day he won't come back."

"Perhaps our new minister can help. He is a young man and may be able to relate to Tommy's troubles."

"It is Tom who truly needs help. I have prayed for years that he would be saved. I pray for Tommy, too, but as much as Tommy hates his father, he also desires to imitate him. Maybe if Tom started coming to church, Tommy would imitate that as he now copies Tom's bad habits."

"You should speak to Reverend Locklin when he gets back from his circuit."

"Reverend McFarland tried to talk to Tom

many times. Once, Tom went after the poor man with the shotgun. The minister stayed away after that." Anguish filled Jane's eyes. "I fear to draw the new minister into this."

Ada had heard about the shotgun incident and knew Jane's husband Tom could be meanspirited. Jane's fears were not without reason. Many stories had circulated over the years about how Tom would pick fights with men in the St. Helens saloons, or how he'd cheated his neighbors one way or another. Once, he had tried to sell a horse to Calvin, insisting that it was a four-year-old when even a city fellow could see the animal had to be at least ten.

"If you told Reverend Locklin all this," Ada suggested, "then he could decide for himself how to approach the situation. He is trained in such matters. There would be no problem with him talking to Tommy, would there?"

"Tom barely tolerates me going to church," Jane replied. "And I never know how he will respond to anything. But I do agree I need to talk to my pastor. This situation is beyond me."

Thirteen

Zack rode at an easy pace, the sun warm upon his shoulders. He felt oddly contented as he steered his horse back to Maintown. He felt like he was going home. He'd been there only a week before setting out on his circuit, but there had been something about the Copeland home, about Mrs. Copeland's warm and welcoming ways after she'd returned to take up her household duties, that had made Zack feel as though he belonged.

This was a new sensation for him. He'd never *belonged* anywhere, even in his ma's house, especially after his stepfather had entered the scene. So rather than feel uncomfortable about the fact that this was not his but William Locklin's life, he decided to enjoy it while it lasted.

He thought back on the last few days of the circuit. He'd held a service on the second Sunday at Bachelor Flat, a mere hour's ride from Maintown. He had met most of the folks the previous Sunday at Maintown, so he had set out alone and then returned to Maintown that same day. He departed on the next leg of the circuit the following Tuesday, accompanied by Calvin Newcomb. They made the journey in two days of easy riding. The ride with Calvin Newcomb to the Deer Island station — which he'd learned wasn't an island at all, though he never discovered the reason for the name — had been more pleasant than he had anticipated. Calvin was a simple, decent man, not a great talker but full of a quiet wisdom that made Zack envy the man's sons. How would Zack have turned out if he'd had a father like Calvin?

Zack recalled one conversation in particular. . . .

"Reverend, have you given any more thought to your employment when you are not riding the circuit?" Calvin had asked.

Back in Maintown Calvin had pointed out that since it was a small circuit, the churches could not afford to pay Zack a full-time wage, so the minister was expected to augment his expenses with other part-time work. The previous pastor, McFarland, had owned a tract of land and had worked this for income. Since Zack had no land, he would need to look elsewhere.

"I haven't much," Zack replied honestly enough. "There's been so much to occupy my time lately."

"That's not surprising, Reverend —"

"Say, Mr. Newcomb, can I request that you call me William? I can't get any others to do it, but I'd sure be honored if you did so." In truth, Zack felt more comfortable with the false name of William than he did with the false title of reverend.

"I'd be honored, William, but then you must call me Calvin. I don't much like formality, either."

"Good. That's settled, then."

"Now, about work," Calvin returned to the former topic, "I don't know how your finances stand, and you don't have to rush into anything, but if you are interested, Clyde Lambert, the manager of the Milton Creek Sawmill, said he'd be willing to hire you part-time."

"I appreciate that and will consider it," Zack said. "But since my room and board is paid by the church, I don't have many other expenses. I'd like to first spend some time getting familiar with my pastoral duties."

"That is a good idea." Calvin was quiet a moment, appearing to consider what he would say next. He seemed reluctant to speak on a delicate subject. Finally he continued. "You might want to think ahead to the future, lad. I . . . uh . . . don't reckon you'll want to be a single man forever."

"I won't be if the girls in Maintown have any say about it." Zack glanced at Calvin, who seemed taken aback by the words; then a sudden grin bent his lips. Zack chuckled, and Calvin joined him.

"I guess the womenfolk aren't as subtle as they think," Calvin said.

"About as subtle as a mallet between the eyes."

Both men laughed heartily.

Appearing more comfortable but still hesitant, Calvin said, "Have you any thoughts on this matter?"

"Of course I'll marry one day, probably sooner than later." Zack answered as he thought William might but kept silent his thought that Calvin's daughters would be his prime candidates.

"A man needs a wife," Calvin said. "Not just for cooking and cleaning and such like. He needs . . . let me put it this way. A woman is like the North Star. I come from a long line of whalers back in Maine, and from them I learned how they used the North Star to steer their ships. That's what a woman does for a man. She gives him direction, maybe even purpose. I figure if I didn't have Ada, I'd be carousing around in saloons, gambling, and drinking away my money."

You mean, having fun? Zack wanted to say. But of course William wouldn't have said that, and in truth, Zack realized he couldn't say it either with total conviction. He lived his life that way, but did he really like his life? Was there something better he was missing?

"With Ada I got something important to live for," Calvin said, "my farm and my family. I don't reckon I could have more."

Zack didn't like the introspection Calvin's words had prompted and replied rather flippantly, "Well, I suppose it would be best for me to work as much as possible and put aside money toward my inevitable plunge into matrimony."

"Marriage isn't quite that bad, William."

"I surely hope not!"

"You find the right woman, and it could be a pleasant experience."

"I've seen some sad marriages, even in my short life, Calvin."

Calvin nodded quietly.

Curious, Zack asked, "What makes a happy marriage, Calvin?"

"I'm no expert. That's for sure!" Calvin laughed. "Ask Ada, and she'll agree. We get storms and choppy seas." He shrugged. "But we enjoy each other's company. I'd say we like each other well enough. Maybe that's all there is to it — just liking each other."

Zack decided that despite his curiosity, the conversation had proceeded long enough. He was only twenty-four years old, and he'd never thought much about marriage, at least not seriously. He definitely had never met the kind of woman a man would consider marrying. And most of the men he'd associated with were die-hard bachelors or had run away from unhappy unions. He had once met a fellow who had three wives in three different towns. He had run away from all three, never bothering to legally dissolve any of the marriages. Zack was seldom around any so-called family men. If he and his friends had happened upon one of this ilk, they were likely to ridicule the poor sot as anchored with a ball and chain. He had never let himself think that such a man was anchored not to a lead ball but to the North Star, and maybe he was soaring through the heavens, his life full of meaning and purpose.

Quickly Zack changed the direction of the

conversation and asked Calvin about the work at the sawmill. They did not return to the disturbing topic of marriage again.

Calvin had returned to Maintown once he'd introduced Zack to the deacons of the church at Deer Island. Zack stayed with one of those families for a few days and preached at the church service on the third Sunday morning. He reused the sermon "Consider the Lilies," with which by now he was becoming quite comfortable. In Deer Island there was also a funeral to officiate. He'd brought William Locklin's books with him and now found that the *Manual for Ministers* was particularly useful, for it gave suggested outlines for various services. Flipping past the section on weddings — ignoring the slightly unsettled feeling that it gave him — he found the section on funerals. All went rather smoothly. No one seemed to mind that he read the service directly from the book. They probably knew he was too new at these matters to have it memorized.

Then he moved on to Columbia City, where he delivered the Sunday sermon — again "Consider the Lilies" — in the afternoon of the same Sunday. A covered-dish supper followed, which enabled him to get acquainted with the church members.

On Wednesday morning after breakfast at the home of the chairman of the Columbia City board of deacons, he headed back to Maintown. On his ride with Calvin from Maintown days ago, they had taken back roads to Deer Island because Zack had told Calvin that he wanted to see some of the countryside. But the folks in Columbia City told him the fastest route back to Maintown would be through St. Helens. Zack had thus far avoided that city, but now he wasn't sure enough of the roads he and Calvin had traveled to attempt taking them alone. He figured he'd simply skirt the city. Then Gilbert Reed, his host, invited himself to ride along with Zack because he had business in St. Helens.

"Pastor," Gilbert said as they rode, "I'm good friends with the minister of the St. Helens Methodist Church, Reverend Barnett, and I know he's been wanting to meet you."

Meeting with other local ministers was one thing Zack felt he ought to avoid at all costs, so he'd have to come up with an excuse.

After a brief pause he said, "I'd like that, Mr. Reed, but today may not be the best time. I want to get back to Maintown before dark."

"Oh, you could take time for a short visit and still make it."

"You don't say?"

As they rode into town, Zack searched his mind for other viable excuses to get out of the meeting. Finally he resigned himself to the inevitable.

St. Helens was a town of some two or three hundred people, three saloons, a large general store, and a couple of hotels. The townspeople had big aspirations, though, hoping to one day be the preeminent port on the Columbia River. Zack thought now about those three saloons and how easily he might get himself enough cash to make it to San Francisco. He thought he could parlay Locklin's few dollars into a nice bundle. But recalling his poor luck at the Portland gaming tables, he reminded himself there was also the risk that he'd lose the money along with his preacher disguise. No minister would be caught around a gaming table.

Giving a covertly wistful glance toward one of those saloons, he caught a far more disturbing sight out of the corner of his eye. His heart skipped a beat, and he quickly jerked his gaze back toward the front. He couldn't be certain, but he wasn't about to turn back for a better look.

He was sure that Beau Cutter was standing on the plank sidewalk in front of the general store conversing with another man. Now that his heart was beating again, it pounded rapidly, and it took all his will to keep from digging his heels into his mount's flanks and flying. Keeping to their slow and easy pace, Zack dipped his head slightly to put his face more into the shadow of his wide-brimmed hat. Dressed as he was in Locklin's duds, Zack would not be immediately recognizable as himself — at least he hoped not.

Calmly he said to his companion, "Mr. Reed, I just saw an old friend. I really must greet him before he gets away. Why, I've already lost sight of him."

"I'll wait," Reed said congenially. "I've got business at Dolman's General Store."

"This may take a while. I'm afraid I'll have to postpone my meeting with Reverend Barnett. But tell him I will look him up at my next opportunity."

Reed seemed reluctant to give up so easily, but Zack kept looking anxiously in the direction his imaginary friend had taken, opposite of where he'd seen Cutter. Reed finally bid Zack good day, and Zack rode off, still at an easy pace. He wound around through back streets, hoping they would eventually take him to the road leading to

Maintown. He kept his pace easy the entire time, ignoring the urging of his pounding heart to run.

He did not feel safe until he was well on his way to Maintown. Maybe that's where his odd feeling of contentment sprang from. Maintown represented a haven for him. Cutter would simply never suspect Zack's crazy plan. And the man could ask all he wanted about a drifter named Zack Hartley, even give a description, and no one was likely to connect that man to the Brethren of Christ minister. Zack had always bemoaned the fact that his looks, though not unsightly, were rather nondescript. Tall, but not strikingly so, light brown hair, brown eyes, average physique — any number of men could fit that description, a fact he now welcomed.

He took one short side trip before returning to his boardinghouse. A couple miles east of Maintown, according to Calvin, was the Milton Creek Sawmill, and here Zack stopped to inquire about employment. He needed to do something else to earn money in order to expedite his departure from this area, even if it meant doing regular labor. For despite the feeling of hominess Maintown gave him, he knew he couldn't stay here forever.

FOURTEEN

Zack's return to Maintown was met with a steady stream of dinner invitations, most from the families of eligible young women, some from homes he'd already visited.

At the Fergus home, the daughter Iris was so blatant in her advances that she even said, "I have just been waiting for the right man to marry, Reverend." The glint in her eye as much as said she had finally found him.

Zack had never in his life been nervous around women, but he was downright afraid of Iris Fergus!

Dinner with the Stoddards was painful in an entirely different way. Mrs. Stoddard was clearly the aggressor there, at least in her unsubtle manipulations of Zack and her shy daughter Sarah. She'd managed to get the two young people alone in the parlor for long periods of time, during which Zack tried to maintain conversation with Sarah, but it would have been easier to coax blood from a turnip. Finally he conjured some pretext to go in search of Mr. Stoddard. The relief in Sarah's expression when Zack took his leave was unmistakable.

But the most disconcerting dinner of all was with the Parkers. Mabel Parker was neither artless nor shy. It was obvious she knew what she wanted, and it was clear she wanted Zack. She also knew how to get it. She was charming and coy, graceful and feminine. She probably would have won the new minister had it been the real Locklin. Even Zack was nearly beguiled by the young woman, but her habit of putting on airs put him off.

The evening had begun with Zack being entertained in the finely appointed parlor.

"My family visited England when I was young," Mabel said in response to Zack's compliment about their lovely home. "Many of our furnishings were purchased there and shipped over. My mother is especially proud of the curio cabinet. It was made to order from her instructions." She went on about several pieces in the room, and Zack quickly lost interest.

Florence Parker chimed in with frequent embellishments. Mr. Parker seemed embarrassed by the bragging but was silent for the most part, though he did converse about other topics. Zack had to admit that of all the families in the area he had visited, the Parkers did indeed have cause to brag. Nathan Parker was half owner of the Milton Creek Sawmill, obviously a profitable business. He also owned a couple of large tracts of rich timberland, a fact that neither Florence nor Mabel let slip by.

Zack could not help being impressed. He was, after all, not a real minister who might be less awed by material possessions. His short stint impersonating English nobility had given him an appreciation for the finer things of life. Marrying into the Parker family could set up a fellow for life. And marrying the attractive, charming Mabel would not be so bad.

As he sipped tea in a fine porcelain cup, he let his mind wander over this prospect. He eyed Mabel, in her stylish linen frock, appreciatively. She noted his gaze and smiled back, not with blatant desire as Iris has smiled at him, nor with the trembling fear that had been in Sarah's one fleeting smile. Mabel's smile was both demure and coquettish, with just a hint of appealing sauciness.

The boyish, unworldly William Locklin would have probably melted completely to the girl's wiles. The far more experienced, even sophisticated, Zack had to work mightily to remind himself of who and what he was and what he truly wanted.

Calvin had mentioned one of the minister's duties that hadn't occurred to Zack — visitation. Zack didn't like the sound of that. He had a vague idea of what it meant. He remembered a minister visiting his parents once when his stepfather had missed church on account of twisting an ankle while working in the fields. The minister had prayed with them and read Scripture and visited somewhat awkwardly with the family for a time until, much to everyone's relief, he departed.

Understandably, Zack would be very uncomfortable doing this sort of thing but knew he could not avoid it for long. Shortly after he returned to Maintown from his circuit, Mrs. Stoddard, as chairwoman of the Ladies' Aid Society, brought him a list of folks who would benefit by a visit from the pastor. He tried to get out of it but quickly learned Mrs. Stoddard was not a woman one easily said no to.

First on the list was the Arlington family. They had a sick child, a matter made worse by the fact that Lewis Arlington had taken a job in Rainier because money was tight, so his wife was alone with their children when Zack made his call. Louise Arlington was a part of the Sewing Circle, and the ladies were trying to help out, but she was still overwhelmed by all that was happening to them.

As Zack lifted his hand to knock on the door, he could hear sounds of chaos inside, children crying, a woman scolding, little feet pattering about. When Louise opened the door, Zack met a woman who was no more than twenty-five and might have been pretty if her hair hadn't been hanging about her face in disarray and her skin wasn't pale with dark circles around her eyes. She was wearing a faded blue calico dress and a stained white apron. A bawling baby was clenched in the crook of one arm. Another crying child, about two years old, was standing next to her, clutching her skirt. In the background a boy, about four, was running about with a feather in his hair and making Indian war cries.

"Why, Reverend Locklin, what a surprise! A . . . pleasant surprise," Mrs. Arlington said. "Do come in."

Zack knew now why the idea of making visitations disturbed him. This woman was up to her elbows in work, and the last thing she needed was to entertain someone.

"I've come at a bad time," he said apologetically.

"It's always a bad time these days," she said with a wan smile.

"Mrs. Stoddard said you might appreciate a visit —" He realized his voice was steadily rising over the din in the background.

"Billy, hush up now!" Louise called to the boy playing Indian. The two-year-old stopped crying upon seeing a stranger and was now hiding behind Louise. The baby was still squawking.

"I can come back —"

"No, please, don't be silly. It's a long ride out here." She pushed the door wide open and gestured for him to enter.

He took a step and nearly tripped over something that turned out to be a laundry basket.

"I'm so sorry," she said. "I was about to hang the laundry when Lizzy started crying."

"Is she sick?"

"A bit of croup, I think. Her little nose is stuffed up. She can't sleep or eat very well." Suddenly Louise bit her lip, which had started trembling. "I never realized how much of a help Lewis is until he took that job in Rainier. He often did the laundry for me and kept the older ones entertained. Sally will soon be home from school, and then — but you don't want to hear all this. Let me fix tea," she added gamely.

"Look, Mrs. Arlington," Zack said with sudden resolve, "I'm sure the last thing you need now is to fix tea for a guest. I could waste your time by visiting and praying with you, but why don't I just pray while I hang your laundry?"

"Oh no! I couldn't let you do that — I mean, hang my laundry! That just wouldn't be right."

"I am quite sure that's why God sent me out here. You just take care of your baby." Zack grabbed the basket and headed outside to where he had seen the clothesline.

He figured this was the best solution for both of them. He had been dreading the moment when he would have to fake a prayer. It was one thing to pretend to pray in a formal way from the pulpit, but it just didn't sit well to do so with the frazzled, needy woman. She'd be much better off with his labor rather than his impotent prayers.

When he left there three hours later, he'd hung all the laundry, washed two days' worth of dishes, coaxed the two-year-old to take a nap, and taught Billy how Indians *quietly* stalked deer in the woods. He also helped Louise rig up a steam tent to help clear the baby's breathing.

He left the Arlington home in a far more peaceful state than when he'd found it. He began to think that there were definitely times when a fake minister was better than a real one.

After that, whenever he was called upon to visit a shut-in or a backslider or others with various needs, he found a way to turn the visit into helping out with chores. No matter what a person's problem, they could always use help around the farm, and few would exchange that for a prayer. He became the most welcome visiting pastor Maintown had ever had.

Two bachelor brothers were on his list to visit. They lived together on their farm, and Zack could see why neither had ever married. They were the crankiest and most cantankerous men he had ever seen. He wondered if Mrs. Stoddard had put them on the list just to test the new minister.

Felix and Fred Baxter were also serious backsliders. They attended church once a year — on Easter Sunday — but this year they had avoided even that because there had been no Maintown pastor. The rest of the year the brothers fought with each other, harangued their neighbors, and got drunk at every opportunity. Somehow they still managed to maintain a fairly prosperous farm. But they were getting older now. Felix had rheumatism, and Fred had frequent stomach troubles.

They were about the only citizens of Maintown to miss Zack's first service. It wasn't Easter, so why would they attend church? Mrs. Stoddard said that old Pastor McFarland had given up calling on them because all his visits to the Baxter farm had ended dismally.

Zack had barely ridden into their yard and dismounted when one of them hobbled out of the barn carrying a pitchfork.

"What d'ya want?" the man growled. He wore a scowl on his creased face with its stubbly gray beard. He looked like he knew how to use that pitchfork to its best effect. From the descriptions Mrs. Stoddard had given him, Zack figured this one was Fred.

"I'm William Locklin, the new minister —"

"And?" the man cut in sharply.

"I was . . . uh . . . well, just visiting the folks hereabouts."

"Ain't got time for such truck."

"I just want to be friendly."

"Ha!" came a voice from behind. "Ya

222

wanta preach at us and tell us we're goin' to Hades!"

Zack turned and saw the man who must be Felix. He was as gray and surly and grizzled as his brother, but he walked with a serious stoop.

"Believe me," Zack said, "that is the last thing I want to do."

"Oh yeah?" challenged Fred. "If that be so, then why don't you do some real good and feed our livestock for us."

With a shrug, Zack took the pitchfork and proceeded to do just that. Then he helped them plant the last of their potatoes. He learned they were late in planting because they'd both been ill. Before he left in the late afternoon, they dared him to return the next day to weed the kitchen garden. He took them up on the dare and discovered that for all their surliness, they weren't bad sorts. When the work was done, he played checkers with them, drank their home-brewed ale, and listened to their stories for hours. They had come to Oregon practically on the heels of Lewis and Clark and knew more about the region than anyone.

Fred and Felix shocked not only Zack but the entire congregation when they showed up at the next church service — and every service after that. Calvin said they were Zack's first converts. Zack smiled amusedly and let it go at that.

FIFTEEN

Even more unsettling for Zack than visiting his congregation was their coming to visit him. First Polly Briggs came by to let him know that her daughter wished to get married on the first Sunday in July after the regular church service.

Zack suddenly felt as if the floor had fallen out from under him. He should have anticipated this, and indeed he'd had a niggling sense that he was overlooking something significant. He could pretend to be a minister, preach, bury people, and do any number of ministerial duties without compunction. But he knew he couldn't marry people and be the cause of two innocents living in sin. He should have seen this coming and had an excuse prepared. Normally he could think pretty fast on his feet, but this was not one of those times.

"Pastor?" Mrs. Briggs prompted after his silence went on noticeably long.

His mind churned but felt more like a wheel spinning uselessly in mud.

"Mrs. Briggs . . . I . . . uh . . . thought you knew." Finally a story lumbered clumsily into his brain. He remembered an important paper among Locklin's things.

"Knew what, Reverend?"

"They didn't tell you?" he said, stalling, trying to fit the pieces of the tale together. When she shook her head dumbly, he continued, "Well, you are aware, I'm sure, of the shortage of ministers —" Someone had mentioned that to him along the way as the reason it had taken so long for the church to appoint a minister to this lightly populated area. "You see, the denomination sent me out a bit prematurely, not wanting to keep you waiting for a minister. They felt certain it would not take as long as it has. . . ."

"What would take as long? I'm confused," the completely befuddled woman said.

Zack hoped the scheme he just concocted was plausible, and he couldn't see why not. "I did not have my official license when I was assigned this post. But everyone thought it would follow soon enough."

"No license?"

"My . . . uh . . . ministerial license, you know. It gives me the legal right to perform my duties, marriages, and so forth."

"Oh, Pastor!" Mrs. Briggs let out a sigh. "I thought it was something serious. You can still marry my daughter even if you don't have this license thing."

"I am appalled, Mrs. Briggs! You would condone your daughter entering an illegal union?"

"Well, here in the West we sometimes have to bend the rules a little. I remember when my family settled in Wisconsin before we came to Oregon. There wasn't a proper minister for a hundred miles. Couples had to be satisfied with a 'hand clasp' marriage until a preacher came along to make it legal. More often than not a couple would have their real wedding with two or three children clinging to them."

Zack hadn't taken this attitude into account, though he knew it to be true. As he was searching in his mind for a rebuttal, Mrs. Briggs continued.

"Reverend, as far as I am concerned, you are a man of God, and that's what matters. A little piece of paper don't change that one little bit."

"I'm sorry, Mrs. Briggs," Zack said, as if with firm conviction, "but it matters to me! If we keep bending the rules, the West will never become civilized. I could never marry someone without the legal prerogative to do so."

"But my Claudia will be heartbroken if she can't marry in July! She has already waited so long for you to arrive."

"At least she won't be forced to live in sin. I am sorry to be so implacable in this, but I must draw the line somewhere. What did the folks do before I came? There surely are not any of these 'hand clasp' marriages about, or I would have faced this dilemma long before now."

"I guess the circuit judge married those who couldn't wait," Mrs. Briggs replied.

"There you go!" Zack felt as if he'd been reprieved from the gallows.

"But I wanted a Christian service for my daughter —"

"I'm sure one of the other ministers —"

"In my own church."

"Perhaps she can wait just a little longer, then," Zack said sympathetically. "I'm sure my license will come soon."

"I guess it can't be helped, then," the woman finally conceded.

When she left, Zack went upstairs to his room and took William Locklin's license from the carpetbag and tucked it deep into the trunk. He should burn it, but there were no matches at hand. He'd ask Mrs. Copeland for some at the first opportunity and finish the job later. Until then that incriminating paper should be safe.

He was distracted from that task when he reached the kitchen and found another of his parishioners there visiting with Mrs. Copeland.

"Hello, Mrs. Donnelly," he said.

"Hello, Reverend." She smiled graciously. "I am so impressed how you remember everyone's names."

"A gift from God," he said wryly, thinking as he spoke that if it wasn't for all the prickly details, this ruse would be like water off a duck's back. The devil was indeed in the details!

"Reverend, do you have a spare moment?" Mrs. Donnelly asked.

"Yes, of course. I was just about to ask Mrs. Copeland for some matches, as I appear to be out. It was a bit chilly in my room last night."

"I'm so sorry, Reverend," Mrs. Copeland said, appearing truly upset by her oversight as hostess.

Zack groaned inwardly. Why couldn't these people be mean and inconsiderate? It would make his life so much easier.

"I'll leave you and Jane to talk while I take care of this, Reverend."

"Thank you," he replied, watching her scurry from the kitchen. "What am I doing?" he murmured, forgetting that he wasn't alone.

"Reverend," Mrs. Donnelly cut into his thoughts, "don't worry about Mrs. Copeland. She lives to do for others, so any need you have brings her great joy to fulfill."

Zack blinked and forced his mind back into focus. "I'll keep that in mind. Would you care to sit, Mrs. Donnelly?"

They both sat at the table and then Jane Donnelly spoke. "Reverend, I would like to talk to you about some . . . ah . . . problems in my family. You haven't met my husband yet. He won't come to church."

"That is too bad. You would like for me to speak to him?"

"That would be nice, but there is more to it than that. You see, Tom has a great deal of hostility toward the church. I'm not sure exactly why, but he does. I no longer even attempt to ask him about church because it . . . well, it makes him very upset. I must say I worry most about our son. Tommy and his father don't get along well, but Tommy does try to emulate his father in many of his bad habits."

"You would think the boy would do the opposite," Zack said.

"Maybe it is not a willful attempt to mimic his father but more an attitude that if his father drinks strong spirits, then why shouldn't he? If his father doesn't have to attend church, then why should he? That sort of thing."

"Do you know why they don't get along?"

"Tom, my husband, is a hard man. He seldom has any good to say about anything, especially his son. That does not serve to endear a man to his son."

"No, it doesn't." Zack nodded with more understanding than Mrs. Donnelly could imagine.

"Add to that the fact that Tom often strikes Tommy —"

"Beats him?" Zack could understand that, as well.

"Perhaps that's a bit strong. I know Tom only does it because he wants our son to grow into a decent young . . . man. . . ." Mrs. Donnelly's lip began to tremble.

Zack thought perhaps she was having a hard time convincing even herself of this. They both knew you couldn't beat decency into a person. More than likely you'd only beat meanness into a man and a total disregard for authority. Zack knew about that, as well. Maybe he'd been lucky enough to leave home before the meanness could take deep root, but the rebelliousness sure had.

While Mrs. Donnelly gathered back her emotions, Zack said, "I'm not sure what I could do about it, Mrs. Donnelly. I could talk to your husband, but if other pastors haven't been able to get through to him, I don't know if I could do any better."

"Perhaps you could talk to Tommy?" she asked. "I fear so for him, that he will . . ." She sniffed and chewed her lip before continuing shakily, "I fear he will run away from home."

Zack nodded. It wasn't an empty fear. "I'll talk to him, of course. Perhaps I can go back with you now —"

"Oh no! Tomorrow would be better. I don't want either of them to think I put you up to this. It . . . wouldn't set well with Tom."

The next day Zack rode out to the Donnelly place. In the short time he'd been in this county, some of the folks had come to him — their minister, they thought — with their problems. He'd listened and responded as vaguely as he could, deflecting as much as possible. But when he couldn't do that he responded with whatever wisdom he thought the real William Locklin would dispense. Sometimes he dished out his own wisdom. These people, he'd found, liked practical horse sense better than bookish gibberish anyway. He rather enjoyed this role because he thought he had more to offer than religious prattle.

But there was something about Mrs. Donnelly's problem that touched him on a deeper level. Tommy Donnelly could have been a younger Zack. At least Zack had had going for him the fact that he was more sharp-witted than Tommy. If Tommy ran away from home, he might not fare as well as Zack had. There had been many times in the last dozen years when Zack had literally survived only by his wits.

When he rode into the Donnelly yard, it appeared deserted. He hadn't made a set time with Mrs. Donnelly, and she hadn't been able to offer more than a general time when Tommy would be there. But hearing a noise in the barn, Zack headed in that direction, dismounting near the doors and tying his horse to a post.

He pushed open one of the doors. "Hello? Anyone in here?"

A figure stepped out from one of the shadowed corners. "Yeah, I'm here. Who are you and what'd you want?"

Zack needed no formal introductions to know this was the elder Tom Donnelly. He was a tall man, three or four inches taller than Zack. He probably weighed a solid two hundred or more pounds. The scowl on his face did not help his coarse looks and neither did the unshaven stubble on his hard jaw. His eyes squinted with a fierce glint.

"Mr. Donnelly?"

"Yeah. Who are you?"

"I'm William Locklin, the minister —"

Donnelly cursed foully. Zack had heard worse in his time but pretended to appear shocked.

"You'll be happy to know," Zack said, "that I haven't come to see you. I was looking for your son."

"You leave my boy alone, too!" the man snarled.

"I make it a habit to visit all my parishioners."

"Well, you'll just have to break that habit where my kid is concerned."

"I don't think so," Zack replied coolly. It took everything he had to maintain civility. This man even looked like Zack's stepfather, and it sent his mind back into the darkest moments of his childhood.

"This is my place," Donnelly said. "You'll do as I say."

"I came to see your son, and I will do just

that," Zack insisted stubbornly. He knew it had less to do with young Tommy than with the fact that Zack refused to back down from this man.

"Get outta my place, Preacher!"

"All I want to do is talk with the boy."

"All you want to do is fill my boy's head with lies — religious lies! I ain't gonna have it."

"Then I'll just talk to him elsewhere, but I *will* talk to him."

"Oh yeah?" Donnelly took a menacing step toward Zack. "I said get out!" Donnelly gave Zack's shoulder a push with his grimy, gnarled hand.

"Don't you touch me!" Zack warned.

"What you gonna do 'bout it, Preacher?" the man sneered. "All you preachers can do is turn the other cheek. Ain't that right?"

"You'd be surprised what a preacher can do," Zack replied. Especially a fake one.

"Oh, you're a tough one." Donnelly pushed Zack's shoulder again. "C'mon, then. Show me what you can do," he taunted, giving Zack a harder shove and then another.

Zack's fist swung fast and sure, making square contact with Donnelly's jaw. The man stumbled back, caught completely by surprise. Zack took the momentary advantage and followed up with another swing into the man's gut. Donnelly was big and solid, but Zack was strong and an experienced brawler. While Donnelly was bent and gagging from the blow to his belly, Zack charged — there was no honor in barroom brawling. Zack had learned you took every advantage you could, or you'd be dead.

The two men tumbled to the floor. Donnelly tried to get in a punch or two but could gain little ground against the barrage Zack aimed at him. Zack's fists pummeled the man until finally Zack realized there was no more resistance from his opponent. He stopped suddenly. Donnelly was lying under Zack, arms raised protectively across his face, totally whipped. Zack rolled off Donnelly. His fists were bloody and bruised but not as badly as Tom Donnelly's face.

"I'm leaving, Donnelly," Zack growled, "because I want to leave."

Donnelly groaned in response. Zack could tell the blighter would be okay, his pride bruised far more than his person.

Zack was still panting when he reached the barn door and strode out. Immediately he saw a figure dart around the corner of the barn, and realizing who that figure was, Zack was suddenly and painfully aware of what he had just done.

"Hey, Tommy!" he called, jogging after the boy.

Tommy stopped and turned to face Zack. "Reverend," he said indifferently, as if he hadn't just witnessed a shocking event.

"Did you see, Tommy?" Zack knew he was going to have to confront the situation. Tommy nodded, but Zack couldn't read his passive expression. "I'm truly sorry," Zack continued. "Sorry you saw such a thing and sorry for what I did to your father."

The boy's brow arched slightly with perplexity. "Why should you be sorry?"

"Why?" Zack hadn't expected quite that response. "Well, because violence isn't right." Zack himself believed those words. He'd never enjoyed violence and had never started any of those brawls he'd been in. He certainly never carried a gun for that reason. What had happened to Ron Sinclair when a gun did stumble into his hand was proof he'd been right. It still made him sick to think he had killed a man.

"My pa deserved what he got," Tommy declared, thoroughly shocking Zack. "You whopped him real good, Preacher!" Tommy grinned.

"It still wasn't right. I lost control. I made myself like him."

"You whopped him!"

Zack could see he wasn't going to get through to the lad, but he felt compelled to try anyway. "I should have talked to him, reasoned with him. That's how you help someone."

"I never thought my pa could get whopped, but he sure can."

Zack figured the only way to get through to Tommy was with actions, so he turned and headed back to the barn.

"What're you doing, Preacher?" Tommy scurried after Zack.

"I'm going to see if he needs help."

"You best not. He'll be madder'n a hornet once he comes to. You might not be able to whop him twice."

Zack considered that and realized Tommy might be right. It would never do if he walked into the barn and another scuffle transpired. He probably only beat the bigger man because of surprise. That wouldn't work again. Besides, another fight might bring out Jane Donnelly if she was home. He couldn't have her see him and her husband brawling.

"You're right," Zack said. "I don't want to risk stirring things up again. You go and take care of your father."

Tommy seemed hesitant but finally went into the barn. Watching him, Zack suddenly wondered how William Locklin would have handled this situation. Certainly he wouldn't have throttled Tom Donnelly! Yet what else could he have done? Turned the other cheek and let the man throttle *him?* Much as Zack didn't like violence, he also didn't think a man like Tom should get away with his vile behavior. A man who abused those weaker than himself did indeed deserve what he got.

Nevertheless, Zack did fear the reaction of the community. This could mean the end of William Locklin's tenure as minister to the good Brethren of Christ in Columbia County, Oregon.

Sixteen

It took only a couple of hours for the story of what happened in the Donnelly barn to spread through the community. Zack heard the first reaction when he came down for supper at the Copelands'.

"Heard you gave that Tom Donnelly what for," his host, Edward Copeland, said.

"We did have an unfortunate altercation this afternoon, I regret to admit."

"Don't you regret nothing. That man had it coming."

Zack gaped at the man. "What I did was deplorable!"

Mrs. Copeland said soothingly, "Now, Reverend, don't be too hard on yourself. Maybe a heavy hand is just what that Tom needs. Lord knows, Reverend McFarland never got far with the man just talking to him."

"I can't believe what I'm hearing!" Zack said.

The next day he received similar comments from others in the community. It seemed Tom Donnelly had been something of a scourge on the town for years. He drank and picked fights at the saloons in St. Helens. He owed money to every person in Maintown and many others in the county. When he worked at the sawmill, he was late and usually drunk, often placing his fellow workmen in danger with his carelessness. Everyone had quit doing business with him because he was as likely as not to cheat them. Despite all this, everyone was too afraid to confront him. Those who tried were usually run off his land with a shotgun aimed at them. The townsfolk had generally fallen into the habit of simply ignoring the man.

The fact that his wife was an upright, decent woman, well thought of by all, probably also led folks to take a light hand with Tom. Any grief brought upon Tom would surely trickle down and hurt his wife.

Zack hoped he didn't run into Jane, for he didn't know what he'd say to her. Maybe ignoring the situation was the right idea. And as the pats on the shoulder continued, Zack was bolstered into thinking he'd done the right thing after all. Why, then, was he nervous when he headed to the Newcomb place the next evening for dinner, which had been arranged before the fight? Oddly enough, he hadn't seen any of the New-combs since his altercation with Tom, and he didn't know what they thought of the incident. It bothered him a little that it mattered. Calvin had gained Zack's respect in ways that few men ever had.

Georgie met Zack at the door. "Hi, Reverend. Let me see them famous fists of yours!"

"Georgie, mind your manners!" Ada said as she strode up behind her son. "Good evening, Reverend. So glad you could make it."

"Thank you for having me," Zack replied, trying unsuccessfully to gauge by her expression what she thought of the fight.

Calvin was descending the stairs. "William, how do you do?" Smiling as he reached Zack, he held out his hand.

"I'm glad I am still welcome here," Zack said, shaking Calvin's hand.

"Of course you are. Come on and have a seat while the girls finish up dinner."

Zack turned and saw Calvin's daughters busy in the kitchen. Maggie waved and smiled. Ellie managed only a tight, polite smile.

"Use the parlor, Calvin," Ada instructed.

"The reverend don't like all that formality, Ada," Calvin said. "You save the parlor for your ladies' tea parties. Me and William will be much more comfortable in the main room."

The main room had no fancy divans as in the Copeland or Parker parlors, but there were a couple of rocking chairs, some stools, and a bench, all sturdy and nice but obviously handmade, probably by Calvin. These were spaced in front of a huge hearth made of river rock. A large rag rug lay on the floor. Calvin directed Zack to one of the rockers as he took the other one.

Boyd came in a few minutes later and joined the men. "That's a fine horse you have there, Reverend," he said.

"Thank you for taking care of her," Zack said.

"We are going to miss you, son," Calvin said to Boyd.

"Where are you going?" asked Zack.

"I work in the lumber camp during the week and board there," Boyd explained. "The last rain caused a mud slide that interrupted work for a bit, but I'll be headed back after church Sunday."

"The girls have everything in hand," Ada said, joining the men and taking a seat on one of the cushion-covered stools. "I so wish he'd take a job at the mill so we'd have him around more. But working in the woods pays more, and Boyd is saving his money to buy a farm."

"Very industrious of you," Zack said. "Perhaps I should try my hand at farming. It might be more my calling than preaching."

"You are doing a wonderful job!" Ada said.

Zack realized he had probably been fishing for some support, though he hated it when other people did that.

Ada went on, "Reverend, you must not be too hard on yourself over what happened."

"That's what everyone keeps telling me," Zack replied, "but I'm especially surprised to hear it from you, Mrs. Newcomb. I know you and Jane Donnelly are close friends."

"It surprises you that I applaud the fact that her good-for-nothing husband finally got his comeuppance?"

The ire in Ada Newcomb's tone was perhaps the most surprising revelation to Zack. He'd known she was one to speak her mind and could be sharp-tongued, but he'd also believed that was mostly show, that she was kind and warm beneath the surface. But the anger she displayed now was uncharacteristically hard-edged.

"Reverend, a man like that would stretch a saint's Christian virtue. And you know, even Christ overturned the money-changers' tables in righteous indignation."

Zack vaguely recalled a story like that in the Bible. "I can only hope now that some good will come of it."

"I saw Tommy," Maggie piped up from the kitchen. "He said he was coming to church again. He said anyone who'd stand up to his pa was worth sitting through the torture of church for."

"Maybe you should go beat up Angus Willoughby," Ellie said. "I hear he's been backsliding."

"Ellie!" Ada gasped.

Even Calvin had a look of shock on his face at his usually circumspect daughter's impertinence.

"Now, Ellie, don't hold back. Tell me what you really think," Zack said with more than a hint of sarcasm.

"Never mind," she said more demurely, obviously taken aback by her parents' reaction.

In spite of Ellie's words, dinner passed pleasantly enough, though the topic of the Donnellys was studiously avoided. Zack noted that Ellie said not another word during dinner, which could have made for an awkward situation except that the rest of the family kept up a steady flow of congenial conversation. Zack felt tense nonetheless. The fact that the whole town and even Mr. and Mrs. Newcomb supported his actions somehow was not enough approbation for him. He hated that Ellie was in opposition. Was it that he respected her opinion, or just that he couldn't bear to have one person around he couldn't seem to charm? Whatever it was, it irked him.

When dinner was finished, the men, including Georgie, retired to the main room with coffee and plates of spice cake. The women cleaned up the dishes.

"William, my wife spoke to Polly Briggs the other day," Calvin began.

Zack groaned inwardly. He'd nearly forgotten the matter of the wedding.

Calvin continued, "She says you won't marry her daughter without your proper license."

"That's true, Calvin. I feel it wouldn't be right."

"Can't you see your way around it this once? The girl was in tears when she heard."

Zack would have bet that William Locklin would have had no problem performing the marriage. There were no doubt countless ministers who operated, especially here in the West, without seminary training or legal documents. But Zack knew that if he performed any weddings and then it became known that he was a fraud, these people would hunt him down far more relentlessly than Beau Cutter ever would. He had to hold a hard line in this, but that was looking less and less plausible given his performance with Tom Donnelly.

"I feel strongly about it," Zack said. He heard a sudden clanking sound from the kitchen.

"Ellie, watch that bowl," Ada scolded.

"Well, then, it might be for the best," Calvin went on. "There's probably some reason the couple should wait to marry."

"It shouldn't be too long," Zack assured.

"There'll be some young fellows around here who will be happy to hear that," Boyd said.

"Are you trying to tell us something?" asked Calvin.

There was sudden silence in the kitchen.

"Well . . ." Boyd paused and glanced toward the quiet kitchen. "I was thinking it was about time me and Kendra took the . . . you know, the leap."

There was a delighted squeal from the kitchen. Boyd grinned as his mother came rushing into the main room. Boyd rose to meet her embrace. Calvin rose and shook his son's hand.

"I haven't asked her official-like yet," Boyd said. "I wanted to tell you first, then ask her pa." Suddenly worried, Boyd added, "He'll say yes, don't you think?"

"He just better," Ada retorted. "You are the finest catch around —" She stopped and glanced toward Zack. "Well, *one* of the finest catches."

Zack pretended he didn't see her pointed look.

Calvin looked toward Zack, "I hope you can marry Boyd and Kendra, William. We'd be pleased."

"That license should come anytime, I'm sure," Zack replied with false confidence.

"The wedding won't be tomorrow. That's for sure," Ada said. "There will be much to prepare. I know Nessa has to make Kendra's dress, and she'll want to order something fine for it. And we both have to finish our quilts for the two of you."

"A proper engagement of three or four months never hurt a marriage," Calvin added.

"Another season in the lumber camp will pad the nest egg well," Boyd said.

Zack knew that Boyd was a timber faller and made good money in season. He was also happy to hear of these practical delays. He'd be long gone by then.

Ellie and Maggie came up to congratulate their brother.

Then Ellie said, "I'm going out for a breath of fresh air. The dishes are done."

As she left, Ada's gaze followed her with a look of consternation.

"Do you think she is still upset about what happened to Tom?" asked Zack.

"She'll get over it, Reverend," Ada said. "But . . . perhaps it would help if you talked to her. I think she is having a hard time understanding it."

"I'd be the last person she would want to talk to, then," Zack said.

"Nonsense. You are her pastor and therefore the best person for the job."

Zack didn't want to do it. He needed to ignore Ellie if for no other reason than ignoring her was the last thing he wanted to do. For some reason that girl always got under his skin — like a bad case of poison oak or a worse case of infatuation. Both equally onerous.

Reluctantly he rose and headed toward the door. He had barely stepped out on the porch when he realized Maggie was right on his heels.

"I doubt it will do any good to talk to her," Maggie said, shutting the door behind her. "Once she gets something into her head, she can be very stubborn."

Zack looked around and was relieved to see that Ellie was not seated anywhere on the porch. Maybe she had walked off to the barn to be alone.

"So you don't think I ought to talk to her?" Zack asked, looking for a way out.

"That's up to you entirely. But just don't let her get to you, Reverend. What you did was a very noble thing."

"Striking a man?"

"Striking a snake!" Maggie corrected emphatically. "Tommy tells me what his pa does, and someone should have whopped him long ago. Makes me realize what a bunch of cowards there are around here."

"Don't you be hard on them like your sister is being hard on me," Zack cautioned. "People just want to live in peace."

"No matter, I'm still proud to know you, Reverend."

Then suddenly Maggie hitched up on her toes and planted a kiss on Zack's cheek. He staggered back against the door in his surprise. She smiled and may as well have said that she wanted to get to know him better. Maybe he wouldn't mind that, either, he thought as he gazed down into her large green eyes now focused upon him so adoringly. He had a strong urge to pull her to him and kiss her properly. Only the fact that her parents were just behind the door restrained him.

"I . . . uh . . . better . . . uh . . ." He had momentarily forgotten why he had come outside in the first place.

"You were going to talk to Ellie," Maggie said in a teasing tone. "But maybe you've found someone more interesting to talk to . . . William."

This raised his brows, her calling him by his given name — well, Locklin's given name. "Now, now, Maggie —"

"Why don't you kiss me, William," she murmured. "I think you want to."

He'd known saloon girls less forward and wizened old men less perceptive. "I don't think so."

"I'm not a child."

"I know that, Maggie. You are a beautiful young woman, and I'd like nothing more than to kiss you —"

"But?" she queried with a bit of a pout.

"Isn't it obvious?" But when she responded with a blank stare, he added, "I'm the minister," as if that was enough.

"Is that all?"

"Let's get to know each other a bit more. You don't know me nearly well enough."

She studied him a long moment before

speaking. He had the feeling she could see right through him, that she was far older than her seventeen years.

"I guess I do need to get better acquainted with you, Reverend," she said, "because I wouldn't have thought you were one to stand on such old-fashioned traditions — not after what happened with Tom Donnelly."

"I'll tell you what," he conceded, "tomorrow after your brother is done with school, why don't the two of you show me one of your fishing holes?"

"The two of us?"

"Most definitely."

Hesitating just a moment, she said, "Okay." She turned back to the door but paused and added, "She's over there." She pointed toward the big willow.

Zack blinked, and it was a full moment before he realized Maggie was talking about her sister. He wanted to follow Maggie back into the house and forget his original reason for coming out. These two sisters were innocent as babes and dangerous as vipers.

He headed toward the willow. Ellie was seated on the swing, her back to the porch. She couldn't have witnessed any of what had just transpired there, though nothing had transpired, had it?

"Do you mind an intrusion, Ellie?" he asked.

"No, I suppose not," she replied, glancing up.

She appeared to not be surprised by his appearance, so he plunged right in. "I think we need to talk about what happened between me and Tom Donnelly. You are upset and I'd like to understand why."

This did seem to surprise her. Moonlight washed over her, bringing her features and expressions into clear focus. Her beauty, as well.

"I'm touched you would take the time to talk to me, that you seem to care about my opinion," she offered.

"I believe yours is the only dissenting voice, so of course I'm curious." He didn't like standing and towering over her, so he sat down upon the grass at her feet. "Tell me your thoughts."

She was quiet for a time, then simply stated, "Violence is wrong, Reverend."

"I am no proponent of violence, either," he said. "But there are times when there is no other choice, or, as your mother indicated, when a righteous violence might be acceptable. I am not saying that what I did yesterday is any of these. But some people only understand the language of violence, and I think Tom is one of those."

"And that makes what you did right? That Mr. Donnelly deserved it?"

"I don't know."

"You should, Reverend. You've studied the Bible. Christ speaks over and over again about peace, turning the other cheek, loving one's enemies. How can you voice confusion over something so clear?"

"Because nothing is ever totally so clear-cut."

"Even the Bible, Reverend?" she challenged.

"Life, Ellie," he said, realizing he had slipped out of Reverend Locklin's skin and was speaking as himself. "And you would do well to learn some flexibility. There are always two sides to a coin. You can't be so unbending."

"I will not bend my principles."

"But you can't let them blind you to seeing into a person's heart or seeing their motives."

"What was your motive, then, for attacking Mr. Donnelly?" Again there was challenge in her tone rather than honest seeking.

His dander rose and he jumped to his feet. "I'll tell you! I looked into the eyes of an evil man. I saw the things he did to his family. I saw a man who would pick on those weaker than himself just because he could." Zack's voice trembled with rising passion. "And I couldn't let it happen again. I wasn't going to let him push me around anymore, criticize me, and make me feel like —" Zack gasped as he realized he was no longer talking about Mr. Donnelly but rather his own stepfather.

Zack's gaze skittered toward Ellie. He saw the shock in her eyes, the disapproval.

Tightly he said, "I better go. Please give your parents my regards. I best not go back to the house."

He spun around, shaking inside, still angry, at himself for so thoroughly forgetting himself, but also at Ellie for sitting there saying nothing, for continuing to stare at him with that look of judgment.

With every step he took to the barn, he hoped she would call after him. He deserved an apology from her. He wanted to know she understood what he was saying. But again, he didn't understand why it mattered.

SEVENTEEN

Ellie watched Reverend Locklin ride away. She wanted desperately to run after him and tell him she was sorry, but she knew she'd be saying it just to appease him, and no one wanted that kind of apology.

But she believed what she believed. If you started saying life was not clearly good and bad, that there were gray areas, you opened yourself up for much confusion. Yet what bothered her most was she knew that wasn't the true reason for her discomfiture. She could be flexible, tolerant, and forgiving to a point. She had only raised these broader issues to cover the one that troubled her most about what Reverend Locklin had done.

If Ellie's father had beat up Mr. Donnelly under the same circumstances, she might have understood and even applauded him a little. But she held Reverend Locklin to a higher standard, not only as a minister but

— and this truly troubled her — as a candidate for her husband.

Was she too inflexible in the matter of choosing a husband? Was that why she was nineteen and not yet married or even engaged? Could no man meet her standards?

Realizing her churning thoughts were making her more distraught rather than offering solutions, she finally rose from the swing and returned to the house. She hadn't realized she'd been out so long. She hadn't even noted the evening chill in the air. Inside, the house was quiet. Maggie, Georgie, and Boyd had already gone up to bed. Mama and Dad were seated in the rocking chairs, Mama with perpetual sewing in her hands, squinting so as to get a few more stitches put in as the firelight began to fade. Dad was thumbing through his Montgomery Ward catalog.

"I was about ready to come after you," Mama said. "You'll get a chill sitting outside so late without a coat."

"We heard Reverend Locklin ride off some time ago," Dad said.

"He asked me to send his regards."

"Something must have happened for him to not stop back in the house before leaving. He even left his coat behind," said Mama.

"We didn't quite agree on something," Ellie said vaguely, hoping that would be the end of it but knowing it wouldn't.

"What did you say to him?" asked Mama.

"You immediately assume it was I who offended him!"

"Well, Ellie, honey," Dad said gently, "you did seem to have a little bee in your bonnet."

"He said I was inflexible and judgmental." She was about to take back the judgmental part when she realized he hadn't actually said that. But she was certain he was thinking it, so she didn't.

"You were pretty unwilling to consider there might be more to what happened than appeared on the surface," Dad said.

"There is more to it than that, though, isn't there, Ellie?" Mama asked.

Ellie looked at her mother, then quickly at her father. She just shrugged. She couldn't say what was really bothering her in front of her father. He was already skeptical of this business of marrying off the minister and might take her confession wrong.

"Calvin," said Mama, "why don't you go on up to bed? I'll be there in a few minutes."

Dad looked from one woman to the other, nodded, and setting aside his catalog, rose. "Don't be too long. It's late."

When they were alone, Mama said, "Now, Ellie, tell me what is really on your mind. I never knew you to be such a pacifist."

"Well, it is true I don't condone violence, and I am bothered that everyone is patting Reverend Locklin on the back. But . . . shouldn't we be able to expect more from our minister? It'd be different if Dad or Boyd had attacked Mr. Donnelly."

"Ellie, the minister is a man just like any other. You don't seriously believe he is perfect. He probably snores when he sleeps, belches when he's alone, and forgets to wipe his boots when entering a house. He is just as liable to make a mistake as anyone else."

"I know . . ." Ellie replied hesitantly.

Mama leaned forward, the light of true understanding in her eyes. "Ellie, did you think that by marrying a minister you'd have the perfect man? Is that why you've always dreamed of that?"

Ellie bit her lip, hating to admit that her mother was right.

Mama reached across the gap separating their seats and grasped her hand. "Honey," she said, "you'll be sorely disappointed in life if you expect perfection from anyone. No one, not even a man of God, can fit the bill."

"I guess I was hoping that if I married a

minister, I'd be that much closer, at least," Ellie said hopefully.

Mama shook her head. "When a woman marries, she can never be truly certain what she is getting."

"You did pretty well with Dad."

"Well, I didn't order him from the Montgomery Ward catalog that way!" Mama smiled at her jest. "It's taken twenty-two years of hard work on my part to get him shaped up."

"Are you saying you change the man you marry?"

"I wouldn't suggest marrying a fellow with the thought that you'll change him to fit your desires. You might end up like poor Jane Donnelly. I hope, however, that you'll start out with good roots, good stock. A man with a good heart. That's why your father has worked out so well. Change happens to people who are willing to be better. Sometimes they need a nudge or two along the way. But if their heart is right, then they are halfway there." Mama rose and went to the cupboard where she kept her sewing things. She took out a box that Ellie knew contained special mementos.

Mama lifted the lid and took out two papers. "You remember these?"

Both papers were children's drawings.

One was of a birthday cake with two candles and some rather lopsided wrapped presents. The other was of a rocking chair in front of a hearth. Scrawled on both in childish writing were the words *Happy Birfday, Mama.*

"Boyd and I drew these," Ellie said. "I made the one of the birthday cake. I must have been five when I drew that."

"Your father and I had been married eight years when you did those. I was expecting Georgie. Your father was a good husband, but like all he had a few faults. One being that he never remembered my birthday. Year after year he'd forget, and year after year I'd get mad, pout, and not speak to him for a day. He just never got the idea. But on this particular birthday, I had determined not to remind your father and to test him. I did happen to mention to Boyd that it was my birthday, and without my knowing it, he drew me this picture and got you to draw one, too. Maggie was too young, I guess, to participate."

"I kind of remember," Ellie said. "He was upset that you didn't have any presents."

"You both presented your pictures at supper. Your father was shocked. He had forgotten once again and was shamed by the fact that his little children had remembered when he had not. Moreover, Boyd's picture of the rocking chair was a lot like one I'd seen at Dolman's store in St. Helens and had hinted that I'd like it for the new baby because our other rocker was old and worn out from rocking not only my three children but from having rocked some of my ancestors' children, as well.

"Next day, when I came in from working in the garden, there was that rocker sitting by the hearth with a ribbon tied around it. Your father has never forgotten my birthday since."

"So you did change Dad, only you let Boyd be your agent."

"I'll admit I did nudge the situation along, but there was no reason to believe it wouldn't be like every other year, and he would go back to forgetting. This time your dad changed himself. I guess what I am saying, Ellie, is that I would still love your father even if he'd kept this bad habit, and believe me, he's got a few bad habits still, but I love him in spite of them. I love him for his heart. I suspect he feels the same about me because, you may not know this, but I have one or two bad habits, too." She added this last deadpan. Then she smiled.

Ellie chuckled with her mother and added more somberly, "I guess I always knew I wouldn't get a perfect husband. But there is more to being married to a minister than that."

"You have set your cap for Reverend Locklin?"

Was there a hint of hopefulness in her mother's tone?

"I was beginning to wonder, the way you seem to avoid him."

"I suppose I changed my mind. I started out thinking I wanted to get his attention, but I don't like the feeling of being a spider spinning a web. Let Mabel have him."

"Mabel would be a terrible minister's wife. For one thing, she would never be able to survive on a preacher's meager wage."

"How about Maggie?"

"Maggie?" Mama started to laugh at the absurdity of this, then paused and added with more alarm, "Maggie?"

"Don't tell her I said anything, Mama, but she got it into her head that she would go after the minister rather than let Mabel win him."

"That only shows her immaturity. I should speak to her."

"Please don't, Mama. You know Maggie. If she thinks you're opposed, that will make her all the more determined. I think if we just let it go, Reverend Locklin will have the sense to choose his mate more wisely. He won't be snared unwittingly by anyone."

If Georgie hadn't been along on this fishing trip, Maggie knew William wouldn't have been either. Nevertheless, she resented her little brother's presence.

For one thing, he'd kept up a steady stream of chatter with the reverend practically the entire ride. But now that they were settled by the pond, Maggie was determined to take better control of the situation. If William Locklin thought this was merely a fishing expedition, he was in for a surprise.

It was a fine afternoon, summer having arrived full-fledged. White puffy clouds sparsely dotted the blue sky, permitting the sun to warm the earth below. A slight breeze ruffled the tall grasses surrounding the fishing pond which, besides the grass, was bordered with a handful of willows, some birch, and a couple of oaks a bit back from the water's edge.

The three fishermen baited their lines and cast them into the smooth blue water. Afternoon wasn't really the prime time for fishing, but this being a school day, it was the only time Georgie could come along. The spring term would go until the middle of July, so Maggie would suggest another fishing expedition on a weekday morning when her brother would be in school.

Propping their poles up with rocks, they reposed comfortably in the grass and waited for a bite. They talked about all manner of things but mostly fishing. William wasn't really a novice. He said he'd fished as a boy in Kansas but had lost interest because his stepfather kept criticizing his technique and was a rather heavy-handed teacher. Maggie had thought she'd heard William was from Maine, but maybe she'd heard wrong or maybe he had moved to Maine at some point.

Eventually Georgie grew bored with the conversation and decided to do some exploring. The last time he had been to the pond, he had spotted a robin's nest and now wanted to see if the eggs had hatched. William said to yell if he found anything but seemed content to mind Georgie's pole in the meantime. Maggie hoped it was because he wanted to spend some time with her.

Finally alone, they talked about one thing and another, and Maggie marveled at how easy he was to converse with, not as she'd imagine it would be with a scholarly man who had been to seminary and must be very intelligent. He talked about simple things, not about religion or philosophy or any such topic. They talked for a while about horses, and he knew more than she thought a city-bred fellow would. He also started talking about his travels, and it surprised her how much he'd seen of the country. He began to tell a story of encountering a storm on a ship from San Francisco to Seattle when he stopped suddenly.

"Oh, that's not an interesting story," he said, looking peculiar. "I wonder where Georgie is?"

"I didn't realize this wasn't your first time in the West, William," Maggie commented.

"Did I say I was on that ship? I meant my grandfather — yes, grandfather. He was quite the seaman."

"I could have sworn you said it was you."

He laughed. "No . . . not me. Say, I've been doing all the talking. Tell me about yourself, Maggie."

"What's there to tell? I have been in the same place for seventeen years and done pretty much the same things." She never thought she was so boring. She hoped that didn't make him lose what interest he seemed to have in her.

"How about your family? Surely there must be stories. Didn't your mother and father come here over the Oregon Trail?"

"Yes, but they don't talk about it much." She was becoming disgusted that she had nothing more interesting than that to tell. Finally she thought of something and, brightening, added, "I'll tell you a huge family secret."

"Maybe you better not do that," he cautioned.

"Well, I can tell only as much as everyone knows —"

"Then it can't be much of a secret."

She scratched her head. Was the only interesting thing she had to say about her family just as boring as everything else? "It is juicy just the same," she insisted. "Have you noticed how my mother and Mrs. Parker don't seem friendly toward each other?"

"Can't say as I have."

"They manage to be civil on the surface, but there is bad blood between them. No one knows why except that something happened when they were girls. They came out here on the same wagon train." She arched a brow, trying to extract all she could from this tiny gem. "I think — I'm not the only one who thinks this — that my mother stole my father from Mrs. Parker."

"And Mrs. Parker has maintained resentment over that all this time even though she married another?"

"Rumor has it that she and Mr. Parker don't have the happiest marriage."

William nodded. "I have noticed they are very formal with each other. Not at all like your parents, who seem comfortable with each other. Your father even told me once how much he enjoys your mother's company. I never sensed a similar feeling with the Parkers."

"And that's why she resents my mother. She got the short end of the stick!"

"That's sad."

Suddenly Georgie's pole began to tremble. "We got a bite!" Maggie exclaimed.

They spent the next few minutes trying to bring in the fish, but when it broke the surface they saw it was too small to keep, so William slipped it from the hook and tossed it back into the water.

"I hope your mother wasn't expecting to cook fish tonight," William said.

"She never plans on it when we fish. Usually if we bring something home, it just becomes a side dish." Maggie thought this was a good time to bring up her plan. "Say, William, how about if we go fishing again next week, maybe Monday. If we get an early start, we'll have much better luck."

"But Georgie will be in school."

Maggie barely restrained a grimace at his insightfulness, then with a resigned sigh replied, "Maybe Saturday, then?" Perhaps she'd think of some way to detain Georgie at the last minute.

"I guess I could if I get my sermon finished."

"It's like you got school assignments to do, isn't it?" Maggie said. "Do you really like being a minister? I was so glad when I finished school. I never want to do another assignment."

"I wouldn't be a minister if I didn't like it," William replied.

Maggie thought his reply lacked enthusiasm. Maybe he didn't really like it. Maybe he'd become a minister to make his parents happy or something. Perhaps that was why he was the most different minister she'd ever seen. She didn't know why that relieved her a little. Perhaps after they married he would quit being a minister and become a farmer instead. She'd like that much better.

"You ever think about farming?" she asked.

"That's mighty hard work."

"I think trying to write a sermon is harder."

"Not if you enjoy it."

"I'm just saying, if you didn't enjoy it, there'd be no crime in quitting and doing something else, would there?"

His brow arched with surprise. "Don't you

think I'm a good minister, Maggie?"

"Oh no! That's not what I'm saying at all. You are a very good minister. It's just that . . ." She didn't know how to finish her sentence. She couldn't very well tell him that she intended to marry him and it would be more to her liking if he was in some other occupation. However, that thought forced her to question her own motives. She wanted to marry the man to win a competition, not because she loved him. On the other hand, she could very easily love him. She was almost certain that if she could kiss him, she'd know if she could fall in love with him. In the moment of silence that descended while he waited for her to finish, she cocked an ear to listen for Georgie. She could hear nothing. He had probably wandered off far enough.

She made an impulsive lunge toward the minister, knocking her fishing pole askew as she did so. She threw an arm around him and bumped her lips so hard against his, one of her teeth bruised her lip. When the awkward maneuver was over, she knew it had to have been the worst kiss in the world.

He was staring at her, shocked. "What was that, Maggie?"

"Don't you know?" Embarrassed by her stupid ineptitude, she focused her attention on straightening out the pole.

"Come here," he said gently and firmly.

Her eyes shot up in surprise, and her heart started thudding loudly inside her. He reached out an arm, encircling her and drawing her near. Her eyes widened with awe as he nudged her closer until their lips were only an inch apart.

"Close your eyes," he murmured.

She clamped her eyes shut and held her breath at the same time. Then his lips touched hers. Her heart raced now, thud-thudding so that it echoed in her ears. She wondered if ministers were supposed to know how to kiss so well.

He held her a moment longer than the kiss lasted. She ventured to open one of her eyes a crack and saw his were open, too. He was smiling.

"That's how it's done," he said. There was good-natured mocking in his tone, but Maggie could see a look in his eyes that said he was going to kiss her again. He leaned toward her.

Then came Georgie's yell. "Hey, I found it!" A loud rustle of the brush followed. He had been closer than she'd thought.

William backed away, but he was still smiling. She was astonished there was no guilt or apology in his expression. She would have thought a minister would be more repentant of such behavior, but she was glad he wasn't. Maybe it would be easier than she thought to get him into another line of work.

Shortly thereafter they headed for home, leaving William at the Copelands' before going on to their place.

As they were tending their horses in the barn, Georgie said, "Hey, Mags, why'd you kiss the minister?"

Maggie nearly dropped the saddle she was carrying to the rack. "Why, you little brat! You were spying on us!"

"It was just an accident," he said defensively. "Are you sweet on Reverend Locklin?"

Desperately, Maggie replied, "Listen here, Georgie, you mustn't ever tell anybody what you saw!"

"I don't know . . . might be too important to keep such a secret from Mama and Dad."

Maggie knew that must never happen. "You keep this quiet, and I'll . . ." She racked her brain for something really enticing. "I'll do your arithmetic for a week."

Georgie seemed to consider this. "The school term will be up soon. How 'bout if you do it till the end of the term?"

That was nearly three weeks, but Maggie

thought it was worth it. She didn't mind arithmetic as much as she did housework. "Okay." She spit in her hand and held it out for him to shake and seal the bargain. When he grabbed her hand, she prayed he'd keep his word.

Eighteen

What am I doing? Zack silently questioned himself as he sat at the desk in his room trying to focus on memorizing another sermon.

Kissing one sister while wanting to kiss the other? Acting as if he had a right to either sister? If he weren't a minister, neither of them would look twice at him. Well, perhaps Maggie would. She was a firebrand, that one! But not straight-laced Ellie. Why, then, was it Ellie who filled his thoughts? And why, as he was kissing Maggie, had he wondered what Ellie would think?

Mrs. Copeland's knock on the door was a welcome diversion, even if her reason was not.

"Reverend, you have a caller," she announced.

He arched a brow. "Who might that be?" Please, not Maggie looking for another kiss!

"It's Miss Mabel Parker."

That was worse. "Can you give her my regrets? Tell her I am working on my sermon —"

"I tried, Reverend, but she said she'd only take a moment of your time."

With a sigh he rose and followed Mrs. Copeland to the front parlor. Mabel was seated on the velvet settee. She was an attractive young woman. Nineteen, like Ellie, she was just as graceful and poised.

"Reverend Locklin, I do hope you don't mind a surprise visit," she said politely.

Her graciousness lost something in the fact that it would have hardly mattered if he had minded. "Of course not," he replied with just as little sincerity, "but I can only spare a few moments. I have a sermon to prepare."

She picked up a package that was beside her on the settee. "These are the shirts my mother altered for you."

He had nearly forgotten that he had given Mabel some shirts a few days ago when she had made yet another visit. Taking the package, he had no choice but to show his gratitude by sitting and visiting. He took the chintz chair adjacent to the settee.

"You may open the package," she prompted.

He didn't see the point, since they were

just old clothes, but she probably wanted him to praise her mother's work. He slipped the string from the package and folded back the paper. Inside were the two shirts he had sent to have the sleeves lengthened and the sides let out. Lying on top of them were some handkerchiefs that were not familiar. He picked up one, noting that embroidered in a corner was the monogram *WL.*

She smiled, batting her thick lashes. "My mother said a man can always use handkerchiefs."

"Do send her my thanks," he said. "I certainly can use them."

"I did the embroidery."

He looked again at the stitching. "Very nice!" he exclaimed, recalling that she had also made one of the fancy blocks on that quilt. When she continued to gaze expectantly at him, he decided she wanted him to offer more. "Your talents amaze me, Mabel. I will think of you every time I use these." Every time I blow my nose? He tried not to grin at the amusing thought.

They visited for a time, with Mabel doing most of the talking. She was articulate and engaging. Yes, this girl would probably have made William Locklin a wonderful wife.

Mabel wasn't his only female caller in the

next couple of days. Iris Fergus came with another dish of cookies, and she, too, engaged him in a brief visit. But her conversation was rather artless and boisterous, reminding Zack of a female mule driver he'd once known.

Sarah Stoddard came to call on Saturday, bringing a frosted apple cake. He happened to answer the door when she knocked, and he thought she looked as if she'd been praying he would not be home. Her cheeks turned pink and remained so during the entire visit, a painful fifteen minutes. As with their previous encounters, he had to propel the entire conversation and practically drag responses from her. Anything she did say was fumbled. He had the distinct impression she was not here of her own volition. Doubtless her mother had put the cake in her hand and shoved her out the door.

Upon consideration of these visits he could comfort himself with one fact. He'd had no desire at all to kiss any of these young women. Perhaps he wasn't as degenerate as he'd feared. It wasn't all the young women of Maintown who stirred him — only two. Peculiar, yes, but still a comfort.

On Sunday, the fourth Sunday in June and his second to preach in Maintown, Zack dressed in the black broadcloth suit Ada Newcomb had altered. It fit perfectly, and he could almost forget who he really was. He had visions of hiding in this safe little enclave for many years. The thought did not make his feet feel itchy at all.

What, indeed, was happening to him?

He walked into the schoolhouse to find it full once again. He was especially pleased to see that Tommy Donnelly had come again. It bolstered his confidence that the altercation with the boy's father had indeed done some good.

Zack preached on the topic of forgiveness, embellishing the good Reverend Markus's words with his own personal take on the subject and making a veiled reference to the fight with Donnelly. He had intended to admit his mistake, mostly by way of appeasing Ellie, but upon seeing Tommy in church, he decided that getting on Ellie's good side was not worth admitting to a mistake that had turned out well. Instead, he used a reference he had come across in Markus's book: "All things work together for good to them that love God, to them who are called according to his purpose." He'd been very pleased to find a bit of Scripture that reinforced his position.

Again, everyone praised his sermon and

clapped him on the back afterward. He could not help thinking that years of drifting and bouncing from one occupation to another had not brought him as much satisfaction and approbation as one month of pretending to be a preacher.

Ellie managed to slip past him while he was engaged with several others of his congregation. She was the only one who didn't make an attempt to shake his hand after the service. Maggie, on the contrary, nearly wrenched his hand from his arm as she pumped it up and down, a grin plastered on her face. He hoped she had the sense to keep quiet about what happened at the pond, but at the rate she was going, everyone was going to guess something was up between them regardless of her silence.

On this particular Sunday the ladies of the church had organized a covered-dish dinner. Because it was a beautiful afternoon, trestle tables were set up in the school yard. One table was laden with a dizzying variety of foods: hot dishes, breads, pies, cakes, and gallons of punch. Zack was directed to take the first place in line, and he made no argument, piling his dish high. He sat at one of the other tables and was soon joined by what was coming to be his usual entourage of young women.

He groaned inwardly. But he also knew he could have probably put a stop to the feminine barrage by simply inventing a fiancée back East who planned to join him soon. He guessed he didn't disdain all the attention that much after all. Besides, he reasoned, keeping the young women distracted with visions of romance would prevent them from paying close attention to the flaws in his performance.

As usual, the glaring absence from the table was Ellie Newcomb. She was sitting at another table with Colby Stoddard. Zack pretended not to notice.

When the meal was finished, the women cleared away the dishes and several of the men set up a game of horseshoes. Zack joined them.

"Say, Reverend," Calvin said after tossing a perfect ringer, "the board of deacons is going to meet Wednesday, and we were hoping you'd join us."

"Be happy to," Zack said as he took his turn.

"We'll meet at the school after supper."

Zack nodded, thinking little of it. He had no idea if it was usual for the pastor to join the deacons' meetings or not. He aimed his horseshoe and tossed, but it went wide of the stake.

He cursed — just an innocent "Shoot!" but apparently the folks of Maintown did not think that appropriate language for their pastor. The word was met by a perceptible silence. It was more surprise than judgment, though a couple of women who were nearby did respond with censoriously raised brows.

With a lame smile, Zack apologized with a simple, "I'm sorry." He decided he'd only make it worse if he tried to say more. The game resumed, and he was more careful after that. And, though being so careful took some of the fun from it, he stuck with the game as long as it lasted because it kept him in the safer company of the men. He noted some of the girls looking over at the game, Maggie in particular. He should avoid her as much as avoiding cursing.

Maggie was just about to walk over and join the horseshoe players. She knew they'd never let her play, since the men seemed to think it was solely their game. But she was as good or better than many of them. So despite the fact she knew they'd reject her, she would try just to needle them.

Then her mother called. "Maggie, come and join us."

The women had cleaned up the food and the dishes and now were seated on quilts spread over the grass. Most had sewing in hand. Ellie, Mabel, and the other girls who aspired to matronly pursuits were with them, as well. Maggie would have rather joined the young kids who were running around the school yard engaged in a game of tag. But she reminded herself that she, too, was now seeking a husband, and that very person had turned when her name had been called and was watching.

William might be a lot more fun than most preachers, but it was a sure bet he'd not appreciate a girl who ran around with the kids. Thus Maggie made herself walk to the quilts. She plopped down beside her mother and tried to look happy about it.

Her mother arched a brow at Maggie's unladylike manner but probably chose to remain silent considering that it was enough she had come at all.

"Why don't you help me with some of these Flying Geese?" Mama suggested. She had already cut a bunch of triangle shapes out of fabric. The larger center triangles were cut from a variety of colorful scraps, while the right-angle triangles, the sky, which would go on each side of the center geese, were of muslin.

"I'll just mess them up for you, Mama," Maggie replied.

"You'll do just fine." She handed Maggie a couple sets of triangles, a needle, an extra thimble, and thread.

Maggie took them because she saw some of the ladies were watching and thought it would embarrass her mother if she sneered at sewing. Normally she wasn't so sensitive to her mother's feelings, but maybe it was time she ought to be. She was no longer a child. Someday, maybe sooner than she wanted to think, she would have to be a part of the group of women. She'd be a biddy whether she liked it or not. There wasn't much more for women to do around here, so if she didn't join them, she'd be all alone, probably even more bored than she was when sewing. Even the women who didn't sew, few though they might be, were sitting on the quilts chatting with the others. None of them would ever consider playing horse-shoes with the men.

With a resigned sigh Maggie threaded her needle, though not successfully on the first or even third try. Then she stuck the needle into the fabric.

"Ouch!" Before her first stitch she had impaled her finger. Quickly she stuck it into her mouth so no blood would get on her mother's precious fabric.

After that Maggie concentrated so hard

on her stitches she couldn't participate in any of the gossip had she wanted to. Glancing over at Ellie, Maggie saw her sister chatting with Mary Renolds while her fingers deftly sewed together her hexagons, the ones she'd been working on for ages.

"Now, you know, Ellie," Mrs. Renolds was saying, "when you get your twelve tops done, we will have a quilting party, and everyone can help you get them quilted. That's what we used to do when I was a girl."

"That will be fun," Ellie replied, "but before you do that, I have to be engaged."

"That won't be long." Mrs. Renolds smiled knowingly. Then she turned to Maggie. "How about you, dearie? How close are you to having twelve complete tops? I know not many girls hold to the old traditions these days, but I am so pleased your mother is passing this one down to her daughters."

For the first time Maggie was embarrassed at her dismal sewing abilities. "I don't have twelve yet," she said truly enough. She didn't have twelve; she didn't have one — not one quilt top finished. Now that she thought of it, even she was astounded, considering all the years she'd had to do the task. Mama had made her start on two or three, but the minute she stopped nagging, Maggie laid them aside. Eventually Mama gave up, no doubt just growing weary with it. Every once in a while she would get Maggie to sew something but never enough to complete a project.

Maggie remembered William's kiss. Could they be married one day soon? And her without a single quilt except for the quilt Mama had made her? She had to change her ways. As if to mock her resolve, she poked her finger again with the needle.

She cursed just as William had earlier, and Mama scolded her soundly. When she finally finished her portion of the Flying Geese pattern, it was lopsided, and some of the stitches were bunched up on one side. She handed it to her mother, who looked at it with pursed lips then quickly put it on the bottom of the pile, probably so none of the other ladies would see it, not that they didn't already know about Maggie's work. Bless Mama, she wasn't going to further embarrass Maggie by saying anything right here. Later, Mama would rip out Maggie's stitches and do it over.

NINETEEN

As everyone was readying to leave the picnic, Ellie got up her nerve to approach Reverend Locklin. She didn't know why it was so hard, but every time she was around him he managed to embarrass her, even if it wasn't on purpose. She'd been thinking for a long time about starting a Sunday school for the children and wanted to discuss the matter with him. It infuriated her that the romantic notions in the air were interfering with spiritual matters. She strode up to him now, trying not to care what others might think. Much to her relief, he said he'd drop by her house on Monday and they would talk more about it.

The next day she couldn't believe how much she was anticipating his arrival. She'd made her grandma's special shortcake recipe and gotten out Mama's good china tea things. Most important of all, she'd made sure Maggie was gone. She'd asked

Mama to send her to help Louise Arlington, who now had two sick children and hadn't been able to finish putting in her garden.

Ellie wasn't certain why she wanted Maggie away. She didn't care that Maggie had set her cap for the minister. It was just that . . . Ellie shrugged. She didn't know. Maggie was just a distraction, and Ellie wanted to discuss serious matters with the minister.

Reverend Locklin showed up promptly at two in the afternoon as invited. Ellie received him in the parlor. He was dressed in his broadcloth suit, which she thought odd because she never saw him in that suit except on Sundays. He was also carrying a bouquet of flowers.

Suddenly Ellie worried he had gotten the wrong idea about this invitation.

Handing her the flowers, he said, "Mrs. Copeland allowed me to pick these for you . . . er . . . your family."

They were bright pink rhododendron blossoms, one purple iris, and some pale yellow daffodils.

"That must be the last of her daffodils," Ellie said. "It was kind of her to send them."

"She's a dear and generous lady," he replied.

Mama put her head into the parlor. "I just wanted to say hello, Reverend, before I scoot to the garden to weed a bit."

"Mama, look at the lovely flowers Reverend Locklin brought us!"

"How thoughtful!"

"It was Mrs. Copeland's idea," the reverend said humbly. "But you have all been so kind to me that I wanted to bring something."

"Anything we do for you, Reverend, gives us great joy," said Mama. "Now, you two children have a nice time. Ellie, the tea water has boiled and is ready to go into the pot."

Ellie thanked her mother and also silently thanked her for vacating to the garden during Locklin's visit. She was grateful yet unsettled, as well. It was almost as if he were paying court. Now Ellie worried that everyone had the wrong idea! But this was about Sunday school and nothing else.

When her mother had departed, Ellie bid the reverend to sit. He sat at one end of the divan, her mother's pride and joy, covered in the best brocaded verona that could be found in the Montgomery Ward catalog. Ellie could have taken the matching chair adjacent, but since the pastor was at the end of the divan farthest from the chair, conversation would have been awkward. She thought she had no choice but to sit on the other end of the sofa.

He smiled as she sat, and she thought she detected a hint of mockery in his expression, as if he'd perceived her awkwardness and was enjoying it. She hugged the opposite arm of the divan, thinking the two feet separating them wasn't enough.

Infusing her voice with an impersonal, businesslike tone, she said, "I know you are very busy, so I will get right to the reason for this meeting."

"Did your mother mention something about tea? I am so parched."

He smiled again, and she found herself growing irritated. That was mockery in his smile. She was sure of it!

She wanted to put him off but could not bring herself to be so impolite. Without another word, she rose and exited the parlor. In the kitchen she took a breath. Why did she feel as though she were stepping off a cliff? Why was her heart racing? Why had she built up this visit so? Why was her hand trembling as she lifted the kettle from the stove?

She had no answers but knew she couldn't go back to the parlor feeling so discombobulated. He'd see right through it, and whereas you'd expect a man of God to show compassion for someone experiencing nerves, she sensed this man would relish it. Taking another breath she filled the teapot on the tray she'd arranged earlier with the other tea things. She fussed with the tray, rearranged the slices of shortcake, checked the sugar bowl to make sure there was enough, though unnecessarily since she'd looked at it earlier.

At last, feeling more composed, she picked up the tray and returned to the parlor.

"You have gone to so much trouble," he said.

Again, she examined his tone but could detect nothing but politeness in it.

"No trouble at all," she said, though it was obvious the opposite was indeed true. At least her hand was steady now as she picked up the pot and filled both cups. "I hope it is strong enough."

"Perfect," he replied.

"Cream or sugar?"

"Neither, thank you," he said and lifted the cup to his lips.

She watched with a kind of morbid fascination, and when she realized she was staring, her cheeks flamed. He'd done it again, embarrassed her without even trying!

"Ellie?"

His tone was so gentle there was no way she could accuse him of mockery.

"Is everything all right?"

"The steam," she said, her voice an octave too high. "The warmth, you know, made me feel a bit flushed."

"Is that so?" He arched a brow. "I think I have inadvertently upset you."

"No . . . no . . . it's just . . . nothing, really."

"If you don't tell me what I've done, I won't know how to prevent it in the future."

"You've done nothing, Reverend Locklin." That was truer than she wanted to admit. He'd done nothing but exist. Apparently that was enough to turn her into a fool. Then something else occurred to her, and she decided to grasp at it. "I was wondering, Reverend, why you wore your suit. I hadn't expected this to be a formal visit." But the tea service mocked her words without his skeptical look.

"I'm sorry. I wasn't sure what to expect. Besides, I did look upon this visit as somewhat special. You see, tomorrow I will begin working at the mill, and then such visits, I'm afraid, will be quite limited. I wanted to make the most of it, I suppose."

"Oh." Somehow this relieved her, though it still did not account for her own behavior.

"Mr. Parker recommended me. I'll work

there three days a week except for the week I go to Deer Island and Columbia City. What with my pastoral visitations, preparing my sermon, and other ministerial duties that might crop up, my time will be very limited."

"I must say, I commend your industry."

"I must begin planning for my future."

The word *future* sent a little thrill through Ellie. Reverend Locklin's future had been at the forefront of everyone's thoughts before he'd even set foot in Maintown. Every girl in town was very concerned with the state of his future. And before she'd met him, his future had mattered very much to her, as well. Not anymore. His future belonged to Mabel or Maggie, or to some girl none of them knew. But not to Ellie.

Why, then, had her heart started racing once again?

"Shall we discuss the Sunday school, then?" she asked abruptly.

He blinked, obviously taken aback by the sudden shift in the conversation. "Yes, let's do so."

At first Zack had been quite amused by Ellie's nervousness. She'd been like a frightened deer caught in the crosshairs of a rifle. He liked it when her poise failed her, not because he was a sadist of some sort but because she was so much more real then. She was the person she was meant to be, not the finishing-school replica she aspired to be.

Why he, of all people, should appreciate genuineness in a person was a question that defied an answer.

In any case, he was sure that was why he found ways to catch her off guard, to shake her little world of manners and decorum. Thus the beginning of this visit had greatly amused him. However, it had taken a startling turn the moment he had uttered the word *future.* Why had he done it? Perhaps he'd thought it would shake her up again. But he hadn't expected the effect it would have on him. It simply was not his way to look too far into the future, certainly not beyond his next scheme.

Yet when he'd said it just now, he'd momentarily forgotten who he was. He'd spoken as a young man looking toward accumulating a nest egg with an eye toward matrimony. He'd said it as William Locklin would have said it. It was too easy to forget who he really was when he was with Ellie Newcomb.

"Sunday school," he murmured.

"What?"

He raised his voice. "Sunday school. You wanted to talk about starting a Sunday school."

"I did."

"So, then . . . ?" he prompted.

"One moment," she said, rising. "I forgot something."

She left the parlor. Zack watched as she gracefully strode away. Her silky yellow hair fell loosely to the middle of her back, its waves swaying with her movements. He felt his throat constrict. He wanted to run after her and bury his face in that silky mass. She made him forget who he was, but he didn't think the good reverend would be feeling this way about one of his parishioners.

She returned with some papers in her hand. "I wrote to the American Sunday School Union for information about starting a Sunday school, and they sent me these." This time she sat in the chair.

"You've been thinking of this for some time, then?" Was he a little disappointed that she hadn't concocted this matter just as an excuse to spend time with him?

"I've been wanting to do this since I returned home from school. But when Reverend McFarland passed away, my father thought I should wait to pursue it until we had a new pastor." She held out the papers, but the distance between them made it awkward for him to see them.

The gentlemanly thing would have been for Zack to move to the other end of the sofa nearest the chair. And he would have, but he hesitated just a moment too long, and in that time, she had moved back to the sofa. Well, that was the more practical seating arrangement if they both needed to look at the papers.

"Ah . . . these . . ." she said, indicating the papers, "are what they sent me. They are outlines of a couple of curriculums they offer."

He stared at the papers, but they were a blur as he caught a whiff of her fragrance. He hadn't noticed it before. It wasn't really perfume but rather something subtler, as if the bouquet of flowers he had just given her had sprinkled its sweet, slightly wild scent about her.

You are Zack Hartley, he told himself. You don't want to get mixed up with a farm girl. You don't want to get mixed up with any woman. They are trouble for you. If they aren't deceiving you, then they are trying to harness you. You don't need that.

"What do you think, Reverend?" she was saying.

"I think . . ." he stopped, forgetting what

he was expected to say. All he could think of was the fragrance coming from her hair and how he wanted to touch that hair.

Before he knew it, the small space between them had disappeared, his lips were touching hers, and his hand was pressing against the silky bouquet that was her hair. She made no resistance. Vaguely he heard the Sunday school papers flutter to the floor.

And for one blissful moment everything was real for Zack.

He wasn't even sure what that meant, except he'd never had a kiss quite like this before — sweet but explosive, uncertain yet passionate.

"Reverend . . ." she murmured suddenly.

Then all reality, or lack thereof, was shattered. She was not kissing him at all. She was kissing William Locklin.

He jerked back until he was safely once more hugging the opposite arm of the sofa.

"I'm sorry. I forgot myself," he said, forcing himself back into the role he was playing. Zack was not sorry at all. He would kiss her again given another chance, but he knew William Locklin would be sorry for making such inappropriate advances.

"It's not . . . you don't . . ." she stammered, her cheeks pure red.

Zack did not enjoy her discomfort at all

this time.

"I should go." He sprang to his feet.

"But we haven't discussed the Sunday school —"

"We don't need to," he said. "I'm sure whatever you want to do will be fine."

"But it will cost five dollars for the materials."

"I'll get you the money," he blurted just to make her happy, just to make a fast exit.

"But the deacons —"

Slowly, his mind began to work again. "Yes. Right. I'll bring it up to the deacons when they meet on Wednesday."

"Reverend . . ." She rose.

Call me Zack, he wanted to say. "Yes?"

She took a few steps toward him. He could have reached out for her again.

"I wanted to kiss you," she said.

He stared, and realizing his jaw had gone a bit slack, he snapped his mouth shut.

She went on, "It was hard to think of anything else, and I thought if we just got it over with . . . well, I don't know. I didn't think beyond that."

That was exactly it, he now realized. He'd wanted to kiss her for the same reason, believing that once it was over and done with, he wouldn't be so obsessed with thoughts of her. Now he could continue on with his plan, no longer distracted by her.

Suddenly something else occurred to him. "You kissed me?"

"I . . . uh . . . I thought so."

"Well, I . . . just wanted to be sure. You see I've never been kissed by a woman . . . *first,* you know." He didn't know if he'd been reprieved or was sinking deeper into an unfamiliar abyss.

"Now you think I'm brazen —"

"No, not at all. You had your reasons. I understand. I really must go." He started to turn.

She grasped his arm. For a moment time seemed to stop. He looked down at her hand. It felt warm even through the fabric of his suit. No, not just warm — hot like a branding iron. When he looked up again into her shimmering blue eyes, he knew he would kiss her again, but this time there would be no doubt as to who was doing the kissing.

"I fear you will no longer like me," she said.

The creaking sound of the front door opening made them both freeze.

"Ma! I'm home! Where is everyone?" yelled Georgie.

"My brother's home from school," Ellie said needlessly.

Zack nodded. But before he turned once again to leave, he added, "I still like you, El-lie." Then he spun around and fairly raced away.

"Hi'ya, Reverend!" Georgie said as they passed each other in the front room.

"Hi, Georgie," Zack said, flinging open the door and continuing on his way.

"Hey, Reverend, I hear the fish are biting down at the pond."

Zack kept walking. The last thing he wanted to be reminded of just then was that pond.

TWENTY

Ellie sat on the parlor sofa for some time before the trembling inside quieted. She had surely made an absolute fool of herself. Yes, Reverend Locklin said he understood and didn't think less of her, but what had she expected? That he point an accusing finger at her and shout, "Scarlet woman!"

His reaction confused her even more. He was so unlike one's typical idea of a minister that she didn't understand why she felt the way she did about him.

Finally she rose, picked up the tea tray, and left the parlor. Georgie was sitting at the table with a handful of cookies.

"Where is everybody?" he asked, chewing an oatmeal cookie.

"Mama's in the garden; Maggie's at the Arlingtons'; Dad is at the mill," she replied in a perfunctory manner.

"What's that you got? Is that shortcake?"

"Yes . . ." she replied, realizing she was

speaking as if through a haze, but she couldn't help it. She could only state the obvious, unable to think clearly.

"Oh, for Reverend Locklin."

"We had company," she said, not really hearing him.

"Hey, was the reverend paying court to you?"

Ellie blinked, the words finally nudging her back to reality. "No! Of course not!" she snapped. "We were just — I don't have to answer all your questions."

"This family gets stranger every day," said Georgie. "Boyd is walking around with his head in the clouds. You are as touchy as a wet cat. Maggie is —" He stopped there, glanced toward the pile of school books on the table, and then said no more.

Ellie brought the tray to the sink. She poured the sugar from the china bowl back into the crock on the sideboard. She was about to put away the shortcake when Georgie took note.

"Hey, is that shortcake?" he asked again. "Doesn't look like anyone even touched it."

"No . . . we didn't."

Georgie shook his head. "Like I said, strange . . . very strange." He reached for a piece.

She jerked away the dish. "You've had

enough sweets."

"Well, someone needs to eat it, since obviously the reverend didn't like it."

"He did so like me — I mean it — I mean — oh, take it!" She thrust the dish at him, and he took it without further argument. She then spun around and left the kitchen. Mama would not be happy that she hadn't washed and put away her good china, but she'd do it later. Right now she had to be alone.

Upstairs in her room she went to the window seat and plopped down, curling her legs up under her. The window looked out on the yard with a perfect view of the willow. No surprise it made her think of the block she'd made for the welcome quilt. How carefully, and yes, almost lovingly she had stitched it. She had put so much effort into it for a stranger. And now that she knew the recipient? Now that she had actually kissed him, looked into the depths of his eyes — warm and kind eyes they were, too. For sure there was a spark of mischief in them, as perhaps no minister should have, and in spite of all she imagined she desired, she rather liked that. Besides, having looked so closely at him, into those eyes, she saw there was goodness in him. As her mother would say, at his heart he was good. Not good for a minister but good for a man. He could have laughed at her impulsive behavior or scorned her, but he had tried to make her feel better. Though he'd been clearly rattled himself, he'd made sure his last words to her had been an assurance that he still liked her.

Would she put as much care into a quilt block for him now? Oh yes!

She knew a kiss was only a kiss. She had kissed Colby Stoddard a couple of times, and she knew she did not love him. In fact, she had tried very hard to love him, for he would have been a fine husband. She gave her head an ironic shake. She had tried as hard to love Colby as she was now trying *not* to love Reverend Locklin.

"Dear Lord, I am so confused," she found herself praying. Only then did she realize how much she needed to give this situation to God. "I just don't know what I want, or what I should want." She remembered something. "I want to want what You want for me, Father. Please show me what you want and what I should do."

Leaning her head against the glass pane, she drew close the sewing basket she kept on the window seat. It was there for just this purpose. She liked to sit at the window and think — and she always thought better with sewing in her hands. She picked up one of her hexagon diamonds. The one she was currently working on needed a few more of the darker hexagons on the outside row to make it complete. There were about ten dark hexagons left. She'd soon have to cut more if she intended to make more diamonds. She loved this pattern and could see it as a special quilt upon the master bed. For that she'd need to make at least as many more as she already had. But she didn't mind. As she had told Reverend Locklin, she so enjoyed each new combination of fabrics that each block was a new adventure, one that had kept her interest for ten years. She had nearly fifty diamonds made.

Digging into the bottom of the basket she took out the very first diamond she had made. It was of light blue and dark blue. Mama had made Easter dresses for her and Maggie of this material when they were young. Examining the diamond, Ellie could tell it had been done by an inexperienced quilter, though by then she had been stitching for four years. Like most girls she had started serious sewing instruction at age five. Even at that, her work was not too bad, for even as a nine-year-old she'd had a steady, careful hand.

Picking up a new hexagon, which was

already basted to paper, she laid it against the last hexagon of the diamond and, using a fine needle and fine thread, sewed them together with a tiny whip stitch. This diamond was green. Many other colors were also represented in the other diamonds. She called it her jewel-box quilt. When she had enough diamond shapes, she would connect them all with a light-colored fabric, probably muslin.

Reverend Locklin thought her perseverance in working with this quilt indicated patience and faithfulness. It was interesting how he had so quickly found the relation between stitching and life. She often saw that connection. Sometimes she thought she enjoyed patchwork so much because she could take plain, even worn, fabrics and put them together into such beautiful shapes. That was just what God did with His Church. Each individual part might not be perfect, but together they made something special.

Well, that might be a bit much, but Mama often used sewing to teach lessons about life, so there must be something to it.

Ellie was about to add the final hexagon to the diamond when the door burst open. She gave a start.

"Goodness, Maggie! You like to scare me

to death," Ellie scolded. "Can't you knock first?"

"What? Knock on my own bedroom door? That's a bit much even for you, Ellie." Maggie gave the door a hard push, and it closed with a bang.

"How'd you get so dirty?" Ellie asked, noting that her sister was indeed nearly covered in grime.

"I wasn't sitting by a window sewing all day. Working in a garden, in case you didn't know, is dirty work." As Maggie spoke she unfastened the straps of her overalls. "Louise is way behind in her garden. She only had a few rows of corn planted and beans. I got in squash and carrots and some turnips."

"That was very nice of you," Ellie commented.

"Nice? Mama forced me to go." She slipped off her overalls and tossed them into a corner.

"Can't you put them into the laundry hamper?"

"I'll get to it later. Mama told me to change and get you so we can help with supper." Maggie rummaged through one of the drawers in the dresser. "Those were my last clean overalls. Now I have to wear a skirt."

"Good thing tomorrow is laundry day."

"How come you got to escape up here in the middle of the day?" Maggie asked as she dressed.

Ellie shrugged. She supposed Maggie would eventually find out that Reverend Locklin had been there. "We had company today. I was . . . uh . . . busy with that."

"Who?"

"Reverend Locklin."

"Really? I wish I'd known. I wouldn't have gone to Louise's —"

"Well, we mostly had business to discuss —"

"With Dad? He isn't even home yet — what do you mean, 'we'?"

"I asked him to come so we could discuss my ideas about starting a Sunday school. That's all." Too late she realized her tone was overly defensive.

Maggie's eyes narrowed with perplexity. "You invited him?" Suddenly her eyes sprang open. "And Mama got rid of me. Ain't that convenient?"

"Now, settle down, Maggie —"

"Don't you talk to me that way!" Maggie railed. "Like I was a child and you are my mother. I won't have it!"

"I was not!"

"So did you change your mind again, Ellie? Now you're going after William. Is that it?"

"It was just about Sunday school!" But she remembered the kiss and could not propel her argument with much force.

"You just have to have every fellow in town, don't you?" sneered Maggie.

"No, it's not that. I don't want him," Ellie protested, though lamely.

"Never mind! I don't want to hear another word. I'm never speaking to you again!" Maggie spun around even as she was fastening the waistband of her skirt. She flung open the door and stormed out.

"Maggie!" Ellie called.

With a groan, Ellie let her head fall back against the window frame. What was she going to do now? If Maggie was this angry over a mere visit, what would she do if she knew Ellie had kissed the minister?

Maggie came tearing into the kitchen, truly like a storm unleashed, then came to a screeching halt. Ada, oblivious to all that had gone on upstairs, turned from the sink where she'd been paring potatoes.

"Maggie, was that you slamming the doors?" she asked. "Haven't I told you a hundred times — ?"

"I won't have it from you, either!" Maggie

cried. "I won't have you treat me like a child, pushing me neatly aside so I won't embarrass you when we have company."

"Margaret Edith! I will not have you speak to me in that tone!"

But apparently Maggie was not ready to curb her anger. "Why should I respect you when you don't respect me? How dare you get rid of me so Ellie could have the minister all to herself!"

"What are you talking about?" Ada's stomach clenched as she began to understand very well what her daughter was getting at.

"Mama, tell me that you didn't send me over to Louise's in order to get rid of me," Maggie challenged.

"Well . . . you . . . ah . . . have it all wrong," Ada stammered.

"Yes or no! Did you try to get rid of me?"

It was not a question Ada wanted to answer because, much to her shame, she knew the answer was yes. Unfortunately, she hesitated too long. Maggie had already yanked open the back door and was racing outside.

Ada sighed heavily. For the first time she realized how things were. She had laughed when Ellie mentioned Maggie's interest in the minister. At the very most, Ada considered it to be a childish whim. Was it more? Did Maggie care more deeply about the minister than anyone imagined?

Making the moment even worse, Ada thought of Calvin's warnings about getting too carried away with matchmaking. Had he been right? Were his dour predictions coming true, with their daughters caught in the midst of the storm?

Was Mother Newcomb right, as well? I'd rather cut off my right arm than have to admit that, Ada thought. Maybe there was still time to repair the damage. Maybe she could clean up the mess before Mother Newcomb ever perceived a thing.

Ada put down the paring knife and headed toward the open back door. Maggie was nowhere in back, but as Ada walked along the side of the house, past the clothesline, and reached the corner of the house, she saw her daughter sitting on the willow swing. Her long legs were sprawled out in front of her, her arms hooked around each of the side ropes. Suddenly tears welled in Ada's eyes. She recalled how often Maggie begged not to be treated like a child, and now Ada saw as clearly as if a fog were suddenly lifted that Maggie was indeed no more a child. Her lithe, mature body dwarfed the swing.

Ada remembered when Calvin had first hung that swing. Maggie had been about four years old and wanted desperately to join the older ones in using it, but the wooden slat seat was a little too high off the ground for her. She'd tried and tried until she finally heaved her little self into the swing. Ada wanted to forbid her to use the swing until she had grown a bit more, but Calvin said they better let her learn, because she was going to use it in spite of them. All that summer Ada feared Maggie would break a bone and had watched her like a hawk whenever she was on the swing.

Now look at her!

Ada dashed away the tears that spilled down her cheeks and approached the swing.

"Maggie, will you forgive me?"

"For what?" groused Maggie.

She never would make anything easy, but Ada knew she didn't deserve a reprieve from her daughter.

"For not being sensitive to your feelings," Ada replied. "I guess I didn't think you'd mind my trying to get Ellie and the reverend time alone —" When Maggie opened her mouth to retort, Ada tried to anticipate her words. "I should have understood that you are indeed old enough to be part of this kind of thing, that you are old enough to understand. But, Maggie, can you try to understand me a little, as well? It's hard for a mother to let her children go. I could lose three of you just like that. And Georgie's not far behind. I want to hold on to you as long as I can."

"The chicks have got to leave the nest, Mama," Maggie said, some of the ire gone from her voice.

"I know." Ada came close to her daughter and placed an arm around her shoulders. "But to me it was just yesterday when your feet were swinging over the edge of this seat, twelve inches above the ground. I need some time to let reality sink in."

"You don't got much time, Mama."

Ada's heart lurched once again. "Are you sweet on someone, Maggie?"

"Maybe."

"N-not the reverend?" Ada implored. She couldn't help it. Was her heart merely set on Ellie having the minister, or was there something else?

"Would that be so terrible?"

"He's quite a bit older than you."

"Only a year more than Ellie."

Ada knew the time had come. She could no longer impose her will on her children as she had when they were young. If Maggie loved the minister, Ada had to stand back.

But she would do as she had when Maggie had learned to use the swing. She would remain close. She would be there to catch her if she should fall.

Twenty-One

Riding down to Deer Island two weeks later, Zack took stock of his situation. Now that he was working at the sawmill, he figured he could save up enough money in a couple of months to leave this place.

There was a way he could leave much earlier —

But, no! He wasn't a thief, and he wasn't about to start with church money. Still, everyone around here talked a lot about God's will. Maybe it was God's will the money had fallen into his hands.

He thought about that deacons' meeting he'd attended. The main topic of discussion was a church building. They thought the time was right to begin serious fund-raising. They thought Zack's youth and enthusiasm was just what they needed to inspire the folks of Maintown to open their purses. Zack had no problem with that. The building committee reported that they had found a nice piece of land for sale about a quarter-mile east of the Copeland place, on the opposite end of town from the schoolhouse. It was a half-acre, and they could get it for two hundred fifty dollars. Actual building costs would be around four hundred with everyone pitching in on the work.

Then Calvin had slapped a leather wallet down on the table. "I think it is time we open an account at the St. Helens Bank and start collecting some interest on this."

"How much do we have there?" Russell Belknap asked.

"A hundred and fifty dollars," Calvin replied. "I don't like to keep that much cash in the house."

"Don't care much for banks," Hal Fergus said.

Apparently the men had had this same disagreement a year earlier, and that's why nothing had been done about the money.

"I care less for some robbers absconding with it," Calvin responded.

"There ain't no robbers round here —"

"I heard someone broke into Dolman's General Store just last week," Nathan Parker said.

"Well, that's St. Helens," Fergus said, as if proving his point.

"I have a thought," put in Lewis Arlington, who had returned recently from Rainier because now not one but two of his children were ill. "Don't Arthur Brennan own that parcel? Maybe he'll take the money as a down payment to make sure no one else gets the land."

"No need," said Nathan Parker, head of the building committee. "Arthur said if we want the land, all we have to do is shake on it, and it's ours when we have the full amount. This money should be earning some interest. That's how you do business." He gave a pointed glance at Hal, who merely grunted in response.

Calvin knew the men looked up to Parker's business savvy, since he was one of the richest fellows in town. He figured this was the best time to proceed and said, "Let's put it to a vote."

Last year, using a bank had been voted down, but this time putting the money in a savings account won by a narrow margin.

To Zack's surprise, Calvin had more to say.

"Reverend Locklin, could you take this to the bank when you go to Deer Island?"

"Me?"

Zack had truly tried to get out of it. He wanted no part in such a temptation, but all the other men were too busy to make a special trip to St. Helens, and he was headed in that direction anyway. Thus, the money had fallen into his hands. These men who didn't trust banks had entrusted *him* with their church building fund!

In the end, Zack had succumbed to temptation. He did not have the money with him. He had buried it at the bottom of his — Locklin's — trunk. He'd tell the deacons he had deposited it in the bank and make up some story about losing the receipt. He wasn't intending to use that money, but he couldn't let it go, either. He was going to keep it for an emergency in case he had to make a fast getaway. Then, just like everything else, he planned to pay it back someday. He may have once or twice rigged a game of poker or sold fake snake oil. He may have concocted one scheme or another to part a fool from his money, but he had never *taken* money from anyone. Most of the time they had been more than willing to give it. He figured he was doing them a service, teaching them to be more careful next time.

He was no thief! But that money weighed upon him like a specter haunting him, intruding even into his dreams. He was beginning to regret leaving it behind. He should have stuck with his original plan —

hide out, make some money at the sawmill, and then, when he had a few dollars and the coast was clear, he could take off for California. That was still the plan. The other was . . . just in case.

Maybe it would be better for everyone if he did take that money and disappear. These people didn't deserve a fake minister. But something more than needing a place to hide kept him here. Something in a blue calico dress with hair like the sun — she haunted his dreams as much as the ill-gotten church building fund. Ellie Newcomb was also another reason he should leave.

When he returned to Maintown after his circuit, Calvin accepted, without question, Zack's story of losing the bank receipt. Why would they doubt him? He was the minister.

Maggie had seen William a few times since that day at the pond, but he wasn't as available as he'd been, what with working at the sawmill now. Then he'd had his circuit, and Maggie had gone to Scappoose with her family for a couple of days to visit her grandparents. Besides all that, her mother kept her busy at home from sunup to sundown. Maybe Mama was purposefully trying to keep Maggie away from the minister.

Those few times she had seen William, they were never alone. They had chatted pleasantly but there were no more kisses. Just to spite Ellie, Maggie wanted to press William for some affirmation of his intentions. But she couldn't bring herself to do it, and not because of Ellie — they were talking again; still the atmosphere between them was chilly. Maggie's reluctance was because she really was not ready for marriage. She wanted to spite them all by snagging the minister, but down deep she knew she'd be hurting herself most of all.

Nevertheless, she was surprised when her mother sent her on an errand to the Copelands'. Of course, Mama probably realized the reverend would be working at the sawmill, so it would be safe to send her.

Maggie found Mrs. Copeland in the kitchen kneading bread dough.

"Mama sent me to fetch the reverend's suit and a couple of other things for her to alter," Maggie said.

"Can you go on up and get them, dear? My hands are a mess."

"He told my mother he would set them out for her."

"He didn't leave anything down here.

They must be in his room." The woman smiled. "I'm sure he won't mind if you go to his room."

Maggie shrugged, not wanting to show her hesitance. Even with her modern thinking, it seemed improper to go into a man's room. The last and only time she had been there was on that first day when half the townsfolk were present, as well. She climbed the stairs and opened the door, feeling almost as though she were entering the Holy of Holies.

Reverend Locklin's room was tidy. She wondered if Mrs. Copeland cleaned it, or if he kept it that way. She looked around and decided it wasn't just tidy. It looked hardly lived in. Well, with working at the mill and riding the circuit, he didn't really spend a great deal of time here. Only the little desk held any personal items — a few books, paper, and pen he must use for preparing his sermons.

The quilt was neatly spread out upon the bed. She had to walk around to the other side to find her block on the part that hung over the side of the bed — the best place to hide a poorly made block. And that block no doubt represented her best work! Maybe she would have done a better job if she'd known William at the time, but most likely this was the best she could ever do.

She looked around, hoping to find a neat stack of clothes ready for her to take, but there was nothing. She thought of Boyd and Georgie's room and how it defied even Mama's constant nagging to stay clean. There were always clothes strewn everywhere. She opened the wardrobe and found both broadcloth suits hanging. She took the one that still needed altering, folded it, and laid it on the bed. In the dresser drawers were clothes that had already been fixed.

She saw the trunk, and it seemed logical that he'd keep clothing he wasn't wearing in there. She was reluctant to open it but at the same time very curious. She realized she knew precious little about William. He'd only spoken of his life that once at the pond, and he had seemed reticent about it once he realized what he was saying. Shouldn't she know more about him if she thought she might marry him?

The answer seemed clear to her as she lifted open the lid of the trunk. Right on top, some clothing lay neatly folded. She could have stopped there but knew she wouldn't. She put a pair of trousers and a shirt on the bed with the suit. Then returning to the trunk, she moved aside the other clothing. On the bottom of the trunk she saw several books, among them *Leather Stocking Tales* and *The Last of the Mohicans* by James Fenimore Cooper. Maggie had read these herself, though her mother had said they were not proper reading for a young lady. Another was *Moby Dick* by a person named Herman Melville. Maggie hadn't heard of this one. She picked it up and glanced at the first chapter. It looked interesting but again probably not appropriate for a girl. She recalled what William had said about a sea adventure on the Pacific Coast, how he'd first said it was his experience, then recanted.

Somehow she thought these books odd for William. These were adventure stories, and though he'd never said anything to indicate otherwise, she had the impression he was a man of the world, a man who lived adventure rather than reading about it. Moreover, she had never seen him read a book for pleasure or even talk of books.

Moving aside some of the books, she found the real prize. A daguerreotype of three people, two older, probably parents, and one younger male, probably sixteen or seventeen years old. Were these William's family? His parents and brother perhaps? None of them looked like William. They were fairer of skin and hair than he was.

Maggie turned over the picture. On the back were the words, "Mama, Papa, and William."

That was strange. Perhaps they were aunt and uncle and cousin. He'd never said anything about relatives he was especially close to, but that was possible. Maybe they raised him. Maybe he was adopted. But to have a brother, a cousin, or adopted brother with the same name?

Replacing this, she saw a larger paper, a certificate of some kind. Lifting it out, to her astonishment she saw what was clearly a ministerial license naming William Edward Locklin as the licensee. This had to be the very license William had told Mrs. Briggs he did not have! Perhaps he had just received it and was going to surprise the congregation with an announcement on Sunday. But why was it tucked at the bottom of the trunk?

Her final and perhaps most disquieting discovery was a leather wallet that had one hundred fifty dollars in it along with a paper verifying the amount and signed by Maggie's father! Maggie had heard her parents talking about how they had given the building fund money to William for him to deposit into the St. Helens bank. William had already been to St. Helens. Why had he not deposited it?

With trembling fingers, Maggie replaced everything, even the clothing, back into the truck just as she had found it. She did not want him to know she had been in the trunk and to suspect she had been snooping.

She sat in the chair by the desk in order to give herself a moment to digest all she'd found. Her mind conjured a dozen logical reasons for everything, for there were indeed many. There need be nothing sinister in any of this, yet her mind, which her mother always said was too imaginative for her own good, also formed many devious reasons. But she shook away each and every one. It was all perfectly innocent, she was certain.

And rather than let her imagination run away, she could ask William himself. He surely had nothing to hide. That would, of course, mean she'd have to admit she'd been snooping.

Propping an elbow on the desk, Maggie bumped a book that was sitting open. Glancing toward it, she saw the chapter title on the open page was "Love Extolled."

He must be working on his sermon, she thought, for beside the book was a sheet of paper with writing on it.

The words "Love Extolled" were at the very top. Below that she read, *This morning we shall explore the miracle of grace — our Savior's astounding grace. This is a difficult concept for men to grasp. How often have I heard men say, "You can't get something for nothing"? This we understand. Even a gift is often perceived with having ulterior motives behind the gesture. . . .*

Maggie turned back to the book. Her eyes moved down the printed page, and she saw the same exact words as were written on the paper. She picked up the book, turned it over, and saw it was titled, *The Sermons of Robert E. Markus.* She flipped through the pages and paused at one titled "Consider the Lilies." She was not one to listen too closely to the sermons in church, nor to remember them verbatim afterward, but what was written on this page sounded incredibly like the first sermon William had preached in Maintown.

Was William stealing another preacher's sermons?

Well, what of it? Maggie found herself answering her own query.

Again, she put everything back the way she'd found it and jumped up from the chair. Mama always said no good came of snooping.

She knew there had to be perfectly good answers to everything she'd discovered. She also knew she wasn't going to try to find those answers. A great sense of protectiveness rose up within her. There were folks who might take these discoveries wrong and think ill of William, and she just couldn't have that.

Was it love she was feeling? Did she love William and thus desire to protect him?

He was, after all, the first man to ever kiss her. She didn't want to think she was the sentimental type who fell in love with the first kiss. Yet he had kissed her, and she had liked it. She felt as light-headed around him as she did around Colby Stoddard.

She just did not know what it all meant and wasn't sure she wanted to. She wanted things to stay just as they were.

She hurried out of the room, nearly colliding with Mrs. Copeland.

"Oh, there you are," the older woman said. "I was coming up to see what became of you."

"N-nothing . . ." Maggie stammered. "I'm fine." Her voice came out in a squeak.

"You look absolutely peaked." Mrs. Copeland frowned. "Couldn't you find the pastor's clothes?"

"Oh . . . uh . . ." Maggie chuckled sickly. "I forgot them." She ducked back into the room, grabbed the suit, and exited again.

"Just the suit?"

"I'll get the rest later. I gotta go." Maggie spun toward the stairs, and suddenly remembering her manners, she paused and offered a quick, "Thank you."

Then she raced down the stairs and outside. She ran halfway home, fearing the entire time she would run into William and he would see guilt spelled clearly on her face.

TWENTY-TWO

Zack was exhausted. He trudged up the stairs after telling Mrs. Copeland he would forego supper. She told him she would keep it warm on the back of the stove in case he changed his mind. In his room he plopped down upon his bed and stretched out, only vaguely thinking of his work-soiled body defiling the fine quilt. But he was too tired to do anything about it.

He'd been up at five in the morning to start work at the mill at six. He'd worked ten hours. In past days they'd had him sweeping up and performing other light tasks, no doubt taking it easy on the minister. But today a couple of fellows had quit, and Zack had been given the job of bucking logs onto the carriage that moved the logs to the saw. Every muscle in his body ached from the grueling labor, and his hands, though he'd worn gloves, were sore and blistered.

He nearly laughed aloud as he thought of his ma's frequent admonishment: "Zack, you work harder than anyone I know to get out of work."

Masquerading as the minister had seemed a lark, an easy way out of his sticky predicament. Now he saw it probably would have been better if he'd just taken a job at one of the lumber camps back in the woods. But that had seemed too much like work.

Then adding insult to injury, Elisha Cook had ridden up after work as he was nearing the Copeland place and asked if he could come back to his place and pray for his ill mother. Mrs. Cook had been suffering with a carcinoma for some time, and it seemed her condition was worsening. Zack had paused long enough to tell Mrs. Copeland he'd be late for supper, then rode with Elisha about four miles to his parents' farm — it was just Elisha and his mother now because his father had run off several years ago.

Zack was growing accustomed to making such calls. He hardly gave it a thought anymore to visit the sick or the troubled. Calvin had once mentioned he'd likely have even more calls later. Some folk were holding off on account of his being new and the folks wanting to "test" him first. Also, word that his license hadn't arrived yet had circulated, so some were probably holding off for that reason, too. If he'd been a real minister, he would have already had several "altar calls" and as a result, a number of baptisms to perform. He'd be counseling folks, knocking on doors, and getting the backsliders to church.

It was easy to sidestep all this by offering one excuse or another or by not seeking out these tasks. He'd rather they think him lazy than inept. Last week in Deer Island he'd officiated at another funeral. He figured there was no harm in doing funerals, since these folks were dead and all. But he knew it would not be much longer until he was fully accepted into the community and more demands would be placed upon him. He hoped to be long gone before then.

He wondered about Beau Cutter. Could he possibly still be looking for him? A man like that had a long memory. Maybe he should cut out of this place when he got his first pay from the mill.

All this thinking was starting to add a headache to his other aches. People talked a lot about "honest, hardworking men," but he was sure it was the dishonest man who worked hardest. Lying and deception did not come easy. Had he realized that when he fell into this scheme, he might have done differently. Yet he was here now, and the best thing was to see it through.

At least tomorrow was Sunday and he'd not have to face the grueling work at the mill for another day. That made him remember he'd been so busy he hadn't finished working on his sermon. He'd copied one from Markus's book but still needed to memorize it. Well, he'd just rest for a few minutes, then eat that supper Mrs. Copeland had promised to keep warm for him. By then he'd be able to face the task ahead.

The Newcombs were spending a quiet evening by the hearth when Jane Donnelly knocked on their door.

"I'm so sorry to interrupt your evening," she said, obviously distraught but still conscientious about propriety.

"What's wrong, Jane?" Ada asked.

"Tom and Tommy went hunting earlier this afternoon, and they have not returned home." She glanced up as Calvin joined them at the door. "You know they wouldn't be hunting after dark."

Calvin probably was thinking the same as Ada. What had they been doing hunting at all in the middle of the day when most men were working? Well, Ada knew what they were doing — shirking real work with the excuse that they were hunting food for the table. Still, Ada didn't know why Jane was so worried. The two layabouts were no doubt passed out drunk in the woods.

"Come on in, Jane," Calvin said, "and tell us why you are so worried. This can't be the first time they are late coming home."

"Even Tom don't miss supper," Jane said a bit defensively.

"You want me to go have a look around for them?" Calvin asked.

"I hate to drag you out at this hour. But . . . oh, I know what you are thinking, and I don't blame you, but this isn't right even for them."

"Maybe they're just lost," Ada offered, though she was certain Tom knew the woods better than anyone.

After confirming with Jane the possible places the men might be likely to hunt, Calvin took his coat from the peg. "Boyd, would you join me?"

"I can go, too, Dad!" offered Georgie.

"Not this time, son. Two of us is enough."

Boyd and Calvin left, and Ada invited Jane to sit down.

Jane hesitated. "I better go back home in case Tom comes back there, don't you think?"

"I'm sure Calvin will go by your house to check," Ada said. "Come and visit with me. Have you had supper?"

"I couldn't eat."

"Then some tea?" Ada asked. "Ellie, would you fix up a fresh pot?"

"I don't want to be a bother," Jane said.

"Of course you're not. Come and sit down."

They sat in front of the hearth that was bright with a nice warm fire. They chatted and Jane helped Ada with some sewing. The next hour passed slowly. Ellie brought tea and joined them with her own sewing while Maggie helped Georgie with a puzzle. It would have been a pleasant, homey scene except for the frequent lulls in conversation and the rising tension as time dragged on.

Ada still believed there was nothing to worry about. Yet what was taking Calvin so long? It was only a few minutes' ride to the Donnelly place and a mile or two into the woods where the men liked to hunt. Of course, searching in the darkness would take time, but Ada did not think Calvin would have to go far before he found the father and son most likely passed out from their moonshine.

Finally, there came the sound of footsteps on the front porch. Ada expected the door

333

to burst open, but nothing happened for several long moments. She could tell by the voices it was Calvin and Boyd. Jane was looking expectantly toward the door, as was Ada, holding her breath.

At last the door opened. Calvin and Boyd entered and hung up their coats before saying a word. That's what made Ada start to worry.

Calvin walked slowly toward the women. "Jane, we found something," he said hesitantly. "I don't know how to say it except right out." But even as he spoke those words, it was obvious he didn't want to say it at all. "We found Tom." Calvin stopped and cleared his throat. "He was . . . ah . . . he was dead, Jane."

Jane gasped.

Ada jumped up, and going over to her friend, she glanced at her husband, who merely shook his head. Ada dropped to her knees beside Jane and took her hand. In the silence that followed Ada noticed some stirring from the children, who had also heard the news. She knew at any moment Maggie would start in with a barrage of questions, for she'd be concerned about Tommy in all this. But Ada didn't think a lot of questions would help right at the moment.

"Children," she said peremptorily, "it is

time you went up to bed."

"But, Mama —" Maggie began.

Calvin cut in gently but firmly. "Go on, Maggie. We'll be up soon to tuck you in."

Maggie was not going to like her father speaking to her as to a child, but they'd talk later, and all would be well. This simply wasn't the time or place for young folks. Perhaps Maggie did understand this, for she followed her brothers and sister upstairs without another word.

Ada turned her full attention toward Jane, now sitting very still and quiet, her face pale and drawn.

Calvin came and pulled a chair close to Jane and sat down. "Jane, I saw no sign of Tommy," he said. "I went by your house afterward, and he wasn't there."

"How — ?" Jane began, but her voice caught on the word and she stopped, fighting back emotion.

"Tom was killed with a shotgun. I expect they were bird hunting, and it was an accident of some sort."

"He . . . he's dead? You are certain?"

"Yes, Jane. I'm very sorry," Calvin replied. "We brought his . . . body back. I laid it in your barn."

Ada couldn't help being relieved that Calvin had the foresight not to bring the man's body here. What a trauma that would have been for the children.

"Where is Tommy?" Jane asked.

"I don't know," Calvin answered.

Ada had the feeling he wasn't telling everything.

"I left a note at your house for him in case he comes home. I told him you'd be staying here."

"I must go home!" Jane started to rise, suddenly agitated. "I must be there for him."

"He'll know to come here," Ada said. "Why don't you stay with us for the night?"

"I . . . I . . . don't know what to do!" Jane lamented in a shaky voice and turned toward Ada. "Ada, my Tom is gone!" Then the tears started as the terrible news finally penetrated her mind.

Ada gathered her friend into her arms, comforting her as best as she could. She didn't know what else to do or say, though there probably wasn't anything to say just then. Instead, Ada prayed silently for Jane and also for Tommy. Where was he anyway? Could he have been involved somehow? Had he finally run off? Only God knew the answers, so it was to God that Ada made her prayer for the boy's well-being.

After a while Jane's tears quieted. "I'm sorry for being such a bother to you."

"Don't even think such a thing!" Ada said. "We are friends." They both knew that was enough, that Jane would do the same for Ada. "Now, dear, I'm going to go upstairs and get a bed ready for you. You must be exhausted."

"I couldn't sleep until I know Tommy is all right."

"I'll wake you the minute Tommy comes," Ada said with confidence, though she feared the boy wasn't going to show up anytime soon. If there had been an accident, he might be afraid to come forth. She didn't want to think of all the other possibilities.

Seeing that Calvin was feeling even more awkward than she, Ada suggested that he fix another pot of tea, and she went upstairs. She found all the children in the girls' room sitting quietly on the bed. It was a remarkable sight, for normally all four together meant a lot of bouncing, bickering, laughter, and noise. It showed Ada just how mature they were becoming, even Georgie.

"Jane is going to spend the night with us," Ada said. "Girls, she'll take your room since it is probably the cleanest. We'll make up a bed for you in with the boys."

"I'll take care of it, Mama," Ellie said.

"Mama," Maggie said, "Boyd thinks Tommy shot his dad. Is that true?"

Ada had forgotten that Boyd had been at the scene of the incident. She thought that might be what Calvin was thinking, as well, considering his reticence.

"We don't know for sure," Ada said with a glance at Boyd.

"Mama, we found Tom in a clearing just west of Asher's Pond," Boyd said. "Dad and I have gone there before to hunt pheasant. It looked like at least two men had been there, and they'd been drinking. The jug of moonshine was nearly empty. It could have been an accident, but if Tom fell where he was shot, he was out in the open, not obscured by trees or anything."

"Of course it was an accident," Ada said. It was monstrous to even consider any other possibility, though, indeed she had.

"Are you gonna call for the sheriff?" Georgie asked.

"Dad told me he would go into St. Helens in the morning," Boyd said.

Maintown had no sheriff or constable of its own. There simply wasn't enough need to support one. Just as there were no elected officials. If leadership was called for, it usually fell to a handful of the leading men — Calvin, Nathan Parker, and Albert Stoddard, for the most part.

"Children," said Ada, "whatever you do,

don't repeat any of this to anyone. Not only could it be hurtful to Jane, but it could start unfounded rumors. And we don't want that."

"Rumors are gonna fly," Maggie said, "no matter what we do."

"Just as long as they don't come from our lips," Ada warned, with a brow arched pointedly toward Maggie.

"I just want to know the truth. I want to know that Tommy is okay," Maggie said.

"That is what we all want," Ada agreed. "Now, let's get this room ready. I fear we will have a long night ahead of us."

That prediction turned out to be right, for even as Ada came back downstairs from preparing a room, Jane broke down again. Grief was settling in, and almost more devastating was fear for her son. She was certain he was lying dead out there, as well, that the two had been attacked by hooligans or thieves. Ada finally suggested that Calvin go after the pastor. Perhaps he'd know what to do in such a situation. At the very least his presence would be a comfort.

But when Calvin returned with Reverend Locklin around ten o'clock that night, the minister looked almost as distressed as Jane. Only then did Ada remember the altercation he'd had with Tom Donnelly. Surely he could not feel responsible in any way for the tragedy. More than likely he just felt too inexperienced to deal with something like this. Maybe it had been a mistake to call him.

"I am so sorry for your loss," the reverend said, in a rote sort of way, not insincerely but as if he was speaking from a litany.

Jane looked at him with surprise. "Pastor, you didn't have to come."

"Of course I did. I want to help you in any way I can."

"Can you pray with me?"

He looked around at Calvin and Ada, almost desperately, before answering. "Yes, let's pray." He paused. "Dear Lord, be with Jane in this time of her grief and comfort her and . . . ah . . . strengthen her." He fumbled over similar ground for a few more minutes until he finally said, "Amen."

Ada realized she had never really heard Reverend Locklin pray an impromptu prayer. The prayers he prayed in church were far smoother and more practiced than the one he'd uttered just now, as if carefully written out beforehand. She had not given it much thought until now. She found it a bit perplexing that she hadn't noticed, but she'd personally had no call to request individual prayer from the pastor, and he certainly had not offered it.

He stayed for about a half hour and then left. He was no more out the door than Maggie hurried down the stairs and slipped outside. Ada didn't question her daughter. Perhaps she desired to pray with the pastor, as well. Ada reminded herself that Maggie was one of Tommy Donnelly's few friends.

Twenty-Three

"William!" Maggie called.

Zack had descended the porch steps and was halfway to where his horse was tied to the front post. He cringed inwardly as he heard the familiar voice call that name. He regretted having allowed her to use his given name because he was certain it meant far more to her than merely a name.

Yet he could not very well ignore her, not when he bore the greatest guilt for encouraging her. He turned.

"What is it, Maggie?" he asked with a weary sigh.

She flew lightly down the steps toward him. She was dressed in her usual overalls, with a yellow shirt. Her hair was loose, brown curls bouncing as she jogged to where he stood. Her tanned, freckled skin glowed in the moonlight, her large green eyes luminous. When he realized how he was appreciating her beauty, he chided himself in view of the recent tragedy. But how could he think straight when he was so tired?

"William, I must talk to you," Maggie said.

"Can't it wait until tomorrow?" he asked. "It's awfully late."

"I have to tell you something because I don't know what I should do about it."

"All right," he replied with a resigned shrug.

Grabbing his hand, she led him to the garden patch. It was backed with a low stone wall that offered a good place to sit. When he realized this was going to take longer than he thought, he tried to be patient, as a good minister would.

"William," she began when they were settled on the wall, "first, you've got to give me your word you won't tell anyone what I am about to say."

Reasonably, he replied, "I can't do that unless I know what you're going to say."

"But you are a minister, so anything I tell you is under some seal of confidentiality."

"That's for Catholic priests —"

"No, it's for ministers, too," she argued. "I read that somewhere. You can't tell no one what a person tells you in confidence."

"Okay, Maggie, if you say so." What could she possibly tell him that he'd want to repeat? If it was about that kiss, he definitely wanted to keep it quiet.

"Well, I talked to Tommy Donnelly yesterday," she continued. "He told me his father had been real hard on him about going to church and that he, that is Tommy, wasn't going to take it anymore. He said that since he saw you beat his father, he was no longer afraid of him. He said next time his father pushed him, he was gonna push back. I'm afraid to tell anyone this because if I do, it may make them certain Tommy shot his father." She paused and took a deep breath. "If the sheriff is called in, do I have to tell him? I know it will just make things worse for Tommy."

Zack hardly heard a thing after her comment about Tommy saying that after Zack had beat up Tom, Tommy said he was no longer afraid of his father. His stomach lurched, and the first thing that came to his mind burst through his lips.

"Are you saying it's my fault?" he snapped.

"What? No, of course not. I would never."

He knew she was telling the truth. It was his own sense of guilt that made him think of blame. But it wasn't his fault. How could he be responsible for how some crazy kid interpreted his actions?

"William, you mustn't for one instant think you had anything to do with what happened. Those two have been at each other's throats since long before you ever came here."

Maggie didn't understand that what she said only heightened Zack's feelings of guilt. Was it a coincidence that years of Tom's abusive behavior finally came to this tragic head so shortly after Zack's fight with him? Even as the case for Zack's blame seemed to grow stronger, he tried to deny it.

"That's right," he said. "No single man can cause events like this."

"But I fear what I know can cause a lot of trouble," Maggie said.

Zack made himself focus on her problem rather than his own. "If Tommy killed his father on purpose, Maggie, he needs to face justice." That's what a minister would say. Then Zack thought of his own situation. He had accidentally killed a man, yet if he had been caught by the law, he doubted anyone would ever believe it had been accidental. He had been in the wrong place at the wrong time, and that alone would have convicted him. Justice was a fine word. It just wasn't always fair. There probably was no conclusive proof whether Tommy had shot his father accidentally or otherwise. But Maggie's information could easily tip the scale toward guilt, and that could hang the boy who, at seventeen, was old enough to be treated as a man. He might be able to get off by pleading self-defense or even temporary insanity by way of drunkenness. Either way it meant a lot of grief for the boy, not to mention grief for Maggie, who would feel she'd betrayed a friend. And Tommy's grieving mother didn't need this, either.

"If Tommy did kill his father," Maggie said, "he deserved it."

Zack was tempted to run and have no part in this. The last time he had tried to help someone, namely Tom Donnelly, the man had ended up dead. Maggie was looking up at him with imploring eyes. She needed her minister's help, and Zack had a funny sense that she needed *his* help, as well. Zack Hartley's experiences might serve better just now than William Locklin's, despite his earlier mistakes.

"Don't say anything to anyone," he said finally. "At least not right away. Let's see how everything shakes out. Tommy might already be long gone and probably better off, too."

"Will they go looking for him?"

"Not without your bit of information. They'll just assume, at worst, that he accidentally shot Tom and ran off because he was scared or couldn't face his mother. They might investigate a little just to make sure it wasn't some stranger who did it."

"What if they ask me point-blank?"

"You'll have to tell them, then. You can't lie. It could make you an accessory or something. You can say you didn't come forward with it earlier because you didn't think it was important. It was the kind of thing Tommy was always saying. Don't just blurt it out, either. Make them coax it from you so it looks like you really have forgotten it."

She arched a brow. "You know, William, for a minister, you sure know how to side-step the truth."

Defensively, he said, "You don't have to take my advice. It still may be that I led Tommy astray."

"No you didn't, William," she rejoined earnestly. "And I will take your advice. I know you're right."

He left the Newcomb place feeling worse than ever, his misery having less to do with his tired, aching body than with a strange queasy feeling in his heart.

Trying hard to attribute that odd sensation to something physical, he hoped some food would help. Mrs. Copeland's stew, still warming on the back of the stove, was tasty even if a bit dried out. But a bowl of it didn't help what was beginning to eat away at him. He went up to his room, and the first thing that greeted him after lighting the lamp on the bed table was the quilt, now a bit rumpled from his taking a nap on it earlier. He didn't want to be reminded that it hadn't really been meant for him.

Turning sharply away from it, he strode to the desk and sat in the chair so he could take off his boots. There he was met with another unwelcome sight — his sermon for tomorrow's service. He prepared new sermons for the first and fourth Sundays of the month, which happened to be the Maintown service. This would be the fourth Sunday in July. He realized this was his fourth new sermon since coming here. It shocked him to realize he'd already developed a routine, a habit, for this life as a minister. In so many ways he believed he belonged here more than the real William Locklin, the man who had never set foot in Maintown, who had never met the wise Calvin Newcomb or his caring wife or their lovely, sweet daughters. He'd conversed with every citizen, supped with almost all of them. He'd played horseshoes with the men, jested with the children, and charmed the women.

"And don't forget, Zack," he told himself sourly, "you also led an impressionable boy to shoot his father."

Bah! He argued with himself. No one knew exactly what had happened out there in the woods between Tommy and his father. I did what I thought was best. Would William Locklin have done any better? He was a strapping fellow who might just as well have thrashed Tom Donnelly. Zack tried to ignore the fact that in a large part he hadn't really been hitting Tom, but rather his own stepfather. He'd had a rage in him William probably wouldn't have had.

With a sigh that closely resembled a groan, he ran his hands through his hair. He was so tired, that was all. Everything would look better after a good sleep. But there was that sermon before him and the reality that tomorrow, despite the tragedy and even because of it, he would have to give these people a church service. By eleven o'clock tomorrow nearly everyone would know what had happened, and they would want the support and comfort of their pastor, of him. Though everything inside screamed that he was an inept fool who was doing more harm than good, he also knew he could not run out on these people when they needed him most. They needed a minister, and he was all they had.

He'd picked a sermon for tomorrow at random from Markus's book. Maybe he should change it to something more appropriate to the current situation. However, there was no way he could copy and memorize a new sermon before morning. He'd have to stay with the one he had already started.

The sermon — "I Will Love Them Freely" — was based on Hosea 14:4. He'd never heard of this book of the Bible and it had taken some searching to find it. The only Bible reading Zack had ever done was the verses he read for these sermons. Maybe someday he would read the entire Bible for himself. Maybe someday he would read one of the sermons with comprehension. Somehow copying and memorizing them didn't make him perceive the contents. He made sure he remained aloof to Markus's words. Even if he wanted to, there was no time for that now, he told himself. I just gotta get this thing memorized.

First he finished taking off his boots. His feet were sore from the long, arduous day. Then, picking up the pages he had copied from the desk, he leaned back comfortably in the chair.

He reread the Bible verse, thankful it was

an easy one to remember. *I will love them freely.* Scoffing, he shook his head. "How am I going to say that with a straight face when I know you can't get something for nothing?" he muttered.

When he went on to read the next paragraph, he saw those very words. *How often have I heard men say, "You can't get something for nothing"? This we understand.* It made him blink as if suddenly waking up.

Was he actually starting to think like a preacher?

It made him take closer notice as he read on. Markus listed examples of how even the most innocent of gifts given by mere mortals are not given entirely without an ulterior motive. Zack immediately thought of that quilt on his bed. Now, there was a gift given with ulterior motives!

He snorted reproachfully. You are not one to judge them, are you? At least they gave you something. You have done nothing but take.

Yeah? He silently debated himself. What have I taken? I give them a sermon every week, a few kind words. I've visited them and helped them with their farm work. Didn't I ride out to the Cooks' today when I was dead tired? And what about comforting a grieving widow tonight? I've been working harder these past two months than I ever have in my life. I don't owe them anything.

Yet every time he looked at that quilt it reminded him of who and what he really was. Well, that's it, then! I'll return this cursed quilt. He jumped up, grabbed the thing, and whipped it from the bed. A corner of it snapped at the lantern beside the bed, sending it flying from the table. Glass shattered as it hit the floor, and in an instant a spark from the flame ignited the spilt kerosene. Flames lapped up the deadly liquid and immediately caught the bottom hem of the draperies.

Once more grabbing the quilt, Zack leaped toward the flame, now shooting up the drapery. His bare foot came down hard on the shards of glass. When he instinctively jerked the foot up, his other foot slipped in the puddle of kerosene, sending him sprawling to the floor. His head cracked against the footboard of the bed, and all around him went suddenly black.

The next thing he knew, a hand was shaking him roughly. "Come on, lad, I can't carry you. You must wake up!" A voice pierced the fog of Zack's consciousness.

He realized hands were attempting to drag him but with great difficulty. He also saw through blurred vision that flames were licking up all around him. That finally spurred him to action. He leapt to his feet, barely noticing in his panic the pain that shot up his leg from his foot, and followed his rescuer to the door.

"I'll get some more blankets for the fire," Mr. Copeland said after seeing that Zack was all right.

Zack saw the quilt was still on the floor and took it yet a third time, using it now in an attempt to smother the flames. But even in the desperation of the moment, it sickened him to use the precious quilt thus. When Copeland returned with more blankets, Zack tossed the scorched quilt into the hall and used one of the woolen blankets to beat at the spreading flames that already engulfed the bed.

It wasn't long before the whole room was alight. Zack and Copeland were forced out the door and into the hall.

"We better get away," Copeland said.

"Mrs. Copeland?"

"She's gone to get help. Come on. It is too much for us."

"I'm sorry," Zack said. "I . . . I . . ."

"You need say nothing, lad," Mr. Copeland said. "Let's go."

Zack scooped up the quilt and raced

downstairs.

A tiny line of light was beginning to brighten the eastern sky when Zack sat down for the first time in hours. Flames still licked up toward the pearl gray sky from the charred remains of the Copelands' fine house. Most of the fire was out, and the little that still burned would be doused before long. He hadn't wanted to quit until it was all out, but less than an hour ago the pain in his foot, which he'd tried to ignore, had gradually turned into a throbbing that made every step an agony.

Not long after the fire started about a dozen men had formed a bucket brigade from the Copelands' well to the house. One of the men had noticed Zack's bare feet and had found him a pair of boots. He had put them on gratefully, not even noticing they were a bit small. Now, after being on his feet for hours fighting the fire, the constriction of the leather, along with the cuts on his feet from the broken lantern, had finally taken their toll.

There wasn't much more to be done now. The house was gone except for two outer walls and the brick chimney. The roof had caved in a few hours ago, sealing the fate of the structure.

The response of the Maintown folk had been heroic. Even before Mrs. Copeland had reached the post office where the fire bell was kept, sleeping folk in the town proper had been awakened by the stench of the fire and had hurried to the scene. Those who lived farther out responded almost as quickly upon hearing the loud clanking of the bell, a sound all feared and none took lightly. Within a half hour twenty or thirty men and women had gathered and formed the bucket brigade. The folk had tried mighty hard to save the place, and though they failed, at least they had prevented the fire from spreading to the homes of neighbors.

Zack still could not believe what had happened. Although he had worked as tirelessly as any to heave water on the flames, he had done so in something of a daze. At first his head was swimming from cracking it on the bedpost, then the pain in his foot began intensifying, but mostly he'd simply been in shock at the swiftness of the disaster. His utter fatigue in missing an entire night's sleep hadn't helped, either.

Lifting his eyes, he saw the scorched quilt lying in a heap in the dirt not far from the garden rock on which he was sitting. What an irony it was the only thing saved from the fire. His things — William Locklin's things — were destroyed. And, of course, nearly all of the Copelands' possessions. Mr. Copeland had been able to save a few things from the lower floor before the roof had caved in, but nothing of much consequence. Oddly, Zack had been wearing his own clothes that day, since they were the most appropriate to wear for working at the sawmill. An inexplicable wave of sadness washed over him as he was struck with just how completely William Locklin's existence had now been extinguished. He felt as if he had lost a friend in the fire.

With a miserable sigh, he decided to focus on the most immediate problem. He lifted up his injured foot and tried to remove the boot. His arms felt like rubber, so weak he could barely budge the thing, and the pain caused by wiggling the boot forced him to stop. He suspected his foot had swelled.

"Can I help you?" came a feminine voice.

He looked up to see Ellie Newcomb approach. "I can't believe I'm too weak to take off my own boots," he said.

She knelt down in front of him and grasped the boot, gently edging it back and forth. He grit his teeth against the pain because he knew the boot had to go and he hated the thought of cutting someone else's shoe, especially since these were all he had. Finally it fell off, and Ellie gave a gasp.

"Your foot is soaked with blood!" she exclaimed. "What happened?"

"The lantern broke," he said dazedly, still reeling from the pain caused by removing the boot.

"Let me get something to clean your foot, and I'll bandage it."

"You don't have to."

"Don't be silly. I must take care of this."

He laid a hand on her arm, lightly restraining her. "Ellie, look what I've done!" When she gave him a puzzled look in response, he struggled to his feet and hobbled to where the quilt lay. He picked it up and carried it back. "It's ruined."

For a moment she seemed confused until it dawned on her what he was holding. "Oh!" she said with distress; then she seemed to regret her response and made an attempt to mask her emotion. "Don't worry about that now, Reverend. You and the Copelands are safe. That's what's important."

He looked at her as if she were uttering gibberish. The scorched quilt in his hands had been the nicest gift he'd ever received. "Freely given . . ." he mumbled.

"It will be okay, Reverend," she said, patting his shoulder. "Honestly, it will. Now, don't move. I'll be right back."

Watching her walk away, he envied her confidence. He wished he could believe her.

Twenty-Four

Ellie was worried about Reverend Locklin. She supposed he had a right to be distressed. His only home had burned down around him along with all his worldly possessions. Funny that he had salvaged that quilt out of everything.

But beyond the physical losses and his injuries, something else seemed to be eating at him. Maybe it was just shock. Perhaps he blamed himself, since the fire had started in his room.

Ellie found her father standing with a group of men watching the last embers of the fire fade to a stream of black smoke.

"It's out, then?" she asked, coming up beside him.

"Yes," her father said. "We'll put a watch on it for the next couple of hours just to make sure."

"Dad, I'm worried about Reverend Locklin. His foot is badly cut, and I think he's in a lot of pain. He's in shock and exhausted, as well. I'd say it's been a full day since he's slept."

"We've made arrangements. He will be staying with us, and the Copelands will go to the Belknaps."

Ellie knew Glennis Belknap was Mrs. Copeland's cousin.

"We ought to get him home right away," Ellie said. "I want to bandage his foot first, though."

"I'll bring the wagon around." Though Dad and Boyd had ridden their horses to the fire immediately upon hearing the fire bell, Ellie and Georgie had come later in the wagon, bringing a jug of coffee for the fire fighters.

She walked with her father to the barn, saying, "I need a moment of privacy." In a corner of the barn, she lifted her skirt and tore away the ruffle of her petticoat. She knew Maggie would laugh at her modesty, but she couldn't have lifted her dress in front of the reverend! With the torn ruffle in hand, she hurried back to where he was still sitting.

"This will have to do for a bandage," she said, "until we get you home."

"Home?"

"You will be staying with us, if you

don't mind."

"What about the Copelands?" he asked.

"They are going with the Belknaps," she explained as she wrapped the ruffle around his bloody foot. With the growing light of dawn, she could see his foot was worse than she'd thought. There was one large shard of glass protruding from it — no wonder it had pained him so! She plucked this out with her fingers but feared there might be some smaller splinters still in the cut.

"What about Mrs. Donnelly?" he asked. "You don't have room for me and her."

"Mrs. Donnelly went home. She couldn't rest, fearing Tommy might come home and not find her there. My mother went with her."

Dad drove up with the wagon. His and Reverend Locklin's horses were tied to the back.

"Can you walk, son?"

"Sure, Calvin." Reverend Locklin struggled to his feet, shrugging off helping hands and nearly collapsing with his first step. He cursed.

Ellie and her father exchanged a look but said nothing. Ellie supposed if her mother were there, she'd chide the minister for his impropriety no matter that he'd had a terrible day and had every right to forget his manners. In any case he grudgingly allowed them to help him to the wagon, where he hoisted himself, again reluctantly accepting help, into the back. Ellie climbed up next to him, and Dad got in the driver's seat. He told them as he snapped the reins that Boyd and Georgie would stay with Colby to watch the house.

"Where's Maggie?" the reverend asked.

For some reason the query disturbed Ellie. Despite how dazed he was, he had noticed Maggie's absence.

"Mama took her to the Donnellys'," Ellie said. "She reckoned if Tommy did come home, it might be good for him to find a friend there."

"He's not coming home," Reverend Locklin muttered.

"Why do you say that?"

"Huh?"

It appeared he hadn't realized he'd spoken out loud.

"What makes you think Tommy's not going home?" she asked again. "You don't think he's —"

"He's scared, that's all. No matter what happened out there, he's just scared."

"But where else would he go? He's only seventeen."

"I was only twelve."

"You were twelve when?"

"When I —" Stopping abruptly, he gave his head a shake. "He's nearly a man," he finally added. "Maybe he'll be better off."

"Without his family, his friends? All alone?" Ellie could not fathom such a thing. When she'd been away at Mrs. Dubois' Finishing School, only as far away as Portland, she'd been lonely even with fifty other girls around her every day. She'd realized then how important her family was to her and that there were no friends like old friends.

Reverend Locklin turned and gave her a strange look, the first time since she found him after the fire that there had been real clarity in his eyes. She couldn't guess what it meant, and he said nothing to illuminate it.

Dad was pulling the wagon into their yard, and Ellie chose not to question the reverend further. She didn't like the sensation that look had given her, or perhaps she'd liked it too much. It had given her a tingle, almost as much as their kiss had. It was as if he were seeing her, really seeing her for the very first time. She'd felt as though in that moment he'd seen who she really was.

With their help, Reverend Locklin hobbled into the house. Ellie bade him sit by the hearth while she went to get some things to tend to his foot.

"You take Boyd's bed," Dad said to the reverend. "He'll be over at the Copelands' for the rest of the morning. And you look like you need at least one good night's sleep. After that, we'll work out other sleeping arrangements."

"I appreciate this, Calvin," the reverend said.

"We are honored to have you." Dad went back outside to take care of the horses and wagon.

After stoking the fire in the stove and putting a kettle of water on to boil, Ellie went to Mama's medical shelf in the cupboard where she kept a supply of bandages, various salves, and herbs of her own making, along with some store-bought things — elixirs for coughs, castor oil, liniment, and stomach tonics. But Mama mostly swore by her homemade concoctions, recipes that had been passed down in her family for generations. The purchased items had for the most part been whims that she said had done little good.

Along with a roll of bandages, Ellie took down Mama's jar of salve made with balm-of-Gilead buds that she always used on more serious cuts. Mama certainly wouldn't begrudge Ellie using it on the minister now, though once when Maggie had gotten down the jar to use on a little finger cut, Mama had nearly hit the ceiling. The buds were not easily procured because they had to be harvested at a very particular time that lasted only a few days. Thus they were to be used judiciously.

When the water was hot, Ellie filled a basin, adding some cold water to make it tepid and also some lye soap. She got a washcloth, a towel, and the other supplies and returned to Reverend Locklin. The poor man had fallen asleep in his chair. She hated to disturb him, but his foot had to be tended to before it festered.

"Reverend Locklin," she murmured quietly, setting the basin on the floor. "I must soak your foot and clean it. Forgive me, please, for waking you."

"What?" he grunted, his eyes flickering open.

"I'm going to put your foot into the water. It will hurt, but it must be cleaned."

"Cleaned?" he muttered. "Can it be cleaned? It's so scorched and soiled . . . can it ever be clean again. . . . It was so nice . . . I liked your house. It was the best part. . . ."

She knew then he wasn't talking about his injured foot. He was still fretting over the quilt. She didn't know what to say, how to allay his grief over that loss. She wished she could promise that the Sewing Circle would make him another. They could, and perhaps they would, but she felt it would be wrong to make such a promise without their consent.

Not knowing quite how to respond, she concentrated on his injury instead. Carefully she removed the petticoat ruffle, then lifted his foot and gently lowered it into the soapy water.

"Yow!" he bellowed, kicking up his foot and splattering water everywhere, only barely missing kicking Ellie in the face.

"Oh, I am so sorry!" she exclaimed. Mama never had this kind of response when she tried to nurse their wounds. Regretfully, Ellie realized she should have made sure he was fully awake before she started.

"What do you think you're doing?" he railed.

"I was just . . . I wanted to —"

But at that moment he let his foot drop to the floor with more force than it could take, and he cried out again, this time with curses.

Ellie's face turned red.

"What's going on in there?" Dad said, coming back into the house.

"I'm afraid I'm not a very good nurse,"

Ellie said in a shaky voice. She was close to tears. She had so wanted to offer comfort and solace to the distraught minister but was only making matters worse.

"No!" Reverend Locklin cut in quickly. "You're doing fine. I . . . I just forgot myself."

"I know you're having a hard time, William," Dad said, "but I do ask that you have a care with your speech. My daughter is of a delicate nature, you know."

"I am so sorry. Please forgive me!" The reverend was definitely awake now.

"Of course," Ellie said. In a steadier voice, she added, "Why don't we try this again? It will burn a little, I'm afraid."

Wryly, Reverend Locklin said, "I already found that out, didn't I?" He offered a smile with his words to allay her distress.

Then, to further display his cooperation he dipped his foot into the basin without any guidance from her. The soap surely burned terribly in the deep cuts, but he made not another sound. She washed away the dried blood and the dirt that had crusted on the wounds when he had been barefoot immediately after the fire started. Glancing up at him once, she saw his eyes were closed, his teeth clenched.

"I hope there's no more glass in there,"

she said. As gingerly as she could, she probed the cut with her fingers just to make sure at least large pieces of glass were gone.

"You know, it actually feels better," he said.

"You are just being brave."

"I'm hardly that, as you could tell before."

"You were taken by surprise."

They were quiet while she tenderly washed his foot. In the kitchen she heard her father rattle about.

"Found some fresh eggs in the hen house," he said. "Anyone else hungry?"

"I'm starved," Ellie said.

"I can't decide if I'm tired or hungry," the reverend said.

"Well, I say you should have a good meal and then sleep for two days," suggested Dad.

"I think I could do just that —" He stopped suddenly and frowned.

Ellie thought she'd pressed too hard on his foot and stopped.

"I forgot — today is Sunday."

"No one will expect you at church today," Dad said.

"This has been hard for everyone," Reverend Locklin said. "Maybe they'll need to get together. Maybe . . . well, maybe I do, too . . ."

"No one was planning on church," Dad said. "But . . . I guess we can get the word out if you truly want to meet. I'll fetch Georgie. He'd love to be useful by rounding up the folks."

"I'll finish fixing breakfast," offered Ellie, "while you go after Georgie. It'll be ready when you return."

Dad appeared relieved to hear that. Ellie knew he would have been willing to pitch in and help in the kitchen since Mama was gone, but he had very little expertise in cooking. Ellie couldn't remember the last time she saw her father cook. It must have been when Georgie was born. He did wrap a loaf of bread from yesterday and a hunk of cheese in a napkin to take to the boys watching the Copeland house.

A few minutes after her father left, Ellie lifted her hands from the basin and, drying them on the towel, said, "I've done as much as I can for now, but it would be good to soak a bit longer. I'll get it bandaged once I get breakfast going."

Ellie sliced up some salt pork and set it in a skillet on the stove. When it was sizzling nicely, she put in some sliced potatoes. Once as she worked she glanced toward the reverend and found him staring at her. She smiled and he smiled back but did not take his eyes off her. That made her self-conscious, but she was competent in the kitchen, so it didn't hurt her performance at all. Finally, when the potatoes were cooking, she returned to her "patient."

"Let's get you bandaged up, shall we?"

He lifted his foot from the water, and she dried it with the towel. As she did so, she carefully examined it. She saw no more bits of glass and hoped that since it had bled quite a lot, it had washed itself out. The foot was swollen, and the cut on the bottom of the arch was deep and quite red around the edges. She smoothed the balm-of-Gilead salve over the cut and then wrapped it with the new bandage.

"How'd you get so good at everything you do?" he asked.

"I guess my mother is a good teacher, and I enjoy this sort of thing — cooking and taking care of people."

"You'll be a fine wife and mother one day."

Though her cheeks surely grew nearly as red as Reverend Locklin's foot, she said sincerely, "I hope so. I can't think of anything I'd rather do."

"I enjoyed watching you. It's been a long time since I've witnessed such a domestic scene."

"You haven't spent much time at your

parents' home, then?"

Hesitating a moment, he shrugged and went on. "I ran away from home when I was twelve. My mother was okay, but my step-father —" He shook his head. "Well, I don't have to think of him anymore."

"You haven't seen your mother since you were twelve?" Ellie asked, unable to hide her incredulity at such a thing.

"She chose her husband over me, so what was the use?" His tone was bitter.

"You've never forgiven them?"

"That would be the Christian thing to do, wouldn't it?"

She thought that an odd thing for him to say. Then she smelled the potatoes and knew they needed tending before they burned. She wanted to return to their conversation, but just then Dad came home and the eggs had to be scrambled, and there wasn't another opportunity. Since the reverend would be staying with them for a while, she determined to learn more about him.

After breakfast Reverend Locklin went up to the boys' room to take a nap before the church service. When Dad went up an hour later to let him know it was time to get ready to go to church, the reverend was asleep so soundly he didn't budge when Dad called.

Dad said he didn't have the heart to wake him.

Ellie and her father went to the schoolhouse by themselves, and she was glad they did because nearly everyone in Maintown was there. Apparently Reverend Locklin had been right about the need of the community to gather together in the face of two tragedies. Though few people liked Tom, the idea of one of their own being shot to death in their own backyard, so to speak, was unnerving. Then on the heels of this to have their beloved friends, the Copelands, who were among the original settlers of Maintown, lose everything in a fire was beyond shocking.

Jane Donnelly and Mama were among the few absent, but Mama had sent Maggie with messages.

Getting Dad and Ellie alone before the service began, Maggie reported, "Mrs. Donnelly is acting real strange. She refuses to leave the house for fear that she might miss Tommy, and Mama is afraid to leave her alone. Mrs. Stoddard is going to organize the Sewing Circle to take shifts staying with Mrs. Donnelly until things settle down." To Dad she added, "Mama says you have to get a funeral for Tom organized as soon as possible 'cause there's an inordinate amount of flies infesting the Donnelly barn, and it's been pretty warm lately."

"In all the excitement I nearly forgot. Leave it to your mother to be practical," he said.

As chairman of the deacons, it fell to Dad to lead the service. He got the business out of the way first, announcing there would be a service for Tom Donnelly tomorrow morning. He requested volunteers to help with the grave digging after today's church service. Usually such labors on Sunday were frowned upon, but all saw the expediency in this case.

With that out of the way, Mrs. Renolds led the group in a few hymns, after which Dad suggested they have an old-fashioned prayer meeting. Again, there was no argument. Everyone seemed to feel the need for prayer, especially in light of recent events, and offered a prayer as they felt led. They prayed for the Donnellys, especially for Jane, whom everyone loved. They prayed for the Copelands, who lost their home, and for the reverend, who had lost his home, too, and been injured, as well. They prayed for other needs in the community: for Mrs. Cook who was failing quickly from her illness; for Albert Stoddard, who was in bed at that very moment from exhaustion after fighting the fire. He'd been ill for some time and as a result had several months ago given up his position as chair of the deacons.

Besides praying for all their needs, the folks also used the prayer time to praise God for their many blessings, of which the tragedies had made them more deeply aware.

Ellie had never felt such a strong bond with her friends and neighbors as she did now. And before she realized it, she was praying out loud, something she seldom had the nerve to do in such a large group.

"Dear Lord, I want to thank you, too, for our pastor you so graciously sent to us. Somehow, no doubt through your wisdom, he knew we all needed this time in church today and made this gathering happen. And though he wanted more than any of us to be here, in the end he was too ill and tired to attend himself. I know he is here in spirit. Bless him now with peaceful rest and heal his injured foot."

She was a little shaky when she finished, but she felt good. The people of Maintown would not soon forget these last two days, and the thing they would remember most was the closeness they all felt in this moment.

TWENTY-FIVE

The last thing on earth Zack wanted to do was officiate at Tom Donnelly's funeral. But he felt he owed it to the town and to Jane, as well, because he could not shake his personal sense of responsibility in Tom's death. Just as everyone had assured him that the fight had been unavoidable, they now assured him he had no blame in the man's death. But he knew what Tommy had told Maggie and thus knew the truth of the matter.

The graveyard sat on a hill just east of the center of Maintown, conveniently adjacent to the property where the new church would be built. Thinking of the new church made Zack realize that among the losses from the fire was that money the board of deacons had given him to deposit in the bank. He'd worry about that later, however. Now he had to put Tom to rest, if that was possible.

Ada had been successful in coaxing Jane

Donnelly from her house for the service. The woman, whom Zack had thought attractive and younger looking than her age when he first met her, now looked haggard and old. Grief bore heavily upon her. Could she have so loved her meanspirited husband? Or was the grief for her missing son?

Having lost all his books in the fire, Zack was forced to improvise the service. But he still remembered what he had memorized for the last Deer Island funeral, so he used that.

There were about thirty folks in attendance. Zack noted that all the ladies of the Sewing Circle were there, most of their husbands, and a few others. He thought the turnout was more likely to support Jane rather than to honor her husband.

"I didn't know Tom Donnelly well," Zack began, noting as he spoke a quiet stir among some of the folks. No doubt they were thinking his fists knew Tom well enough. He went on with the words he'd delivered in Deer Island. "But God knew Tom and loved him, and so we must find comfort in that." There was something else in that service about the deceased going to a better place, but Zack knew he couldn't say that with a straight face where Tom was concerned. Instead, he decided he'd better just cut it short. Mrs. Donnelly didn't look as though she could stand for much more anyway.

He concluded by quoting a Scripture he'd memorized for that earlier funeral, " 'God is our refuge and strength, a very present help in trouble . . .' " Zack paused, because as he spoke, the words echoed in his head in such a way that for the first time he really heard them. Maybe it was because this sleepy little village was experiencing some serious troubles and they were demonstrating how very true those words were. Ellie had told him about the prayer meeting yesterday. She had praised him for making it happen and said that because of it the people had found God's comfort. He wished he'd been there but then reminded himself that he did not deserve God's comfort. God did not comfort fake ministers.

Yet still he envied these people.

"Reverend?" came Calvin's quiet voice.

Zack realized he'd been quiet for much too long. He continued with the recital of the Scripture, trying hard not to hear it but failing as the words reverberated in his own ears. " 'God is our refuge and strength, a very present help in trouble. Therefore will not we fear, though the earth be removed, and though the mountains be carried into the midst of the sea; though the waters thereof roar and be troubled, though the mountains shake with the swelling thereof.' "

Two months ago those words had been a rote blur of *thereof*s and *therefore*s. Now they made uncanny sense.

Somehow Zack managed to get through the rest of the service. He tried to speak words of comfort to Mrs. Donnelly afterward, but he knew his words were empty, hollow. Fortunately, she was anxious to leave, so he was spared further contact. Ada took her home, and everyone else dispersed. Usually after a funeral there would be a gathering in the bereaved one's home, but there hadn't been the time or the heart to prepare something.

Zack rode back to the Newcomb house, unable to get those words from his mind. "God is our refuge . . ." It was probably because he had just lost his home, or refuge, so to speak. Yet deep down he knew that wasn't entirely the case. Until coming to Maintown he could barely recall ever having a refuge. The last time had been when he was eight. That's when his father had died. Leon Hartley had been out in a blizzard trying to round up some cows that had gotten loose. He had caught cold and developed a lung infection. Within a week he was dead. Zack barely remembered his father. The little he knew was that he was a quiet man who worked hard. He usually left to go work in the fields before Zack woke up. Then more often than not, Zack was asleep before his father came home. He remembered, too, that because they were so poor, his father was gone a lot working for hire on other farms, often far away. Zack had no picture in his mind of what his father looked like, though his mother often said Zack favored him greatly.

Within six months of his father's death, his mother, out of desperation, married the first man to come along — the stepfather. There was no refuge for Zack after that. The stepfather's children came first. There were three of them — an older boy and girl, and a boy a year younger than Zack. They got served first at the table, and Zack got what was left, usually a few scraps. They got the new clothes; Zack got the hand-me-downs. When they did something bad, Zack got blamed, and he got the whipping. His mother never interceded because she so feared being left alone. By the time he was nine, he tried to run away but was dragged back. He ran away at ten and was dragged back again. By then he realized he was too young and needed to wait until he was older and smarter or until he could stand it no longer, which happened to be when he turned twelve. They didn't catch him that time. They didn't drag him back. His stepfather probably thought Zack was finally old enough to make it on his own and didn't even bother looking for him. Zack would never know. He didn't look back — ever.

Then followed twelve years of moving from place to place to place. Always moving. No wonder he was growing attached to Maintown. He'd already been here two months, longer than any place since San Francisco, and he'd been there only a few weeks, during which time he had not let himself get attached. He'd made no lasting friendships.

He had no idea why it was different here in Maintown. Maybe if he had come as Zack Hartley, he would have remained as detached as always, but something had happened to him when he had slipped into William Locklin's skin. Pretending to be the minister had somehow forced him to let down his guard.

Regardless of how it had happened, he knew this place had become more of a refuge than any other place he'd been in his life. That's why he was still here when he should have run long ago, like when Mrs. Briggs had first approached him about the wedding, or when he'd beat up Tom Donnelly, or when he'd kissed two innocent sisters. It was stupid and foolish and dangerous to stay. He should run. He'd already hurt the Donnellys, and he knew he would hurt the Newcombs before he was through. Yet . . .

Riding into the Newcomb yard after the funeral gave him such an odd feeling of belonging that turning away from it would be like stepping from light into darkness again. And he had not the will for it just then.

The next few days were doubtless the best Zack had ever experienced. He was made to feel a part of the Newcomb family. With Boyd gone back to work at the lumber camp, Zack shared the boys' room with Georgie, just like an older brother. But his favorite time was sitting around the table with the family for meals. There was always the buzz of congenial conversation. Zack remembered mealtimes at his home as a child — they had been silent, grim. His stepfather began the meal saying grace, a long, solemn prayer that Zack closed out of his mind by thinking of other things. The children were not permitted to speak unless spoken to, but the adults were not much interested in their children's lives, so they seldom addressed them. Likewise, Zack's mother and stepfather appeared little interested in each other, seldom speaking.

The Newcombs had much to say to one another, inconsequential stuff for the most part, but even Georgie's adventure tales of catching a big fish or winning a game of marbles on the playground were listened to raptly. The women talked as much as the men and were taken seriously. Calvin may have been bored listening to Ada talk about a new quilt pattern she'd found in the latest *Godey's,* but he never showed it.

When Zack had first arrived in Maintown, his initial impression of the Newcomb family was that Ada "ruled the roost." But he saw now that Calvin, in a quiet way, was clearly the head of the family. The man just didn't seem to feel that he had to lord it over his clan in order to prove himself.

Only one thing marred this pleasant time. Zack was frequently plagued with pangs of conscience. He couldn't count how many times he was on the verge of telling Calvin the truth about himself, but he never found the nerve to do it. He knew that he feared not punishment for his crime but rather Calvin's disappointment in him.

So when that small voice said, "Confess," a stronger voice said, "No!"

Because of his foot, which was swollen and sore for a few days, he was not expected to work at the mill, to ride his circuit, or to make visitations. He spent all day at the Newcombs' trying to help around the farm as much as possible, but Ada would scold him every time he did something she considered to be too much. She let him carry laundry or churn butter or do other household tasks, which, of course, put him in close contact with Ellie and Maggie. He shouldn't have been as pleased about this as he was, and he didn't want to enjoy them as much as he did, each for a different reason.

One afternoon Zack was particularly restless. Ada and Maggie had gone to bring some food to Mrs. Donnelly. And Georgie, with school now out for summer break, had gone with his mother to help with chores at the Donnellys'. Calvin was working at the mill. Ellie had gone out to work in the garden. Zack thought it a bit odd that no one feared leaving him alone with Ellie. The town's burning desire to marry off the minister had faded a bit, no doubt dimmed by recent events. And he thought Ada was probably starting to think of him more as a member of the family than as a marriage candidate for her daughter.

Zack had been instructed to elevate his foot for an hour because it was starting to fester and swell again. But after a half hour he simply could not stand the solitude another moment. His thoughts had returned to the funeral and the unsettling feeling that Scripture had given him. He put on his boots — a larger pair had been found for him — and hobbled outside, using a cane that had belonged to Ada's father.

Zack wasn't surprised that his aimless wandering ended up at the garden. He stood quietly and watched Ellie before she noticed him. She was kneeling in the dirt, canvas gloves on her hands, straw bonnet on her head, wearing a green calico dress. She was plucking weeds around the vines of green beans that stood nearly two feet tall on the stakes they were tied to. He could tell she was deep in thought and had not heard him approach. He didn't want to disturb her, nor did he want to interrupt watching her while she was relaxed, absorbed in her work, and obviously enjoying herself. When she knew he was around, she always became guarded and awkward.

When he shifted his weight to take some pressure off his injured foot, he snapped a twig, and she looked up.

"Hi," he said and limped closer.

"Hi, Reverend," she said. "I wish the plants grew as well as the weeds." With her gloved hand she wiped away a trickle of sweat from her brow.

"The plants are looking quite good," he replied. "At least the corn was knee-high by the Fourth of July."

"Yes, it is looking quite good."

He went over to the garden wall, but before settling down he asked, "Do you mind if I rest for a few minutes?"

"I'm ready for a rest, too." She rose lithely and, taking off her gloves, came to the wall. "Can I join you?"

"I was hoping you would. I'm getting what sailors call 'cabin fever.' "

"But you can't let your foot dangle like that. Just a minute . . ." She jumped up and fetched the bushel she'd been tossing weeds into, dumped it out, and carried it back. "This should do." She overturned the bushel and put his foot up on it for him.

"I can't believe such a small cut is causing so much trouble," he said.

"It wasn't small," she replied. "Mama thinks there may still be glass in it. She thinks if it doesn't get better in a few days we should take you to the doctor in St.

Helens. He may have to put in a stitch or two."

"I have never been to a doctor in my life."

"Well, let's not worry about that until the time comes." She paused before adding, "It must be hard to be idle. I imagine you are worried about your circuit."

He didn't know how to respond to that. The fact was he had considered playing up his injury just to have an excuse to get out of the circuit. Without the wise Dr. Markus, Zack was going to be pretty lost in the pulpit. But he waited too long to reply.

"Is something wrong, Reverend?" she asked.

"I suppose after all that has happened, I don't feel competent to mount a pulpit —"

"What?"

"I have questions."

"You mean, like a crisis of faith?"

"Yes, that's it." Even as he realized this was the perfect answer to his sermon problem, he also realized these words were true in another way. They were probably the truest words he had spoken since coming to Maintown.

"I suppose it doesn't help having everyone telling you that none of this is your fault."

"I know you mean well, but it doesn't help. Why would God let these things happen? You are all good people. You don't deserve any of this. I have never met finer folks than the Copelands, yet they have lost everything."

"Things happen. It is life — not your fault, not God's fault, either, Reverend."

"Would you not call me that!" he said more sharply than he'd intended. The title had begun to sting him a little more sharply every time it was used.

"We've been over this, Rev — well, we have discussed this before."

"Is there nothing else you can call me?" he implored. "I know. Call me Zack," he added impulsively.

"What are you talking about?"

"Call me Zack or Zacchaeus."

"Why that?" she asked with a dubious chuckle.

"I always liked that name."

"I like it, too." Then she went on in a singsong tone, "Zacchaeus was a wee little man, a wee little man was he. He climbed up into a sycamore tree, for the Lord he wanted to see. . . ." She trailed away, a little embarrassed.

"I didn't know there was a song." He'd had no idea that his odd given name belonged to anyone except his grandfather. He'd hated the name Zacchaeus and had shortened it to Zack even before he had left home.

"It's just a song I learned when I was young. Mama would tell us the story from the Bible, and we sang the song."

"It's from the Bible?"

"Of course. You know, the story of the man who couldn't see Jesus over the crowds, so he climbed the tree . . . you remember?"

"Ellie, pretend for a minute that I'm not a minister and that I don't know a thing about the Bible," Zack said, feeling suddenly reckless. Maybe it was like a thief returning to the scene of the crime because down deep he wanted to be caught. "I want to hear it as if for the first time. Tell me the story."

Appearing bemused by the odd turn of the conversation, she went on, "Well, Zacchaeus was a short man, and he couldn't see Jesus because of the large crowd of people. So he climbed up into a tree. When Jesus walked by, he looked up at him and told him to come down, for he was going to Zacchaeus's house today. This surprised everyone because Zacchaeus was a publican —"

"A publican?" he asked.

"You know —" When he gave her a censorious look, she finished without further question. "He was a tax collector, not a popular person back then and regarded by all as a sinner."

"Then what happened?"

"Zacchaeus was thrilled to have Jesus in his home. His heart was touched and he repented of his evil ways, giving half of his wealth to the poor and restoring to those he had cheated in his taxing. And Jesus forgave him."

"Just like that, Jesus forgave this man who was obviously a lowlife type?"

"Of course, Reverend. That's what God's love is all about, isn't it? I'm not certain of the exact reference, but I know it says in the Bible that Christ came not to call the righteous but to call sinners to repentance. But, Reverend, you know all this."

There was distress in her tone. It would be quite vexing to someone like her if her minister fell from faith. He winced inwardly as she used *Reverend* again, though seeing her distress he didn't have the heart to correct her. Suddenly he had never appreciated his own name more and longed to hear it from the lips of others. Even Zacchaeus would have been preferred over that title of Reverend or the name stolen from a dead man.

"Yes, of course," he lied. "But even a minister needs to be reminded of these things now and again."

She took his hand in hers and turned her gaze so that he had no choice but to look into her eyes. After only a moment he was desperate to look away. He could not bear that look of caring and genuine tenderness. Yet at the same time he was so mesmerized by the depth of those blue eyes that he felt glued in place.

Then she said, "I would pray with you . . . William."

Hearing her say that name sickened him. It was worse than when she called him Reverend, because she was now doing it to please him, despite that it made her uncomfortable.

A voice in his mind cried, *Run! Run! Run!*

But he didn't run. He wasn't sure his legs would have carried him anyway. He sat there and let her pray, trying with what will he had left to shut out her sweet petition to God.

TWENTY-SIX

Shortly after Tom's funeral the sheriff came to Maintown. He was not alone. The Methodist circuit minister, Joshua Barnett, accompanied him. While the sheriff went to the mill to speak with Calvin, the minister stayed at the house to visit with Zack, who began to feel like Daniel in the lions' den, a Bible story he did happen to know.

Ada served them tea in the parlor, and Zack tried to get her and the girls to remain, but Ada declined.

"I'm sure you men would like some time to yourselves to talk about your work." She and the girls left him alone with the minister.

Barnett had some books that he handed to Zack. "I heard about the fire and thought you might like some reference books to replace yours. I can spare these as long as you need them, my boy." Barnett was a good twenty years older than Zack. He was tall and hefty but appeared fit, for the rigors of riding a circuit could not help but keep a man's physique sound. His head was balding, and the hair that remained rimmed a large bald spot like a monk's tonsure. It was black, streaked liberally with gray. He wore wire-rimmed glasses over pleasant blue eyes and generally seemed a good-natured sort.

"Thank you very much," Zack said, taking the books and seeing with a quick perusal that none were books of sermons. Maybe they would offer him some help anyway.

"I have been wanting to meet you, Reverend Locklin," Barnett said. "But you know how our work keeps us busy. I'm sorry it was this tragedy that finally got me to be neighborly."

"I understand completely," Zack replied. "I, too, have wanted to meet you and the other pastors. But, alas, time does get away from us."

"How are you holding up, my boy? Many an older, more experienced man would be hard-pressed to find the inner resources to deal with such difficult events."

"Well . . . ah . . . trusting God helps." For some odd reason, when Zack had first come here, spouting religious verbiage had come more easily than it did lately. Now, when such words should flow after much usage, they had begun to stick in his throat. Today, however, he would have to put on his best performance, for if anyone was going to see through his ruse, it surely would be a man of God.

"Well, Reverend Locklin, you must feel free to come to me if you need assistance."

"That is kind of you, but you know what the Bible says — God helps those who help themselves."

Barnett smiled quickly; then that was replaced by a perplexed expression. Zack feared he had somehow offended the man.

Finally Barnett said, "Many use that reference, but it is not truly in the Bible, of course."

Zack grimaced. He was in trouble now. Surely the man didn't expect him to have read and studied every word in the Bible. Zack decided to be frank. "I didn't know that."

"A common mistake of lay folk."

Zack waited for the man to point an accusing finger. Instead he went on in a patient tone.

"I am afraid I part with the commonly held notions about self-reliance. The Bible does say, 'My grace is sufficient for thee, for my strength is made perfect in weakness.' "

Zack braced himself for what he'd feared most — a theological debate with a real man of God. Hoping to nip this in the bud, he nodded and said dismissively, "Yes, of course, Pastor." Then he quickly added, "In any case, my losses were the least of any here, Reverend Barnett, but I do appreciate your offer."

"May I change the subject, then?"

"Of course." Zack swallowed. Now what? he thought, unable to feel any sense of reprieve.

"I must ask you about Robert Markus."

Zack nearly dropped Ada's fine teacup. Was that man going to ever haunt him?

"Ah, dear Pastor Markus," Zack said, trying to mask his apprehension.

"You knew him well, then?" asked Barnett.

That little *Run! Run! Run!* alarm began sounding in Zack's mind. The minister's seemingly innocent question had the sound of a trap.

"I served in his church in Boston for a time," Zack responded as evasively as he could.

"I had the honor of attending one of his tent meetings," Barnett said, "in his younger days, before he went to Boston. You must know, of course, that he started out a Methodist."

"Of course." Zack paused, waiting for the trap to snap shut on him. But it didn't. Barnett just nodded in response.

Zack relaxed a little. He'd passed the hardest test of all with flying colors. But he didn't let down his guard, especially when Ada invited Barnett to stay for lunch. There were only a few more difficult patches during the meal, but Ada saved him when she asked about folks she knew in Barnett's church and got the conversation turned to news and gossip about locals. Barnett had to leave right after the midday meal because he had an evening service in St. Helens. Before going, he suggested that the local denominations get together later in the summer for a camp meeting. Zack heartily approved of the idea and offered his help in the planning, knowing that he'd be gone before it ever happened. Probably.

Maggie was nervous the entire time the sheriff was there and continued to worry even after he went to find Dad. Oddly, William seemed every bit as nervous as she was, though she had a feeling it had more to do with Reverend Barnett's visit than the sheriff's. He had turned white when the man had introduced himself as a fellow minister. She wondered about that as she did her chores that afternoon but didn't know what to make of it. She was more worried about her own problems.

Though the sheriff showed absolutely no interest at all in Maggie, she was in a cold sweat the entire time he remained at the house. She was certain if her parents knew she was withholding important information, they would be upset. She felt like a liar, though she had said nothing at all. Twice she almost blurted out what she knew to the sheriff but then thought of poor Tommy and how it could ruin his life. That sealed her silence. She prayed Tommy was long gone, then hoped it was okay to pray such a prayer if Tommy had indeed shot his father.

At supper Dad talked about the sheriff's visit. He'd taken off work at the mill in order to show the sheriff the place where they'd found Tom's body. He also went with the man to question Mrs. Donnelly. None of this investigating had yielded anything new. The sheriff drew the obvious conclusion: Tommy had shot his father, probably accidentally, and had run away out of fear. The sheriff would send out a bulletin to other constables in the county to be on the lookout for Tommy and to take him into custody for questioning if they found him. No one was anxious to accuse a seventeen-year-old boy of murder.

Maggie should have been comforted that it appeared the matter would simply fade away. But still she could not sleep that night or the next, haunted by terrible dreams when she did manage to nod off for brief moments. No wonder she was cranky and out of sorts the next couple of days. No wonder she reacted as she did when she looked out the kitchen window and saw William talking to Ellie in the garden.

She had seen the two of them together an awful lot since he had come to stay with them. What was going on? Had Ellie changed her mind yet again about William? And Mama seemed to be conspiring in their favor. She was letting Ellie shirk her chores while piling more and more work on Maggie.

If that wasn't enough, Mama constantly sent Maggie up to Mrs. Donnelly's house with food or merely to check on the woman. Most of the time there was someone from the Sewing Circle there to keep the grieving widow company and take care of the household chores, but Mama wanted Maggie to help with the outdoor chores — feeding the chickens, milking the cows, weeding the garden, things that Jane or Tommy would have normally done. Jane wasn't doing any chores now. She merely sat in a rocking chair with sewing in her hands, never putting a single stitch into it. Sometimes the ladies would get her to talk for a bit, but usually after a few words she'd lapse into silence and stare into space.

Mama said Maggie's presence might be a comfort to the woman because she'd been Tommy's only friend. But Maggie feared the time would come when it might occur to Mrs. Donnelly to ask her what she and her son had talked about. Maggie didn't know if she'd be able to lie to Mrs. Donnelly, even though she thought the woman would be better off not knowing.

All this weighed on Maggie, and she knew it was petty to be thinking of romance at a time like this when people were suffering serious hurts. But she couldn't help it. She felt terribly put upon. Whether on purpose or not, Mama was favoring Ellie, just because she was older and more of a lady. Ellie could just as easily feed the Donnelly chickens, though, of course, she didn't even feed the Newcomb chickens these days. The only outside task she did was the gardening, and that was because she liked it. She did the sewing, the mending, the cooking, and the housecleaning.

Maggie hated those chores, but she knew very well no one cared about that. If Mama thought she was old enough to marry, she might take Maggie's training in these matters more seriously. Maggie had forgotten her frequent declarations that she wasn't about to marry for many years. She forgot that until recently she used to jump at the chance to clean the hen house rather than cook or sew.

What was happening to her?

She only knew that as she watched William and Ellie laugh together, it set her teeth on edge.

"Maggie, aren't those potatoes done yet?" Mama asked.

Suddenly Maggie realized she was helping cook supper, a job she'd just told herself that only Ellie did. Well, of course I have to peel potatoes! Who else is going to do it if Queen Ellie is off wooing Prince Charming?

She gritted her teeth during supper but nearly lost all control of her temper when she thought she saw Ellie and William exchange a covert glance, like sweethearts with a secret. William had kissed Maggie. Did it mean nothing to him? Did he take her no more seriously than anyone else?

Everyone would see her much differently if she was married. She now knew it had been foolish of her to think she ought to wait. Only married women, or those who were close to marrying like Ellie, were of any consequence.

She decided that after supper she would approach William and get the truth from him. Was he courting Ellie or not? But while Mama was serving cake, Elisha Cook came to the house asking for William. Mrs. Cook didn't have long to live and could the reverend come pray over her? Mama didn't think it would be good for William's foot to ride so far, but the reverend did not even hesitate. He left immediately.

Maggie had another sleepless night.

The next morning Mama and Ellie were busy setting up the quilt frame in the front yard. The Sewing Circle was coming to meet at the house. Mama hoped it would get Mrs. Donnelly out of her house for a time and get everyone back to some comfortable normal activities.

Maggie saw William stride out the kitchen door, so she hurried after him. He'd come in late last night, long after she'd gone to bed, though she had been awake and had heard his footsteps as he climbed the steps and strode down the hall, still with a slight limp, to Georgie's room. She'd thought about catching him then, but there was too much risk of waking Ellie or the others. In any case, if he was now headed back to the Cooks' or on some other errand, she could not bear to wait another day before talking to him. Besides, she had put on a dress in preparation.

He was indeed heading toward the barn. She jogged toward him, then slowed to a more sedate pace when she was near.

"Are you planning to go out today?" she asked.

"Yes, I was."

"Are you sure you ought to? Mama didn't think you should be riding."

"I had no problem riding out to the Cooks'," he said. "My foot is much improved."

She thought he was a bit defensive, but perhaps he had a right to be, since it did sound as if she was interrogating him.

Changing her tone, she said, "I — we're all worried about you, William."

"I know." He smiled.

It gave her courage to go on. "William, before you go, can we talk a moment?"

"Of course, Maggie."

"Not here," she said, taking his hand and

leading him behind the barn where they would be hidden from the view of Mama and Ellie, who were still working in the front yard and had been joined by a few of the Sewing Circle women.

The rock wall that backed the garden extended several feet behind the barn as a retaining wall. Maggie's heart began thudding as she and William sat down on the wall. She hardly noticed the wild scent of the broom growing profusely among the grass like a yellow sea on the hillside. A bumble bee, looking for flower nectar, buzzed around their heads for a few moments, reminding Maggie that it was a lovely summer morning and one day she would look back on this as a very special day.

"So, Maggie, what's on your mind?" William asked. "Are you still worried about the sheriff?"

"I think I am safe for the time being," she said. She didn't want to just blurt out what was on her mind. "How is Mrs. Cook?"

"She doesn't have long. But she seems ready to meet her Maker."

"You must have stayed with her a long time. It was late when you came in."

"You were awake?"

"I haven't slept well lately." She sighed.

"My mind has been in great turmoil, over Tommy and . . . well, over you, William, as well."

"Over me?"

"Having you here in our home these last few days has been special."

"I've seen so little of you."

"Mama keeps sending me to Mrs. Donnelly's, but she can't keep us apart forever." Maggie's heart was pounding like a hammer in her chest.

"Us?"

"William, I think it is time we made public our feelings for each other." There. It was said, and she thought she'd done it very maturely.

Why did he look like he had just swallowed that bumble bee?

"Maggie . . . Maggie . . . I . . ." He blinked a few times, opened his mouth but uttered nothing else.

"You're hesitant, I know," she soothed, "because of your secrets. But they don't matter to me. I . . . ah . . . love you, William." She ignored how difficult it had been to get the word *love* out of her mouth.

"You love me?" he rasped. Then he blinked and added, "Secrets? What secrets?"

"They have all burned up in the fire, and it's just as well," she said. "I don't care why you hid your preaching license or the church building money. Or why you have a photo of the family of someone else named William."

"You . . . searched my room?" He seemed to be having trouble breathing.

"Accidentally, when I went to get some of your clothes for Mama to alter." Now she was feeling defensive. Maybe it had been a mistake to mention the things she'd found in his room.

"Maggie, how could you?"

"I said I don't care about any of it. I have secrets, too. You and I — we share secrets." She nodded encouragingly.

"What are you saying?"

"It's just that . . ." Why was this so hard? It was what she wanted. "I think it means that we belong with each other. William, I want us to get married!"

Jumping up, he stared incredulously at her. Finally, chuckling nervously, he said, "Oh, you almost had me! Maggie, you are quite the jester! Ha, ha!"

He may as well have lit a match to a fuse. "Why, you — you miserable rat!" she railed. "You low-down dirty — snake! You deceived me, you —"

"Maggie, hush! Your mother will hear!" he looked frantically around.

"My mother! Ha!" She gave a derisive snort. "She'd just think it was a joke, too. That's what I am to you all — just a joke! Did you laugh hard after you kissed me, William? Was that a joke, too? Is your name even William? Is it Zack, or Zacchaeus? Oh yes, Ellie told me all about that! Who are you — ?" She stopped abruptly as she saw a stark look of panic on William's face. "You do have a secret, don't you? Who are you, William?"

"Maggie, stop while you are ahead," he said rather desperately.

She grasped his arm, suddenly hating herself for her outburst. "I'm sorry, William. What I said before is true. I don't care about your secrets."

"You should care," he murmured. Then, with a shake of his head, added, "I have to go."

"We can still be married," she pleaded. "We can keep each other's secrets."

"Don't ever beg for a man's affections," he said with a hard edge to his tone. "You are better than that . . . better than me. Don't forget that."

He turned and walked away.

She wanted to run after him, but tears began to spill from her eyes and she didn't want her mother or Ellie to see her cry and start asking questions. And why should she go after him anyway? He had just rejected her. She was doomed to always being thought of as a child.

TWENTY-SEVEN

Why should he be surprised by any of this? Zack had pushed this insane scheme further and harder than it could possibly have stood. He'd known someone was going to get hurt, yet still he had pushed.

Now there was no question about what he must do. He strode as quickly as his sore foot allowed to the front of the barn, all the while waiting to hear Maggie's footsteps running after him, her voice calling his name. But another voice, feared no less, reached his ears.

"Reverend Locklin!"

It was Ada's voice.

"Come see what we're doing."

He knew he must leave this place — not only the Newcomb house but Maintown, too — yet he had to do so in the least conspicuous way possible. Ignoring his hostess and riding off right before her eyes was sure to raise questions. So he turned from his goal of the barn and walked to where a half dozen ladies were gathered around the frame that Ada and Ellie, after refusing his offer of help, had carried outside earlier. On the frame was spread a quilt. He knew that's what they must want him to see, so he perused it carefully. It was made of red cloth and a white material Zack thought was probably muslin. Unlike the welcome quilt, this was of a single uniform design. Light and dark tones combined with squares and diamond shapes to form a pattern that was almost three-dimensional, while at the same time there was a central star shape that seemed to be spinning.

"It's a very nice quilt," he said.

"Mary Renolds made it," Ada said.

"I made it several years ago and tucked the top away in my cedar chest," Mary explained. "I suppose I was waiting for just the right moment for it to be quilted and passed on to the right person." She smiled. "When I told Ada and Emma Jean I had a quilt of this pattern in my chest that only needed to be quilted, we laughed, and though in a way it is silly, it is also rather perfect, too. Don't you think?"

Zack had no idea what she was talking about and was fast losing patience. He didn't have time to solve riddles. Maggie might chose any moment to appear and accuse him of any number of indiscretions.

"He doesn't know what you are talking about," Emma Jean said. "And who could expect him to with such a ramble? Reverend, the pattern of this quilt is called Bachelor's Puzzle." She smiled, arching a brow. He still didn't know what she meant.

"We thought it was fitting," Ada said.

"This is all very interesting, ladies, truly it is," he said. "But if you would excuse me, I have a rather pressing errand to attend to."

"Of course, Reverend," Emma Jean said, but apparently she wasn't about to let him off so easily. "First, let us clarify ourselves. Mary has donated this quilt to a special cause. If you like it — I know it is not blue — but if you would accept it, we want to present it to you to replace the quilt lost in the fire. Once it is quilted, of course."

"Which we plan to do today," put in Ada.

"You want to give me this quilt?" he asked, incredulous. This was almost more unexpected than Maggie's marriage proposal. "Why?" he gasped.

"It is our way of assuring you that you are part of our family," Ada said. "The first quilt was given to a stranger, so in a way this has even more meaning. And we want you to know one thing — the quilt may be called Bachelor's Puzzle, but there is no puzzle in our minds as to how much you mean to us, Reverend."

"You shouldn't say that," he replied through a constricted throat.

"Look, we've gotten him all embarrassed," Polly Briggs said.

Then Jane Donnelly, who had been sitting quietly in a chair by the frame, rose, came to Zack, and took his hand. "We are so thankful God sent you to us, Reverend."

He wanted to scream, "How can you of all people say that after what I did to your family?" But she did not blame him and never had. He did not understand any of it.

He just knew he had to get away — now!

"Thank you all so much. I'm . . . ah . . . real touched." But inside he was saying, *Keep your quilt. Save it for someone who deserves it.* "I really must go."

As he turned to leave, he saw Ellie out of the corner of his eye. He'd been studiously trying to avoid looking at her the entire time, though he had been acutely aware of her presence. For a brief wild and crazy moment he thought of staying. He could cajole Maggie out of her nonsense. He could —

But his inner alarm — *Run! Run! Run!* — drowned out all indecision.

This time he heeded the warning and hurried to the barn, where he saddled his horse. Unfortunately, he was not lucky enough to make the clean escape he'd desired.

"Reverend Locklin, are you all right?" Ellie asked on entering the barn.

"Ellie," he said, "I'm in a hurry. That's all." The words came out sharply in his need for haste.

"Oh."

"I guess I hurt the women's feelings." He had to say something. He was leaving forever, yet even now he didn't want them to hate him. How ridiculous was that? *They are going to hate me no matter what, once they figure out what I've done. She is going to hate me.* That's what pained him most. *When I am gone, she will think of me only with revulsion.*

And the craziest part of this entire fiasco was that he cared what Ellie thought of him. When Maggie had been uttering her proposal, he'd been wishing it were Ellie instead, even though he knew he could never marry either sister. Because once such words were spoken, it would mean the end of the game. He'd been too selfish and weak to stop when he should have. He'd even foolishly started to think this could be his life. But his life was out there, a drifter with no friends, no family, and no bed upon which to lay a pretty quilt.

"Zack . . ." she murmured.

His head jerked a double take at the unexpected sound of his true name on her lips. "What — ?"

"You told me to call you Zack."

"I have to go . . . I have to leave." Desperately he looked around. For a way of escape? But she had called him by his name. Did she know about him after all? Did that mean he could stay?

"You haven't hurt anyone's feelings," she said. "They actually thought you might be choked up and too embarrassed for them to see, so that's why you hurried off."

"Why did you come, then? Did you want to see me cry?" Give me a minute and I will, he thought sadly.

"No. I just wanted to be sure you understood. I guess I was afraid you might think they were making fun of you. When I saw what Mrs. Renolds's quilt pattern was, I tried to get them to put off the presentation."

"You mean the Bachelor's Puzzle? It is rather funny when you think of it." But there was no amusement in his tone. All the girls had wanted to catch the bachelor minister, while the minister wanted the one girl who didn't want to catch him. It was

412

funny and puzzling and sad, very, very sad. "You were against it all from the start, though, Ellie. Wisely, you knew it presented too many opportunities for people to get hurt."

"That is the irony, isn't it? I was against the romantic tomfoolery, and yet . . ." She lifted her eyes to meet his.

For a moment he forgot what he was about to do, who he was, and who he wasn't. For that brief moment he was just a man looking into the eyes of an angel.

Then she finished, "And yet, it was I who fell in love with the minister . . . no, no — in love with *you,* William . . . or Zack . . . or whatever name you'd be happy hearing."

"Oh, Ellie!" he groaned. "Don't say such a thing. You don't know my name or what I am or who I am."

"I love you, whoever you are. Do you love me?" she entreated.

He returned her gaze, looking into her eyes for a long time before he spoke. How he wanted to tell her what he felt, that he'd never been happier than when he was with her, that he had never felt more real, more whole. He wanted to say that he loved her. But as much as he tried to tell himself otherwise, he knew she loved Reverend Locklin. She didn't know Zack. She couldn't love him.

He gave her the only response he could. He grabbed his horse's reins and swung into the saddle and rode away, ducking as he cleared the barn door. He did not look back, but he couldn't help seeing all the women watching him as he rode away. A few waved innocently. But soon Ellie and Maggie would tell them all what a cad he had been, and they would be relieved they hadn't bestowed him with yet another quilt. He thought of that scorched quilt he still kept, now tucked away in a drawer in Georgie's wardrobe. He wished he could go back for it, to keep as a reminder of the dangers of staying too long in one place.

He got about a quarter of a mile down the road when he saw a rider approach and groaned when he recognized the horse as belonging to Calvin. It seemed making a clean escape had been doomed from the beginning. If he were a religious man, he'd probably believe God was conspiring against him.

"Hello, William," Calvin said, reining in his mount.

There was a tightness around his lips and a tenseness in his tone that was not natural to him. He couldn't possibly know what had just happened.

"Hello, Calvin," Zack replied coolly, still determined to make a quiet getaway.

"I've just come from St. Helens. Several members of the board of deacons got together last night and decided to make a loan to the Copelands to help rebuild their house."

Zack listened, again, his patience growing thin.

Calvin continued. "The Copelands have done so much for the church and the community, we felt getting them a roof over their heads took precedence over building a new church."

"That's a very thoughtful gesture —" Zack began, then stopped abruptly when he suddenly put together what Calvin's words meant. Again the urge to dig his heels into his mount's sides and flee assailed him. But he was beginning to sense that he didn't deserve to escape his crimes, and God appeared to agree.

Calvin wore a pained expression. "I went to the bank to withdraw the building fund money —"

"And it wasn't there," finished Zack. "It's true. I never put it into the bank." He was prepared to take his medicine. "You may as well know the truth, Calvin. I didn't steal the money. I never used it. I kept it only for an emergency. But it got burned up in the fire. The money is gone."

"But, William —"

"Let me finish." Zack pushed ahead, anxious to have it all out before he lost his nerve and dug in his heels. "I am not William Locklin. He died. I found him on the trail where he'd been thrown from his horse and injured badly. I had nothing to do with his death, I swear that to you. I tried to help him, but he was hurt too badly. I was on the run and needed a place to hide out for a while. Taking Locklin's identity seemed to be the answer. I didn't think it would hurt anyone."

Taking a few moments to absorb all this, Calvin finally asked, "You are wanted by the law?"

"No, I am not. I owed money to a hoodlum in Portland. A fellow named Cutter." Zack added this last to give his confession veracity. "There was a scuffle, and I accidentally shot one of his friends. Sinclair was his name. You must believe me — I am not wanted by the law. But the hoodlum was after me for killing his friend. He would have killed me if he had found me."

Calvin's disappointed sigh and his look, as much rueful as sorrowful, was enough to make Zack wish he *was* wanted by the law, could turn himself in and go to jail as punishment for his crimes. If Calvin was wondering what punishment to mete out, his look of disappointment, in itself, was worse than prison.

"All this time you lied to us, to the church," Calvin said. "You made a mockery of all we believe in."

"That was never my intent!" But Zack knew that had been the inevitable result. "I just . . . I didn't mean . . ." Any defense was weak, even if he could make one or get it past the lump of gall in his throat.

"You best leave, William, or whoever you are," Calvin said with great regret.

"That's what I was doing now. I was leaving. I finally realized it had gone too far. I wanted to confess to you. So many times I tried but just didn't have the courage. I didn't want you folks to hate me."

Calvin appeared to ruminate on that, no doubt questioning how coincidental it sounded that Zack happened to be leaving at just the moment he was found out.

"Go, then," Calvin said, "and don't ever show your face around here again."

Zack started to spur his horse forward but stopped. "Calvin, I'm sorry."

Calvin made no response, and Zack didn't wait for one. He rode off at a hurried trot.

TWENTY-EIGHT

News of the fake minister spread quickly though Maintown. After the encounter with William on the road, Calvin had rode into his yard, only to find a half dozen of the worst gossips in town right there. He saw no reason to keep quiet what William had just confessed. Why should he? Besides, he was angry, an emotion rare to him but now so strong he wanted the world to know about the evil man who had hoodwinked an entire community.

As expected, telling six ladies was like lighting six fuses that ignited the entire church and the town. The townsmen quickly organized a meeting that very evening at the schoolhouse. Everyone even remotely related to the church showed up. Calvin thought the group resembled a lynch mob rather than a congregation of Christians. If the fake William Locklin had been there, truly only God could have spared his life.

Come to think of it, maybe God wouldn't have, either.

The man had scorned God, indeed mocked God, by speaking His words in a perfidious manner.

Several of the men present rebuked Calvin, as well.

"You let him go?" Nathan Parker demanded. "You let him just ride away?"

"How could you be so foolish?" Hal Fergus railed.

Part of Calvin did regret what he had done. But he hadn't had much of a choice. He'd had no weapon with which to compel the man to stay. His action had likely spared that miscreant a tar and feathering. Calvin was angry, but he knew his anger derived mostly from the fact that he had genuinely cared for the lad. He felt as if this William imposter had wronged him personally. He had let him go because he feared his own anger, as well as the anger of the whole town. If they acted on that anger, he feared it would wound the already beset town beyond healing. He thought it best if the "minister" just disappeared and the town's ire dissipated on its own.

The upshot of the meeting was that Nathan Parker would go into St. Helens and speak with the sheriff to see if criminal charges could be brought against "Locklin." It seemed a toothless gesture to Calvin, since their man no doubt was long gone by now. But no one listened to his voice of reason.

Parker went into town the very next morning. What he discovered and later reported to Calvin was that the sheriff could find nothing criminal in "Locklin's" actions, especially since he had performed no marriages. However, when Parker mentioned the stolen — his interpretation of Calvin's explanation — church money, the sheriff was pleased to say that now he had a criminal case. Parker pressed charges. The sheriff said he would send out a bulletin bearing a very good likeness of "Locklin," thanks to Parker's detailed description. These bulletins went as far as Astoria to the west and Portland to the east.

Maggie was sickened by all that had happened. She felt it was her fault. If she hadn't pushed "William" into a corner as she had, he might have gone on forever as the town minister. That's what she wanted more than anything — for things to go on as they were. She didn't care that he was a fake minister. She had kind of guessed that anyway when she had found the questionable things in his trunk. She didn't feel like the rest of the town did, that she had been deceived. She was glad he wasn't a minister.

She was especially upset when she learned that criminal charges had been made against him and he could go to jail for what he had done. Down deep, she didn't feel he was the criminal or evil sort many in Maintown were now making him out to be.

She tried to defend him to her parents.

"Dad, when you saw William on the road that day," she said one evening as the family was gathering for dinner, "I am sure he really was leaving town like he told you."

"What do you know of this, Maggie?" Dad asked.

Maybe if she told the truth, they would not think so badly of him and perhaps even drop those charges. He shouldn't go to jail.

"One thing I know," she replied, "is that what he said about the money is true. I saw it in his room —"

"What were you doing in his room?" demanded Mama. All that had transpired had been quite upsetting to her. She had liked "William," too, and had been the most vocal promoter of getting him married off. She well knew that given a little more time, this . . . fraud would have surely married one of their local girls, and she would have felt it was, in large part, her fault.

"I went to get his suit for you to alter," Maggie said defensively. She should have sensed her danger and stopped then, but she never did know when to stop. "He had the money tucked into the bottom of his trunk like he had no intention of using it."

"And you never said anything about this?" Dad asked.

"I . . . uh . . . well, I figured there was a good reason for it," she stumbled on. "Maybe he didn't trust banks or something. But the important thing is that he didn't use the money. It did burn up in the fire."

"Why are you defending him?" Dad asked. It was a question, but Maggie sensed there was hope behind it. Dad had liked "William" and maybe was looking for a way to spare him the worst punishment for what he had done.

"I really don't believe he meant to hurt anyone. Why else would he leave immediately after I proposed to him?"

"You what!" screeched Mama.

Maggie blinked. What had she just said? She hadn't intended on telling that much of the truth! But maybe it would make them finally understand. "Well, I did. I asked him to marry me, and he turned me down. A few minutes later he met Dad and said he was leaving town. He knew it had gone too far. He was trying to spare me."

"What had gone too far?" Dad asked sharply. It seemed like his anger was suddenly ignited once more. "Did he do something to encourage you?"

"No, Dad!" She decided this was not the time to mention the kiss. "I just didn't want any of the other girls to get him. I thought everyone would finally take me seriously if I was married. And, well, William and I had become friends."

"I don't know what to say." Dad sighed.

But Mama did know exactly what to say. "Margaret Edith, you better be telling the truth! And if you are telling the truth, you should be ashamed of yourself! Your behavior only proves how immature you are. I can almost sympathize with the reverend."

"I know he didn't mean no harm!" Maggie insisted.

"I think she's right," Ellie put in.

All heads swung in her direction. Up until now Maggie had been surprised by Ellie's response to all that had happened. She had thought her sister, who could be self-righteous at times, would speak loudly against William's fraud. Instead, she had been very quiet since the revelation. She had not talked at all to Maggie about it.

Maggie had known it was because her sister was mad at her. Their interactions of late had been quite chilly. But now, she too was defending William?

"I don't believe he was a truly bad person," Ellie went on. "I talked to him often, and I don't believe everything he said was a lie. Now thinking of some of our conversations, I believe he regretted what he was doing. He just got caught up in the masquerade and couldn't find his way out."

"It seems you girls knew him better than I thought," Dad said. "You didn't propose to him, too, did you, Ellie?"

"No, Daddy." She shook her head. Her lip was trembling and moisture filled her eyes. "I just told him I loved him." Tears spilled from her eyes.

"Oh my!" Mama groaned, then fanning herself with a hand, she sank down onto one of the kitchen chairs. Maggie had never seen her mother attacked by the vapors, but the woman now alternately turned pale and then flushed Turkey red.

Dad looked at Mama. And Maggie knew the full measure of her father when he remained silent. He could so easily have said to his wife, *I told you so!*

Her voice shaky with emotion, Ellie added, "Dad, I believe that at the end, God was convicting Zack of his mistakes."

"Then," Dad said, "we will let God deal with him. Zack? You say his name is Zack?"

"I don't know. He once asked me to call him that. I thought it was a jest. But maybe it was just getting harder and harder for him to keep up the false identity."

"Dad, you say God will deal with . . . him, with Zack," Maggie said, "but there are still those charges against him."

"I cannot change that," he said. "The money is missing, and the majority of church members want legal justice."

"Then he truly is in God's hands," Ellie said with a note of hopefulness in her voice.

Somehow Mama managed to get dinner on the table, and everyone tried to eat, but it was an unusually silent meal, and the silence extended for the rest of the evening. Maggie wished she had Georgie's homework to do as a distraction, but with school out now there was no arithmetic. She played a couple games of checkers with Georgie but received little joy from beating him and finally quit. Mama and Ellie sewed by the light of the kerosene lamp, and Dad read his seed catalog. Everyone seemed relieved when Dad finally rose, stretched, and announced it was time for bed. Maggie would have gone upstairs earlier, but she hadn't relished the idea of being alone.

Georgie lingered in Maggie and Ellie's room for a few minutes. "You sure the reverend wasn't lying 'bout everything?" he asked.

"We'll never know," Ellie said.

"But you said —"

"I was speaking mostly of his heart, Georgie," Ellie explained. "I suppose he had to keep telling lies to cover up other lies."

"But lying is wrong," Georgie said, perplexed. "It's breaking a commandment and all. How can his heart be right if he's breaking commandments?"

"We all make mistakes, Georgie. It doesn't mean we are evil in our hearts."

Maggie added, "I've told lies, Georgie. Do you think I'm evil?"

"No, I guess not." But he punctuated his words with an impish grin. "Still," he went on more earnestly, "I hope you're right 'cause I don't want to think I liked an evil person. When we was sharing my room, we talked some. I tried to ask him about the Bible 'cause I thought that's what a minister would want, but he'd always change the subject, and we talked about more common stuff, like problems at school and how I didn't want to finish school 'cause it seemed useless. He told me I should finish. It would make my parents proud. I asked him if I should kiss Cissy Fergus."

"What did he say to that?" Maggie asked.

"He said to never kiss a girl unless she wanted to be kissed. I asked him how to know if she wanted to, and he said the best way was to ask her. But he said if you have to ask, then she probably don't."

"Georgie," Ellie said, "it is possible that the only time Zack wasn't himself was when he was in the pulpit or doing ministerial things."

"Do you think he was a Christian?" Georgie asked.

"That is not for us to judge."

A few minutes later Georgie reluctantly left. It had surprised Maggie that he had become friends with Zack, too.

Zack . . . she liked that name better than William. She wondered what his last name was.

When she and Ellie were under their covers and the lamp was out, Maggie wasn't ready for sleep. She knew she must finally talk to her sister about their fake minister.

"Ellie, do you really love him?"

Ellie didn't answer for a long time. Maybe she wouldn't. She might be upset that Maggie had proposed marriage to him.

Finally Ellie responded. "I told him I

loved him. But who did I love? If he wasn't real, how could my love be real?" Her voice was thin and shaky. It seemed as if she had been holding in her emotions about this for a long time, but now that the truth about her feelings was out, she was unable to control them.

"Maybe you loved what you saw in his heart, the part that was real."

"I'm awfully confused," Ellie admitted. "It is hard to quit loving once you start. But I'm furious, too, that he lied to us. How can you be so mad at someone and still in love?"

"Why did you defend him, Ellie?"

"Because I don't think I could love someone who was evil." After a long pause she went on, "And you, Mags? What about your love? You were ready to marry him."

"I never said I loved him."

"You didn't?"

Now Maggie was thoughtfully silent. She had told Zack she loved him. But Mama was right. She was too immature to know anything about love. When he left her that day behind the barn, she had never been so relieved. She'd cried, yes, but most of those tears had been from humiliation. What would she have done if he had accepted her proposal? She'd be engaged now and planning a wedding, and in six months she'd be . . . married! No girl had ever been happier to see a man run.

"No, I didn't," Maggie answered. "And I am pretty certain he didn't love me either, even after I kissed him."

"You kissed him?"

"I just wanted to see what it would be like."

"I kissed him, too," Ellie confessed.

Maggie laughed.

"You're not mad at me?" Ellie asked. "I wasn't trying to steal him from you."

"Even if sometimes I thought you were, I know it ain't true. I suppose if a man really loves a woman, another woman couldn't steal him away."

"That makes me feel so much better."

With another chuckle, Maggie added, "But I do feel sorry for him, for William or Zack or Zacchaeus or whatever. The poor fellow had enough on his hands trying to pretend to be a minister. We sure made it worse by throwing ourselves at him."

"Still, he did something very wrong in impersonating a minister," Ellie said.

"I hope he doesn't go to jail."

"I hope he doesn't, either. Maybe God won't mind if I pray for him."

"I'll pray for him, too," Maggie said, and she did so right then and there, silently. She prayed he would repent of his sins and return to Maintown — not for her, though, but for the person who really did love him.

Across the hall Ada was experiencing a rare bout of humility. She glanced over at her husband and didn't know if he had fallen asleep yet. The lamp was out and in the moonlight flowing through the window she could only discern a vague lump beside her.

"Calvin, are you awake?"

There was a long pause, so she thought he must be asleep.

Then he mumbled, "No."

"How can you sleep at a time like this — ?" she began to rail and then realized this wasn't the best way to begin an apology. "Calvin, I've got to say something. I . . . well . . . I was . . . wrong."

This made the vague lump turn and sit upright. He looked at her with pure wonder.

"Oh, stop that!" she said, chuckling quietly. "Well, I deserve it. I deserve to hear you say 'I told you so.' "

"I'm not going to say it, Ada."

"No. I want you to. Go ahead. Say it."

"Wouldn't be right. Be like kicking you when you are down."

"Calvin! You say it right now! I mean it!" she demanded.

Calvin smiled. She saw the twitch of his lips in the moonlight. "I told you so, Ada," he deadpanned.

"Humph!" she responded. "How could I know the man was a fake?" Pausing, she added with as much humility as she could manage, "Thank you, Calvin."

"You think Ellie was right about him?" he asked.

"If not, then we are the biggest fools ever." Thinking about it a moment, she added, "I don't think he ever meant to play us for fools."

"Maybe not, but that doesn't make me feel any better."

"Ellie loves him." Ada said that because it was finally dawning upon her.

"Probably not anymore," Calvin replied.

But Ada knew a woman's mind better than her husband did, and she didn't think a woman could turn her love on and off like one of those electric lights she'd seen once when visiting Portland.

Twenty-Nine

Ellie knew that what she was doing was foolishness. Mama had hinted at it, though she had still offered to help. As she sat on the porch with the damaged "welcome quilt" spread over her knees, Ellie tried to define why she wanted to repair it. The answer was not clear to her, but when Georgie had dragged it down from his room one day asking if he should take it to the barn to use for the animals, Ellie had been compelled to rescue it.

"No, Georgie, maybe it can be fixed," she'd said.

Mama had raised a brow. "Some things can't be fixed, Ellie."

Ellie knew her mother's words referred to more than a quilt.

But Mama had helped Ellie wash the quilt in a bath of white soap, shaved and dissolved in boiling water, to which was also added ammonia. That had cleaned away the soil the quilt had picked up after the fire when it had been dragged through the dirt, and it also removed some of the minor scorching. But there were still several stubborn marks remaining that Mama said to leave until the frayed, burned places were patched, at which time the quilt could stand a more vigorous washing. When the quilt was dry, Ellie had begun the tedious task of patching. Some small holes burned by hot embers she had been able to darn, but the larger holes needed patching. Mama still had some of the backing material that could be used to patch holes in the back, but for the blocks on the front, Ellie had gone to the individual makers to get scraps. She hadn't told them what she was doing. She thought some of the ladies might be adverse to the idea of repairing the quilt most of them regretted making in the first place.

Strangely, one of the worst damaged blocks was Jane Donnelly's. It had been in the corner used to beat out flames. It was almost beyond repair, and Ellie thought she might just remake the whole block. It was a fairly simple pattern called Shoofly. With some trepidation Ellie paid Mrs. Donnelly a visit.

"Oh yes, I have some scraps left," Mrs. Donnelly told Ellie after inviting her into the house. They were seated at the kitchen table. "Do you plan to make another blue quilt?" When Ellie hesitated, Mrs. Donnelly smiled. "Are you trying to fix the welcome quilt?"

No one had thus far asked her so directly. She suspected no one wanted to talk about the quilt. But now she was forced to answer honestly.

"Yes, Mrs. Donnelly. Is that all right with you?"

"You don't need my permission to do so."

"Your blessing, then?" Ellie implored. "You, more than anyone, have a right to protest, to want the quilt and the memory of . . . well, of why we made it, buried forever."

"Do you think I hate our erstwhile minister?" Pausing only a moment, she answered her own question. "I don't. I don't blame him for anything that happened to my family."

"But maybe if he'd been a real minister, he would have given better advice and restrained his violence. And things might not have happened as they did." Ellie didn't know why she was changing her defensive stance regarding Zack. She was mostly trying to sort through everything and understand her own oft conflicting reactions.

"In an odd way I believe he took his duties as minister rather seriously," Mrs. Donnelly said.

Ellie gasped at the surprising comment.

Mrs. Donnelly smiled, adding, "He didn't have to talk to Tommy as I requested. He didn't have to do a lot of things he did, like help Louise or sit up for hours with Mrs. Cook. He could have found excuses not to do those things just as he found an excuse not to marry Claudia Briggs. He probably would have been safer to avoid us as much as possible. But I think he liked us and wanted to help us. The real William Locklin was young and inexperienced and might have made mistakes, as well. But I am not convinced that the way our William dealt with Tom and Tommy was wrong. He helped my Tommy be strong. He gave him courage not to take his father's abuse, something I was never able to do. That needed to happen. If it brought about the unfortunate events in the woods, then . . . I don't know."

Ellie had the feeling Mrs. Donnelly might have said, "Then so be it." Could she be glad that the elder Tom was gone? That was a question that should never be asked or, for that matter, answered.

Mrs. Donnelly rose from her chair, went

to her scrap box in a corner of the kitchen, and dug through it until she found some large pieces of the fabrics she had used in her block.

"Take these and fix that quilt," she said.

"Thank you. I'm afraid I may have to remake most of your block, as it was damaged pretty badly."

"Do that, then. I think the quilt should be preserved. I know your mother has a good stain remover made of soap and alcohol and rosemary, but I have always had very good results by rubbing a paste of cream of tartar on stains. It may work on the scorch marks."

"I'll definitely try it."

Ellie left still feeling confused yet also somewhat vindicated. If Mrs. Donnelly, who had been hurt the most since Zack came to town, could feel benevolent toward him, then perhaps Ellie was not as far off in her perception of the man as she sometimes felt. Some further confirmation had come from another area. Dad had gone to Portland and corroborated much of Zack's story. Without implicating Zack, Dad had learned a man named Sinclair had indeed been killed shortly before Zack showed up in Maintown. He also learned there was a crime boss named Cutter. The police had never heard of Zack, at least beyond the Maintown flyer they had posted on their Wanted board.

Ellie fixed her attention back to the quilt and the patch of muslin she was appliquéing to a hole on the back. The afternoon light was fading and casting the corner of the porch where she worked into shadow, but her stitches were small and even nonetheless. She wanted to finish this patch, for then the back would be finished and she could concentrate on the front. She had already repaired some of the front, but Mama had suggested completing the back in order to give better support for the more exacting work on the front. She had been impatient to get the front looking nice but took her mother's advice nevertheless.

About half the blocks on the front would need some repair or at the least some concentrated stain removal. Her own block had a big burned patch right in the middle of the sky. Maggie's fans had been lower, opposite from the edge used to beat out flames, and therefore unharmed.

Ellie still couldn't believe that Maggie had proposed marriage to William. Then after rejecting her, he had immediately left Maintown, though not before Ellie had also thrown herself at him. No wonder he had decided to run! Could that truly have been his reason? Or rather than doing the honorable thing, was he merely fleeing the entanglements of matrimony? Perhaps it was a bit of both. But she was still convinced that his conscience had begun to be seared by his charade.

Ellie finished the last stitch on the muslin patch. Was she working on this quilt because she hoped he would return for it? No. He would never return. The quilt could be fixed, but the wounds of what he had done in the community were too deep for any needle and thread to repair.

At the sound of approaching horses she lifted her eyes. Three strangers were riding into the yard. A chill ran up her back. They were rough-looking sorts.

"Mama!" she called in alarm. Somehow she sensed these men were not on a friendly visit. She and Mama were alone in the house. Dad was at the sawmill. Maggie and Georgie were off somewhere.

Ada heard her daughter's call and came out to the porch, a bit perturbed because she had work to be done and didn't want to waste any more of her time fixing that quilt. She hadn't protested her daughter's determination to repair the quilt because she had thought it might help Ellie put recent events behind her. But she had forgotten that once Ellie put her mind to something, she had a tendency to become rather mulish about it.

Immediately, however, Ada saw why her daughter had called her. Three strangers had ridden into the yard, and they looked like roughnecks. Certainly some rough sorts came to Maintown, especially when the lumber camps opened for the season, but these men did not appear to be lumberjacks. For one thing they wore revolvers strapped to their waists, a sight seldom seen in these parts. Farmers and lumberjacks did not wear such weapons. These men were also dressed differently, in expensive-looking boots and hats with traveling dusters over nice trousers. They looked like lawmen or gunfighters.

Ellie came and stood by her mother. Ada resisted the urge to take her daughter's hand. She didn't want Ellie to see that she was trembling a little.

"Hello, ma'am," one of the men said.

He lifted his hat, revealing pale hair. He was a handsome man but hard-edged like a good knife.

"Good afternoon," Ada said stiffly, mostly to hide her nerves. "What can I do for you?"

"We're looking for a fellow," the pale-haired man replied. Staying mounted, he rode close to the porch, took a paper from his coat pocket, and reached it down to Ada.

Ada opened the paper and saw a pen drawing of Zack, as she had recently learned to call him. She remembered him telling Calvin that hoodlums from Portland were looking for him.

"You seen him?" the stranger asked.

Ada had the almost overwhelming urge to lie, to protect Zack from these men. But she was not accustomed to lying. "Yes, he was here for a time, but he left more than a week ago."

"You know where he went?"

"He never said. He more or less just disappeared."

"You don't know what direction he went?"

"If he was smart, he would have hightailed it as far from here as possible. He didn't leave any friends here, that's for sure. I expect he went to Astoria where he could get passage on a boat."

"He never gave any indication of where he might go?"

"Why do you want to know? Are you the law?" A moment after asking it she realized the question was a mistake. But her curiosity had gotten the better of her.

"We just have some business with him." The man scowled. "But whether we're the law or not, you better be telling me the truth. He's a scoundrel that don't deserve protecting."

"Ha!" Ada barked gamely. "The last thing I want to do is protect that no-good charlatan. If I could help you, I would. You are welcome to him."

The man studied her for a long, uncomfortable moment. Maybe she had overdone it, but then, what she said was true, wasn't it? She didn't care what happened to that fraud.

Without even a word of thanks, the three riders wheeled around their mounts and rode away.

Ada's knees suddenly felt weak, and she swayed on her feet. Ellie put a steadying arm around her.

"Are you all right, Mama?"

"Those are bad men," Ada breathed.

"And they are looking for Zack," Ellie said tremulously.

Ada wanted to comfort her daughter, but perhaps it was best for Ellie to see what kind of man this Zack was, to be involved with that sort of men. She had always told her children, "You are judged by the company you keep." Then again, those men certainly were not friends of Zack's. If they were his enemies, what did that say about him?

■ ■ ■ ■

Beau Cutter didn't know if he should believe the woman or not. Yet after what he'd heard about Hartley from some fellows in St. Helens, he could see no reason why she would protect him. Then again, women were strange creatures.

"Let's go into town and ask around," he told his companions.

"Town? You mean back to St. Helens?" asked one.

"No. This town, or what there is of it." Someone in St. Helens had directed him to the Newcomb place as the best place to get information on Hartley, so Cutter had gone directly there. Now he rode back to the town, which consisted of a post office and a few houses.

There was no one in the post office, so Cutter went to the adjacent store where a woman was working behind the counter and two men were looking at a display of hunting knives.

Cutter tipped his hat at the female clerk. He knew that in these small villages you caught more flies with honey than with vinegar.

"Afternoon, ma'am," he said congenially.

"What can I do for you?" asked the woman, a middle-aged farmwife who probably kept the store for her husband.

"I'm looking for this man." Cutter took another handbill from his pocket. He'd left the last one with the Newcomb woman.

The woman nodded. "Yeah, he was here. Left over a week ago."

"Do you know where he went?"

"Don't know. Don't care."

Cutter could tell he wouldn't get more from the woman and was about to fold up the handbill and replace it in his pocket when one of the customers spoke up.

"Hey, I think I seen that fellow." He turned to his companion. "Bill, didn't we meet him up at Samuel's camp?"

Bill moved closer and peered at the handbill. "Sure, that was him."

"When was that?" Cutter asked.

"Well," said the first man, "we first saw him six, seven days ago, worked with him a few days, then me and Bill quit. You ever work a lumber camp? It's blistering work, that is!"

"We figured there ought to be an easier way to make money," put in Bill.

Cutter frowned. What would Hartley be doing in a lumber camp? Was he foolish enough to have stuck around these parts after what he did to the folks here? Could be these lumberjacks were mistaken. But thus far Hartley had never done the expected, so why should he start now?

THIRTY

Zack had not traveled more than twenty miles from Maintown. After making his confession to Calvin, he had headed toward Astoria. There he could get a boat and fairly quickly be long gone from Maintown, the Newcombs, and everyone else. Though his situation had not improved from when he had first left Portland, except that now he had a better horse and a little money from his pay at the sawmill, he knew going any other direction was foolish.

But he had ridden less than a mile from the Newcomb farm when he realized he couldn't leave this place, not forever. Only as he was forced to flee town did he know just how much the last couple of months had meant to him. Maybe if he faced everyone and confessed his misdeeds, they would forgive him and accept him back, not as their minister, of course, but just as a neighbor. For the first time in his life he could see himself settled down in one place, perhaps working a small farm, raising children with a wife.

The appeal of this dream made him rein in his horse and head north instead of west. He could get work for a while in a lumber camp — not the one Boyd worked at but one he'd heard of near Veronia, where he wouldn't know anyone. He'd give the folks in Maintown time to cool off and then he could return. Why shouldn't they accept him back? He hadn't done too badly toward them. He'd given some of them good counsel. He'd gotten the Baxter brothers back to church; he'd consoled the Cook family.

Yet he knew he didn't deserve to be accepted by them, that any good he had done had been thoroughly offset by his lies. If he returned, it would have to be in utter humility. He would have no problem with that, either. And even if they rejected him, he still knew he had to face these folks. He had to look each one in the eye and apologize for what he had done. Slithering away like the snake he was did not sit well with him. Maybe living in William Locklin's boots had done him some good. The old Zack would have had no qualms about hightailing it out of town one step ahead of the law.

But this new fellow wanted to be a better man.

Nevertheless, practicality told him he best wait until the folks simmered down and he could return without fear of being strung up by his toes. Two days later he rode into Thomas Samuel's lumber camp and got hired. And it wasn't long afterward that he began to lose his resolve. For one thing he remembered the missing money. They might forgive him for the lies, but one hundred and fifty dollars was a small fortune. They could not forgive that. If he returned, he would doubtless be prosecuted and jailed.

Zack was put to work with a crew building a skid road, which would be used to move cut logs from the forest to the river. Oxen would haul the logs on the skid road to the water, where they would await the first big rain of the year, usually in November, to be carried by water to the nearest seaport.

At the end of his first day of work he went to the mess hall for supper. Among the fifty men gathered who worked the camp at various jobs, Zack saw a familiar face.

"Hey, Reverend!" called Tommy Donnelly.

For a brief moment Zack considered ignoring the call. But the last thing he wanted was for attention to be drawn to him, and it certainly would be if the men thought he was a minister. Tommy was about to call out again, so Zack waved back and hurried over to the boy.

"Hi, Tommy," Zack said.

"What you doing here, Rev —"

Zack cut in, "Tommy, I'd appreciate it if you not call me" — he pitched his voice lower — "Reverend."

"Why not?"

"I'll explain it to you later, okay?"

"What'll I call you, then?"

"Zack."

"But ain't your name — ?"

"I'll tell you later." In the din of fifty men hunkering down for a meal, Zack could have conversed easily enough without being heard, but he was suddenly nervous. Maybe there were more men here who knew him. Some lumberjacks had come to his services, now that he thought about it. He looked all around but didn't see any other familiar faces.

After supper he and Tommy went outside to talk. The August night was warm, lit by a full moon, the fragrance of cut wood strong in the air. They hitched themselves up on the edge of the wood retaining wall that bordered a slope of wooded land at the back of the bunkhouse.

Knowing that Tommy was a bit slow in grasping things, Zack began as directly as he could. "Tommy, I was just pretending to be a minister. My reason for doing so is a long story, but mainly I just needed to hide out for a while."

"Was it a joke or something?"

"No, not at all. There were some men pursuing me, and I didn't think they would ever find me if I was a minister, using a different name and all."

Tommy rubbed his chin, nodding as if he really understood. Maybe he did. It wasn't such a complex story when boiled down like that.

"But you preached sermons, and you buried folks. I . . . well, I was looking on, hidden in the woods, when you buried my pa." A hint of anguish flickered across the boy's brow; then he brightened. "It was a fine service, too. You done a good job. You sure you ain't no real minister?"

"Everyone thought you were long gone," Zack commented. He was just as curious about Tommy's story as the boy was about his.

"I weren't never exactly sure my pa was dead till I saw the funeral. I couldn't leave before I was sure."

"Why, Tommy?"

"If he weren't dead and I left, who'd be there to protect my ma?" Tommy said matter-of-factly.

Zack's stomach tightened. Was it true, then? Tommy killed his father on purpose? Afraid to ask that direct question, Zack tried to skirt the issue. "Did your father hurt your mother, too?"

"Not while he had me around."

"Is that why you never left before now?"

"I figured my pa had to beat on someone — someone weaker than him. If not me, then surely it'd be my ma."

Zack had always wondered why Tommy had stuck it out under such deplorable conditions for so long. Now he had to question his own actions when he had left home so young. Had his departure merely opened his mother up to take his stepfather's abuse. He had never considered that until now.

"That's most admirable, Tommy," Zack said with all sincerity.

Tommy shrugged, then said, "Reverend, if you wasn't a real minister, does that mean my pa wasn't buried proper, and his soul is floating out there somewhere like a ghost or something?"

"I don't know."

"Well, he don't deserve no better anyway." For a seventeen-year-old, Tommy's tone held a man's share of bitterness.

"Do you want to talk about what happened in the woods?" Zack asked. Maybe it was true that confession was good for the soul. Perhaps it would help ease Tommy's bitterness if he could talk about that day. Zack hardly realized how naturally he fit back into the role of counselor. Maybe being a minister had indeed rubbed off on him.

"I know folks think I kilt my pa of a purpose."

"Most are ready to believe it was an accident."

Tommy shifted uncomfortably. Finally he said, "But it weren't a accident. I shot him, Reverend —"

"Zack." Zack didn't want Tommy to confuse any of this with some spiritual confession. If Tommy wanted to talk as if to a friend, fine, but nothing else.

"Okay, Zack. I shot my pa. That lowdown, dirty —" He stopped abruptly, then went on, "Hey, if you ain't no minister, I can cuss in front of you, can't I?"

"Yeah, you can, but I get the gist of what you mean," Zack replied. "Your father pushed you to do what you did, right?"

"He was drunk," Tommy said. "He was aiming his shotgun at me and then he fired a couple of times — into the air, but still it scared the stuffing outta me 'cause his aim ain't none too steady when he been drinking. He told me he was gonna make a man of me, not some churchified sissy. He was real mad I had started going to church, you see. I started to run and he run after me, but he tripped over a rock and went down, letting go of the gun. I grabbed the shotgun and aimed it at him. I wanted to scare him like he scared me, but he just laughed at me. Said I didn't have the guts to shoot him, and he came toward me again. I knew if he got hold of the gun again, he'd kill me for sure. So I fired. I fired two or three times, even after he went down. I just couldn't stop. When I realized what I had done, I ran."

"It sounds like self-defense to me, Tommy."

"What's that mean?"

"It wasn't murder. A fellow can kill to defend himself. That's the law."

"Don't matter much, does it? My ma probably hates me for what happened."

"She knows what kind of man your father was," Zack said. "I don't think she'd hate you for defending yourself. I do know she is worried sick about you."

"I don't want her to feel bad."

"She's your mother. She loves you." Zack had never before regretted what he'd done in leaving his mother. Now he understood as never before how selfish he'd been. His mother had loved him, too, even if she had been too weak to protect him. He had caused her suffering and pain she did not deserve.

"I miss home terribly," Tommy said woefully. "That's why I only got this far. I thought maybe I could go back home someday."

"You and I are a lot alike, Tommy."

Tommy laughed with a snort. "Me and you? I wish I was like you, Zack. Why, you're smart, and all the girls like you. You was brave enough to beat up my pa. The folks in Maintown thought real high of you. They just snicker at me."

"They don't think highly of me anymore."

" 'Cause you faked being a preacher?"

"Because I lied to them and used them. They probably believe I was mocking them and their God."

"Was you?"

"No," Zack replied unequivocally. On the contrary he had never respected people more. And as for their God . . . he had never intended mockery. But now he saw that every time he had prayed a prayer and preached a word without meaning it, he had been showing contempt for those very things. It didn't matter that in the last few days since leaving town he'd brought back to mind many of the things he had memorized and realized the truth of the words, the words of Reverend Robert E. Markus and of his God. Could he ever make up for what he had done?

"Are you ever going back?" Tommy asked.

"I don't know. What about you?"

"Be easier going back with a friend."

Zack nodded.

Over the next several days, Zack and Tommy talked a lot about these things. If one's first impression of Tommy was that he was slow-witted, Zack quickly saw that the boy possessed a great deal of wisdom.

"I don't think the folks in town would hold a grudge against you," Tommy said one day. "I think they'd forgive you."

"How can you say that when many of them were never very nice to you?"

"Well, the folks that matter. Like the Newcombs." Tommy arched a brow knowingly. "The Newcombs matter most, don't they? 'Specially since you're sweet on Ellie."

Zack's jaw went slack. "What makes you say that?" He had never believed his feelings were that obvious.

"I seen the way you looked at her, like a sick mule or something. I looked at Maggie like that sometimes, but she never looked back at me in the same way. But Ellie, she looked at you with them same pining eyes."

"I'll be honest with you, Tommy. I want to go back, swallow my medicine, and try to make it there. I liked Maintown, the people . . . and Ellie Newcomb."

"Then you should."

"I'm afraid."

"But you stood up to my pa."

"It's a lot easier to beat up someone with fists than to face them with humility."

"I guess I can understand that," Tommy said. "I'm afraid to go back, too. But you know what? It ain't no fun to live in fear. I done that for too long with my pa."

Zack smiled. "You are so right!"

They finished out the week at the camp. Zack's pay was one dollar and fifteen cents a day, so six dollars and ninety cents in one's pocket was nothing to sneer at when a man was considering starting a new life. And it wouldn't hurt having some money if he failed in Maintown and had to hit the road again. But something inside him gave him confidence that he might find a way back into the hearts of the citizens of Maintown. When that confidence faltered,

Tommy helped to bolster it. And he did the same for Tommy.

Together they rode back to Maintown, Zack on William Locklin's nice horse and Tommy on his father's mule. They were two misfits hoping to find a place to call home.

They were riding along the banks of Milton Creek, its water low in the midst of summer, just a few miles from Maintown proper when Zack saw the three riders approach and knew immediately that they were not local folk. They were not dressed as farmers, their horses were too good, and they had pistols strapped to their waists, along with carbines in their saddles.

Zack had no weapon. Tommy still had his pa's shotgun hanging from his saddle.

As they came closer to the strangers, Zack suddenly desperately wished he could reach that shotgun. He recognized Beau Cutter.

"So we finally meet!" Cutter shouted over the hundred or so feet that separated them.

"Tommy," Zack said quietly, "don't make a sudden move, but get ready to make a run for it."

"You know them men?"

"Yeah."

"Run where?"

"You just run the minute I give the word." Zack hoped if he remained behind and had it out with Cutter, Tommy could get away.

"We ain't far from the Carlsons' deserted shack," said Tommy. "We could hole up there —"

"You run home, Tommy, fast as you can." Then Zack saw Cutter go for his rifle. "Now!" Zack barked to Tommy.

Tommy had his shotgun in hand. "I can pick 'em off —"

"Now!" Zack ordered again.

"But —"

Zack realized Tommy wasn't about to desert him without good reason, so he added, "You gotta get help."

This seemed to make sense to Tommy, who probably didn't realize no one in Main-town was about to help out the fake minister.

As Tommy tossed the shotgun to Zack, he said, "The shack's just south, less'n a quarter mile." Then he dug in his heels and took off. At that same moment Cutter fired, missing Zack by a few inches.

One of Cutter's men had his rifle aimed in Tommy's direction.

"Leave the kid be," Zack shouted. "He's nothing to you."

Cutter called off his man and said, "It's only you I want, Hartley."

"He might go for help," one of the men said.

"No one in that town is gonna help him," Cutter said. "That so, Hartley?"

"I've no friends back there. That's true," Zack replied.

Zack knew he couldn't lift and aim the shotgun before Cutter or his men fired their own weapons. So his options were few. He could let Cutter pick him off like a sitting duck, or he could give him a moving target. The moving target had little chance of getting far, but a small chance was better than no chance at all. Zack dug in his heels so hard that his horse reared. A rifle fired and missed, then Zack took off. A couple more shots flew over his head. If he didn't get shot first, his horse would probably end up breaking a leg going at such a pace on this rough trail. Nevertheless he headed south. The trail quickly led down into a small valley that opened out into a meadow. The tall grass likely hid all manner of hazards, potholes, rocks, buried roots. But Zack was heartened by the sight of the shack dead ahead. He raced toward it in a zigzag route, hoping to avoid the rifle fire behind him. One shot took his hat clean off his head.

Fortunately, he and William Locklin's fine horse made it to the cabin in one piece.

Zack leapt to the ground before the animal came to a full stop. With the shotgun in hand, he ran to the cabin. Inside he found a musty, ramshackle heap. There was a hole in the roof, letting in enough light to show this place had not been fit for occupation for many years. He heard a couple of varmints scurry away underfoot to some dark corner. But the first thing Zack did was barricade the door by sliding the bar through the rusted metal carriers, still in good shape. Then he cracked open the shotgun and found it fully loaded. Tommy probably had intended on using it to hunt game while he was on the run.

Zack snapped the gun back together and squatted on the dirt floor by a window that had no glass but half of a shutter intact. He could hear Cutter and his men taking positions around the cabin.

"You're surrounded, Hartley!" shouted Cutter. "You may as well give up."

"What'll you do if I surrender?" Zack asked reasonably enough.

"I'm gonna kill you!"

"But, Beau, that doesn't give me a whole lot of motivation, now, does it?"

"What did you expect?"

"You know I didn't mean to kill Sinclair. You can't kill a man for an accident."

"We wouldn't have been in that alley in the first place if you hadn't welshed on the money you owed me."

Zack didn't like the direction this was taking. He peeked through the opening in the window. Cutter was behind some trees, maybe within range of the shotgun. But Zack was no sharpshooter, not even close. That was one reason he was not fond of carrying a gun. Another reason was that he wasn't crazy about shooting people.

Still, he didn't want to die.

He decided this might be a good time to practice something for real that for the last months he had been pretending to do — pray.

"Well, God, I'm in a fix and I don't know how to get out of it. Could you find it in your heart to help a miserable reprobate? I would promise you I'll follow the straight and narrow if you do, but I remember reading — or was it in one of my sermons? — that it isn't a good idea to try to make deals with you. But I was already intending to be a better person. Now I'd just like the chance to see if that's possible. But not at the expense of Cutter. I mean, if I can turn good, so can he. Would it be asking too much to get out of this fix without anyone dying?"

Pausing, Zack decided it was a pretty convoluted prayer. He needed practice, that was for sure.

Finally he finished, "See what you can do anyway, God. Ah . . . amen and thanks."

It was nothing like the fancy prayers he'd prayed as a minister. Many of those he had lifted directly from Markus's book, and others he had fashioned in the same style. He was smart enough to pray a religious-sounding prayer, but even he knew that for God to hear, it had to come from the heart. So this time he avoided all the book jargon he'd adopted before.

He heard some movement outside. Could be Cutter's men would try to get closer to the cabin. There was only the one door and one window, so entry would be difficult. They might try to burn down the shack. Zack thought it would be too ironic to have two shelters burned down around him in the space of a month.

Cautiously he looked out the window. He saw the flicker of a shadow about twenty feet from the shack to the left. Then, *bam!* A shot blew the remaining shutter off the window. Zack ducked safely away. Keeping down, he stuck the shotgun through the window and fired — just to remind them he wasn't exactly helpless.

After a half hour Zack realized this had all the makings of a regular standoff. All Cutter had to do was wait for Zack to die of thirst. Why hadn't he taken a moment to grab the canteen from his saddle before racing to the shack? Suddenly Zack was feeling very dry.

He knew Cutter was not about to wait three or four days. He would make a move long before then. Probably soon.

When Zack heard the sound of horses, he thought for a minute that Cutter was attempting to rush the place. Risking a look through the window, he saw that was not it at all. Maybe it was the answer to his prayers.

"I've got men with weapons trained on you," shouted the familiar voice of Calvin Newcomb.

"This ain't none of your business!" Cutter shouted in response.

"You are wrong there," Calvin said. "We are not gonna have gunfighting in our town, you hear? It is our business to keep our town peaceful."

"You the sheriff or something?"

"You might say that. Now put away your weapons and leave."

Cutter chuckled. "I can't do that. And I doubt a bunch of farmers can make me."

"Like I said, I've got a half dozen men

with weapons. One is aimed right at your head."

Zack could see Calvin, Nathan Parker, and Stan Wallard. Who else was in the woods with Cutter and his men in their gunsights?

"Listen here," said Cutter. "I am only seeking justice. The fellow in the shack murdered my friend. And he owes me two hundred dollars."

"As I understand it, the killing of your friend was an accident," Calvin replied.

"My friend is still dead, and I'm gonna have justice —"

"You mean vengeance."

"Why are you defending him?" Cutter asked. "I heard what he did to you folks."

"That's our business. There's just not going to be any more killing. It's your word against Zack's. There are no witnesses to prove it wasn't an accident or the law would be after him. I looked into the matter, and the police in Portland have closed the case. But if you kill Zack Hartley today, there *will* be witnesses, and you will be hauled in for murder. You best accept the fact that your friend's death was an accident, or you will likely end up hanging."

There was a long pause. Good old practical, wise Calvin! He had spoken pure horse sense. Cutter had to be thinking it over. If he killed Zack now or even sometime later, everyone would know who had done the deed. Also, another killing might open up the case of the alley shootings. Both of those deaths were accidental or at the least self-defense, but an investigation would hurt Cutter in any case.

Finally Cutter said, "Well, he still owes me two hundred dollars. That is fact. I got his signed marker to prove it."

Zack only owed Cutter one hundred dollars, but of course Cutter would have added steep interest.

"He will pay back every penny," assured Calvin.

Zack could pay back six dollars and ninety cents and saw no possibility to repay the rest, not honestly — and he really was determined to walk the straight and narrow. Maybe Cutter would be willing to wait a few years for his money.

As if reading Zack's thoughts, Cutter said, "I want my money now. Then maybe I'll be able to forget that polecat exists. Two hundred plus interest, mind you. Three hundred ought to do it."

"That's outrageous!" shouted Nathan Parker. For once Zack could appreciate Parker's business savvy. Maybe he could negotiate the amount down.

"I only owed him one hundred to begin with." Zack decided it was time to chime in.

"What about all the trouble you put me through?" reasoned Cutter.

Zack didn't think this would be a good time to mention all the trouble *he'd* been through in the last months. It hadn't been a lark pretending to be a minister. But with one of his "victims" negotiating on his behalf, it was probably best to leave that out.

"We can come up with one hundred and fifty — in a week," Parker said.

We? Zack wondered what he meant by that.

Calvin said, "I will bring it to you in Portland."

After another pause, Cutter said, "Okay. I'll be waiting at the Cranston Hotel, Saturday at three o'clock. You be there, or I am coming after all of you. I can round up twenty men who will blow your stinking village off the map."

Cutter called in his men, and Zack heard them ride off. He rose then and slipped away the bar from the door of the shack. Suddenly he was more nervous than when he had three gunmen shooting at him. Now he had to face the people he had wronged.

The other Maintown men were riding into the clearing with Calvin, Parker, and Wallard. There was Lewis Arlington, Elisha Cook, and Tommy Donnelly. Tommy was holding the reins of William Locklin's horse.

"See? I got help," Tommy said, grinning proudly.

"I don't know what to say." Zack strode forward, feeling very small and vulnerable. "Thank you, all of you."

"Like I said, we aren't gonna have no more killing in our town if we can help it," Calvin said.

"But what about the money?" asked Zack. "I'll never be able to pay back Cutter."

"We'll figure something out," Calvin said. "Now, come along. It's almost suppertime."

"Just like that?"

"Unless you think you have a better place to go."

Zack shook his head. "I have no place else to go. Maintown is my home."

THIRTY-ONE

He would not look her in the eye. Though his gaze swept over the entire congregation, it refused to rest upon her. Nevertheless, Ellie was proud of him. This could not be easy, facing people you had wronged and asking for their forgiveness. He wasn't standing in the pulpit this time but rather on the same level as the people.

"I want you to know," Zack said to a full schoolhouse the very next day after his rescue at the Carlson cabin, "that I don't think I could have done what I did if I had known any of you beforehand, because since I have come to know you, I have gained great respect for each of you and for your faith. The longer I was here, the more I hated what I was doing. Yet as I came to admire you, I found it harder to confess — I just couldn't face having you despise me."

His eyes roved over the group again,

lingering a moment on various ones. He seemed determined to look them in the eye as he confessed. This time Ellie kept her gaze averted, concentrating on her hands folded in her lap. She did not want to make him any more uncomfortable than he was. This was not the time to confront the words spoken between them the day he had left. Maybe later, if there was a later. Her father had said that Zack decided to abide by the decision of the church as to whether he could stay in Maintown or not. Many were still hurt and angry. But Ellie was praying their hearts would be changed by the humility he was showing now.

"I can tell you how sorry I am," Zack continued, "but you have no reason to believe me. I understand I must work to regain your trust, if not your respect. I ask you for the chance to do so. I haven't known a real home since I was eight years old. I ran away from home when I was twelve and have never let myself be in one place long enough to make attachments. Being in Maintown has made me want to settle down someplace for the first time in my life. But if you can't stand the sight of me and want me to clear out, I will. But . . ." His voice broke a little and he paused, swallowing once or twice before going on. "With God's

468

help, I will try to be a better person. Thank you."

The schoolhouse was utterly silent as he walked down the center aisle and exited. The silence lasted for several minutes until Dad, feeling everyone had had time to consider what had been said, rose.

"Our church has never had a situation like this," he said, "where we had to decide whether or not to accept a person into the fold. We have always accepted any who came through those doors."

"But this is different," Arliss Briggs said. The Briggs family was the most upset by all of this. Claudia was still brokenhearted about the postponement of her wedding. Polly was upset they had waited for fake papers when, had they known the truth, they could have had the wedding at the Methodist church in St. Helens or had a judge perform the ceremony.

"That is why a decision like this has to be made," Dad said. "That is why we have to vote. But let me tell you that I have talked to the young man, and I believe he is truly repentant of his actions. In fact, Zack came here without much of a faith, a man back-slidden from his religious upbringing. He now professes what I feel is an honest faith in God. The Word of God says, 'All things

469

work together for good to them that love God, to them who are called according to His purpose.' Good, indeed, has come out of this unfortunate circumstance. A soul has been brought into the fold of God through it all!" Dad stopped abruptly, looking a bit flustered. His voice had grown rather intense at the end of his speech, almost like a preacher expounding from the pulpit. He was not accustomed to delivering speeches. "Anyway, we have a fine chance here to build upon the work of God."

"Let's get this vote over with," groused Felix Baxter. "But let me tell you, any who vote nay ain't gonna be much welcome at my place!" It was a rather empty threat, for few would have desired to visit the Baxters — even the newly reformed Baxters were a bit hard to take.

"How do we vote on this?" Elisha Cook asked.

"How about yea or nay?" suggested Dad. "If you are ready, let's go ahead. How many wish to accept Zack Hartley into our congregation?"

Ellie held her breath. Then a chorus of "yeas" rose to the rafters. She let out her breath and smiled.

"How many don't want him?" Dad asked.

The question was met with silence. Polly

and Arliss Briggs and Claudia squirmed a little but remained silent.

Zack was waiting outside. He had obviously heard the response of the people, but when many swarmed over to him, slapping him on the back and shaking his hand, his expression was filled with wonder and relief.

A few, like the Briggses, shook Zack's hand grudgingly. It would take time to win them over, but at least they were willing to give him the chance. After the meeting Nathan Parker would go into St. Helens and have the criminal charges against Zack dropped. The issue of the money still had to be dealt with, not only the building fund that had burned in the fire but also the debt owed the man from Portland. As far as the debt went, the deacons, who were all unanimous in accepting Zack into the church, planned to take up a collection over the next couple of days. Nathan Parker offered to make up the difference with his own money, which Zack could work off at the sawmill. Zack also said he would repay the building money, too. It might take years for him to clear this debt, but if it kept him in Maintown, Ellie couldn't be happier, even if it seemed Zack was keeping his distance from her.

It was quite a while before she even spoke

to him. First he insisted on riding to the churches in Bachelor Flat, Deer Island, and Columbia City to apologize to them, as well. Dad rode with him to offer his support. When Zack returned, he went to stay with the Donnellys. Jane and Tommy were going to need much help to put the farm back in order after weeks of neglect, so Jane invited Zack to stay. Under the circumstances, Dad thought it would be best if he didn't stay with the Newcombs.

Jane needed Zack's help even more after the sheriff paid a visit to the farm. Ellie heard the story directly from Jane, who told it to Mama when she came to visit them one afternoon.

"Ada, Zack has been such a support to me since the sheriff came," Jane had said.

"I still can't believe he came after Tommy," Mama said. "Everyone knows what happened to Tom was an accident."

Jane shook her head dismally. "It's an election year, and Sheriff Haynes needs a good arrest to prove he's been doing his job. But it didn't help that Tommy confessed. Zack argued with the sheriff, trying to convince him it was an accident. Then Tommy piped up and said it wasn't an accident. He said if Zack could take his medicine like a man, so could he. Tommy said he shot Tom in self-defense. Well, the sheriff said it would need a jury to decide if that was so."

"Couldn't Sheriff Haynes just let Tommy stay home in your custody?"

"No, he wouldn't budge on that. He said Tommy ran once, and he could run again."

"You poor dear!" Mama was almost in tears. "To watch him take your boy away. How awful!"

"Zack took it almost harder than I did," Jane said. "He already felt responsible for what happened, and then for Tommy to say he was again following Zack's example made him nearly despondent."

"Tommy is truly in jail?"

"Until there can be a trial. And who knows how long that will take?"

Jane also told Mama what a hard worker Zack was. He was so grateful for the place to stay that he refused to take any pay beyond his room and board. But unbeknownst to him, Jane donated fifty dollars to the collection for his debts. It turned out that her ne'er-do-well husband, who was quite a spendthrift where his farm and family was concerned, had stashed away a sizable nest egg. Jane had always believed he gambled and drank away their money, which he had, but apparently his gambling had been profitable lately, for she found a cashbox among his things with several hundred dollars in it.

Though the Donnelly place was less than a half mile from the Newcombs', Ellie still did not see Zack. She knew he was purposely keeping away from her and probably from Maggie, as well. Perhaps it was wise. He certainly didn't need any female complications right now while he was trying to put his life in order. In a way she admired him for this. She heard from her father that he was working day and night — at the Donnelly farm and at the sawmill.

Ellie hated having her feelings so up in the air. The last time she had spoken to him, she had told him she loved him. Then she had discovered he wasn't who she had thought him to be. Over and over she asked herself if she still loved him. Had she been in love with the minister or the man? Where did one leave off and the other begin? To complicate matters further, she was finding that now as she observed him from afar and hearing of his recent behavior, her feelings were not dissolving. Rather, they were, amazingly, still present. The man he was showing himself to be was perhaps even more desirable than the perfect minister she had once thought him to be.

About two weeks after Zack's return, Ellie

finished repairing the welcome quilt. There remained a few stains, but for the most part it looked very nice. She thought it was just as well that it wasn't perfectly restored, because the flaws would be a reminder of all that the quilt represented. But now Ellie didn't know what to do with it.

She spread it out before her mother and asked, "Should I give it to him, Mama?"

Mama rubbed her chin thoughtfully. "I don't know. It might be a reminder of a time in his life he'd rather forget. He is trying to start new."

"I wouldn't want it if I were him," Maggie chimed in. "It was made for someone else, and he will always know that. I don't know why you worked so hard to fix it."

"I don't know, either," Ellie said. "I just had to."

"Let's keep it here for now," Mama said. "It will be a reminder of how silly we were."

"I don't think it was silly —" Ellie began.

"You sure did when we gave it to him," Maggie said censoriously. Most of the time all was healed between her and Ellie, but there were occasional moments when Maggie's old ire would slip through.

"Like Dad said, 'All things work for good.' I think it is possible that this quilt might have helped to open his eyes." Ellie turned to her mother. "Mama, you always say when you sleep under a quilt you can't help but feel the love with which it was made. Think of all the nights he slept under this quilt. And don't forget, it was the only thing he saved from the fire."

Mama ran her hand over the quilt, gazing at it as if for the first time. "You may be right." There was a sadness in her eyes as she added, "But, Ellie, you didn't want to put a lot of stock in the quilt when we first made it for him, and it would be wise if you didn't do so now." She reached up and tucked one of Ellie's yellow curls behind her ear. "Zack Hartley is a different person now. Maybe a better person, but still different."

"I am a different person, too, Mama," Ellie said.

Mama gasped and looked at Ellie as she had a moment ago looked at the quilt, as if seeing her anew. "Oh, my dear child!" was all she said.

Ellie tucked the quilt into her hope chest. But she couldn't stop thinking of Zack. Several times she decided to go up to the Donnelly place but changed her mind. She was afraid because Zack had never responded to her declaration of love. It wasn't only her own feelings she was protecting. It was Zack's, as well. If he had to reject her, she knew it would hurt him terribly to do so.

THIRTY-TWO

Zack was doing the evening milking in the Donnelly barn. Maggie watched him a moment before making her presence known. She had to smile because he was having to fight the cow. She doubted he was much experienced at farm work.

"Listen here, Betsy, this is gonna happen one way or another," he warned the animal. "So you may as well submit!"

"That how you woo all your female acquaintances?" Maggie asked as she strode closer.

Zack laughed. "Never had this much trouble with human females."

"Scoot over." Maggie grabbed another milking stool and set it next to Zack. "I've milked a million cows — well, the same cows a million times."

"This is my first."

"Hold on like this." She grasped Betsy the same way she had her dad's cows many times. "Don't tug or squeeze. Coax gently but with authority. The milk wants to come out. You don't need to manhandle the cow."

A steady stream of milk flowed into the bucket, and Betsy ceased her restless side-stepping.

Zack gave it another try, and the results were much improved. "Maybe I'll be made into a farmer yet," he said.

"Maybe a better farmer than preacher." She immediately regretted the glib remark, for he turned suddenly solemn. It was still a tender subject. "I've missed you, Zack," she said with equal solemnity.

"Look, Maggie —"

"Let me finish," Maggie interrupted. "I miss the friend you had become. I'm sorry I ruined it with all that marriage foolishness. Don't avoid me because you're afraid my heart is broken or something."

"It's not?"

"Well, you have a high opinion of your effect on women, now, don't you?"

"You did propose to me."

"I know now I didn't want to marry you," she confessed. "I just wanted to prove something to everyone else."

"You wanted to be the one to win the minister?"

"Something like that," she replied with a

shrug. "I don't know what I would have done if you had said yes. I like you, Zack, but I don't . . . well, you know, love you."

"I guess I was avoiding you because I was afraid I had hurt you." He concentrated on Betsy for a few moments. The milk was flowing nicely now. "I'm sorry I didn't talk to you sooner."

"I didn't come here for an apology, and I never expected one. You've done your fair share of apologizing anyway."

Then the flow of milk slowed and Zack rose. "I've gotta do the other cow."

"Milking doesn't wait," Maggie said.

They took their stools and moved to the next stall. Zack slipped the bucket in place and began. He was definitely a fast learner. He might make a farmer after all.

Maggie was glad to have finally talked with Zack. She sensed his relief when she clarified her feelings toward him and realized it must have weighed upon him, too. But that wasn't the only reason for this visit.

"Zack, you know I ain't the only one you've been avoiding," she said.

"I know."

"Ellie told me what she said to you."

He looked up, a bit astonished. "She did?"

"We do talk. We're sisters."

"She must truly hate me," he said.

"No wonder you've been avoiding her if that's what you believed."

"She'd have every right."

"If you knew Ellie at all, you'd know she wasn't the kind of person to hate anyone."

His hands slowed. He nodded thoughtfully and then his hands resumed their steady milking rhythm. He was quiet, and hard as it was, Maggie kept quiet, too. She began to question her wisdom in coming. She had thought Zack and Ellie were too afraid to make any move toward each other, and all they needed was a little boost. Yet she really didn't know how Zack felt about Ellie. Her only clue was that Ellie was a far more perceptive girl than Maggie had ever been, so she probably wouldn't fall in love with someone without a hint that her feelings would be reciprocated. But it wasn't impossible. Maybe Zack didn't love Ellie. For all Maggie knew, he might love Mabel Parker!

Maggie chuckled in spite of herself. She just couldn't be that dense.

"What's so funny?" Zack asked.

"We are all just a bunch of ninnies," Maggie replied, still smiling. "I'm impulsive, Ellie's confused, and you're afraid. And if we don't watch it, Mabel Parker is gonna do what her mother did with my mother and move right in and blindside us all."

"I thought your mother stole Mrs. Parker's beau."

"Well, I don't know exactly what happened, but if so, that would mean that Dad and Mrs. Parker had once been sweethearts, and I just can't see that."

"Maybe there was someone completely different, and after the two girls fought over him, he went off and married someone else."

Maggie arched a brow at this new twist on the old tale. "I suppose we don't always end up with the one we think we'll end up with."

"I always figured I would never marry at all because that would mean settling down," Zack said. "And I sure never knew any gals I wanted to settle down with. Most of the girls I knew were the saloon-gal type."

"You knew saloon gals?" Maggie's eyes nearly popped. She had guessed Zack was a man of the world, but this was almost more than she could imagine. Not only had she never been in a saloon, but when they walked by the ones in St. Helens, her mother always made them walk on the opposite side of the street.

"I'm not proud of it," he said. "But now look at me. I'm milking cows, I got a steady job, and I'm in debt up to my armpits —

just like a regular family man."

"Except you ain't married." Maggie realized she was talking to Zack just as she would talk to a friend. She liked that so much better than that earlier nonsense behind the barn.

"I've not known many decent women, not until I came here," Zack said. "And I'm not sure I deserve one."

"Is that why you are afraid . . . ah . . . of Ellie?"

His lips twitched in a reluctant smile. "Are you playing matchmaker, Maggie?"

"I'm just trying to get everything back on track."

More earnestly he replied, "Everything that happened before is in the past. All has changed, hasn't it?"

"Not Ellie's feelings."

"What!" he exclaimed, unconsciously taking a hard tug on the cow, who responded by giving her hindquarters a corresponding hard swing, right in Zack's face, nearly knocking him off the stool.

Maggie grabbed the bucket to keep it from toppling over.

"It had to be said," she added, a bit defensively.

"Do you know this for certain?" He eyed her keenly. The milking was forgotten now.

"Maybe not for certain, but don't you think you ought to find out?"

"You are right about me being afraid," he said. "I've hurt too many folks around here. I care far too much about her —" He stopped, flustered.

It was enough, however, for Maggie to know she might be more perceptive than she gave herself credit for. "You're afraid of hurting her, and she's afraid of hurting you." Maggie scratched her head trying to think of something. Finally it came to her, a word she'd learned in a spelling bee at school. "This is a regular conundrum."

"William Locklin would know what that word means but not me," Zack said.

"It means, you dolt, that someone better get off his . . . uh . . . milking stool and talk to someone else before you both end up an old maid and an old bachelor."

The next day was sunny and warm, but there was a crispness in the air that hinted summer was drawing to a close. Ellie saw merit in all the seasons, but the winters in these parts could be awfully long and gloomy, the sun an infrequent visitor, rain far more frequent. But winter did mean more time to devote to quilting, so that was something.

Still, it was hot and lazy now, as summer should be. It was certainly too hot to be indoors, especially with bread baking and the house almost unbearably hot. Mama had let Ellie escape outside for a few minutes and had even let her take her sewing with her, probably hoping that she would get to the mending. She found a spot on the porch where the willow branches lent a nice shade and dragged a chair there. She had a half hour or so before it would be time to fix lunch and then start the afternoon chores.

In Ellie's sewing basket the mending was on top: a pair of Georgie's trousers with a tear, a couple of socks with holes in the heel, and Dad's work shirt with a rip in the sleeve. Under these were Ellie's patchwork projects. She should do the mending, because it had a way of piling up, but it had been days since she had been able to do any stitching for enjoyment, not since she had finished the welcome quilt. Mama was keeping everyone busy with preparations for Boyd and Kendra's wedding, planned for October, only a little over a month away. They had decided to have a double wedding with Claudia Briggs and her fiancé. The Methodist circuit rider said he would come and perform the ceremony, which, it was decided, would be held at the Newcomb home. The Brethren of Christ denominational headquarters in Boston had been notified of the demise of William Locklin. Dad and Zack had stopped by the grave on their way to Portland to pay the money owed the man Cutter. Zack had also notified the Locklin family, writing them a long letter, as if from a friend, which, in fact, he felt he was to the departed minister.

But the church headquarters had no more available ministers to send at this time, so the Columbia County folks were in the same position they had been before Zack had come along. Zack had actually been a pretty good minister, and there were some among his heartiest supporters, like the Cook family, who had suggested he remain their minister. Many of the folks could remember a time when any man with a "call" could be a preacher. But Zack had shrugged off these comments. Dad said Zack had developed a deep respect for the office of minister and insisted he wasn't worthy.

Ellie had reserved judgment on this matter. She did not care if he was a minister or not. She just wanted to talk to him again. She wanted to get to know the real person he was. But she was not as bold as Maggie.

She had told Ellie about her visit with Zack and said she had told him she really hadn't meant her marriage proposal and was sorry for the trouble it had caused. Maggie had a kind of gleam in her eye that indicated she was holding something back. Why she would choose now to be reticent, Ellie didn't know, but it was frustrating.

Ellie pushed aside her mending and withdrew her hexagon diamonds from the basket. It always soothed her frustrations when she worked on them. What would she do if she ever finished this quilt?

She was laying one of the basted hexagons on another so as to whip-stitch them together when she heard a horse approach. She looked up, and a thrill surged through her when she saw it was Zack. She never expected to see him now. She thought he would be working at the sawmill.

"Hi, Ellie," he said, dismounting. He tied the reins to a post and strode to the porch.

"Hello . . . Zack." The name still had a strange feel on her tongue.

"Mind if I come up?"

"Of course not."

He strode up the steps, but just then Mama came to the door, wiping a towel over her brow. Obviously the heat in the house was getting to her.

"Oh, hello, Zack," she said, surprised to see him there.

"Hello, Mrs. Newcomb. I hoped it would be okay for me to come uninvited."

"You are always welcome here," Mama said. "We've missed having you around."

"Thank you, ma'am."

Mama's eyes flickered from Ellie and back to Zack. "Well, I best check that bread. You'll stay for lunch, won't you?"

"I'd like that, Mrs. Newcomb, but I don't have much time. I got off work early from the sawmill because it's time to cut Mrs. Donnelly's hay."

"You plan to do that by yourself?" Mama asked.

"There are four farms ready, including yours. We will all share the work."

"Calvin mentioned he might be off early today. I'm glad you will be in the co-op. Hay cutting is grueling work. Well, I best get lunch on, then." Mama ducked back into the house.

Zack came and stood before Ellie. "I won't stay for lunch if you don't want me to."

"Mama said you are welcome here." Though she had been wanting nothing more than to talk to him, now that he was here before her, she was unsure of herself.

He said, "I need to talk to you."

"You could have talked to me at any time," she said. Was it her fear that made her suddenly defensive?

He paced for a moment and then turned to face her. "Ellie, I was so ashamed. It was hard enough facing everyone else. But you . . . after what you said . . . after me running off and leaving those words just hanging. I would have rather faced a hundred angry congregations."

"But you must have known I wasn't angry —"

"How could I have known? You never said anything."

"I tried to smile —"

"It's not your fault. It was up to me to speak. And I did sense you weren't angry, but I didn't feel I deserved your forgiveness."

He hooked a footstool with his boot, pulled it over by her, and dropped down upon it.

She didn't like the sense that he was kneeling at her feet, but she had a feeling he had done it purposefully, as better than towering over her.

Finally he went on. "Ellie, yesterday Maggie came to see me, and she told me how mistaken she was in her proposal. After that it was so much better between us. So I knew I had to come and give you that same chance. Then maybe we can be friends . . . at least."

"Are you saying it will never be all right between us until I take back what I said?"

He shrugged, confusion creasing his brow. "Well . . . I . . ." He paused, appearing to ponder his words.

Ellie was quiet, letting him have all the time he needed.

At last he said, "Ellie, when I ran out of here, you were a big part of the reason why I only got as far as Veronia, why I didn't clear out completely. I couldn't stand the thought of never seeing you again." He glanced at her hands, then reached over and picked up the half-sewn hexagon diamond she was holding. He smiled. "I realized I wanted to settle down. I was sick of the wandering life. But I knew it wasn't going to be easy. I needed someone at my side, someone who could spend ten years carefully and tenderly piecing together scraps of cloth with never a desire to quit, because she could envision that the end product would be worth it."

She wrapped her hands around his, crushing the diamond between them.

"I am that kind of person, I know," she

said. "That's why I couldn't get real angry at you or hate you for what you did. When Dad told us how you confessed to him and how terrible you felt, I realized you might take some time." She smiled coyly. "You can't love patchwork if you don't love the prospect of taking scraps and putting them together into a beautiful whole design. But Zack, don't get me wrong. I do that with cloth. Only God can do it with people."

"Maybe He will use you as His needle?"

"I like that. The 'needle' of God. There's a sermon topic."

"Ellie, I won't be preaching any more sermons."

"I know that, and don't ever think it matters to me." As she spoke the words, she knew more than ever how true they were. At one time she had thought she wanted a minister because she wanted someone perfect. Zack had made her realize she wouldn't have enjoyed that at all, not that she could have found perfection even in a minister. "It only matters what is in your heart, Zack, be you minister, farmer, mill worker, or whatever."

"That's good, because the love in my heart is all I can offer you!"

"Love?" she said breathlessly.

"Yes," he said and quickly added, "but I

don't expect you to speak those words to me again right away. You've got to have time to get to know the real me, to see how you feel then."

"That's wise. But —"

Just then Dad rode into the yard. He dismounted and tied his horse to the post next to Zack's. Coming up the porch steps, he said, "Hi, Zack, Ellie."

Though Zack had quickly dropped Ellie's hands before Dad dismounted, Dad still gave them a peculiar glance. Well, Zack was seated at her feet. It did indeed look strange. What would Dad think if he knew Zack had just declared his love for her? Somehow she didn't think he'd be surprised.

"We still going to work on the hay this afternoon?" Dad asked Zack.

"Yes, Mr. Newcomb."

"You staying for lunch?"

"Yes, sir. Mrs. Newcomb invited me."

When Zack was their minister, he had called Ellie's father Calvin. Now he was addressing him as "sir" and "Mr. Newcomb," giving the proper respect a suitor gives to a girl's father. Suddenly she had no doubt that Zack was indeed her suitor and they would eventually marry, because even though she ought to get to know him first, she could not deny what was in her heart.

BACHELOR'S PUZZLE PATTERN

Ada Newcomb and her sewing circle friends would have used templates to make this block and would have hand pieced it with several tricky Y seams. But I am convinced that if these ladies had a rotary cutter and today's quick-piecing methods, they would have happily embraced them. Here is the quick way to make this block in a 12″ finished size.

Fabrics: background (BG), light (L), medium (M), dark (D)

Cutting: From background
    Two 3 7/8″ squares, each cut once on diagonal
    One 4 3/4″ square

From light
    Four 3 7/8″ squares, each cut once on diagonal

From medium
  Four 3 7/8″ squares, each cut once
  on diagonal

From dark
  Four 3 1/2″ squares

Sew together the triangle pieces so that you have 4 half-square triangle units of medium/background and 4 medium/light units.

Next, sew four light triangles to each side of the 4 3/4″ square.

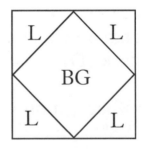

Arrange these pieces, half-square triangles and center square as indicated in diagram and sew together in rows as indicated.

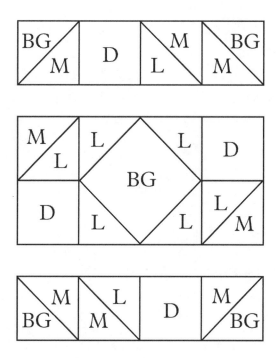

QUILT DRIVE

In honor of Judith Pella's newest series, PATCHWORK CIRCLE, Bethany House Publishers is hosting a quilt drive for those in need. The following is a list of charitable organizations that accept quilt donations. **If you would like to donate a quilt to one of these, visit *www.judithpella.com/quilts* to make a Good Faith Commitment and receive a free Bethany House novel!** Be sure to let us know which organization you will send the quilt to. We will post a virtual quilt block to Judith's Web site to recognize each donation.

Convoy of Hope
A Christian compassion organization that meets physical and spiritual needs: mobilizes resources, and trains churches and other groups to conduct community outreaches, respond to disasters, and direct other com-

passion initiatives in the United States and around the world.

Vineese Childs
330 S. Patterson, Springfield, MO 65802
417-823-8998 • www.convoyofhope.org

Home to Home, Inc.

Equips "local churches and pastors to minister through friendship, outreach, evangelism, and discipleship to our local Jerusalem in the name of Jesus."

Wayne Wingfield, Affiliate Director
326 Habersham Rd., Suite 103, High
    Point, NC 27260
Email: info@hometohomehp.org
Go to www.hometohomehp.org for more
    information.

Lutheran World Relief

Distributes quilts to people around the world: those fleeing conflict, suffering from a disaster, living in chronic poverty, or refugees.

Brenda Meier, Director for Parish and
    Community Engagement
Email: bmeier@lwr.org
Go to www.lwr.org/parish/quilts.asp for

more information.

Oklahoma Campers on Mission

A Christian camping organization whose women sew for needs in the communities where their men build, restore, and remodel buildings, especially churches. Your quilts will go to children who are victims of recent diasters.

Fran deCordova
Trinity International Church
1329 NW 23rd, Oklahoma City, OK
 73106-3617
Email: kidscomfyquilts@cox.net

For more information go to www.bgco.org/com, then click on the "kids comfy quilt" link.

Sewn-N-Love

Provides quilts to cancer patients and their families.

Sandy Wilson, Co-founder
Email: info@sewn-n-love.org
Go to www.sewn-n-love.org for more information.

United Methodist Committee on Relief Sager Brown Depot

Dispatches tons of supplies worth millions of dollars to points around the world, domestic and international.

Kathy Kraiza, Executive Director
Phone: 337-923-6238
Email: director@sagerbrown.org
Go to www.sagerbrown.org for more information.

Wrap Them in Love Foundation for Children

Collects donated quilts and distributes them to children in need around the world.

Ellen Sime
2522 A Old Hwy 99 S, Mt. Vernon, WA 98273
Phone: 360-424-9293
Email: admin@wraptheminlove.org
Go to http://wraptheminlove.org for more information.

Boise World Relief

Your made-with-love quilt will welcome a refugee family to a new life in Idaho, cheering their hearts and their homes.

H. Renee Hage, Director
6702 Fairview Avenue, Boise, Idaho
  83704
hrhage@wr.org

Minneapolis-St. Paul World Relief
Reaches out to refugees and immigrants; partners with churches to provide tangible help to needy families while embracing them with God's love and care.

Woubejig Shiferaw (Docho), Volunteer
  Coordinator
1515 East 66th Street, Richfield, MN
  55423
Email: Minnesota@wr.org

Sacramento World Relief
Provides refugee resettlement for family reunification, including case management, donated home goods and clothing, immigration services, and tutoring.

Betty Eastman, Assistant Director/Fiscal
  Officer
4721 Engle Road, Suite #11, Carmichael,
  CA 95608
Email: BEastman@wr.org

Seattle World Relief

Their mission is to be the hands, feet, and face of Jesus Christ to refugees and immigrants. Your quilt will go to a recently arrived refugee family.

Kelly Pearson
Web site: www.wr-seattle.org
Email: kpearson@wr.org

Tri-Cities World Relief

Assists new refugees with basic needs such as food, blankets, and furniture.

Scott Michael
2600 N. Columbia Center Blvd., Suite 206
Richland, WA 99352
Email: SMichael@wr.org

World Relief-Spokane

Works with church partners to help refugees and immigrants begin new lives.

Linda J. Unseth, N.W. Regional Director
1522 N. Washington, #204, Spokane, WA 99201
Email: lunseth@wr.org

For more information on regional World

Relief offices, go to www.wr.org and then to "Where We Work."

ABOUT THE AUTHOR

Judith Pella has been writing for the inspirational market for more than twenty years and is the author of more than thirty novels, most in the historical fiction genre. Her recent novel *Mark of the Cross* and her extraordinary four-book DAUGHTERS OF FORTUNE series showcase her skills as a historian as well as a storyteller. Her degrees in teaching and nursing lend depth to her tales, which span a variety of settings. Pella and her husband make their home in Oregon.

VISIT JUDITH'S WEB SITE:
www.judithpella.com